D0568904

BEYOND THE DA VINCI CODE

This edition published by Barnes & Noble, Inc.

Produced and packaged by The Book Laboratory Inc.

Design: Amy Ray
Production Manager: Priya Hemenway
Art Research: Jeannine Jourdan

2005 Barnes & Noble Books
M 10 9 8 7 6 5 4 3 2 1

ISBN: 0-7607-6625-8

Printed in Singapore

BEYOND THE DA VINCI CODE

FROM THE ROSE LINE TO THE BLOODLINE

The Unauthorized Guide to Dan Brown's Best-selling Novel

SANGEET DUCHANE

BARNES & NOBLE BOOKS
NEW YORK

CONTENTS

PART THREE THE HOLY GRAIL

PART FOUR LEONARDO DA VINCI

PART FIVE MODERN TIMES

INTRODUCTION

Dan Brown's novel *The Da Vinci Code* has not only been a massive best-seller but has stirred up an unprecedented amount of controversy for a work of fiction. A *New York Times* article reported that more than ten books about the novel were set for release a little over a year after its publication. Most of these books were by Christian writers who feared that the book might be "sowing doubt about basic Christian beliefs."[1] Less than two years after the novel first came out, more than fifteen related books are now on the shelves.

As a result of all the controversy, Brown's book may be one of the most nit-picked in history. He has been taken to task for errors on a variety of topics, including guns, airplanes, the layout of Paris, and Christian history. There is no question that Brown brought much of this criticism on himself by asserting that the novel is more than a work of fiction. On the first page he has a statement titled "Fact" that claims the Priory of Sion is a real organization, gives information about the religious organization Opus Dei, and then adds, "All descriptions of artwork, architecture, documents, and secret rituals in this novel are accurate."[2]

Brown uses a few other techniques to suggest that the story behind his story is true. First, he supplies the most controversial "information" through two characters: Robert Langdon and Leigh Teabing. Langdon is a professor of religious symbology at Harvard and has written a textbook on religious symbology. Teabing is a religious historian and a reputable author. These credentials give some credibility to their statements. There is, of course, no professor of religious symbology at Harvard, and neither Langdon nor Teabing behave or speak like academics.

Another technique Brown uses to make his story sound credible is to have these two characters produce a bibliography, wave to a shelf of books, or say that all academics agree or that the subject has been extensively documented, whenever their statements are particularly extreme.[3] Almost invariably, the statements being made by Langdon or Teabing at these moments are rejected by scholars or

OPPOSITE PAGE *Astarte Syriaca* by Dante Gabriel Rossetti (1828–1882).

extremely controversial, never something that could actually be proven. When books do exist to support Langdon's or Teabing's points, they are rarely academic, rather they are often written by what Langdon's agent so colorfully calls "pop schlockmeisters looking for a quick buck."[4] Brown's techniques have provoked the wrath of academic critics.

Brown also has indicated in the book's Acknowledgments and in interviews that he did an extensive amount of research for the book. Given the number of errors Brown makes that could have been avoided by careful research, his critics debate whether he has been gullible, sloppy, intentionally dishonest, or all of the above in insisting his work is true and based on careful research. Brown claims in his interviews that he is convinced that his story is true, and we cannot know whether or not he really believes that.

Errors aside, he has told an entertaining story, created delightful puzzles, and, perhaps most important, brought vital issues up for public discussion. The success of Brown's book indicates that he has touched a nerve in his discussion about the history of Christianity's relationship to women and the sacred feminine.

Many critics, particularly Christian scholars, have wondered aloud how the public could be gullible enough to believe Brown's story. These critics might do better to ask themselves why the public might feel it has been misled. It is an unfortunate reality that biblical and Christian scholarship over the last centuries in Europe and America has been strongly biased. The history of biblical times and the Bible itself have been studied from a perspective that is male, white, and mainstream Christian. In the last two or three decades, as more women have received academic positions and new documents have been discovered, there has been a massive reevaluation of the role and position of women in early Christianity. We are still in the middle of that reevaluation, and there are no easy answers yet. Although the academic mainstream still holds a traditional Christian perspective, many of us have begun to question long-held beliefs about the history of Christianity and women.

This uncertainty and the realization that past "expert opinion" may not have been so expert after all has left the public feeling that it has been given a false story. Many are sincerely trying to find out as much as they can about early Christianity. Dan Brown has made errors in his story, but he points to a fascinating new look at history that may revolutionize our understanding of Jesus, women and Christianity, Christian legends, and the Holy Grail.

This book looks at the story beyond *The Da Vinci Code* and addresses issues such as the possibility that Jesus was married; the evidence that Mary Magdalene was one of his leading disciples; the record of the Goddess in the Jerusalem Temple; and the possible connection between Mary Magdalene and the Grail. It will also examine why *The Da Vinci Code* is so popular, and where we go from here with the issues that the novel has raised.

PART ONE

The Early Church

CHAPTER ONE
WAS JESUS MARRIED?

Is There a Historical Record?

Dan Brown's character Sir Leigh Teabing says that the marriage of Jesus and Mary Magdalene is a matter of historical record and that Jesus could not possibly have been celibate given the Jewish customs of the day. This has provoked Christian writers to claim that most reputable scholars agree Jesus was not married.[1] Are either of these assertions true?

The reality is that there is no definitive evidence on the marital status of Jesus. We cannot prove he was married, and we cannot prove he was not. Both options are possible, and both plausible.

Though most of the information we have about Jesus is found in the New Testament, and many commentators on this topic seem to treat the New Testament as a historical account, it is not always historically accurate. The gospels were meant to convey the "good news" of the Christian message. They were written for the purpose of teaching new Christians, not as historical records. The four New Testament gospels have many contradictions and inconsistencies among them and compared with other historical records. For example, though the Gospel of Luke tells the story of Mary and Joseph going to Bethlehem because of a census (Luke 2:1–7), the historical information we have tells us the census was taken when Jesus was ten years old and applied to Judea, not to Galilee, which was under a different government. According to Luke's genealogy for Jesus (Luke 3:21–38), the family connection to Bethlehem was in the distant past, several generations before. There is no conceivable reason why Joseph would have been ordered to go there to register for a census. A census of Joseph and his family would have been taken in Nazareth.[2]

The Gospel of Matthew tells a completely different story. In that version Joseph and Mary flee to Egypt because Herod is killing Jewish firstborn sons (Matt. 2:13–15). We have records of numerous atrocities committed by Herod, but

ABOVE Miniature from *The Book of Hours* by the Master of James IV of Scotland. Joseph and Mary went to Bethlehem for a census, according to the story from the Gospel of Luke, but there is no record of a census taken at that time.

OPPOSITE PAGE *Noli me Tangere* by Frederico Barocci (1535–1612).

Flight to Egypt from *John of Berry's Petites Heures* (14th century). In the Gospel of Matthew, Mary and Joseph flee to Egypt after they have been warned by an angel that Herod will try to kill Jesus.

Massacre of the Innocents by Fra Angelico (ca. 1400–1455). Herod's soldiers are shown killing male children, illustrating the story that appears only in the Gospel of Matthew. There is no historical record that such a massacre actually took place.

there is no record that he killed firstborn sons. This story is most likely based on the story in Exodus 1:15–18.[3]

The stories of the journeys to Bethlehem and Egypt were probably used to show that Jesus had fulfilled prophecies that the Messiah would come out of Bethlehem and Egypt (Matt. 2:5–6, 15), rather than to record historical events.[4] Because a primary purpose of the New Testament gospels was to establish doctrine by attempting to prove Jesus was the Messiah or was divine, we must use them with caution as a source of historical information.

The New Testament tells us nothing directly about the marital status of Jesus or of any of the male disciples. It was the general custom of the time to refer to women in terms of their relationships to men, such as Mary, the wife of Clopas, or Mary, the mother of James. If a woman was described as a wife or mother, we can surmise that she was married. No such information is given about the men.

We know that Peter was married, because Jesus healed his mother-in-law (Matt. 8:14–15; Mark 1:29–31; Luke 4:38–39), but we hear nothing about his wife. Since we hear nothing of other wives either, we might conclude that most of the male disciples of Jesus were not married and that Peter was probably a widower. Paul, however, tells us that this was not the case. In a letter to the community at Corinth, he says, "Do we not have the right to be accompanied by a believing wife, as do the other apostles and the brothers of the Lord and Cephas [Peter]?" (1 Cor. 9:5) In other words, by the time of Paul, probably from the late forties to the sixties of the first century, many male disciples, including Peter, were traveling around with their wives.

It is possible, of course, that the apostles Paul talks about all married or remarried after the crucifixion, but that would certainly argue against any theory that Jesus advocated celibacy. Some commentators have even claimed that the "wives" Paul talks about were not really wives but preaching partners who traveled with the male apostles. That seems to be a case of shaving a square peg to fit it in a round hole. Paul's statement is straightforward—the men were traveling with their wives—and he most likely meant what he said. We can conclude that many of the male disciples of Jesus were probably married at the time they were with Jesus, but their marital status was not mentioned in the New Testament.

ABOVE *Saint Peter Preaching* by Fra Angelico (ca. 1400–1455). In European art, Peter is shown traveling and preaching alone, though the letters of Paul tell us he had a wife who traveled with him.

The gospels of the New Testament were written from 40 to 110 years after the crucifixion of Jesus. It is unlikely that any of the gospels were written by people who were present at the events described. We have no reliable information about the identity of the writers or where the gospels were written. The figures of Matthew, Mark, Luke, and John were attached to the gospels through later legend.

Stories about Jesus were passed on through oral transmission during the first century after his death, and the written text contains only a very small portion of the information that was once available in the oral tradition. The events recorded in the gospels were the ones considered important by the writers or redactors.

The four gospels of the New Testament are inconsistent on many points, including what Jesus said in certain situations like his trial, what others said to him, and what events took place. This inconsistency may be partly due to variation in the oral tradition. (See Chapter Four.)

Jesus heals Peter's mother-in-law. Mosaic from Chora Church, Istanbul (14th century). This story is the only indication we have that Peter was married.

Were There Celibate First-Century Jews?

There are three main possibilities regarding both the marital status of Jesus and his teachings about marriage. The first is that Jesus was unmarried and celibate, and taught that celibacy was superior to marriage. This was the view of the early Church, and though most Protestant churches have rejected the Catholic Church's teaching on asceticism and a celibate clergy, there seems to be a strong emotional reaction among many Christians to the possibility that Jesus was sexually active.

The popular writers that Dan Brown relies on reject this first possibility. Brown has Langdon say that it was not possible for Jesus to be celibate because celibacy was condemned in the Judaism of his time. In this the author is incorrect.

According to Flavius Josephus and the Jewish philosopher Philo of Alexandria *(left)*, there were at least two Jewish groups of the time that practiced celibacy: the Essenes and the Therapeutae. A younger contemporary of Jesus, the Roman Pliny the Elder, wrote that a community of Essenes was located around Qumran, where the Dead Sea Scrolls were found.[5] Pliny, however, claimed that the community was all male and completely celibate. Archaeological evidence of female burials at Qumran shows that either this is not the same community Pliny was referring to or he got some of his facts wrong. The second is the more likely, and it raises questions about the accuracy of the other accounts as well.

The Dead Sea Scrolls and Josephus indicate that a few male members of the community remained celibate in the same way men were bound to abstinence during a holy war.[6] The majority of Essenes were married and engaged in sexual intercourse for purposes of procreation, though not for pleasure.[7] The Essenes, therefore, were sometimes celibate, but they did not challenge the Jewish tradition of marriage or the necessity of procreation.

The Therapeutae, who lived outside of Palestine, had both men and elderly women as members and seemed to choose celibacy as a way of life. They lived in isolation in separate communities and did not include women of childbearing age, so they did not interfere with or reject procreation.[8]

It was clearly possible for a Jewish man of the time of Jesus to choose celibacy without being considered an outcast. But the possibility does not prove that Jesus actually did so or even make it probable. We know that the Essenes and the Therapeutae were celibate because Josephus, Philo, and Pliny all found the groups' sexual practices worth mentioning. Celibacy was not unknown at the time, but it was unusual enough to be remarked upon.

Brown has Langdon say that it was not possible for Jesus to be celibate because celibacy was condemned in the Judaism of his time. In this the author is incorrect.

Did Jesus Advocate Celibacy?

"For John the Baptist has come eating no bread and drinking no wine, and you say, 'He has a demon'; the Son of Man has come eating and drinking, and you say, 'Look, a glutton and a drunkard, a friend of tax collectors and sinners!'"

Why then, if Jesus was celibate and taught celibacy, was there no comment about it? In the New Testament Jesus is criticized for behavior outside the norm, such as eating with tax collectors (Matt. 9:10–13; Mark 2:15–17); healing on the Sabbath (Matt. 12:9–14; Mark 3:1–6; Luke 6:6–11; John 5:1–18, 9:1–41); allowing his disciples to pick food on the Sabbath (Matt. 12:1–5; Mark 2:23–28; Luke 6:1–5) and eat without washing their hands (Matt. 15:1–9; Mark 7:1–23); failing to fast (Matt. 9:14–17; Mark 2:18–22; Luke 5:33–38); casting out demons (Matt. 12:22–32; Mark 3:22–27; Luke 11:14–23); and claiming the power to forgive sins (Mark 2:1–12). But the New Testament gospels do not record any question or comment about Jesus' teachings on celibacy.

The lifestyle of Jesus as described in the New Testament did not resemble those of the communities practicing celibacy. The Essenes and Therapeutae were very concerned about strict observance of the law and about issues of purity. Jesus, on the other hand, is portrayed in the New Testament as being opposed to strict ideas about purity and regulations. He healed on the Sabbath, stated that the Sabbath was made for humanity, not the reverse (Mark 2:27), said that what came out of the mouth was more important than what went into it (Matt. 15:10–20; Mark 7:14–23), and pointed out the difference between how he and John the Baptist were seen by their contemporaries:

> *For John the Baptist has come eating no bread and drinking no wine, and you say, "He has a demon"; the Son of Man has come eating and drinking, and you say, "Look, a glutton and a drunkard, a friend of tax collectors and sinners!" (Luke 7:33–34)* [9]

Given these differences, it is unlikely that Jesus was a member of the Essenes or the Therapeutae, and scholars do not usually argue that he was. Some simply argue that since celibacy was not unknown, Jesus may have been celibate without attracting too much attention because of it.

Saint John the Baptist Preaching by Anastagio Fontebuoni (1571–1626). John lived a very ascetic life and may have been celibate. Jesus, however, did not live an ascetic life, but ate and drank with people shunned by the respectable Jewish society of his time.

It would certainly have been unusual for Jesus to teach the superiority of celibacy over marriage. The passages of the New Testament that are usually cited in support of the theory that Jesus advocated celibacy are all subject to other interpretations. For example, some have claimed that because Jesus praised women who did not bear children, he meant that childbearing was less good than celibacy.[10] In fact, Luke says only that Jesus predicted a time when things would be so bad for the Jews that people would say that women who had never had children were blessed (Luke 23:2–29; see also Matt. 24:15–19; Mark 13:14–23). It would be reasonable to say that it would be easier to not have children than to see your children die in the coming apocalypse, or to say that it would be difficult to try to escape while pregnant or with a nursing child, but it is a stretch to make this statement into an argument for celibacy.

It would certainly have been unusual for Jesus to teach the superiority of celibacy over marriage.

In an earlier passage in Luke (Luke 20:27–40),[11] Sadducees ask Jesus a question about the resurrection. It was the Jewish custom for a brother of a man who died without children to marry the widow and raise the children on behalf of the dead brother. So the Sadducees asked Jesus if a woman married seven brothers in succession, which brother would she be married to after the resurrection? Josephus tells us that the Sadducees did not believe in the resurrection,[12] however, so we have to question the accuracy of this account.

The Marriage of the Virgin by Bernardo Daddi (1290–1349). Many believe that Jesus was a supporter of marriage.

Flavius Josephus, copper engraving from a pre-1900 European edition of his history *The Antiquities*. Josephus was a leader in the Jewish first-century revolt. He surrendered to the Roman general Vespasian and curried favor with him by predicting that Vespasian and his son Titus would be emperors. When Vespasian became emperor, Josephus was released and given Roman citizenship. He settled in Rome to write several works of history.

In the story, Jesus answered that people will not marry after the resurrection. The most obvious meaning of this is that life after the resurrection will not be the physical life as we know it, with sexuality and procreation. However, it does not necessarily follow that marriage and procreation in this life are any less virtuous because of that. Considering the admonition of God in the Genesis account to be fruitful and multiply (Gen. 1:22) and the widespread Jewish belief that procreation was an essential part of their covenant with God, it would take a much stronger statement than this to prove that Jesus meant to criticize marriage simply because he said it did not continue after the resurrection.

There is one last statement attributed to Jesus as a direct endorsement of celibacy, in Matthew 19: 10–12. In that story Jesus has just spoken against divorce, and his disciples object:

> *His disciples said to him, "If such is the case of a man with his wife, it is better not to marry." But he said to them, "Not everyone can accept this teaching, but only those to whom it is given. For there are eunuchs who have been so from birth, and there are eunuchs who have been made eunuchs by others, and there are eunuchs who have made themselves eunuchs for the sake of the kingdom of heaven. Let anyone accept this who can."*

The first question we must address is whether this is an authentic saying of Jesus. This statement appears only in the Gospel of Matthew. If this was intended as an endorsement of celibacy and Jesus really had taught something so radically opposed to mainstream Jewish thought, would it be likely that the other gospel writers would not have heard of it? Would they have left it out if they had heard of it? Some would say yes, but there is no proof to substantiate that claim.

Statements from a wide variety of people, from Paul to the great teacher of the Essenes, who is described in the Dead Sea Scrolls, might have been attributed to Jesus in the oral tradition. Statements were also attributed to Jesus after his death. People of antiquity believed in literal prophecy—people could speak for God directly. For example, in one of his letters Paul says that Jesus spoke to him about a physical problem and said, "My grace is sufficient for you, for power is made perfect in weakness" (2 Cor. 12:7–9). Paul puts this forward as a direct quote of Jesus, and many of his contemporaries would have accepted that, even though we do not know that Paul ever met Jesus in his lifetime. Paul and his contemporaries did not have the same definition of historical quotes that we have. Quotes "from Jesus" may not have come from Jesus while he was alive.

If the comment about eunuchs is an authentic statement of the historical Jesus, does it actually mean that he advocated celibacy? If Jesus was referring to celibacy, why talk about eunuchs? For one thing, eunuchs are men, and a discussion of eunuchs excludes women, something Jesus is rarely portrayed as doing. There is also a major difference between celibacy and castration. Was Jesus advocating castration in this statement? Legend says that the Christian writer Origen believed so at the turn of the second century and castrated himself,[13] but Christians in general have not agreed with this interpretation. So why talk about eunuchs if he meant celibacy?

Origen, 16th century engraving. Legend says that Origen castrated himself because he believed that Jesus recommended castration. Other Christians have concluded that Jesus was talking about celibacy.

ARGUMENTS AGAINST CELIBACY

A significant group of biblical scholars believe that the statement about eunuchs has been misinterpreted. The Jesus Seminar, formed in 1985, consists of a group of qualified scholars, including well-known writers John Dominic Crossan, Marcus Borg, Karen Armstrong, and Karen King. It started as a group of 30 and grew to more than 200 trained specialists. The group met, debated, and voted on the authenticity and meaning of statements attributed to Jesus in the New Testament and the *Gospel of Thomas*. They voted anonymously by dropping colored beads into a box.

The Jesus Seminar scholars voted that the statement attributed to Jesus in Matthew 19: 10–12 was not authentic, but part of it reflected a statement probably made by Jesus. That part, in the Jesus Seminar's own translation, was: "There are castrated men who were born that way, and there are castrated men who were castrated by others, and there are castrated men who castrated themselves because of Heaven's imperial rule."[14] Seventy-seven percent of these scholars voted that this statement was one of many similar statements in which Jesus included people within Judaism who were marginalized by practice. This included the poor, toll collectors, prostitutes, women generally, and children. Men who had been castrated or who did not have fully developed testicles, they argued, were excluded from Temple service and could not be fully men within the group.[15] The Jesus Seminar report states that the scholars were:

"In any case, the sayings on castration should not be taken as Jesus' authorization for an ascetic lifestyle; his behavior suggests that he celebrated life by eating, drinking, and fraternizing freely with both women and men."

> *overwhelmingly of the opinion that Jesus did not advocate celibacy. A majority of the Fellows doubted, in fact, that Jesus himself was celibate. They regarded it as probably that he had a special relationship with at least one woman, Mary of Magdala. In any case, the sayings on castration should not be taken as Jesus' authorization for an ascetic lifestyle; his behavior suggests that he celebrated life by eating, drinking, and fraternizing freely with both women and men.*[16]

The scholars of the Jesus Seminar are not necessarily correct, and more conservative scholars would no doubt disagree with the group's decision. The point is that ample basis for disagreement exists and scholars do not agree with each other on this or most other points in biblical scholarship.

It is interesting to note that none of the statements about celibacy attributed to Jesus appears in the *Q Gospel*, the text that has been reconstructed from Matthew and Luke and is believed to have been written before any of the New Testament gospels. (See Chapter Four.) *Q* includes Jesus' opposition to divorce but says nothing about eunuchs or other possible references to celibacy. While this does not prove that the statement in Matthew 19: 10–12 is inauthentic, it tells us that Jesus was not portrayed as an advocate of celibacy or castration in that early level of the Christian tradition; he was portrayed as an opponent of divorce, which might be interpreted as a support of marriage.

When Paul advised people not to marry because the end of the world was near, he did not say that this teaching came from Jesus (1 Cor. 7:25–40). In fact, the first record we have that someone claimed to base his celibacy on the celibacy of Jesus came almost a century after the crucifixion.[17] If Jesus was celibate, why was his celibacy not invoked sooner as a justification of the practice?

We can conclude that while it is possible that Jesus was celibate and taught the superiority of celibacy, it is by no means certain that he did either.

Entry into Jerusalem by Fra Angelico (ca. 1400–1455). Jesus rides into Jerusalem on a colt, fulfilling a prophecy for the return of the Jewish king.

Jesus the Prophet

There is a second possibility that Jesus was celibate because he was a prophet but did not teach celibacy to others. The Jewish scholar Geza Vermes has argued that there was a tradition for some Jewish prophets to be celibate, and to those who saw Jesus as a prophet, his celibacy would not be unusual.[18] The New Testament tells us that some people did see Jesus as a prophet. In Mark, when Jesus asked his disciples who people said he was, they replied John the Baptist, Elijah, or one of the prophets (Matt. 16:13–14; Mark 8: 27–28; Luke 9:18–20).

It is generally believed that John the Baptist was celibate. Though we have little reliable historical information about John, his extremely ascetic lifestyle as described in Mark 1:4–8—he wore garments woven from camel hair and ate locusts and wild honey—gives support to this idea. We have seen that according

Bulgarian icon showing scenes from the life of Elijah (18th century). Some people believed that Jesus was Elijah reborn.

"Lo, I will send you the prophet Elijah before the great and terrible day of the Lord comes..."

to the New Testament accounts, Jesus had a very different lifestyle from John and was perceived by others as his opposite (Matt. 11:18–19; Luke 7:33–34). John's celibacy then would not indicate that Jesus was celibate. Some prophets such as Isaiah had sons (Isa. 8:1–4), so being a Jewish prophet was not necessarily equated with lifelong celibacy. Jesus could have been both married and a prophet. If he was a celibate prophet who did not go against the Jewish teachings on marriage, Jesus could have been celibate without being challenged about it or having his celibacy mentioned.

THE MESSIAH AND KING

The New Testament accounts are not consistent about how Jesus was perceived. Some people thought Jesus was Elijah, but according to Malachi, Elijah was to be the forerunner of the Messiah: "Lo, I will send you the prophet Elijah before the great and terrible day of the Lord comes"(Mal. 4:5). The Gospel of Matthew says that John the Baptist was Elijah (Matt. 17:10–13; see also Mark 9:9–13).

There are several indications that some people perceived Jesus as the kingly Messiah, who would lead the Jews to freedom. Jesus was accused at his trials before the Sanhedrin, Pilate, and Herod of being the Messiah and the king of the Jews (Matt. 26:63, 27:11; Mark 14:61–62, 15:2, 9, 12, 18; Luke 22:66–71, 23:2–3, 37; John 18:33, 19:14). According to gospel accounts, Jesus rode into Jerusalem on a colt and was hailed as Messiah or king (Matt. 21:1–11; Mark 11:1–11, Luke 19:29–40; John 12:12–19). If this event really took place and some people proclaimed Jesus king, such a proclamation would explain the nervousness of both the Jewish and Roman authorities and their motivation for his execution. A belief that the king of the Jews had returned could lead to an uprising, whether the claim was true or not. All the gospels say that the inscription on the cross of Jesus identified him as the king of the Jews (Matt. 27:37; Mark 15:26; Luke 23:38; John 19:19).

It is less likely that people would proclaim a celibate man king than recognize him as a prophet. There is no record in Jewish history of a celibate king. A king was expected to produce heirs. If people did proclaim Jesus king of the Jews and if the authorities took the claim seriously, that at least raises questions about the claim that he was celibate.

A Married Man?

The last possibility is that Jesus, like the vast majority of Jewish men of his time and his age group, was married. This possibility is consistent with the fact that no outsiders are portrayed as questioning Jesus about his marital status or his views on celibacy, and it is consistent with the portrayal of Jesus in the *Q Gospel* as strongly opposed to divorce, but not an advocate of celibacy.

Several popular writers and Dan Brown argue that this is the only possible option. Jesus must have been married because he was a rabbi. While it is true that rabbis were generally married, there were prophets such as John who were not married. Jesus could have been a religious teacher, gathering large crowds and disciples, even if he was unmarried.

Lamentation Over the Dead Christ (detail) by Fra Angelico (ca. 1400–1455). The *Gospel of Philip* says that three women traveled with Jesus, his mother, his sister, and Mary Magdalene. Here three women mourn his death.

THE GOSPEL OF PHILIP

The text generally relied on to "prove" that Jesus was married, and the one Dan Brown calls a historical record, is a second- or third-century apocryphal gospel, the *Gospel of Philip*. Two sections of text are relevant to the marital status of Jesus, one that is fragmented and one that is not. The intact text reads:

> *There were three [women] who always walked with the Lord: Mary his mother and her sister and Magdalene, the one who was called his companion. His sister and his mother and his companion were each a Mary* (Gospel of Philip *59:6–11*).[19]

Many writers and Brown's character Teabing claim that the Aramaic word for companion here clearly means wife. The text, however, is in Coptic, not Aramaic, and most likely a translation of a Greek original. *Koinonōs* is a Greek word.[20] Further, as we have seen, nothing is very clear in this area of scholarship. The term *koinonōs* does not always mean a spouse. It generally refers to a person engaged in some kind of fellowship or sharing with another: marriage or a spiritual or business relationship. In the Bible the term is used for a spouse (Mal. 2:14), a religious companion (Philem. 17), a coworker in proclaiming the good news (2 Cor. 8:23), and a business associate (Luke 5:10).[21]

The word koinonōs *may have been used because the writers of this gospel considered Mary Magdalene more than a wife, since she was also the spiritual companion of Jesus.*

St. Mary Magdalene by Piero della Francesca (ca. 1420–1492). The *Gospel of Philip* portrays Mary Magdalene as the disciple most intimate with Jesus. This is very different from the Roman Church's portrayal of her as a prostitute.

The family relationship of Jesus with the other two Marys mentioned in this section suggests that Mary Magdalene may also have had a familial relationship with him. The main argument against this is that the word for "wife" used in the rest of the *Gospel of Philip* is different.[22] From this some scholars argue that the text means Mary Magdalene was the spiritual consort of Jesus.[23] Being a spiritual companion would not preclude her from also being his wife, and scholars are divided whether this partnership would include "marital and sexual dimensions."[24] The word *koinonōs* may have been used because the writers of this gospel considered Mary Magdalene more than a wife, since she was also the spiritual companion of Jesus.[25]

The Dead Christ with the Madonna and Mary Magdalene by Agnolo Bronzino (1503–1572). The mother of Jesus and Mary Magdalene are often portrayed as the women who mourned him.

The fragmented section of text reads:

> *And the companion of the [...] Mary Magdalene. [...loved] her more than [all] the disciples [and used to] kiss her [...]. The rest of [the disciples...]. They said to him, "Why do you love her more than all of us?" The savior answered and said to them, "Why do I not love you like her? When a blind man and one who sees are both together in darkness, they are no different from one another. When the light comes, then he who sees will see the light, and he who is blind will remain in darkness."* (Gospel of Philip *63:34–35, 64:1–9*)[26]

Popular writers hail this as proof that Jesus loved Mary Magdalene as a man loves a woman and had a sexual relationship with her. Many Christian writers argue that the kiss referred to is metaphorical and means that Jesus transferred spiritual knowledge to her or initiated her. Again, there is no way to determine for certain which is true, and scholars do not agree.[27] There is little doubt that this gospel presents Mary Magdalene as a close spiritual disciple of Jesus, but does it also portray her as his wife and/or sexual partner?

Christ and Mary Magdalene by Auguste Rodin (1840–1917).

If Jesus was married, why then was there no mention of his wife or children in the New Testament?

LATE TEXTS

Not everyone would consider the *Gospel of Philip* a reliable historical source, since it is dated from the second to third centuries. To dismiss such texts as nonhistorical without consideration, however, would be a mistake. Scholars used to dismiss the Gospel of John in the New Testament as a historical source, since it, too, is often dated to the second century. In recent years studies have shown that some of the descriptions of events in the Gospel of John, particularly of the events around the crucifixion, are more consistent with what we know from other historical records than accounts in the remaining three New Testament gospels. Now many scholars believe that parts of John are based on very early accounts, probably preserved in a written form.[28]

This experience should remind us that documents written down in 140 or 160 might be based on more accurate historical information than accounts written in 80 or 90. There tends to be a bias in biblical studies that New Testament texts are more accurate and reliable than apocryphal documents, but this may not always be a valid assumption. At the very least, the *Gospel of Philip* tells us what some early Christians of the second or third centuries believed to be true about Jesus and Mary Magdalene. We know that they considered her a leading disciple, probably the disciple closest to Jesus, and they may also have believed she was his wife or lover.

Some modern scholars find that last point quite believable. While it is true that few scholars have argued openly for the theory that Jesus was married, there are some good reasons for that. One is that the topic raises a great deal of emotion, as reaction to *The Da Vinci Code* has shown. The other is that there is no proof that Jesus *was* married; there is just the possibility. Given the lack of evidence, it is little wonder that scholars have not wanted to risk their careers on such an argument. Under cover of anonymity, however, we have seen that members of the Jesus Seminar expressed their belief that Jesus was not celibate. So the statement that virtually all reputable scholars believe Jesus was single and celibate is simply not true.

THE WIFE OF JESUS

This brings us to an important question. If Jesus was married, why then was there no mention of his wife or children in the New Testament? As we have seen, wives and children were not generally mentioned in the gospels. If the wife of Jesus was

Mary Magdalene, a woman mentioned repeatedly in the New Testament as well as apocryphal gospels, why was she not called Mary the wife of Jesus in more texts than possibly the *Gospel of Philip*? This takes us into the realm of pure speculation. It is possible that Mary Magdalene was known in her own right before her marriage and that she continued to be known in the same way after the marriage.

There is another plausible explanation why the family of Jesus was not mentioned in later Christian texts. If Jesus really was executed because the authorities thought he or others claimed he was the king of the Jews, then any heirs of Jesus, particularly his male heirs, would have been in danger. Herod killed some of his own children over questions of succession.[29] Herod's son Antipas, who came into power in Galilee, or the Roman authorities in Judea would have been willing to get rid of a putative claimant to the throne of David, even if they did not believe the claim.

Some support for this theory is found in the historical account that the Roman Emperor Domitian had the descendants of Jesus traced and brought before the Roman authorities in 90. The Romans found only two grandchildren of a brother of Jesus. When those grandchildren appeared they were simple farmers who worked thirty-nine acres of land with their own hands, and they were released.[30] Had Domitian found a direct descendant of Jesus, the result might have been different.

Carrying of the Cross from *John of Berry's Petites Heures*, the result of a collaboration between miniaturists Jean le Noir (1331–1375) and Jacquemart de Hesdin (active about 1380–1415). Christian artists often portray Jesus in close association with women.

Questions We Can Answer

Given the lack of solid evidence on this question one way or the other, it might be more productive for us to look at what lies behind the question. Why has *The Da Vinci Code* raised so much interest in this topic? Why are people attracted to or touched by the image of a Jesus who is a loving husband and loving father? On the other hand, why are so many people upset and distressed by the image of a sexual Jesus? What are the underlying ideas about sexuality that makes this distressing? These are at least questions we have a chance of answering. We cannot answer the question of whether or not Jesus was sexual or married, at least perhaps until another cache of lost Christian documents is discovered.

CHAPTER TWO
MARY MAGDALENE IN THE NEW TESTAMENT

Dan Brown has Langdon and Teabing make several claims about Mary Magdalene. They say she was the wife of Jesus, the mother of his daughter, the person Jesus asked to found his church, and the true Holy Grail. By the end of the novel she is treated like a Goddess[1] and as the representative of the lost sacred feminine.

We will now look to see what the New Testament—the gospels and other writings accepted by the early institutionalized Church—can tell us about the woman Mary Magdalene, her relationship to Jesus, and her position in the early community.

Women at the Time of Jesus

To understand Mary Magdalene's role, we need to reevaluate commonly held ideas about women's roles in first-century Jewish Palestine. Christian scholars have long argued that women were subjugated in Jewish culture, and that Christianity saved them from that subjugation. This ignores the fact that Jesus and the women with him were all Jews and that whatever they did was within Jewish tradition. Recently, several scholars have begun to challenge this view.[2] They point out that the standard Christian view is based on two very unreliable sources of information.

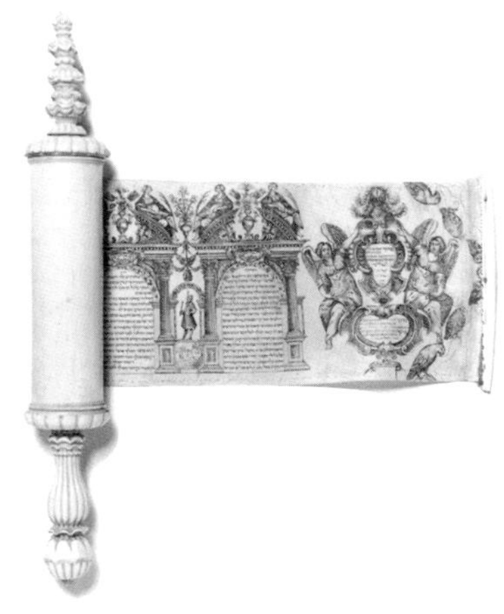

ABOVE Esther Scroll. Ancient Jewish scriptures are not good indicators of attitudes toward women in first-century Palestine.

OPPOSITE PAGE *Penitent Mary Magdalene* by Titian (1488–1576).

JEWISH TEXTS

The first source used is the Hebrew Scriptures, known to Christians as the Old Testament. Some of the Hebrew Scriptures restricted the role of women in antiquity, and many scholars have assumed that women were still treated in that way in the first century. That would be like scholars 2,000 years from now assuming there is no divorce in predominantly Christian cultures of the twenty-first century because the New Testament forbids it. We know that divorce is very common and

Deborah moving with Barak and 10,000 men to Kedesh against Sisera. Illustration from the Psalter of St. Louis (13th century). Deborah was a judge, or leader, or Israel, who advised Barak to go to war. He would only do it if she accompanied him, which she did, and they won the battle.

that Christian scriptures do not necessarily reflect modern views about divorce, marriage, and sexual mores. In the same way, ancient Hebrew Scriptures are not reliable indicators of first-century Jewish culture.

The other unreliable source of information about women's roles in first-century Palestine is the material written by rabbis 100 to 200 years or more after the time of Jesus. For one thing, we know that the writings of those rabbis arose out of only one segment of Palestinian society, the sect of the Pharisees. These rabbis wrote in a different time and different culture than the one in which Jesus lived; the Jews had been defeated by Rome, the Temple destroyed, and the people dispersed.

Women in Jewish history had filled various leadership roles. Deborah was a prophet and judge, or leader, of Israel at one time (Judges 4:4–24). Hulda was the prophet the king's messengers sought out when they needed to understand a book found in the Temple (2 Kings 22:14–20). Queen Shulamit inherited the kingdom of Judea from her husband Alexander in 76 B.C.E. because he recognized how much the people respected her. Her reign lasted ten years and became known as the golden age of the Hasmoneans.[3] In the Diaspora the roles of prophets, kings, and priests disappeared from Jewish culture. Only the role of rabbi, the lawgiver, was left, and this was traditionally a male role.[4]

Some of the later rabbinic writing expressed fairly negative views toward women, but Christian writers one hundred years after Jesus also displayed very negative attitudes toward women. Neither the Jewish nor Christian writings of later centuries are reliable sources of information about the roles of women in first-century Palestine.

THE NEW TESTAMENT

We have very little information about the culture at the time the New Testament was written because much was destroyed or lost when the Jewish people were defeated and sent into Diaspora. Though it is not always a reliable historical document, certain sections of the New Testament were written in times much closer to the life of Jesus than the writings of the rabbis and can therefore give us insight into what those writers thought about the roles of women in relation to Jesus. One obvious point emerges in the New Testament stories: No one objected when

Jesus traveled with women and taught them. Though modern scholars have claimed this was shocking behavior in the first century, the New Testament writers clearly did not think so.

In his surviving letters, Paul mentions women he calls apostles and women he has worked with who are heads of house churches, the houses where the community gathered. He seems to accept this role for women as perfectly normal.[5] The letters that condemn women and require them to submit to men were not written by Paul. These are called the deutero-Pauline letters or the Pastoral letters.[6] Most scholars now believe that they were written by a follower of Paul in his name, probably within a few decades of Paul's death. There is nothing in the New Testament, aside from the deutero-Pauline letters, to indicate that women traveling with Jesus, being taught by him, or serving as leaders in the early movement was shocking or even unusual. The disciples are surprised that Jesus talks to a strange Samaritan woman at the well in the Gospel of John (John 4:27), but that is because Jews and Samaritans were estranged (John 4:9).

Saint Paul Preaching at Athens by Raphael (1483–1520). Paul traveled widely and worked with many women as church leaders and teachers.

Another point illustrated in the New Testament accounts is that women were out in public interacting with men. Wherever Jesus goes, women seem to be there. They are praying in the Temple (Luke 2:36–38, 13:10–17, 21:1–4), in the crowds (Matt. 14:21, 15:38), touching him (Matt. 9:20–22; Mark 5:25–34, asking for his help (Matt. 15:21–28; Mark 7:24–30), talking to him (John 4:1–42), and anointing him (Matt. 26:6–13; Mark 14:3–9; Luke 7:36–50; John 12:1–8). Scholars of the past have claimed that Jewish women were segregated, but if some women were, it was probably only the wealthiest who could afford to be. Many women in the New Testament stories are out and about their business everywhere Jesus and the disciples go.

Jesus and the Samaritan Woman by Duccio di Buoninsegna (b. ca. 1255, d. 1319). The disciples of Jesus were surprised when he talked to a strange Samaritan woman at a well, because Samaritans and Jews were estranged. The Samaritans worshiped on Mt. Garazim, while the Jews centered their worship on the Temple in Jerusalem.

INSCRIPTION EVIDENCE

Another possible source of information about the first-century culture is inscription evidence. Bernadette Brooten's research supports the claim that women held leadership roles in Jewish communities.[7] Reviewing Jewish inscriptions ranging from 28 B.C.E. to 500 C.E., Brooten discovered that women were sometimes described as heads of synagogues, leaders, patrons, elders, mothers of the synagogue, and priests.

Ancient Roman fresco. Few people were literate in the first-century Roman Empire, but women were clearly among those who could read and write.

Some synagogues had side rooms, but there is no evidence that they were used to seclude women.

This inscription evidence has been known for a long time, and its interpretation has been one of the most extreme examples of bias in this area of scholarship. The predominantly male scholars of the past said that these kinds of inscriptions about men meant that the men actually held the positions indicated. The inscriptions about women, on the other hand, could not mean that women held such positions. Why? Because, the scholars said, they already knew that women did not hold positions of power. Inscriptions concerning women meant that women held *honorary* positions or indicated positions that the women's *husbands* held.[8] As a result of this circular reasoning, the information about women's roles in first-century Jewish communities has been distorted.

Scholars have also argued that women were relegated to balconies in the synagogues of that time. Brooten has shown there is little archaeological evidence to support the argument that there were galleries in Palestinian synagogues, and no evidence at all that there were galleries in Diaspora synagogues. Some synagogues had side rooms, but there is no evidence that they were used to seclude women.[9] Past scholars also have claimed that Jewish women were secluded from the men in the home. Again, archaeology has shown that in much of Galilee the houses were too small to have allowed that. The houses in areas like Capernaum were very small.[10] A group of any size, like Jesus traveling with a group of twenty or more disciples, would have had to meet outside, where they would not be segregated.

We can conclude that some women held leadership positions in first-century Jewish culture, acted independently, and handled their own finances. Women probably interacted openly with men in many situations, and none of this behavior appears to have been shocking to their contemporaries. This is not to say that the culture was completely egalitarian. It was a patriarchal culture, but exaggeration and distortion of the evidence about the roles of women have led to the conclusion that women could not have held positions of leadership around Jesus. That conclusion is now being challenged.

Holy Women Near the Tomb by Maurice Denis (1870–1943). In the Gospel of Luke, the two men in dazzling clothes speak to the women as though they were present while Jesus taught his disciples. Western interpretations and Western art have long assumed that Jesus taught only men, not a mixed group of disciples. There is every indication that Jesus taught women too.

The Women Around Jesus

The women traveling with Jesus are rarely mentioned in the New Testament. In the Gospel of Mark we do not hear about the women until they are standing by the cross, and then the Markan writer says that they have been with Jesus since Galilee (Mark 15:40–41). This means that when we read the earlier New Testament stories, we should consider whether the women were present. For example, in the scene at the tomb in Luke, the two men in dazzling clothes speak to Mary Magdalene and her female companions:

> *"...Remember how he told you, while he was still in Galilee, that the Son of Man must be handed over to sinners, and be crucified, and on the third day rise again." Then they remembered his words, and returning from the tomb, they told all this to the eleven and to all the rest. (Luke 24:6–9)*

The clear meaning is that the women at the tomb were also present at the earlier discussion with Jesus. The account of Jesus telling these things to the disciples is

If women held religious leadership positions in Jewish society, as the evidence indicates, and were equal disciples of Jesus, the possibility that they played leadership or other major roles in the Jesus movement seems much more likely.

found in Luke 9:18–22. The story begins, "Once when Jesus was praying alone, with only the disciples near him…" (Luke 9:18). A traditional interpretation would have assumed that when Jesus was alone with his disciples, he was with the male disciples or the twelve. This image has been reinforced by Christian art, but clearly the Lukan writer does not understand it that way. When Jesus speaks to his disciples in the New Testament he is often speaking to both women and men. The New Testament writers use the same term for both male and female disciples.[11]

If women held religious leadership positions in Jewish society, as the evidence indicates, and were equal disciples of Jesus, the possibility that they played leadership or other major roles in the Jesus movement seems much more likely.

Mary Magdalene in the Gospels

Mary Magdalene is the only person who is present at the cross at the time of the crucifixion in all four gospels of the New Testament. She is also the only woman at the tomb in all four gospels. In the first three gospels other women go with her, and in the Gospel of John she goes alone. There is reason to think that the account of her going alone may be the oldest.[12] In the gospels of Matthew and John, Mary Magdalene is also the first person to see the risen Jesus (Matt. 28:9–10; John 20:11–12). In Mark, Mary Magdalene is listed first among the women who traveled with Jesus and ministered to him.

MARY MAGDALENE IN THE GOSPEL OF LUKE

The Gospel of Matthew tends to agree with Mark in its presentation of Mary Magdalene, but there is additional and alternative information about Mary Magdalene in the Gospel of Luke. This is significant, because we will see that the Gospel of Luke is problematic on the subject of Mary Magdalene in particular and women in general. Luke says:

> *...The twelve were with him, as well as some women who had been cured of evil spirits and infirmities: Mary, called Magdalene, from whom seven demons had gone out, and Joanna, the wife of Herod's steward Chuza, and Susanna, and many others, who provided for them out of their resources.(Luke 8:1–3)*

ABOVE *The Evangelist Luke* by Simeon Spiridonov (ca. 1690). The writer of the Gospel of Luke provides the least flattering portrayal of Mary Magdalene and the other women around Jesus.

OPPOSITE PAGE *Sermon on the Mount* by Fra Angelico (ca. 1400–1455). Most Western Christian art shows Jesus teaching only male disciples, but the gospels say women traveled with him too.

This has a very different meaning than the text of Mark. In Mark the women minister to Jesus alone, and the word "minister" can be understood as a spiritual ministry. In Luke the women's ministry is defined as financial. The men are called as spiritual disciples, but the women come because they have been healed of demons and disease and to provide financially for all the disciples, not just Jesus. Also, in Luke a real disciple is one who has given up all possessions (Luke 14:33), and these women have financial resources. For the writer of Luke, apparently only the men were true disciples.

At one time the Gospel of Luke was thought to be favorable toward women, and certainly it is very inclusive of women and has more stories involving them than any other New Testament gospel. Over the last two decades many scholars have begun to point out that the writer of Luke has another agenda as well. He wants to include women, but, at the same time, to severely restrict their role.[13] In Luke the women close to Jesus are not leaders or questioners or (usually) prophets. They are women who know their place—the place the writer of Luke thinks is proper.

In order to achieve this effect, the writer of Luke edited the material in the Gospel of Mark. He used some parts of Mark but changed or deleted other parts. The story of the Syrophoenician woman who convinced Jesus to heal her daughter even though she was a Gentile (Mark 7:24–30) was omitted. The discussion

Miniature from the Psalter of 1260 for the Cistercian Abbey at Basel, Switzerland. The anointing woman in Mark and Matthew anoints the head of Jesus, but the women in Luke and John anoint his feet. This is an unusual portrayal of both stories. Scholars differ on whether there were two anointing incidents or two versions of the same story.

between Peter and Jesus about what the disciples have left behind them to follow Jesus (Mark 10:28–29) was changed to include the word "wife" but not "husband," so that the discussion can be understood to concern only men (Luke 18:28–29). The prohibition against divorce (Mark 10:9) was omitted, but the proscription against remarriage was kept (Mark 10:11; Luke 16:18).

Anointing Women

Some of the changes were larger. For example, the anointing woman in Mark 14:3–9[14] was an unnamed woman who poured costly nard over the head of Jesus. Jesus described her as one who had seen his coming death, which made her a prophet of sorts, a person of penetrating insight who had seen more than the others. Jesus said, "Truly I tell you, wherever the good news is proclaimed in the whole world, what she has done will be told in remembrance of her" (Mark 14:9).

The anointing woman in Luke is a sinner who repents and washes the feet of Jesus with her tears and anoints them with ointment. Jesus is portrayed in the story as the insightful one; he understands the heart of the woman and of his host. The woman is forgiven, but she displays no insight, only her repentance of sin. We will see that this was the image of Mary Magdalene promoted by the Western Church, but there is no evidence at all that the anointing woman in this story was Mary Magdalene.

The Gospel of John tells a different version of the story of a woman anointing the feet of Jesus (John 12:1–8). She is not a repentant sinner but Mary of Bethany. She appears in the story as a close disciple of Jesus who expresses herself to him quite confidently. She understands Jesus' power to heal when others doubt him.

Scholars continue to debate whether there was one anointing story that got changed or two different incidents. If there were two stories, the writer of Luke left out the story of a woman as a prophet that appeared in Mark. If there was only one story, then the writer of Luke changed the woman from a prophet to a sinner, a point with which all the other gospel writers disagree. The Lukan story of a repentant woman became so popular with the Church that the anointing woman of Mark and Matthew has been virtually forgotten and, contrary to the prediction of Jesus, very little has been told in remembrance of her.

Christ in the house of Martha and Mary by Alessandro Allori (1535–1607) In the story from the Gospel of Luke, Martha complains to Jesus because her sister Mary is not helping her serve. Jesus tells her that Mary has chosen the better part. In first-century Christianity, this story had a different meaning than it would today.

Mary and Martha

The story of the sisters Martha and Mary of Bethany is another good example of the Lukan perspective. In that story Jesus comes to their house and Mary sits silently listening to Jesus while Martha is bustling about serving them. When Martha complains to Jesus that Mary is not helping, he tells her that Mary has made a better choice than she has (Luke 10:38–42). In Western culture, where the idea emerged that a woman's place was in the home, this apparent message from Jesus that education is more important than housework was welcomed. Within the culture existing at the time the Gospel of Luke was written, however, it had a very different meaning.

Jesus driving seven demons out of Mary Magdalene from *The Book of Hours* (1460–1470). This is a questionable story found only in the Gospel of Luke.

We know from the letters of Paul and from Acts, also written by the author of Luke, that the early Christians had house churches and the people who served in those churches had priestly functions.[15] The writer of Luke clearly limited that role to men (Acts 6:1–6). Many scholars believe that the intended message of the story of Mary and Martha in Luke is that women should sit silently and listen and not try to take positions of leadership in the Christian movement.[16]

Seven Demons

All this information about the Gospel of Luke is important because that gospel contains a claim that has been used to denigrate Mary Magdalene. It says that Jesus drove seven demons out of Mary Magdalene when he healed her (Luke 8:2). In European Christianity the seven demons were linked to the seven deadly sins, and this idea was used to identify Mary Magdalene as a terrible sinner before her redemption. The allegation is only found in one other place—Mark 16:9, but the last section of Mark 16:8 and 16:9–19 were endings added by later editors, most likely taken from the other gospels.[17] These sections cannot be used to support the historical accuracy of the claim that Mary Magdalene was cured of seven demons.

In considering whether this is a historical account it is useful to ask: What would it mean to be cured of seven demons? In the Jewish culture of the time the number seven was the number of totality: seven days in each lunar phase or week, seven observable planets making up the universe, the seventh day as the Sabbath. When Jesus is emphasizing the importance of forgiveness, he says to forgive not just seven times but seventy times seven—an infinite number of times (Matt. 18:21–22). Someone who had seven demons would have been totally possessed.

The New Testament gives us a good idea of what it might look like to be possessed by seven demons. The Gadarene (Matt. 8:28–34) or Gerasene (Mark 5:1–20; Luke 8:26–39) demoniac was possessed by several demons. He lived naked and was so violent that he was left chained outside of the village. In other words, he was uncontrollably insane. If Mary Magdalene were totally possessed by demons, it follows that she, too, would have been uncontrollably insane. Is it likely that no one except the writer of Luke would have heard of this? It is noteworthy that no other sources mention this "fact" about her, except for the editorial addition to Mark that can be traced to Luke.

Popular writers have tried to argue that casting out seven demons means that Jesus brought Mary Magdalene to full consciousness.[18] That is not a likely interpretation of Luke, whose writer was least likely to promote Mary Magdalene. Nowhere else in the New Testament is the casting out of demons linked to higher consciousness. When Jesus healed the Gadarene demoniac, the man wanted to go with him, but Jesus refused. There is no indication that this man was then fully awakened. We only see that he had been cured of insanity. The villagers were shocked to find him clothed and sitting quietly with Jesus.

If, as the evidence indicates, this story about Mary Magdalene and the seven demons is not historical, the obvious question is why the writer of Luke would have included it. It is possible that he wished to harm Mary Magdalene's reputation, and, if so, he certainly succeeded. It is also quite possible that he truly believed the story and still have been mistaken about it.

A quick look at the New Testament shows that Mary was a very common name. A study of first-century inscriptions has demonstrated that it was one of the most common names for women in Palestine at that time.[19] We can also see that characters in the New Testament stories were often confused with each other. Perhaps a story was in circulation that Jesus drove seven demons out of a woman named Mary and the writer of Luke or his community associated that woman with Mary Magdalene. The lack of corroboration for this story in the many other texts that discuss Mary Magdalene argues against the historical accuracy of that association, but it may be true that Jesus healed a woman named Mary of a terrible condition.

The Gate of Hell with the seven deadly sins. Illustration from the *Book of Hours of Catherine of Cleves* (1435). In the Middle Ages the seven demons from Luke's gospel were associated with the seven deadly sins, emphasizing Mary Magdalene's role as a former sinner.

The Loyal Disciple

The New Testament gospels agree that Mary Magdalene was a disciple of Jesus who traveled with him, ministered to him, and stood by him when most or all of the male disciples had fled in fear. From her actions at the crucifixion and the tomb, it would appear that her ministry was much more than financial, though she might well have been a wealthy woman. She was the first witness to the resurrection at the empty tomb and the Apostle to the Apostles in relaying that information. According to Matthew and John, she was also the first witness to the risen Jesus.

The Supper at Emmaus by Caravaggio (1573–1610). In the Gospel of Luke, Jesus appears to two travelers on the road to Emmaus after his resurrection. The two travelers are shown as male in Christian art, but only one of them is identified as a man in the gospel.

In the Gospel of Mark, the first of the New Testament gospels to be written, there is no report of a post-resurrection vision of Jesus. One of the endings added later says that Jesus appeared first to Mary Magdalene, then to two travelers, and then to the eleven (Mark 16:9–19). This does not reflect the view of the writer of Mark, but rather the view of later editors. This version combines the stories in the other three gospels, but rejects the claim in Luke that Jesus appeared to Peter alone. In Matthew, Jesus appears first to Mary (Matt. 28:1–10) and then to the eleven in Galilee (Matt 28:11–20). In Luke he appears to two travelers on the road to Emmaus, and when they hurriedly return to Jerusalem, they find that he has appeared to Peter (Luke 24:13–35). It is not clear who he appeared to first. In John, Jesus appears first to Mary Magdalene in Jerusalem (John 20:11–18), to all the disciples (John 20:19–29), and then to seven fishermen, including Peter (John 21:1–19).

Visions and Authority

These contradictory stories tell us that there was no clear version of the story and there was a great deal of controversy about the first post-resurrection appearance. One more account about these appearances is found in a letter of Paul, which says that Jesus appeared first to Peter [Cephas], then to the twelve, and then to 500 disciples (1 Cor. 15:3–11). Of course Paul was not a first-person witness to any of that, since he was an opponent of Jesus at the time. He says that he has been told this, and we know from another letter that when he went to Jerusalem he spent most of his time with Peter (Gal. 1:18–24). Paul's statement presents the possibility that Peter claimed to have been the witness to the first appearance. The writer of Luke may have gotten his information about Peter from Paul's letters or what he had heard about Paul's writing. Information he uses in Acts, which he also wrote, shows some familiarity with Paul's writings. It is very interesting that the other gospel writers rejected or had not heard that version of events.

Mary Magdalene and the Other Apostles. Illustration from the Albani Psalter, Hildesheim (12th century). As the first witness to the empty tomb, Mary Magdalene takes the news of the resurrection to the other disciples. For performing this role, she is known as the Apostle to the Apostles.

Why is the question of the first vision so important? According to Paul, it is the vision of Jesus that confers authority on the community leaders. Paul claims authority because he says that Jesus appeared to him. That appearance made Paul an apostle. Jesus appeared to him last, so he was the last of the apostles (1 Cor. 15:3–11). It follows that whoever Jesus appeared to first was the first of the apostles.

On the basis of our current information, we cannot say which, if any, of those accounts of visions were historically accurate, but we can tell that from the beginning there was dissension about the authority of those who witnessed Jesus' appearance. Paul and Luke say Peter was the first witness to the risen Jesus, while in Matthew, John, and the text added to Mark the first witness was Mary Magdalene.

LUKE AND PETER

With this in mind it is very interesting to note that the writer of Luke did not only edit material from Mark that concerned the role of women, he also edited the material from Mark about Peter, possibly in order to portray Peter in a

more favorable light. The writer of Luke gave Peter more prominence in several places than the other gospel writers and deleted critical material.

For example, in all of the first three gospels, Jesus predicts that Peter will deny him (Matt. 26:3–35; Mark 14:26–30; Luke 22:31–36). In Mark and Matthew, Peter contradicts Jesus and appears as a weak man who continually refuses to face the truth about himself. In Luke, Peter does not deny the truth of what Jesus says but declares his loyalty. Luke adds the following statement made by Jesus: "I have prayed for you that your own faith may not fail; and then once you have turned back, strengthen your brothers…" (Luke 22:32). Mark's story of Peter's weakness is transformed into an endorsement of Peter's leadership.

In Mark and Matthew, Jesus tells all the disciples he will make them fishers of men (Mark 1:17; Matt. 4:19), but Luke has Jesus speak directly to Peter (Luke 5:10). In several other places, Luke gives Peter prominence that he does not have in Mark. The most important example, for our purposes, is in the story of organizing the Last Supper. In Mark and Matthew, Jesus sends "disciples" to prepare the meal (Mark 14:13; Matthew 26:17), while in Luke he sends Peter and John. This is significant because, as we will see in our discussion of Leonardo's painting *The Last Supper*, in Mark Jesus arrives for the supper with the twelve (Mark 14:17–18) This indicates that at least two other disciples besides the twelve were present at the meal—those who had gone ahead to prepare it. By naming two members of the twelve as the ones who prepared the meal, Luke changes this meaning.

The writer of Luke also left out material in the gospel of Mark that was critical of Peter. In Mark, when Jesus announces that he must suffer and die, Peter takes him aside and rebukes him. Jesus rebukes Peter for this, calling him Satan (Mark 8:31–33; see also Matt. 16:21–23). Luke leaves this section of the narrative out completely. Later, when Jesus is in the garden of Gethsemane, the disciples with him fall asleep. In Mark and Matthew, Jesus rebukes Peter for this (Mark 14:37; Matt. 26:40). In Luke, the disciples are sleeping "from sorrow," and Jesus speaks gently to all of them (Luke 22:45–46).

From these editorial changes to the Gospel of Mark and the portrayal of Peter in Acts, we can theorize that the writer of Luke was an advocate for the authority of Peter. This possible bias makes it clear why his writings about Mary

"I have prayed for you that your own faith may not fail; and then once you have turned back, strengthen your brothers…" (Luke 22:32)

OPPOSITE PAGE *The Agony in the Garden* by Master of the Trebon Altarpiece (late 14th century). While Jesus prays before his arrest, Peter and some of the other men fall asleep. This is one of several stories showing the weakness of Peter.

Magdalene must not be taken at face value. In Acts, Peter and Paul are the leading apostles and Mary Magdalene does not appear at all. Acts has frequently been taken as reliable account of the early Church and used to support the proposition that Mary Magdalene was not a leader in the early community. Quite a few scholars do not believe this is accurate. The consistency with which Mary Magdalene appears in the New Testament and, as we shall see, in other texts as well; the consistency with which her name was used; and the portrayal of her as the witness to the crucifixion, resurrection, and the risen Jesus all indicate that she was extremely well known in the early community and that the gospel writers could not have left her out.[20]

Why, we might ask, would Mary Magdalene be so well known in all the varied and widespread communities of the New Testament gospels? Why would a significant number of people be willing to believe that she was not only the first witness to the resurrection but also the first witness to the risen Jesus? The most obvious explanation is that she was present and active in the early community and was believed to have received authority from Jesus.

Mary Magdalene was portrayed as a prostitute and repentant sinner by the Roman Church, and this view of her was made official in the late sixth century by Pope Gregory who was called "the Great."

The Western Church and the Prostitute

If this is the way Mary Magdalene is presented in the New Testament, why do most people in the West think she was a prostitute? Mary Magdalene was portrayed as a prostitute and repentant sinner by the Roman Church, and this view of her was made official in the late sixth century by Pope Gregory, who was called "the Great." We do not know if Gregory made up this portrayal of Mary Magdalene or merely made existing stories "official."

The presentation of Mary Magdalene as a prostitute was achieved by conflating several female characters in the New Testament accounts: Mary Magdalene, Mary of Bethany, the anointing sinner in Luke, and sometimes the adulteress in John 8:1–11 were all combined into the figure of Mary Magdalene. The Church justified this combination because the story in Luke of the anointing sinner came right before the verses saying that seven demons were driven out of Mary Magdalene. In Gregory's reasoning, that made Mary Magdalene a repentant sinner.

Where the idea of a prostitute came from is not clear, but it may have arisen because Luke's sinner had unbound hair and appeared to be a loose woman. Mary of Bethany was thrown into the mix because the writer of John says that she was the one who wiped the feet of Jesus with her hair, and the adulteress is sometimes thrown in because she is a sinful woman. Mary Magdalene was also associated with the various anointing women because she went to the tomb to anoint the body of Jesus and is often portrayed in art carrying an ointment jar.

The writer of Luke was an expert, telling stories full of heart and emotion. The image of the repentant woman bathing the feet of Jesus with her tears and drying them with her hair was so touching that it became very popular. The story in the Gospel of John where Mary Magdalene searched for Jesus until she found him was equally touching, and the image of Mary Magdalene as the perpetually sorrowful repentant sinner grabbed the popular imagination. She became an immensely popular saint in the Middle Ages.

Of course, even the most cursory reading of the New Testament would reveal that there was no real basis for this portrait of Mary Magdalene, but that point of view was not welcome. In the sixteenth century France's leading Christian humanist, Jacques Lefèvre d'Étaples, pointed out that there was no support in the New Testament for the claim that Mary Magdalene was a prostitute. His work stirred up a controversy, but in the end Lefèvre d'Étaples was accused of heresy and driven from his position at Paris University.[21] It was not until 1969 that the Catholic Church reconsidered the question and agreed with Lefèvre d'Étaples that there is no evidence that Mary Magdalene was a prostitute or should be combined with the other characters in the New Testament stories.

Today, several popular writers are using the early Church's technique of conflating characters to portray Mary Magdalene as something sensational. For Margaret Starbird she is a pagan priestess,[22] and for Lynn Picknett and Clive Prince she is a sacred prostitute and sexual initiatrix of Jesus.[23] They achieve these results by combining the character identified as Mary Magdalene in the New Testament with the unidentified anointing women in the various stories.

The Woman Taken in Adultery (detail) by Rembrandt (1606–1669). Jesus saved a woman taken in adultery by telling her accusers to stone her if they were without sin themselves. Since they were not, they left her alone. This woman, along with the sinner woman in Luke and Mary of Bethany, has been combined with Mary Magdalene in the process of turning Mary Magdalene into a prostitute.

RIGHT Martha of Bethany with a spoon and kettle from *The Book of Hours of Catherine of Cleves* from the first half of the 15th century. Martha was sometimes portrayed in Christian art as a housekeeper, but the role of service at communal meals in early Christianity was more like a priesthood.

OPPOSITE PAGE *The Sisters of Bethany*, sculpture by John W. Wood (1839–1886). The gospels indicated that there were several remarkable women around Jesus. Here Martha and Mary of Bethany are portrayed as affectionate sisters instead of as the competitors who appear in the Gospel of Luke.

Remarkable Women

The assumption that seems to underlie this conflation of characters is that there could not be very many remarkable women around Jesus, so any outstanding woman has to be combined with a named character. The New Testament accounts, however, speak of a group of women who traveled with Jesus (Mark 15:40–41; Luke 8:1–3), and the stories of the visits of Jesus to Mary and Martha in Bethany show that they were close disciples as well. We will also see in Chapter Three that some of the apocryphal gospels spoke of a group of seven prominent women who were disciples of Jesus. Because we know that there was a group of women close to Jesus, we cannot be justified in combining all the stories into one or two characters just because some of the names have been lost. Since Mary Magdalene was so well known in many communities, it is unlikely that her name was lost. It is much more likely that the anonymous stories, such as the anointing women in Mark and Matthew, are about other women.

One more argument is used to justify combining Mary of Bethany with Mary of Magdala, the argument that Magdalene is actually a title and not an indicator of Mary's place of origin. A woman could not be from both Magdala and Bethany, but she could be Mary the Magdalene from Bethany. Margaret Starbird uses this argument,[24] and the claim has been made before in popular writings. Scholars have always rejected this theory for a very good reason. The correct translation of the Greek is Mary, a woman of Magdala—clearly an indication of the place from which she originated.[25]

Conclusions

If we disregard all the efforts to combine her with other women, what does the New Testament tell us about Mary, the woman of Magdala? At one level it tells us that she was one of the women who traveled around with Jesus and ministered to him and perhaps to the other disciples as well. It tells us she was one of the witnesses to the crucifixion and the resurrection, and that a significant number of people in the community believed she was also the first witness to the risen Jesus. At a slightly more subtle level it tells us that she was so well known in the various communities of the New Testament writers that her name and the stories about her were remarkably consistent. This is significant when we see how many names have been lost and how much inconsistency there is about other characters in the accounts. Conflicts in the New Testament accounts tell us that there was a difference of opinion in the community about whether Peter or Mary Magdalene was the first witness to the risen Jesus. From Paul we know that this may mean that a conflict between the authority of Peter and the authority of Mary Magdalene as the first apostle existed in the communities of the New Testament writers.

Ἡ ἁγία
Μαρία
Μαγ
δα
λη
νή
SAINT
MARY
MAG
DA
LE
NE

CHAPTER THREE
OTHER VIEWS OF MARY MAGDALENE

Mary Magdalene in the Eastern Church

Mary Magdalene was never called a prostitute by the Eastern Church, and she was not combined with other female characters from the gospel accounts. The feast days of Mary of Bethany and the anointing women from the gospels of Mark and Matthew have always been separate from hers. There was also a widespread legend in the Eastern Church that Mary Magdalene was a preacher after the crucifixion.

The story says that Mary went to Rome and told the emperor what Jesus had taught and that he had risen from the dead in three days. The emperor said that a man could no more rise from the dead than an egg could turn red. At that point Mary picked up an egg and it turned red. This is one explanation given for the tradition of red Easter eggs in Eastern Christian countries.

The story is almost certainly not true, but it is interesting because it portrays Mary as a teacher and preacher who not only traveled on her own but also had the courage to go straight to the emperor. Considering that the Romans had just executed Jesus, it is unlikely she really did that. Nonetheless, she is remembered as a woman of great courage who participated fully in spreading the teachings of Jesus.

...she [Mary Magdalene] is remembered as a woman of great courage who participated fully in spreading the teachings of Jesus.

The Gnostic Gospels

There are many texts outside of the New Testament that also mention Mary Magdalene. These are often referred to as the Gnostic Gospels, but even Elaine Pagels, who wrote the excellent book by that name, no longer uses that term.[1] The problem is that scholars do not have an accepted definition of Gnosticism, and it is virtually impossible to distinguish between Gnostic and orthodox ideas in the early centuries of Christianity.

OPPOSITE PAGE *Mary Magdalene Holding a Red Egg*, 20th century icon.

Christ Pantocrator, painted by a Greek artist working for Archbishop Constantine Cavasilas, in Ohrid, between 1262 and 1263. In the apocryphal gospels Jesus is often called the Savior, a role he also plays in mainstream Christianity.

There are three main criteria associated with Gnosticism. One is that the Gnostics recognize the authority of gnosis or an individual experience of knowing. The second is that the Gnostics were radical dualists, considering the material world as evil and only the spiritual as good. The third is that Gnostics have an elaborate alternative cosmology. Sometimes scholars talk about Gnosticism in terms of only one of these characteristics, and only rarely in terms of all three.

These characteristics tended to be recognizable in some sects after the fourth century or so, but the documents found at Nag Hammadi often do not fit these criteria.[2] In early Christian texts it is difficult to distinguish between New Testament and apocryphal texts on these points. For example, Paul gets both his authority and, apparently, much of his information from at least one vision of Jesus. Is that Gnostic? He goes on at length about the superiority of the spirit over the flesh (Romans 8). Is that Gnostic? The *Gospel of Mary* involves a vision Mary had of Jesus. Paul claims to have had a vision, and all the gospels except Mark report post-resurrection visions of Jesus. When does a vision become Gnostic? In many ways, some of the texts found at Nag Hammadi are less Gnostic than New Testament texts, so labeling them Gnostic is too often just a way of discrediting them or disregarding them.

As Harvard professor Karen King has pointed out, there never was a group of people called Gnostics. Gnosticism is not a religion or a belief system. It is an academic category created by mainstream scholars to categorize early Christian groups. To paraphrase King, scholars had three basic categories: too Jewish, just right, and not Jewish enough. These three categories translated into Judaism, Christianity, and Gnosticism.[3] Despite all the evidence to the contrary, there is a pervasive belief that "real" Christianity existed from the time of Jesus to the present, and all other points of view are just heresies that have sprung up along the way.

The evidence we have demonstrates that there has always been diversity in Christianity. Early Christians were not Gnostic or orthodox; they were simply Christian. Many of the apocryphal texts were written before any clear ideas of orthodoxy had been formed. To call them Gnostic is a way to make them "other" than Christian and disregard them. Yet the apocryphal texts are as valid an indicator of what some early Christians believed, as any New Testament text.

Nag Hammadi Texts

The dating of the apocryphal texts varies from 50–70 C.E.[4] for the Gospel of Thomas to the third-century for the *Pistis Sophia*.[5] Many, but not all, of the texts were discovered in Egypt at Nag Hammadi in December 1945 by brothers who were digging for *sabakh*, or soft soil, to fertilize their crops. As they dug around a boulder they discovered an earthenware jar almost a meter high. After smashing it, they found thirteen leather-bound papyrus books, which they gathered up along with some loose papyrus to take home. They kept the books, which might be valuable, but discarded the loose papyrus in the straw used to start fires. Their mother burned much of it in the oven.

...the apocryphal texts are as valid an indicator of what some early Christians believed as any New Testament text.

Shortly after the discovery the brothers avenged their father's murder by killing his enemy, hacking off his limbs, and devouring his heart.[6] Fearful that the police would discover and confiscate the books while investigating the murder, they asked a local priest to keep one or more of the books. The value of the manuscripts was discovered by someone who saw one in the priest's possession. The manuscripts were then sold on the black market, where they eventually came to the attention of the Egyptian government.

The government managed to confiscate ten and a half of the books and place them in the Coptic Museum[7] in Cairo, but a large part of the thirteenth book was smuggled out of Egypt and offered for sale in the United States. The Dutch scholar Gilles Quispel persuaded the Jung Foundation in Zurich to buy it, only to discover that pages were missing. He traveled to the Coptic Museum to review the texts there and discovered that they contained the *Gospel of Thomas*, fragments of which had been found in the nineteenth century.

Dan Brown claims that the Church prevented the publication of these texts, but the Church had little influence with the Egyptian government. The delays in publication were mainly due to political and scholarly infighting and litigation over ownership.[8] Everyone knew that being involved in the translation and pub-

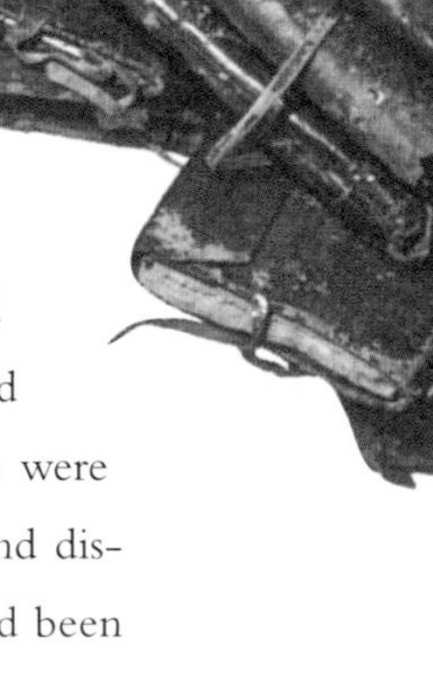

The Nag Hammadi texts were fragmented and damaged, but they have given us very valuable information about the diversity of early Christianty.

lication of such remarkable texts could make a career, as indeed it has for many. *The Nag Hammadi Library in English* was finally published in 1988.

The real tragedy of this story is that many of the missing pages of the codices that we have were undoubtedly used to light an oven, and more than one of the codices that were sold on the black market have never been recovered. In interpreting the documents that we have, it is good to keep in mind that much is still missing. With such incomplete information we need to be careful about drawing final conclusions.

The texts from Nag Hammadi and other apocryphal texts found over the past few centuries present a very different picture of Mary Magdalene than the way she was portrayed by the Roman Church.

The texts found at Nag Hammadi were clearly hidden because they were no longer allowed by the new Church. Many have assumed that the codices came from a Gnostic library, but it is quite possible that they came from the library of orthodox Christians who found it necessary to hide them when a new hierarchy forbade them. Elaine Pagels has theorized that the texts might have been buried by a monk from the nearby monastery of St. Pachomius, to save them from destruction.[9]

The texts from Nag Hammadi (*below*) and other apocryphal texts found over the past few centuries present a very different picture of Mary Magdalene than the way she was portrayed by the Roman Church. This raises questions about Mary Magdalene's role in the early Christian community and the reason why this view of her was lost in or disregarded by the Church.

Doubting Thomas by Guercino (1591–1666). In the Gospel of John, Thomas is portrayed as the one who doubted the resurrection of Jesus. This portrayal may have been because the community where the Johnnine gospel was written had a different candidate for first disciple—the beloved disciple that legend has identified as John.

The Gospel of Thomas

The *Gospel of Thomas* is what is known as a saying gospel, a collection of sayings attributed to Jesus similar to the hypothetical Q *Gospel*. (See Chapter Four.) Many believe that the sayings gospels were written down during the life of Jesus or shortly after and made up the earliest level of written Christian texts. When the *Gospel of Thomas* was first discovered, most orthodox scholars believed that it was based on the New Testament gospels and dated it to the second century for that reason.

This assumption of reliance on the New Testament was questionable and soon challenged by numerous scholars. Several scholars now date the *Gospel of Thomas* to as early as 50, before any of the New Testament gospels.[10] Most scholars agree, however, that some of the sections, most particularly the last saying, logion 114, were added later.[11]

The Apostle Thomas by Nicolas Frances (ca. 1424–1468). The apostle Thomas is portrayed as the leading disciple in the *Gospel of Thomas*. He was horored as a leading figure in Syria and as the founder of Christianity in India.

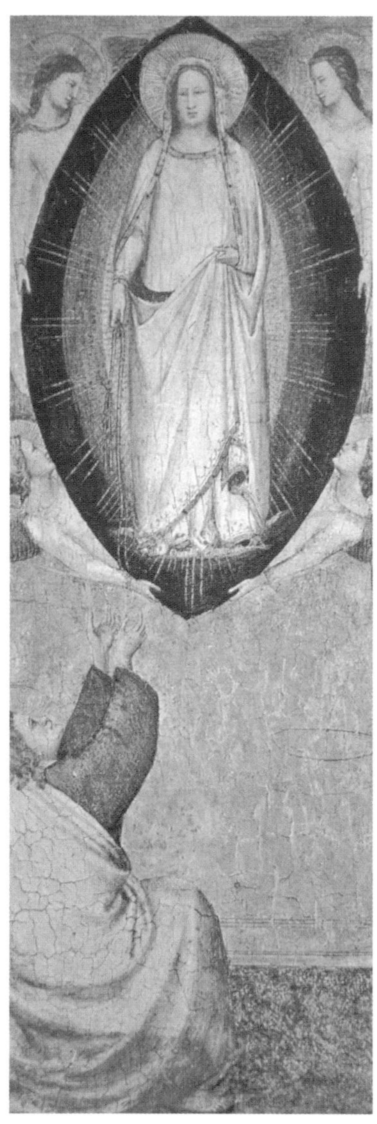

The Descent of Mary's Girdle to the Apostle Thomas by Maso di Banco (active 1320–1350). In one legend, Mary the mother of Jesus was taken into heaven. As she was taken up, she dropped her girdle to Thomas. This legend may have come from a community that promoted Thomas as the most important disciple of Jesus.

In this gospel, Thomas, who is described as the twin of Jesus, emerges as the leading disciple. Jesus praises him as no longer needing a master (35:4–7). Several disciples question Jesus and one more is mentioned by name. The questioners are Peter and Mary Magdalene, who ask two questions each, and Matthew, Thomas, and Salome, who each ask one question. James the Just is named as the leader of the community after the death of Jesus (34:25–27).

We see that Peter and Matthew have a mistaken conception of Jesus. Mary Magdalene and Salome are superior to them in understanding, but still inferior to Thomas.[12] The last logion, 114, is significant in that it is a portrayal of tension between Peter and Mary Magdalene:

> *Simon Peter said to them, "Let Mary leave us, for women are not worthy of life."*
>
> *Jesus said, "I myself shall lead her in order to make her male, so that she too may become a living spirit resembling you males. For every woman who will make herself male will enter the kingdom of heaven."* (51:18–26)

This is thought to be a later addition to the text in part because it contradicts an earlier saying that:

> *When you make the two one, and when you make the inside like the outside and the outside like the inside, and the above like the below, and when you make the male and the female one and the same, so that the male not be male nor the female female...then you will enter [the kingdom].* (37:20–30)

The belief that the spiritual ideal was male instead of beyond gender and beyond duality, as the earlier logion indicates, was most likely due to the later influence of a different philosophy. The relevant point for our purposes, however, is that Peter is portrayed as attacking not just Mary Magdalene but Mary as the representation of all women, who, he claims, are not worthy of spiritual life. This is misogyny in an extreme form, since it does not just challenge the role of women as spiritual leaders, it excludes them from spirituality altogether.

The writer of logion 114 appears to believe that women are inferior and must become male to enter into salvation. But even so, Peter's desire to exclude women completely is too extreme to be acceptable to that writer. The question for us is why Peter is portrayed in such a fanatical way. Why is his attack on Mary Magdalene and women in general so vicious? What historical information or legend did the early Christians rely on to form this image?

The Gospel of Mary was discovered in the late nineteenth century, and eventually three different fragments, two Greek and one Coptic, came to light.

The Gospel of Mary

The *Gospel of Mary* is dated to the late first or early second century, with the majority of scholars favoring a second-century date.[13] Many scholars accept the argument that this gospel, like the *Gospel of Thomas*, was based on the New Testament. Karen King has demonstrated that the phrases that are claimed to be dependent on New Testament texts are so short and found in so many Christian texts that they cannot be used to prove any dependence.[14] If the *Gospel of Mary* is not dependent on New Testament texts, it may have been written in the first century.

This gospel was not part of the Nag Hammadi find, though it is often included in publications of those texts. The *Gospel of Mary* was discovered in the late nineteenth century, and eventually three different fragments, two Greek and one Coptic,[15] came to light. King believes that the discovery of so many fragments indicates that the text was widely distributed.[16] Because of differences in the surviving texts, it is clear that at least two versions of this gospel were in circulation.

The first six pages of this gospel are missing, so the section we have begins with the end of the Savior's farewell to the disciples as he prepares to ascend into heaven. The disciples are supposed to go out and teach, but they are afraid that they will be killed as Jesus has been. Mary kisses and comforts them and encourages them to be resolute, saying that Jesus has made them human beings or perfect humans,[17] meaning something like fully evolved people or saints.

"Did he, then, speak with a woman in private without our knowing about it? ...Did he choose her over us?"

Jesus Ascending to Heaven by William Hole (ca.1890). Several of the apocryphal gospels claim to be conversations between the risen Jesus, the Savior, and his loyal disciples. Though only men are present in Christian art, the apocryphal gospels report that women were present too.

Peter calls her "sister" and asks her to tell them something Jesus has told only her, because Jesus loved her more than other women. To Peter's dismay, Mary does not relate some personal anecdote but launches into a description of a teaching from Jesus that illustrates that she is not only the most beloved *woman*, she is the most beloved *disciple*, because she has been given a teaching the others have not received. Andrew, Peter's brother, objects that the teaching is strange. Peter says:

> *Did he, then, speak with a woman in private without our knowing about it? Are we to turn around and listen to her? Did he choose her over us?* (BG 8502 10:3)[18]

Mary weeps and asks Peter if he thinks she is lying, and Levi comes to her defense. He calls Peter a "wrathful person" or "hothead," depending on the translation, and says that if the Savior found her worthy it is not Peter's business to reject her. The Savior's knowledge of her is reliable and he loved her more than the other disciples. At this point either Levi or all the disciples go out to preach, depending on the version.

This gospel does not portray Mary Magdalene as the opponent of the twelve, as some commentators have claimed, or place the Gnostics against the orthodox. The disciples in general do not attack Mary or criticize her, and there is no indication that they support Peter against her. Instead of reflecting some kind of doctrinal dispute, this story appears to address the criteria for authority in the early Christian movement.[19]

In Mary Magdalene's case, she has been chosen by Jesus and has displayed her courage and understanding in supporting the other disciples. Peter, on the other hand, has displayed fear, jealousy, and anger. The fact that Peter is consistently shown as the one who attacks or criticizes Mary Magdalene is not likely to be accidental.

The Gospel of Philip

This text, which we have already examined in Chapter One, was written by Valentinian[20] Christians around the end of the second or beginning of the third century.[21] It uses Syriac words and discusses Eastern sacramental practices, so it was probably written in Syria, perhaps in Edessa or Antioch. It appears to be a collection of various literary types and may have been a compilation done by a community.[22]

As we saw in Chapter One, scholars differ on whether this gospel refers to actual sexual relationships or to sexual practices. Even if Mary Magdalene was not the sexual companion of Jesus, she was portrayed in this gospel as his spiritual companion and spiritual consort. Her relationship to him was intimate and made her, if not literally, then figuratively part of his family.

. . . [Mary] was portrayed in this gospel as his spiritual companion and spiritual consort. Her relationship to him was intimate and made her, if not literally, then figuratively part of his family.

The Pistis Sophia

The *Pistis Sophia* was most likely written in Egypt, since it refers to the Egyptian calendar and to Egyptian mythological names, and is usually dated to the third century.[23] It was not part of the Nag Hammadi find but exists in only one manuscript that was discovered in London in 1773.

This text concerns a conversation between Jesus and his disciples that takes place after the resurrection. Mary Magdalene plays an important role as a questioner, asking more questions of Jesus than all the other disciples put together. In Book III, for example, she speaks fifty-three times, while John speaks five times, and Peter and Salome one time each. Peter, of course, objects to the extent of her participation.

> *My Lord, we are not able to suffer this woman who takes the opportunity from us, and does not allow anyone of us to speak, but she speaks many times.* (58:11–14)[24]

> *My Lord, let the women cease to question, that we may question.* (377:14–15)

Mary expresses her concern over this attitude:

> *My Lord, my mind is understanding at all times that I should come forward at any time and give the interpretation of the words which she [Pistis Sophia] spoke, but I am afraid of Peter, for he threatens me and he hates our race [or sex].* (162:14–18)

Jesus encourages Mary to speak out:

> *Mariam, thou blessed one, whom I will complete in all the mysteries of the height speak openly, thou art she whose heart is more directed to the Kingdom of Heaven than all thy brothers.* (26:17–20)

ABOVE *Rendering of the Tribute Money* (detail) by Masaccio (1401–1428). In *Pistis Sophia*, Jesus identifies John the Virgin and Mary Magdalene as his two top disciples, but mentions Mary Magdalene first.

OPPOSITE PAGE Sophia (Wisdom) from *The Book of Wonders* by David Jors, 16th century. Sophia as the feminine embodiment of wisdom was an important figure in the apocryphal gospels.

Jesus also affirms Mary Magdalene as one of his top two disciples, and mentions her first of the two:

"But Mary Magdalene and John the Virgin will be superior to all my disciples." (232:26–233:2)

> *But Mary Magdalene and John the Virgin will be superior to all my disciples.* (232:26–233:2)

This is because she has become Spirit:

> *When she finished speaking these words, the Savior marveled greatly at the answers to the words which she gave, because she had completely become pure Spirit.* (199:20–200:3)

Mary Magdalene by Jose Antolinez (1635-1675). Jesus, in *Pistis Sophia*, identifies Mary Magdalene as one of his two most superior disciples and as pure spirit.

Mary also explains Jesus' meaning to Philip (72:5–22), answers Salome's question and is thanked by both Salome and Jesus (338:1–339:4), and asks Jesus questions on behalf of the male disciples (201:8–25; 296:7–12; 311:17–24), including one instance when the male disciples become too frightened to understand what Jesus is talking about (218:1–219:22).

The Sophia of Jesus Christ

The *Sophia of Jesus Christ* was included in the texts found at Nag Hammadi and is dated to the late first or early second century.[25] There are two Coptic manuscripts and one Greek fragment of this gospel. Most scholars agree that this was a Christianized version of an earlier text, *Eugostos*, which was also discovered at Nag Hammadi.

In this story, nineteen disciples are still loyal to Jesus after the resurrection, the twelve men and seven women. This group gathers in Galilee and Jesus appears to them and answers their questions. The entire group asks two questions, while five of the nineteen disciples ask individual questions. Philip, Matthew, Thomas, and Mary Magdalene ask two questions each, while Bartholomew asks one.

This group of nineteen disciples appears to be viewed as the ones who received the highest teachings from Jesus and who themselves were authorized to teach.[26] It is significant that this text identifies a group of women who are among the leading disciples after the death of Jesus.

Saint Philip by Peter Paul Rubens (1577–1640). In the apocryphal gospels, the apostle Philip is frequently portrayed as a disciple who understood Jesus well.

The Dialogue of the Savior

There is only one copy of the *Dialogue of the Savior* text, a partial, heavily damaged version found at Nag Hammadi, dated by most scholars to the early second century.[27]

This text is another dialogue between the Savior and the disciples in which Matthew, Thomas, and Mary Magdalene are singled out by name. No other woman is mentioned here, and at times Mary Magdalene assumes the role of spokesperson for all the disciples. Mary is praised by the narrator as "a woman who had understood completely" (139:11–13), and the Savior says that she makes "clear the abundance of the revealer!" (140:18–19). In other words, she understands and can explain the Savior's message.

The grouping of Mary Magdalene with Thomas, Philip, and Matthew is not unique to this text. In the *Pistis Sophia* Mary Magdalene is the main questioner, while Thomas, Matthew, and Philip are the official scribes. In the *Sophia of Jesus*

Philip, Matthew, Thomas, and Mary Magdalene ask two questions each, while Bartholomew asks one.

Three Women at the Tomb. Icon from central Russia (17th century). The *Epistuala Apostolorum* preserves a different version of the story of Mary Magdalene and two other women going to the tomb.

Christ, Mary Magdalene, Judas Thomas, and Matthew are model disciples. In another Nag Hammadi text, the *Book of Thomas the Contender*, Thomas and Matthew are entrusted secret teachings, and Thomas, Matthew, and Mary are all featured questioners in the *Gospel of Thomas*. These consistent portrayals of Mary, Thomas, Philip, and Matthew as the leading disciples after the death of Jesus, show no evidence of competition. That behavior is reserved for Peter.

The First Apocalypse of James

This text was found at Nag Hammadi, and though another version of the text exists, it is not available for study.[28] The word "first" was added to the title to distinguish it from the subsequent text by the same name, also found at Nag Hammadi.

This text is not usually used in studies of Mary Magdalene because it consists of a dialogue between the Lord and his brother James, though this text makes it clear that James is not the material brother of Jesus (24:15). The text is interesting in relation to Mary Magdalene, first because James asks a question about (possibly seven) women who have been disciples. James is amazed at how powerful the women have become in their knowledge of themselves (38:15–20). Even more significant, the Lord advises James about several of those women. The first two are Salome and Mariam (Mary Magdalene), and scholars believe the second two are Martha and Arsinoe. Unfortunately, the fragmented text does not allow for unambiguous interpretation. Either the Lord says James should encourage the woman[29] or that he should turn to them for instruction.[30]

The Epistuala Apostolorum

This document is significant because it is a strongly anti-Gnostic text, probably from Egypt in the second century,[31] which indicates that Mary Magdalene's prominence was not limited to groups now called Gnostic. There is an Ethiopic[32] version of this text and a fragmentary Coptic one.

The document is a resurrection narrative and includes the story of Mary Magdalene, Martha, and Sarah going to the tomb, where Jesus appears to them. In the Ethiopic text, Mary goes to the other disciples to tell them Jesus has risen, but they do not believe her. Sarah goes next, but they do not believe her either. In the Coptic version Martha goes first, and then Mary Magdalene and neither woman is believed. Finally, the Lord goes with them to convince the others.

Here we have another example of Mary Magdalene as one of the first recipients of a post-resurrection vision of Jesus. We also see that Martha and the unknown Sarah are identified as women close to Jesus.

The Apostle Peter by Feofan Grek (Moscow, 14th century). Though mainstream Christianity considers him the founder of the Church, Peter is portrayed in the apocryphal gospels as a hot-headed man who does not really understand Jesus. He is frequently in conflict with Mary Magdalene and makes insulting comments about her and other women.

Recurring Themes

In-depth analyses of these texts would fill a complete volume, and, in fact, several have already been written.[33] For our purposes it is enough to say that these documents are consistent on a few important points.

MARY MAGDALENE: THE MOST INSIGHTFUL DISCIPLE

Mary Magdalene is consistently portrayed as one of the three or four leading disciples of Jesus. She is identified as the companion of Jesus, superior to the other disciples, pure spirit, and a woman who has understood Jesus' teachings completely.

PETER AND MARY MAGDALENE

Another consistent theme in these gospels is the conflict between Mary Magdalene and Peter. Some commentators have argued that this reflects a historical conflict between Gnostics and orthodox Christians, and the Gnostics have simply chosen Mary Magdalene as their representative. This theory ignores the fact that Mary Magdalene is not shown in conflict with other members of the twelve, or with the twelve as a group. Her conflict is consistently with Peter and, in the *Gospel of Mary*, with his brother Andrew. To assume that Peter represented all of orthodox Christianity to early Christians is to impose modern ideas onto antiquity. Peter was not the first and foremost leader of the community in the first

We have consistent portrayals of Mary Magdalene, both in the New Testament and in the apocryphal texts, as the leader and the most remarkable woman in the community, but that does not mean that other women were not remarkable in their own ways.

century; James was the leader in Jerusalem, Paul in the areas he proselytized, Thomas may have been a leader in Syria, and so on.

Ann Graham Brock, in her excellent book *Mary Magdalene, The First Apostle*, has pointed out that the depictions of Mary Magdalene in these apocryphal texts are not dependent on each other. Given that these texts were written over a long period of time in a variety of locations and by groups holding different points of view, it is clear that the tradition of a dispute between Peter and Mary Magdalene did not reflect a local conflict or concern.[34] A strong argument can be made that this widespread retelling of the conflict indicates an equally widespread tradition of an actual conflict between these two historical figures. Whether or not such a conflict ever took place, it is likely that many early Christians believed it did and that the portrayal of the conflict was not simply metaphorical.

THE GROUP OF WOMEN

A last theme is that there were several women, in addition to Mary Magdalene, who were well-known disciples. One of these is Salome, a person we have seen in the Gospel of Mark as one of the two women who accompany Mary Magdalene to the tomb (Mark 16:1–8). Her name is not mentioned in the Gospel of Matthew (Matt. 28:1), and in Luke she may be among the "other women" (Luke 24:10), but she is not named.

Another woman mentioned is Martha, whom we know from both Luke and John. Some commentators have wondered why her sister Mary is not named as well, but it is possible that the portrayal of Mary of Bethany and Martha in the Gospel of Luke reflected their actual history. Mary, who was portrayed sitting quietly and learning, may have lived a life of study and contemplation, and so was not mentioned as a teacher or leader in apocryphal texts. Martha, who is shown bustling around, may have lived a life of active service. This would account for her mention in these texts as a leading woman in the community.

Mary the mother of Jesus is not usually portrayed as a teacher or community leader after the death of Jesus, but she does appear as one of the questioners in the *Pistis Sophia*.

Who then were the seven leading women disciples who were loyal to Jesus after his death? We have several candidates. We know Mary Magdalene was among them, and it's very likely Salome was too. Other candidates include Martha, Arsinoe, Mary the mother of Jesus, Sarah, Mary the mother of James, Joanna, and Mary the wife of Clopas. This list of possibilities illustrates how little is known about the women close to Jesus and how little the chroniclers cared to tell about them. Though we hardly know anything about these women, we know enough to hesitate before we assume that all the women around Jesus can be conflated into the figure of Mary Magdalene. We have consistent portrayals of Mary Magdalene, both in the New Testament and in the apocryphal texts, as the leader and the most remarkable woman in the community, but that does not mean that other women were not remarkable in their own ways.

Mary the mother of Jesus is not usually portrayed as a teacher or community leader after the death of Jesus, but she does appear as one of the questioners in the Pistis Sophia.

Founder of a Church

Does the frequent representation of Mary Magdalene as a leading disciple mean that Dan Brown is right and Mary Magdalene was the person Jesus asked to found his church? That question presumes that Jesus wanted someone to form a church, and this is not at all self-evident.

Mary Magdalene is portrayed as a teacher and a woman of understanding, but she is not seen as the enforcer of a hierarchy or someone who wanted to dictate to others. It may have been the intention of the Peter-and-Paul stream of Christianity to form a hierarchical church, establish dogma, and enforce a spiritual correctness that resulted in its ultimate victory over other early forms of Christianity. Our evidence indicates that this was not the approach Mary Magdalene would have taken.

OPPOSITE PAGE *The Three Marys at the Tomb* by unknown artist (German 1460–1480). Both New Testament and apocryphal texts describe a group of women who were disciples of Jesus.

CHAPTER FOUR
EVOLUTION OF THE EARLY CHURCH

Dan Brown's characters spend a considerable amount of time discussing the development of Christianity. The author's general view seems to be that Christianity was formed by a group of people who admired Jesus as a wise man and prophet but did not believe he was God. In this line of thinking, thousands of pages were written documenting the life of a prophet, but Constantine had the gospels rewritten to present Jesus as God. In the Council of Nicaea he forced the Church to accept the doctrine that Jesus was God. The original documents now make up part of the secret Grail treasure.

The true history of Christianity is much more complex. Many influences led Christians to identify Jesus as God long before the time of Constantine. Though Constantine had some influence on the development of Christianity, it was not nearly as overwhelming as Brown argues.

ABOVE *Conquest of Jerusalem by the Romans* by Nicolas Poussin (1594–1665). In 70 C.E. the Romans conquered Jerusalem, destroyed the Temple, and forced the Jews to scatter to other parts of the world. Christianity began to emerge in the world of the Jewish Diaspora.

OPPOSITE PAGE *Coronation of the Virgin* (detail) by Fra Angelico (ca. 1400–1455).

Influences on Early Christianity

The religion that we know as Christianity evolved in a very different arena from the one in which Jesus lived. He lived in a Palestine where the Jewish people, though under the control of Rome, had a certain amount of autonomy. They had the Temple as a physical center for their religious practice, a priesthood, and a line of kings, as well as their own law and the power to enforce it. The modern concept of Christianity emerged after the Temple was destroyed, the people had dispersed, and the culture was broken.

When Jesus was executed, the people around him had to make sense of it. Those who thought he was the promised Messiah had to come to terms with what that meant. There were many ideas about a Messiah in first-century Palestine, but perhaps the most popular was that the Messiah would free the Jewish people from Roman domination. Instead, Jesus was killed by the Romans, and approxi-

Conversion of St. Paul by Hildesheim (15th century). Saul of Tarsus was a persecutor of Christians until he had a vision of Jesus. He changed his name to Paul and became one of the most active promoters of his own understanding of Christianity.

mately forty years later the Jewish people were defeated and devastated by Rome. Could Jesus still be the Messiah? If so, what did being a Messiah mean?

The group that became the orthodox Christians focused on explaining the spiritual meaning of the death of Jesus as the Messiah. In general, this group put more emphasis on the significance of his death as salvation, than on his teachings as a path to salvation. Other Christians, such as the writer of the *Gospel of Mary*, seemed to focus more on the content of the teaching of Jesus as the way to salvation, rather than on the significance of his death.

As Christianity evolved from a Jewish sect to a world religion, it borrowed from some traditions and was borrowed from by others. Much of the borrowing centered on defining who Jesus was, his nature, and the meaning of his death.

A JEWISH SECT

In the years after the death of Jesus, the group that was to give rise to Christianity was not a separate religion but a sect of Judaism. James, the brother of Jesus, was the leader in Jerusalem. The group in Jerusalem, which included Peter, went to the Temple every day (Acts 2:46). The members of this group, then, considered themselves observant Jews and understood the work of Jesus within the boundaries of the covenant of God with the Jewish people.

The transition of Christianity from a Jewish sect to a Gentile religion was a gradual one…

When Paul converted to Christianity, he, too, focused on the Jewish community. He began his work by going to the synagogues in Jewish communities outside of Palestine. Eventually Paul and others would argue that the gospel—or good news—was for everyone, and that Gentiles did not need to become Jews before they could become Christians. Specifically, that meant that men did not need to be circumcised. Since circumcision was the sign of God's covenant with the Jewish people, this took Christianity outside that covenant and redefined it. This radical change led to a break between Paul and the Jews in Jerusalem.

The transition of Christianity from a Jewish sect to a Gentile religion was a gradual one, and Judaism deeply influenced the development of Christianity. Religious innovation was frowned upon in antiquity. New religions and new ideas were considered dangerous superstitions. Perhaps because of that, Christians continued to claim Judaism as the ancient roots of Christianity, even renaming the

Hebrew Scriptures the "Old Testament." The Old Testament was then superseded in importance by the New Testament.

One Jewish group, the Essenes, appears to have had a significant influence on Christianity's evolution. It is fairly certain that Jesus was not an Essene because of his relaxed attitude toward the law, but Essenes may well have been attracted to Christianity later, particularly after the fall of Jerusalem and the destruction of the community at Qumran.

The Essenes were an apocalyptic group who expected a Messiah and a final destruction of the world. They may have influenced the interpretation of Jesus as Messiah or the expectation of the end of the world that was so prevalent in the early Christian community. The Essenes also had a hierarchal organization similar to the one that was eventually formed in the institutionalized Church.[1]

The designation of twelve apostles is similar to the council of twelve laymen at Qumran. Jesus might have used this symbolism himself after his contact with John the Baptist, who many believe was an Essene. The symbolism may also have been adopted by the disciples after his death.[2] Two additional links between early Christian practice and Qumran are the concepts of communal goods, sometimes put into practice by early Christians, and the community meal, which became an important part of Christian tradition in the first century, eventually leading to the sacrament of the Eucharist.

The designation of twelve apostles is similar to the council of twelve laymen at Qumran.

MYSTERY RELIGIONS

As Christianity gained more non-Jewish converts, the other religions of the Greco-Roman world began to have more influence. There was a group of religions that are called oriental religions or mystery religions. Three of those were major competitors of Christianity, and they most likely influenced the development of Christian ideas.[3]

Cybele and Attis

The first major competitor was the religion of the Great Mother, Cybele. This religion was extremely popular in Rome in the first century and as far west as the British Isles. The worship of Cybele as the Great Mother began in the prehistoric culture of the Phrygian Empire in what is modern Turkey. In 204 B.C.E. the

Mystical Wheel by Fra Angelico (ca. 1400–1455). The idea that twelve men represented Israel is older than Jesus. The mystical wheel of heaven from the Book of Ezekiel shows twelve prophets in the outer wheel.

The worship of Cybele as the Great Mother began in the prehistoric culture of the Phrygian Empire in what is modern Turkey. In 204 B.C.E. the Sibylline Oracle in Rome predicted that Rome's enemies would be defeated if Cybele was brought to Rome.

Sibylline Oracle in Rome predicted that Rome's enemies would be defeated if Cybele was brought to Rome.[4] In 191 B.C.E. the small black meteorite that was the focus of her worship was moved to a temple in Rome.

At some point in the development of her myth, Cybele was linked with Attis. *(See photo of marble bust, right.)* In that story Zeus, the great philanderer, propositions Cybele but she turns him down. Not one to take rejection lightly, Zeus masturbates on her while she sleeps, and she gives birth to Agdistis, a hermaphrodite of great power. He is so powerful and wild that he disturbs the Gods, and they either castrate him or convince him to castrate himself. The flow of blood produces either an almond tree or flowers. Nana, the river's daughter, comes along and eats the almonds or tucks the flowers in her bosom and becomes pregnant in virginal conception. Her father does not believe she is a virgin, and when she gives birth to Attis, he leaves the baby exposed among the reeds by the river. The baby is found and raised by shepherds.

As Cybele watches Attis grow into a man, she is struck by his beauty and falls in love with him. In one version of the myth, the castrated Agdistis is now a woman and seduces Attis, which makes Cybele very jealous. In another version Attis falls in love with a nymph. In all the versions Cybele is madly jealous of other women, and when Attis is supposed to marry a princess Cybele disrupts the ceremony, causing Attis to run into the woods. He lies down under a pine tree, castrates himself, and bleeds to death. He does this either because Cybele's jealously has driven him mad or because he regrets causing her such pain. Where he has bled, violets grow.

When Attis dies Cybele is sorry for what she has done and takes the pine tree, the body, and the violets back with her to her cave, where she mourns him for three days. On the third day she, either alone or with the help of Zeus, restores him to life. In one version, Cybele recognizes the castrated Attis as her daughter and conveys all her sacred mysteries to her.

Worshipers of Cybele had several powerful rites to celebrate this myth. Once a year they would carry a pine tree covered with violets to Cybele's shrine and mourn for three days, and on the third day they would celebrate the resurrection of Attis. They were told, "The god is saved, and for you also will come salvation from your trials."[5] Worshipers were also promised immortality and practiced a form of baptism called the taurobolium, borrowed from Mithraism. The devotee bathed in bull's blood and was buried in a pit covered with boards, then rose to a new life, purified of sins.

The would-be priests of Attis castrated themselves during a yearly festival, after ecstatic music and dancing. Since these priests castrated themselves for the sake of heaven, this religion may be the context for the saying about castration that is attributed to Jesus (Matt. 19: 10–12).

The birthday of Attis was celebrated on the winter solstice, when the life-giving light begins to return to the earth in the Northern Hemisphere. According to the ancient calendar, the solstice fell on December 25, but in our modern calendar it falls around December 22.[6]

The Sibyl of Cumae by Michaelangelo (1475-1564) on the Sistine Chapel, Rome. The Sibyl was a Roman prophetess who recommended bringing the worship of the Goddess Cybele to Rome.

Isis and Osiris

The next major competitor of Christianity was the Egyptian religion of Isis and Osiris. Osiris was the son of the Goddess Nut and ruled for twenty-eight years as pharaoh. He was also sometimes portrayed as a Creator God who had created the earth and constellations. He civilized the people of Egypt and taught them to use the flooding of the Nile to irrigate their crops. Osiris's brother Set (or Seth) was jealous of him and wanted to usurp him. According to the story, Set gathers a group of accomplices who plan how to kill Osiris. They secretly take his measurements and have a beautiful sarcophagus made to fit him. Set takes the sarcophagus to a party, where everyone marvels at it. He tells the guests that he will give it to anyone who can fit in it. One by one they try it, but when Osiris

Resurrection by Matthias Grünewald, (ca.1475-1528). Jesus was not the only God to be resurrected in three days. Attis was also brought back to life on the third day after his death.

Basalt relief from the sarcophagus of Nes-Shutfene (Saqqara, 4th century B.C.E.). The sperm arises from the dead Osiris to impregnate his wife Isis. Becaue of this, Horus is born from a kind of virgin birth.

lies down inside, Set's accomplices rush out, slam the sarcophagus shut, seal it with lead, and throw it in the Nile. And so Osiris dies.

His sister/wife Isis is devastated by the news of his death and is determined to find his body so that he can be given a proper burial and journey to the underworld. The sarcophagus had washed up on the riverbank in Syria and a tamarisk tree had grown around it. The tree had such a wonderful aroma that the king had it cut and brought to the palace to be a pillar there. Isis hears about this and gets a job as a nursemaid to the infant prince by braiding and perfuming the hair of the queen's servants. She nurses the child by letting him suck on her thumb and decides to give him immortality by slowly burning away his mortality in the fire.

This plan is ruined when the queen finds the baby in the fire, and Isis is forced to reveal who she is. When they hear her story, the queen and king open the pillar and give her the sarcophagus.

Once again Isis has to find the body so she can give Osiris a proper burial.

Isis takes the body of Osiris back to Egypt, and by extracting his essence from his dead body, she conceives the infant Horus in a form of virginal conception. Shortly after, Set accidentally stumbles upon the hiding place of the sarcophagus, and he becomes so angry that he chops up Osiris's body into fourteen pieces and scatters them. Once again Isis has to find the body so she can give Osiris a proper burial. She finds thirteen pieces, but his penis had been eaten by a fish and cannot be recovered. Nevertheless, she completes the burial service, and Osiris is resurrected to rule as the king of the underworld.

Horus later avenges himself on Set but loses an eye in the process, giving rise to the Eye of Horus symbol. In one version of the myth, Horus and Set continue their battle of good and evil, and on the day Horus wins, his father Osiris will return to rule the world. He will bring with him all those who had been loyal to him, so the bodies of the dead were embalmed in antiquity to preserve them for the return of Osiris.

This group had two major festivals. On March 5 they celebrated the end of winter, and from late October to early November, the death and vindication of Osiris.[7]

Mithra

The final major competitor of Christianity was Mithraism, a religion popular among Roman soldiers that honored the ancient Persian God Mithra. Although limited in its appeal since women were not included, Mithraism nevertheless had a strong influence for centuries.

Mithra (also Mithras) was originally a God from the Persian tradition of Zoroastrianism. This religion envisioned a struggle between good and evil in the form of two Gods: the good Ahura Mazda and the evil Ahriman. At the end of their lives, humans would be judged and either go to a form of celestial heaven or be pulled down into a pit. Much like Jesus in the New Testament, Mithra was a lesser deity who came to help humans in their struggle. He would personally guide them after death, and at the end of the world Mithra would conduct a final judgment of humanity and would cause fire to consume the evil.

The Caesarea Mithraic medallion is a marble disk that shows Mithra slaying the bull in the upper portion. In the lower part Sol is kneeling before Mithra (on left), Sol and Mirhra banqueting (middle), and Mithra riding the bull (right). Mithra kills the bull in order to fulfill his role as savior. According to one legend, he killed the sacred bull reluctantly when the good God, Ahura Mazda, told him to. When the bull died, plants, animals, and all beneficial things flowed from it.

The Caesarea Mithraeum. Low benches, suitable for reclining to eat and drink, flank the walls to left and right. A beam of light from an aperture in the vault illuminates the altar area.

Mithraism was a secret religion; little textual evidence about its beliefs or practices exists, therefore, except what was written by its enemies, clearly not a reliable source. We do have many artifacts and surviving temples, however, which were underground caves often featuring a painting of Mithra killing a bull. The killing of the bull was in some way connected to overcoming sin or the unconscious and restoring peace and plenty to the world. Over time, Mithra himself becomes the bull, sacrificing his life for humanity, resurrecting, and ascending into the celestial heaven of Ahura Mazda, from which he will return to judge the world.

The worshipers of Mithra had several rituals so close to those of Christianity that they were commented on by early Christian writers. Tertullian claimed that the worshipers were baptized with water, which was said to remove sins,[8] and Justin Martyr wrote about a sacrament where the followers of Mithra consumed consecrated bread and water.[9] Some modern Christians argue that the worshipers of Mithra took rituals from the Christians and not the reverse. We have no way of knowing which tradition did the borrowing; it may have gone both ways. We do know that the rituals of these two religions were remarkably similar.

In his Roman myth, Mithra was portrayed as the God of Light, the spiritual sun, and associated with the Roman Sun God Sol Invictus. The birthday of both Sun Gods was December 25, the winter solstice, when the light returns to the world. As we will see, the Emperor Constantine attempted in some ways to combine or unify the religions of Christianity, Sol Invictus, and Mithra by making December 25 the birthday of Jesus as well. This day has become the most widely celebrated holiday of the Western world.[10]

These myths and rituals demonstrate that the early Christian view of Jesus and the purpose of his life was consistent with contemporary ideas of other religions. Gods were born through virgin births; they acted as mediators between humanity and God; sometimes they died or were killed, often for the sake of humanity; they were resurrected; and their resurrection symbolized the salvation of humanity. Apparently, ancient as well as modern commentators noticed these similarities. In the second letter of Peter, written by an anonymous writer probably around 80–90,[11] the writer defends against claims that Christian beliefs are reworked myths. "For we did not follow cleverly devised myths when we made known to you the power and coming of our Lord Jesus Christ, but we had been eyewitnesses of his majesty" (2 Pet. 1:16).

Last Judgement by Fra Angelico (ca. 1400–1455). Both Jesus and Mithra were expected to judge humanity after the end of the world.

PHILOSOPHY

Many of the educated elite in the ancient world engaged in philosophy and left the mystery religions to the majority. Several philosophical ideas may have influenced Christianity. The first was Stoicism, the philosophy of Seneca, Epictetus, and Marcus Aurelius. For the Stoics only matter was real, but God permeated everything and gave order to the universe. The universe operated according to a divine plan that even God must obey, and human happiness lay in following that plan as well.

By the second century Stoicism was being edged out by Platonism, a form of dualism that separated matter and spirit and taught either that spirit was superior to matter or that matter was evil. The last major philosophy was Cynicism, which flourished at the time of Jesus. This system taught that salvation was to be found in a return to nature and a natural way of being.[12]

In the second letter of Peter... the writer defends against claims that Christian beliefs are reworked myths.

Creation of the New Testament

Dan Brown has Teabing claim that the Bible "has evolved through countless translations, additions, and revisions. History, Teabing says, has never had a definitive version of the book."[13] This is an exaggeration, but the evolution of the New Testament is more complex than most people realize.

...even after the tradition of written gospels began among the educated, the oral tradition continued unabated among the vast majority of Christians.

THE ORAL TRADITION

Jesus is depicted in the New Testament as a traveling teacher who speaks both to crowds of thousands and to a small group of his disciples. He teaches them orally and sometimes responds to their questions. This picture is consistent with the experience of most people of that time, who lived in a predominantly illiterate culture. For the most part, only the educated elite and some people in business could read and write.

We have evidence that some sayings of Jesus may have been written down at a fairly early time, but the stories about Jesus and the contexts in which he was supposed to have spoken the sayings were not written down until at least one generation later. For example, several sayings of Jesus were placed in the context of a sermon on a mount in the New Testament gospels. The sermon may have been a literary construct in which to present a group of similar sayings, instead of a historical event. It is also important to keep in mind that even after the tradition of written gospels began among the educated, the oral tradition continued unabated among the vast majority of Christians.

Questions arise about the accuracy of the oral transmission, which have led to hot debates. The inconsistencies in the various accounts in the New Testament and apocryphal texts, not just in the sayings of Jesus but in the descriptions of events, substantiate the argument that the oral tradition was not very accurate and that stories and sayings changed as they were passed on. The material was passed on by various groups: the crowds who heard Jesus talk, the people they communicated with, the disciples who were with Jesus and learned from him, people taught by the apostles, and converts like Paul. The information would have been diffused through ever-expanding levels of oral transmission.

OPPOSITE PAGE *Christ Preaching and Bystanders* (detail) by Pietro Perugino (ca. 1450–1524) and Bernardino Pinturicchio (1454–1513). Jesus taught his disciples and spoke to crowds. His teachings were oral and were passed on in an oral tradition for many years.

The Arab Tale-Teller by Emile-Jean-Horace Vernet (1789–1863). The stories of Christianity were passed on by word of mouth in many situations similar to this portrayal of an Arab teller of tales.

Any translator will admit that translation involves some interpretation of concepts and ideas.

So was the information in the oral tradition distorted, resulting in the variations we find in the various texts? Some scholars have argued that there was no distortion, because people in oral cultures had perfect memory, a skill that has been lost in written culture.[14] This theory has been seriously challenged—there is no evidence that the oral transmissions scholars have been able to study in modern times function that way.[15] One commentator argued that the inconsistencies in the New Testament result from Jesus saying the same thing differently in different places.[16] In other words, everyone had perfect recall and only Jesus was inconsistent. Even if that were true, it would not explain the inconsistency in descriptions of events.

There is no doubt that written culture has affected our ability to memorize and repeat verbatim, but the things we know about memory were most likely as true in antiquity as they are today: Some people have better memories than others. Human memory is very imperfect and is affected by our emotions, beliefs, and capacity for understanding. We are incapable of passing on an understanding that is greater than our own, and we tend to understand based on the beliefs and experience of our own past.

As we saw in Chapter One, people in antiquity did not always distinguish between what Jesus said in visions and what he said in his physical life. Any number of people besides Paul may have relayed "quotes" they received in visions. Some scholars also theorize that common sayings like the golden rule were attributed to Jesus, whether he said them or not.

The oral transmission took place between seventy and a hundred years before the New Testament gospels were completed in written form. The transmission took place across geographical boundaries in the Middle East and Europe, across religious and cultural groups, and through a variety of languages. We know that Jesus spoke Aramaic, and even if he could speak Greek as well, some of the sayings and stories would have been passed on in Aramaic. Since the New Testament was written entirely in Greek, this means there was at least one language translation involved, and very likely more. Greek was the language of the educated, but the oral transmission would have taken place in the various spoken languages of a variety of regions. Any translator will admit that translation involves some interpretation of concepts and ideas.

It is important to remember that the oral tradition that came to the New Testament writers had most likely come through many layers of interpretation and understanding, and the written tradition represents only a small part of the oral tradition available at the time.

St. Paul, an enamel and gilt roundel from a 10th century Venetian book cover.

THE WRITTEN TRADITION

For more than a millennium, Christians believed that the New Testament was written by disciples of Jesus with firsthand information. They also believed that the biblical texts were inspired by God and were therefore infallible. When this view was challenged by objective biblical scholarship in Europe in the nineteenth and early twentieth centuries, the new discipline was very controversial.[17] By now most scholars agree that the New Testament was not written by people with first-hand information, but was written based on many years of oral transmission and a few early written texts.

We do not know who wrote the New Testament texts or when or where they were written. Legend associated the New Testament texts with names like Matthew, Mark, Luke, and John, but these legends arose in the second century or later and are connected to the belief that the early disciples or people who knew them wrote the gospels and Acts.[18] The majority of modern scholars agree that the writers are anonymous.

Saint Mark Cutting a Pen by Boucicaut Master (active about 1405–1420). An artist's portrayal of the writer of the Gospel of Mark.

The first three gospels are called the synoptic gospels—synoptic means seen together—because they are interconnected. The Gospel of John is clearly based on some of the same oral tradition, but most scholars do not believe it was based on the written texts of the first three gospels. Many scholars believe the Gospel of John is based on an earlier written tradition that some scholars have named the *Gospel of Signs*.[19]

Most biblical scholars also agree that Mark is the oldest of the four gospels, written about 70 C.E., around forty years after the death of Jesus. Matthew was next around 80, followed by Luke about five years later. John is the latest, dated from 100–150. These texts were written, as we have seen, not primarily as historical accounts but as teaching tools. They were written by the educated elite and may only partially represent the beliefs or understandings of the majority of practitioners.

Saint Mark and Saint Peter by Fra Angelico (ca. 1400–1455). There were many legends about the men who wrote the New Testament. We have no reliable information about who any of the writers were, but legends filled in the blanks. One legend said that Mark wrote down the sermons of Peter, and Peter is sometimes shown dictating the gospel in Christian art.

Mark was most likely an original composition based on about forty years of oral tradition. Matthew and Luke used the Gospel of Mark and other sources as well. One source is believed to be the hypothetical Q *Gospel*, short for the German *Quelle* or "source." The theory of Q is based on a collection of Jesus' sayings that appear in both Matthew and Luke. The wording is so similar in the two gospels that the sections must be based on a common written source, though no copy of that document has been found. Until a copy is found, the gospel must remain hypothetical. Dan Brown claims in the fictional aspect of his novel that Q is part of the Grail documents and might have been written by Jesus himself. It is unlikely that Jesus would have collected his own sayings and much more likely that people in the early community wrote them down during his life or shortly after his death.

Matthew and Luke also include information that came from other sources, written, oral, or both. The Gospel of Luke starts out, "Since many have undertaken to set down an orderly account of the events that have been fulfilled among us..." (Luke 1:1–2), so it is likely that the writer had more written sources than Mark and Q, in addition to the oral tradition of his community.

We should keep in mind that some of the sources used in the written tradition were probably inaccurate. The writers of Matthew and Luke used only a portion of the material from Mark. Matthew used about 90 percent, while Luke used only about 50 percent.[20] We cannot be sure why they did not include other parts of Mark, but it may have been because they thought they were erroneous. For example, Luke may have excluded the story of the Syrophoenician woman (Mark 7:24–30), not only because it portrayed a woman arguing with Jesus, but also because in that story Jesus says that his work is only for the Jews. The writer of Luke was obviously an admirer of Paul and supported Paul's ministry to the Gentiles. He may have believed that Mark's portrayal of Jesus was flawed or that the situation had changed, and though Jesus worked primarily with Jews, it did not help to emphasize that when taking the good news to a mixed Jewish and Gentile population.

The inclusion of the Gospel of John in the New Testament was controversial at an early period. Suspicion of this gospel is not surprising, since it presents a different picture of Jesus in several respects. While the Jesus of the synoptic gospels tends to speak in short, somewhat pithy statements, or statements and parables strung together, the Jesus of John gives developed lectures on topics like light, truth, and his nature. Jesus performs no exorcisms in John, speaks much more about himself, and shows little concern for the poor or oppressed.[21]

Saint Matthew the Evangelist by Guido Reni (1575–1642). The evangelist Matthew takes dictation from an angel, illustrating the belief that the New Testament gospels were divinely inspired.

EDITED TEXTS

Is Brown correct in writing that the biblical texts have been heavily edited? Many scholars believe that the Hebrew Scriptures, known to Christians as the Old Testament, were revised a few times over the millennia and were not yet final in the first century.[22] Most of the theories Teabing puts forth, however, have to do with the New Testament, so that work will be our focus. Have the texts of the New Testament been edited with additions and revisions?

To some extent, yes, but it is difficult to say how much. The writers of the New Testament gospels are often called redactors, meaning compilers or editors, to indicate that they were not creating original works but compiling and editing material from earlier written and oral sources. We have already seen that the redactors of Matthew, and particularly Luke, modified or deleted material from Mark. Two endings—a short and a long—were added to Mark. We do not know if the original manuscript of Mark ended abruptly and later copyists thought it needed a longer ending, or if the original manuscript was damaged. The surviving version of Mark ends abruptly, with the women fleeing from the tomb and making no report of the resurrection. Since the narrator of Mark would not be able to tell the story of the resurrection and the women's visit to the tomb unless the women *had* told others what happened, it is easy to see why later editors might have thought something was missing from the story.

Secret Mark

According to some scholars, there is also evidence that text was removed from the Gospel of Mark. In 1958 the scholar Morton Smith found a copy of a letter written by the early Church father, Clement of Alexandria (150–213), at the Mar Saba monastery near Jerusalem. This letter referred to another version of the Gospel of Mark, called Secret Mark, which Clement thought should not be made public. Some scholars dismiss this version as a second-century Gnostic revision,[23]

The Resurrection of Lazarus by Juan de Flandes (active 1496–1519). The story in Secret Mark appears to be another version of the raising of Lazarus from the dead that is found in the Gospel of John.

while John Dominic Crossan and Helmut Koester think Mark was derived from Secret Mark, with offending passages removed.[24]

The first fragment of Mark that was either added or deleted tells the story of Jesus raising a young man in Bethany who has just died, very similar to the story of the raising of Lazarus in the Gospel of John, but with significant variation. The following text of the story is controversial, because Clement said the Carpocratians, a sect founded by Carpocrates of Alexandria, combined it with "carnal lies" in their teachings:

> *Then, the man looked at him and loved him and he began to call him to his side that he might be with him. And going from the tomb, they went to the house of the young man. For he was rich. And after six days, Jesus instructed him. And when it was late, the young man went to him. He had put a linen around his naked body, and he remained with him through that night. For Jesus taught him the mystery of the kingdom of God.*[25]

The Carpocratians no doubt interpreted that as some sort of homosexual encounter, and so Clement thought it was best to leave that story out of the gospel.

"He had put a linen around his naked body, and he remained with him through that night."

There is one more interesting section of text that Clement says appeared in Secret Mark. After he teaches the young man, Jesus leaves Bethany and goes to Jerico, "and the sister of the young man whom Jesus loved was there, as well as his mother and Salome. And Jesus did not receive them."[26] It is unclear why this text was objectionable. It may be because it was understood as Jesus rejecting his own mother and not the mother of the man Jesus loved, as the text is ambiguous. It might be because Jesus is described as loving a young man, a theme we see again in the Gospel of John. It might also be because Jesus is portrayed as rejecting Salome, who was probably well known in the early Christian community. Salome is mentioned in Mark 16:1, as well as the apocryphal texts, as one of the women at the tomb. We do not have this kind of evidence of additions or deletions from the other gospels.

MANUSCRIPTS AND TRANSLATIONS OF THE NEW TESTAMENT

As we mentioned above, the New Testament was written in Greek, the common language of the educated in the Roman Empire, in the way Latin would become the common academic and ecclesiastical language of Europe. One of the earliest translations of the New Testament was a Syriac translation called the Diatessaron (Gospel of Harmony), made by Tatian around 160. That version was suppressed in the fifth century and only quotations survive.

The Virgin from The Deesis Cycle, icon from the Monastery of St. Nicholas, Moscow. In the Gospel of Mark, the family of Jesus went out to restrain him when the crowds said he was out of his mind. His mother and brothers went to where he was teaching and sent for him. He replied that the people around him were his mother and brothers (Mark 3:21; 3:31–35). This is a very different relationship with Mary than appeared in later Christian legend, but is consistent with the text in Secret Mark.

Latin

In the early centuries of Christianity a few translations were done into Latin, but they were unreliable. In 382, Pope Damascus commissioned Jerome to do a new translation of the Old Testament and New Testament. Jerome took twenty years to complete this task, translating much of the Old Testament from Hebrew texts instead of the Greek translation or Septuagint. He used previous Latin translations more in the New Testament and relied less on Greek texts. Jerome's translation into Latin is called the Vulgate. It was first translated into English in the sixteenth century and called the Rheims-Douai version. The Vulgate has been translated into many languages, including several modern English translations.[27]

English

The Roman Church taught that the Bible could only be read with permission by those trained and authorized by the Church. Vernacular translations of the Bible were often forbidden. As part of his rebellion and instigation of the Protestant Reformation, Martin Luther translated the Bible into German and made it available to the people. Translations into English were met with more difficulties. When William Tyndall wanted to translate the Bible in the sixteenth century, he had to leave England and go to the Continent, where he also experienced opposition. He finally managed to publish 18,000 copies in 1526, but Cuthbert Tunstall, Bishop of London, bought many of them and burned them in public displays.

By the next century there were two favorite translations available in England and the king, King James I of England and Scotland, ordered a new translation that was to be used in all churches in England. It was to have no marginal notes. A

Egarton Papyrus 2, one of the earliest versions of the New Testament. The Egarton Papyri and other early texts show that it is virtually impossible that Constantine had the Bible rewritten.

group of fifty-four experts was appointed, and they decided to base their translation as closely as possible on an earlier translation, the Bishop's Bible. The first King James Version was published in 1611. It was revised in 1870, when approximately 30,000 corrections were made in the New Testament translation, most on the basis of better Greek texts.[28] The American version was called the American Standard Version.

Since 1611 more than 250 English translations have been made of the Bible, many to incorporate newly discovered manuscripts that provided new information. A complete text, the Codex Sinaiticus, was discovered at St. Catherine's monastery in Sinai in 1844, and another text was found in the Vatican Library and published in 1868–1872. The Chester Beatty papyri, dated to the first half of the third century, were purchased by Chester Beatty, probably in Egypt, in 1930–32. In addition, as the study of archaeology expanded at the end of the eighteenth century, thousands of scraps of texts on papyri were found in dumps in the Egyptian desert.[29]

Does any of this support Brown's theory that the New Testament was rewritten at the time of Constantine? The Chester Beatty papyri date from a century before the time of Constantine, and a substantial portion of the New Testament also dates to 200.[30] On the basis of these texts, there is no evidence that the New Testament was rewritten in the fourth century at the direction of Constantine.

FORMATION OF THE CANON

Dan Brown claims that the New Testament was not formed until the time of Constantine, and his critics claim that the New Testament canon was already formed by the second century.[31] They are all partly right. The canon of the New Testament was fairly well formed among one faction of Christians by the end of the second century. That was the faction that won the theological struggles and became what we know as today's Christians. In this case the victors not only got to write history, they chose to preserve or not preserve the manuscripts. In many cases it was not necessary to destroy texts. If texts were not preserved or copied, they deteriorated and were lost.

Other factions did not agree on the selection of the four gospels,[32] but most of their gospels have been destroyed or lost, so we have very little information on what the differences were. We also do not have reliable information about the number of gospels that were lost.

The final decision on the composition of the New Testament was made at the Council of Carthage in 397.[33] Constantine played a part in the process that led to this decision, and that might be the basis for Brown's claim that he had the Bible rewritten. Constantine ordered Eusebius to put together fifty Bibles with approved texts to make an official Christian Bible, but since none of the fifty have survived, we do not know which texts were selected. It is possible that Constantine's Bible had an influence on the Council of Carthage, but we cannot say for sure.[34]

Constantine and Jesus

Teabing says that Constantine wanted to make Jesus into a deity, so he had Christian representatives take a vote at the Council of Nicaea on whether Jesus was human or divine. Teabing claims that the New Testament gospels were edited to portray Jesus as divine, while the other texts such as the Nag Hammadi text and the Dead Sea Scrolls show Jesus as human. In truth, the dispute was not nearly so simple.

Though Constantine was hailed as the patron of Christianity, when seen from another point of view, he progressively became a more intolerant leader. In 324 he allowed all religions, with only a limited favor toward Christianity. From 324 to 330 he was struggling against his co-Caesar, Licinius, who supported the pagans, and was probably supported by them in turn. Perhaps as a result, Constantine became more antagonistic toward all forms of paganism. After defeating Licinius, Constantine set out to destroy paganism and all alternate forms of Christianity.[35] In this he merely joined forces with the orthodox Christians, who had already been fighting against and condemning alternate forms of Christianity for 200 years. Constantine's authority gave them more power to enforce their views. His primary purpose seems to have been to force agreement and create one unified Roman religion. In that he failed.

No one knows for sure whether Constantine converted to Christianity as a real believer or used Christianity for political purposes. We do know that he was

Though Constantine was hailed as the patron of Christianity, when seen from another point of view, he was progressively becoming a more intolerant leader.

The Triumph of the Cross (detail) by Agnolo Gaddi (active 1369–1396) depicting the dream that led to Constantine's conversion. The Christian historian Eusebius reported that Constantine became the defender of Christianity after a vision and dream. Soon after noon one day he saw a cross of light in the sky above the sun with the words CONQUER BY THIS. That night in a dream, Jesus told him to make a likeness of what he had seen and use it to protect his armies in battle. Constantine's military successes were attributed to this symbol.

No one knows for sure whether Constantine converted to Christianity as a real believer or used Christianity for political purposes.

not baptized until his deathbed. On the other hand, he definitely considered himself a prominent figure in Christianity, and Eusebius called him "almost another Christ." Constantine moved the capital from Rome to Byzantium, where he had a church built with thirteen coffins as pillars—twelve for the apostles and one for him.[36] He also declared Sunday a legal holiday and said that Jesus was a manifestation of the unconquered sun. Until then Christians had celebrated the Saturday sabbath of Judaism. Now they celebrated the day of the sun. This appears to have been another of Constantine's efforts to combine existing religions. As we have seen, he also had the birthday of Jesus celebrated on the day the unconquered sun is born, the winter solstice.[37]

COUNCIL OF NICAEA

The Council of Nicaea was held in 325 by order of Constantine. He paid the expenses for the bishops, but attendance was mandatory. They were ordered to come and sort out the differences among the various groups of Christians. The dispute about the human and divine natures of Jesus that Dan Brown refers to was between Arius and his followers and the orthodox faction. Arius believed in the unity of God and did not believe that there was a separate son of God who was of the same essence. Arius's theory was that the Logos was created—the first in Creation and before all else. He also thought that the Logos combined with the flesh of the man Jesus so that Jesus did not have a human soul. Jesus was neither God nor fully human.

The council debated whether Jesus was of the same essence as God the Father. The majority voted that Jesus was of the same essence as the Father, and Constantine backed them up. This debate made it clear that 300 years after his death, Christians still had a variety of ideas about who or what Jesus was. Neither Arius nor the orthodox faction at Nicaea, however, argued that Jesus was an ordinary human prophet or only God. For Arius, Jesus was human in form but had a different soul, the Logos. The orthodox faction said that Jesus was both fully human and fully God.

The Condemnation of Arius (Crete, 16th century). Arius was condemned by the majority of bishops and Constantine at the first Council of Nicea. He later regained the favor of Constantine.

At the end of the Council of Nicaea, Arius and his supporters were excommunicated and many other alternative views besides Arianism were officially condemned. Constantine did not seem very concerned about the theological issues involved in these disputes. He was more concerned about having a Christian consensus—a concrete and enforceable set of beliefs. Arius was punished after Nicaea because he and his people would not compromise and join in a unified Church.

When Arius agreed to compromise the next year, Constantine reconvened the Council of Nicaea and ordered the Church to reinstate him. Some orthodox bishops refused, causing Constantine to penalize them and shift his favor to Arius. Arius died in 336, but Arians remained in favor with Constantine until his death the next year and continued to be in favor with his son, Constantius, until his death in 361. The orthodox faction eventually won their point and Jesus was declared of the same essence as God the Father, but this point was not finally settled because of Constantine, nor did it happen during his lifetime.[38]

The Holy Trinity by Andrei Rublev (ca.1370–1430) is an icon showing God in Trinity as He appeared to Abraham in the form of three angels (Genesis 18:1). In the middle Christ is represented as a chalice, formed by other angels, which symbolizes Communion. An understanding of the nature of Jesus eventually emerged in Christianity, centuries after his death. The prevailing view is that God the Father, Jesus, and the Holy Spirit are three aspects of one Godhead.

Teabing also claims that there is more information about the life of Jesus the man in the Nag Hammadi texts and the Dead Sea Scrolls than in the New Testament, but this is not generally true. Many of the texts found at Nag Hammadi are revelation texts about teachings of the risen Savior and do not concern or contain stories about the life of Jesus. The *Gospel of Thomas*, which is a collection of the sayings of Jesus, is an exception and might be what Brown had in mind. Most scholars do not think the Dead Sea Scrolls are about Jesus at all.[39] However reliable or unreliable we may consider the New Testament accounts, these and the *Gospel of Thomas* are the best sources of information we have at the present time about the life of Jesus the man.

DISCOVERING HIS NATURE

Decisions about the nature of Jesus, the purpose of his life, and the significance of his death were not made at Nicaea. That council was just one step on a long road of interpretation and development that was influenced by a wide variety of ideas and beliefs. Perhaps the most important point for modern people to realize is that the Christian dogma on these points, which is accepted as truth by many, was not agreed upon until close to 400 years after the death of Jesus. This agreement was possible only because alternative views had been forcibly repressed. In modern Christianity that diversity has returned, and we have Unitarian, Trinitarian, and many other views of the nature of God and Jesus.

ABOVE *The Transfiguration*, a detail from an iconostasis beam at St. Catherine's Monastery in Sinai. The story of the transfiguration of Jesus in the New Testament shows that Jesus was considered more than human at a fairly early date.

PART TWO

The Sacred Feminine

CHAPTER FIVE
THE GODDESS AND SEXUALITY

Dan Brown portrays Robert Langdon as an expert on the Goddess and has him claim that women were once celebrated as an equal half of spiritual enlightenment until the Christians defamed the Goddess. In truth, history is always more complex than that, and the attack on the Goddess began long before Christianity.

Archaeological excavations have revealed that the early civilizations of the Upper Paleolithic and the Neolithic worshiped a form of the Goddess. Most human figures found in excavations were female figures, often with exaggerated sexual characteristics. Male energy was represented in animal form, such as the bull. These artifacts date back as far as the third millennium B.C.E.[1]

This information is not well known because many early scholars dismissed these cultures as "fertility cults" and made moralistic judgments about their apparent celebration of or emphasis on sexuality.[2] It is only in recent years that both scholars and popular writers have begun to take another look at this early religious development. Though claims have been made about a time of the Great Mother Goddess when the Goddess ruled and life was idyllic, life has probably never been idyllic. Nevertheless, there does seem to have been a time when Goddesses, sexuality, and the creation of life were accorded much more value than they have been given in Christian culture. This is partly because Christian culture grew out of several preceding cultures in which the Goddess was in the process of being demoted.

At the earliest level of surviving myth, the Goddess is often portrayed as mother and creator or as a participant in creation. For example, in an early Babylonian myth, the saltwater Goddess Tiamat mates with her beloved, the freshwater God Apsu, and gives birth to creation. In a later level of this myth, one of their sons, Marduk, kills Tiamat, hacks her body in half, and uses half to create the earth and half to create the heavens. There is a shift from creation through natural birth to creation through physical violence. Women

TOP The Venus figurine of Willendorf.

BOTTOM Goddess statue from Haute Garonne in France.

OPPOSITE PAGE *The Birth of Venus* by William-Adolphe Bourguereau (1825–1905). Goddesses like Venus and Aphrodite were very sexual and celebrated their sexual attractions.

predominate in the first, and men dominate in the second. Tiamat became the Hebrew sea monster Tehomot.[3]

The students might well have been shocked, because though there definitely was a Goddess in the Temple, she was the Goddess Asherah…

Most commentators attribute this shift in attitude toward the Goddess to a series of invasions by nomadic tribes who worshiped a dominant male God.[4] As many religious groups, including Christians, would do after them, these invaders took over the Gods and Goddesses of the conquered people and then redefined them to suit their own beliefs. Goddesses were usually allowed to survive, but they assumed a more and more subservient position with respect to the Gods. Many early modern scholars called them consorts of the Gods instead of Goddesses, which meant that for many years most of the public did not even know that some of the Goddesses had existed.[5]

This is a very superficial overview of a long and complicated evolution, but the essential point is that the mythical and practical domination of the Goddess began long before Christianity. Though Christianity—along with several other religious traditions—continued the process, Christianity does not bear the sole blame for the subjugation of the Goddess or the feminine aspect of the divine. The process began in Judaism centuries before the time of Jesus.

The Hebrew Goddess

RIGHT Small figurine of the Goddess Asherah or Astarte. The two Goddesses have been confused since antiquity.

In *The Da Vinci Code*, Robert Langdon laughingly recalls how shocked his Jewish students were when he told them that the Shekinah was the consort of Yahweh in Solomon's Temple and that priestesses had ritual sex with men. The students might well have been shocked, because though there definitely was a Goddess in the Temple, she was the Goddess Asherah, and the only sexual practitioners we know for sure who were in the Temple were male.

Asherah was worshiped by the Canaanites and was probably already present in Canaan when the Hebrew tribes invaded. The Hebrews seem to have accepted her as their own. A pole, stylized tree, or sometimes an actual tree called an asherah was used to worship her. Because Hebrew does not use capital letters there is some dispute about the word "asherah" when it appears in the Old Testament: When is it referring to the Goddess and when it is referring to the item of worship?

It is clear that there was some representation of the Goddess in the Jerusalem Temple until the seventh century B.C.E., when the king threw it out (2 Kings 23:6). We also know that the asherahs were connected to the worship of both Asherah and Yahweh, but it is not certain that Asherah was his consort. That interpretation is based on one inscription on a storage jar found at Kuntillet Ajrud on the border of the Sinai. It is sometimes translated as a tribute to Yahweh and his consort Asherah, but the translation is controversial.[6]

Illustration of the Hebrew prophet Elijah who challenged the priests of Baal to a magical duel. He called upon Yahweh to light the fire in front of him. When Baal did not light the other fire, the crowd attacked the priests of Baal and killed them.

The story of Asherah in the Old Testament shows that she was more tolerated by the Hebrews than the male Canaanite Gods were. In one Old Testament story, Queen Jezebel had the priests of Yahweh killed (1 Kings 18:3–4) and gathered the prophets of Baal and Asherah. The Hebrew prophet Elijah came and challenged the 450 prophets of Baal to a magical battle. He said that 400 prophets of Asherah were also gathered, but he did not challenge them (1 Kings 18:19). When Yahweh defeated Baal, the people killed the prophets of Baal (1 Kings 18:20–40). No mention was made of the prophets of Asherah, and they were apparently left alone.

Despite this kind of attack, the worship of Baal and Asherah continued in the Jerusalem Temple until the time of King Josiah in the mid-seventh century B.C.E. Josiah, upon his father's death, became king when he was only eight years old. When he was eighteen, the high priest of the Temple found a book of the law that no one could understand. Josiah told them to take it to someone who could explain it, and they took it to the prophet Huldah. She said that Yahweh was furious because the people had honored other Gods and that he would destroy the people. Because Josiah was devout, Huldah said that he would die before this happened (2 Kings 22:8–20).

Josiah was incensed and went on a rampage against other Gods and Goddesses.

Josiah was incensed and went on a rampage against other Gods and Goddesses. He took the vessels made for Baal and Asherah and others out of the Temple and burned them. He also took the Asherah or her symbol from the Temple, burned it, beat it to dust, and sprinkled it on graves to defile it. He sacked and defiled the high places and destroyed the sacred poles, and he

Baal, the chief God of the Canaanites (Syrian statuette from 1400–1200 B.C.E.), was also worshiped by some Hebrews. His statue was once in the Temple in Jerusalem.

Clay figurines representing Asherah or Astarte, the Caananite Goddesses (ca. 1200 B.C.E.).

destroyed and defiled the shrine Solomon had built to honor Astarte and others (2 Kings 23:4–20).

According to the biblical account, Yahweh was not appeased, and Nebuchadnezzar of Babylon conquered Judah and took many of the people captive. Josiah died before he had to witness this. The prophet Jeremiah tried to tell the people of Judah who were in exile in Egypt that Judah had been defeated because Yahweh was angry at their worship of other Gods, and, though he did not say it—Goddesses. Jeremiah said that Yahweh threatened to completely annihilate the people in Egypt if they did not stop this worship (Jer. 44:1–14).

The people, however, refused to listen. They thought all the problems started after they stopped honoring the Queen of Heaven and said that they were going to make cakes with her image and pour out libations to her as their ancestors had done. It is clear that the women were the ones responsible for the ritual to the Goddess (Jer. 44:15–19).

Jeremiah told the people that their honor of the Queen of Heaven was the reason for their ruin:

> *The Lord could no longer bear the sight of your evil doings, the abominations that you committed; therefore your land became a desolation and a waste and a curse, without inhabitant, as it is to this day. It is because you burned offerings, and because you sinned against the Lord and did not obey the voice of the Lord or walk in his law and in his statutes and in his decrees, that this disaster has befallen you, as is still evident today.* (Jer. 44:22–23)

Jeremiah represents the official view of the Hebrew priests in this story. It is fairly clear that the Hebrews were not monotheistic until the Babylonian exile, and that they became monotheistic because their prophets told them they had been defeated and taken captive as punishment for their worship of Gods and Goddesses other than Yahweh. Many of the people clearly did not agree with that view. They thought the disaster had been caused by a neglect of the Queen of Heaven and perhaps other Gods or Goddesses as well.

The Prophet Jeremiah Mourning Over the Destruction of Jerusalem by Rembrandt (1606–1669). The prophet Jeremiah warned the Hebrew people who fled to Egypt after the Babylonian invasion to give up the worship of the Queen of Heaven, but many of the Hebrews refused. They thought their troubles resulted from a neglect of the Goddess. Jeremiah insisted that Yahweh was punishing them for disloyalty.

The Old Testament claims that Josiah put aside all household Gods, as well as mediums, wizards, and idols (2 Kings 23:24). He may have thought so, but archaeological excavations show that around that time images identified as Asherah or Astarte, Goddesses who were sometimes interchanged with each other, began to appear in residential areas. They also were found in caves where rituals seem to have been performed.[7] We have no information on the purpose or use of these figures, but it is likely that Asherah or Astarte or some form of a Goddess continued to be worshiped in private or used for magical purposes when their public worship was prohibited. This is consistent with what the people in Egypt said to Jeremiah. The kings and priests could destroy and defile the high places and destroy the images of Asherah and Astarte, but they could not prevent the people from honoring the Goddess.

TOP *The Fall of Adam and Eve* by Jacobo Carrucci known as Pontormo (1494–1557).

BOTTOM *Adam and Eve—The Fall of Man* by Raphael (1483–1520). Christian artists often portrayed the snake in the Adam and Eve story as female.

When Josiah was clearing out the Temple, "He broke down the houses of the male temple prostitutes that were in the house of the Lord, where the women did weaving for Asherah" (2 Kings 23:7). There is evidence that in non-Hebrew cultures, women sometimes served in the temples of the Goddesses as holy women. (They did not call themselves prostitutes.) The only clear evidence we have of sexual activity in the Jerusalem Temple was that men were acting as prostitutes in the Temple. Women were present at the Temple, engaging in ritual activity in the service of Asherah. Their ritual activity, however, was weaving.

Adam, Eve, and the Serpent

The myth of Adam, Eve, and the serpent found in Genesis was a story meant to explain why there is evil and suffering in God's good creation, but it also plays a role in the subjugation of the Goddess. The Persian Zoroastrians explained that there were two Gods, one good and one evil, in constant struggle, very similar to the way many Christians see the struggle of God and Satan. The Hebrews did not like that explanation and said instead that evil and suffering was the result of disobeying Yahweh. Adam and Eve were cast out of Paradise for disobedience.

There is another level to this myth that would have been clear to the people of the time and to the people of Europe when the Christians carried the myth there. We have seen that the tree or the sacred pole was associated with Asherah or the Goddess. The snake also appears to have been associated with her. Josiah was not the first zealous reformer to attack her. His great-grandfather Hezekiah, "...removed the high places, broke down the pillars, and cut down the sacred pole [Hebrew asherah]. He broke in pieces the bronze serpent that Moses had made, for until those days the people of Israel had made offerings to it; it was called Nehushtan" (2 Kings 18:4). So Hezekiah cut down the sacred pole of Asherah and threw out the snake that he appears to have associated with her.

The snake was related to Goddesses in other cultures as well, including Egypt and Greece, and was connected to prophecy. The oracle at Delphi was called the Pythia, and she had a python in the shrine with her.[8] Ishtar was sometimes shown sitting on a throne holding a staff with two serpents wrapped around it,[9] a staff later associated with the God Mercury.

These associations have led some commentators to conclude that the symbolic meaning of the myth was that all evil and suffering in the world results from listening to the Goddess, in this case, Asherah, instead of the male God Yahweh.[10] Whether or not that was the intent of the writers of Genesis, the myth would most likely have been understood that way by those familiar with the symbolism. When the myth was carried into Europe, where the snake and sacred trees were often associated with Goddesses, it would have carried the same message.

He lived with the animals, feeding, drinking, and sleeping with them.

THE EPIC OF GILGAMESH

An earlier version of the Adam and Eve myth appears in *The Epic of Gilgamesh*, which also has an earlier version of Noah's story (Gen. Chapters 6–10). It would appear that this epic, dated to about 2000 B.C.E., was an important source for the writers of Genesis.

In that early version of this myth, the Sumerian love Goddess Aruru created a noble savage from clay called Enkidu. He lived with the animals, feeding, drinking, and sleeping with them. They accepted him as one of them, until Gilgamesh sent a priestess to him to initiate him into the mysteries of love. After his initiation Enkidu was more wise than the animals, and they shunned him. The priestess covered his nakedness with part of her garment and brought him back to Gilgamesh.[11] Eve in Genesis is called the mother of all living (Gen 3:20), a title also used for the Goddess Aruru, the creator in this earlier version.[12]

The earlier version of the legend shows that the story was originally connected with a Goddess as creator and a priestess as the initiator into sexuality. Enkidu is created from clay by a Goddess, initiated into sexuality, and has to be clothed when he becomes wiser than the animals. If we interpret the Genesis myth with that myth in mind, we see that Adam and Eve are created by a male God out of clay (or Eve from Adam's rib). Eve, in the role of the priestess, receives information from the guardian of the sacred tree of the Goddess, and both she and Adam are initiated into the mysteries and become as wise as the Gods. When this happens, they cover their nakedness. The male God is so angry with their actions that he casts them out of Paradise. In the early version of the

Noah's Ark painted by an unknown Mexican artist (16th century). The earlier version of the Noah story appears in the Sumerian legend *The Epic of Gilgamesh*. This legend was a source for the writers of Genesis.

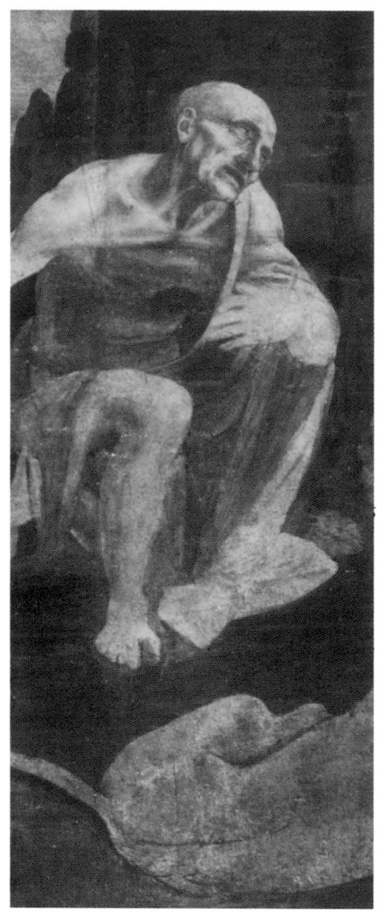

Saint Jerome by Leonardo da Vinci (1452–1519). Jerome was one of the most adament opponents of Jovinian, who argued that celibacy was not superior to marriage. Jerome was a vehement supporter of celibacy and helped determine the Church's approach to sexuality.

myth, the message seems to be that it is natural for a human to become more wise than the animals and that sexuality, as taught by a priestess, is an important part of that process. The message of the Genesis version seems to be that any lesson taught by the Goddess or priestess is evil and those who follow it deserve severe punishment.

CHRISTIAN VIEWS

When the Adam and Eve myth was adopted as part of the Old Testament into Christianity, it was closely connected to the issue of sexuality, though sex is not explicitly mentioned in the Genesis version of the myth. Some believed that the sexual act was the sin that caused all suffering, while the majority saw sexuality as the direct result of sin.[13]

For the Romans and many earlier cultures, sexuality had been a good remedy for death, as it led to birth and regeneration. Sexual energy had to be controlled, but it was basically good. In contrast, the belief began to emerge among Christians in the second century that sexuality was either the cause of death instead of the remedy for it, or the result of a fall from immortality.[14] This was the view of the theologians and was never really accepted by the majority of people in everyday life, who continued to marry and have children. Nevertheless, these ideas came to color an entire culture's ideas about sexuality.

In the third century Jerome wrote that Adam and Eve would have lived in the paradise of virginity if they had not sinned.[15] Augustine said that humanity would always have reproduced through sex, but without sin there would not have been any passion involved.[16] Marriage was approved because it was mentioned in the Bible, but it was considered inferior to celibacy.

A third-century monk named Jovinian had the audacity to argue that marriage was as virtuous as celibacy and that celibates should not be so proud. His writings were destroyed, and we only know about them from the spirited attacks people like Jerome and Augustine made on his writings.[17] He was flogged and exiled because some celibate women decided to marry as a result of his arguments. Some historians have actually made it sound like Jovinian seduced them himself.

The official Church view on marriage by the end of the third century was that it was permissible, but not as virtuous as celibacy. Because it was not as virtuous, it would not gain as high a place in heaven. Sexuality was not a sin within marriage as long as it was for procreation and not solely for pleasure. It was best for married people to remain celibate if possible.[18] It is still the teaching of the Roman Catholic Church that sex is permissible only for purposes of procreation, and that is what underlies the Church's opposition to birth control.[19] Sex with birth control is sex simply for pleasure, and that is considered a sin.

Early Christians began to use the Adam and Eve myth to blame women for all the suffering in the world and for their own suffering. The second-century writer Tertullian said:

> *You are the devil's gateway...you are she who persuaded him whom the devil did not dare attack... Do you not know that every one of you is an Eve? The sentence of God on your sex lives on in this age: the guilt, of necessity, lives on too.*[20]

Augustine emphasized that the suffering of pregnancy and childbirth are not natural but punishment for Eve's sin:

> *What passed to women was not the burden of Eve's fertility, but of her transgressions. Now fertility operates under this burden, having fallen away from God's blessings.*[21]

According to Genesis, one of Yahweh's punishments for women was that they should be subjugated to men, perhaps as the Goddess was subjugated to Yahweh. The pangs of childbirth would increase and women would desire their husbands, who would rule over them (Gen 3:16). This led early Christian thinkers to conclude that women had more sexual desire than men and both needed and deserved men's domination. This view is still held by some conservative Christians today.

The official Church view on marriage by the end of the third century was that it was permissible, but not as virtuous as celibacy. Because it was not as virtuous, it would not gain as high a place in heaven.

Noli Me Tangere by Titian (1485–1576). In the Gospel of John, Mary Magdalene searches for the body of Jesus in the garden where he was buried, and finally finds him after mistaking him for the gardener. He tells her not to hold onto him, because he has not yet ascended to the Father (John 20:13–18). She is usually portrayed in Christian art on her knees, but in the gospel she is standing.

The Christian Goddess

The Goddess was not completely forgotten in Christianity. Both of the leading Marys of Christianity, Mary the mother of Jesus and Mary Magdalene, have been associated in some way with the ancient Goddesses. Eve was connected to the Mother Goddess with the name "mother of all living," and both Mary the mother and Mary Magdalene were called the new Eve. Mary the mother was the new Eve because she obeyed God, and in doing so she made up for Eve's disobedience. Mary Magdalene was called the new Eve because she was known in the Western Church as a repentant sinner. Her intense repentance was also repentance for original sin.[22]

The story of Mary Magdalene in the Gospel of John, where she looked for the body of Jesus in the garden and found him alive, at first mistaking him for the gardener (John 20:15–17), was also connected to the story of the woman searching for her beloved in the Song of Songs and to the story of the Goddess Isis searching for the body of Osiris that had been dismembered and spread over the earth. In small ways, then, Mary Magdalene was associated with aspects of the Goddess.

There is no question, however, that Mary the mother became the official Christian Goddess. Though theologians would argue that she is not a Goddess at all, the Church quite intentionally gave her many of the characteristics of former Goddesses. She is often shown seated with Jesus on her lap in the way Isis was shown seated with Horus on her lap and similar to the way Ishtar, Queen of Heaven and Goddess of childbirth, was depicted with a child in her arms.[23] Despite the prophet Jeremiah's spirited denunciation of the Queen of Heaven in the form of Asherah, Astarte, or Ishtar, Mary the mother was given that title by the Church, and Mary being crowned as the Queen of Heaven became a popular theme in Christian art. We will see in the next chapter that flowers associated with the various Goddesses in Europe became associated with Mary instead.

So the Church did not just defame and destroy the Goddess, as Dan Brown has Robert Langdon claim. It usurped her and changed her, the way victors have been doing for millennia. Mary the mother is not the old Goddess. She technically has no powers of her own and is praised for purity and obedience. Purity in this case translates into virginity, which gives the clear message that sex is impure.

Though she is a mother (despite her lack of sexuality), she is primarily a role model for celibacy and obedience.

This is a far cry from the earlier Goddesses who had powers of their own. They also often represented a celebration of sexuality as the source of the miracle of life and regeneration. The virgin was only one aspect of the Goddess in earlier traditions. With Mary the mother the message has changed. The celebration of her is no longer the celebration of the role of the female in sexuality and reproduction; it is a celebration of the victory of spirit over flesh.

This small clay sculpture of lovers on a woven bed (ca. 2000 B.C.E.) may be an early representation of the *hieros gamos* ritual.

Hieros Gamos

Dan Brown has Langdon claim that *hieros gamos*—Greek for sacred marriage—celebrated the reproductive power of the female. He says, "Historically, intercourse was the act through which male and female experienced God. The ancients believed that the male was spiritually incomplete until he had carnal knowledge of the sacred feminine. Physical union with the female remained the sole means through which men could become spiritually complete and ultimately achieve *gnosis*—knowledge of the divine. Since the days of Isis, sex rites had been considered man's only bridge from earth to heaven."[24]

In this description Brown seems to be combining several different rituals. The *hieros gamos* ritual was one in which the king mated with the Goddess, who was represented in the flesh by her priestess, to ensure the health and fertility of the land and people. In the process of the ritual, the king displayed the sexual virility needed to rule the land, and the Goddess gave her blessing for fertility and for his rule. By completing this ritual, he took on her authority to rule. The ritual was performed when the king was crowned, and often on a yearly basis during his reign.

The ritual probably originated in Sumer, not Egypt, as Langdon claims, and was practiced in so many cultures over such a long period of time that it is very unlikely there was only one ritual. The actual sexual contact may have taken place privately in the temple or in public, but it was not a group event. It involved the king and the priestess.

Herodotus of Halicarnassus (ca. 484–425 B.C.E.), the Greek historian, reported that Babylonian women of that time were required to go to the temple one time and have sexual intercourse with one stranger.

Brown mentioned another tradition in which holy women had sex with men in the temple of the Goddess. Herodotus of Halicarnassus (ca. 484–425 B.C.E.), the Greek historian, reported that Babylonian women of that time were required to go to the temple one time and have sexual intercourse with one stranger. In doing so, a woman made herself holy in the sight of the Goddess and could return home or continue in the temple if she wished.[25] We do not have the kind of detailed information Brown's character Langdon claims to know about the meaning of this ritual for the man or woman involved. We know that the woman was made holy by the experience and it may have been a religious experience for the man as well, but we do not know.

There were many other instances of sexual rites involving groups in widely different religions. Little is known about the practices of the Greek mystery religions, but the worshipers of Dionysus, among others, were said to have sexual rites. There were also sexual rites in Europe, related to the fertility of the fields and the harvest.

Langdon's description of sex rites, in particular that a man seeks God in the climactic instant when his mind goes blank, may have more in common with modern Western understandings of Tibetan and Taoist tantric practices than with any Middle Eastern or European sexual rites.

THE RITUAL

In the novel, Sophie describes the ritual she sees in the novel—the men wearing black and the women white, with everyone masked—and Langdon claims to recognize this as *hieros gamos*, where the Grand Master and his wife are having sacred sex in front of the group. Langdon mentions the movie *Eyes Wide Shut* as an example of secret societies practicing *hieros gamos*, but says that the moviemakers got the ritual wrong.

Brown is telling a good story in this section, but the details of the ritual he describes are not known as *hieros gamos*. People wore masks at the sexual "ritual" in *Eyes Wide Shut*, but the women involved were call girls, not priestesses. The sexual activity was not about honoring the sacred feminine or the Goddess. It seemed to have much more to do with the rich entertaining themselves.

In the novel, the people at the ritual chant, "I was with you in the beginning, in the dawn of all that is holy, I bore you from the womb before the start of

day…"[26] This quote actually comes from a vision of the twelfth-century mystic Hildegard of Bingen.[27] The chant used in the *hieros gamos* ritual in Sumer was much more sexually explicit.

This ritual dialogue was recorded in Sumerian texts before 2000 B.C.E. It takes place between the Goddess Inanna and her legendary husband, the shepherd Dumuzi. The ritual would have been performed by the priestess of Inanna and the king.

INANNA
My vulva, the horn,
The boat of Heaven,
Is full of eagerness like the young moon.
My untilled land lies fallow.
As for me, Inanna,
Who will plow my vulva?
Who will plow my high field?
Who will plow my wet ground?
As for me, the young woman,
Who will plow my vulva?
Who will station the ox there?
Who will plow my vulva?

DUMUZI
Great Lady, the king will plow your vulva,
I, Dumuzi the King, will plow your vulva.

INANNA
Then plow my vulva, man of my heart.
Plow my vulva.
My eager impetuous caresser of the navel,
My caresser of the soft thighs;
He is the one my womb loves best,
My high priest is ready for the holy loins.
The plants and herbs in his field are ripe.
O Dumuzi, your fullness is my delight.
Let the bed that rejoices the heart be prepared.
Let the bed that sweetens the loins be prepared.
Let the bed of kingship be prepared!
Let the bed of queenship be prepared!
Let the royal bed be prepared!

Watercolor drawing from a 15th century manuscript of *Aurora consurgens*, sometimes attributed to Thomas Aquinas. This androgynous image is an allegory of wisdom. The south wind, represented by an eagle, gradually unites the two opposites.

One of the most touching love stories of all time is in the Old Testament Song of Songs. Those lovers, illustrated here, epitomize the sacred in relationship. Christians have treated the Song of Songs as an allegory, instead of as a story of sexual love.

CHRISTIAN RITUAL

Did the Christians ever use sexual rituals? This is not clear. The *Gospel of Philip* talks about a ritual or sacrament of the bridal chamber, but like the kisses Jesus bestowed on Mary Magdalene, it is not clear if the ritual of the bridal chamber was literal or metaphorical. The writers of the *Gospel of Philip* believed that the ideal state of humanity was androgyny, though perhaps not literal physical androgyny.

> *If the woman has not separated from the man, she should not die with the man. His separation became the beginning of death. Because of this Christ came to repair the separation which was from the beginning and again unite the two, and to give life to those who died as a result of the separation and unite them. But the woman is united to her husband in the bridal chamber. Indeed those who have united in the bridal chamber will no longer be separated. Thus Eve separated from Adam because it was not in the bridal chamber that she united with him.* (Gospel of Philip 70:10–23)[28]

We do not currently have enough information to be sure what the bridal chamber actually was. We only know that the healing of gender division was viewed as a spiritual issue in this community and one that they believed Jesus himself came to resolve.

The Sacred in Relationship

The form of Christianity that predominated and formed much of European and American culture has rarely seemed concerned with resolving gender issues. By insisting that Jesus was single and celibate, emphasizing celibacy over sexuality, and failing to value women, many feel that Christian culture has lost a sense of the sacred in sexual relationship—a loss of something profound that humanity needs in order to become whole. This sense of loss has inspired many claims about pagan sex rituals in popular books.[29] As sensational as the idea of sexual rituals might be for some, most people would not consider those rituals as a practical way to change cultural attitudes about sexuality or regain a sense of the sacred in relationship. A claim that Jesus and Mary Magdalene engaged in sex rituals does not do much to remedy that loss. More readers appear to be touched by the idea that Jesus might have been a loving husband and a loving father than by the idea that he engaged in sexual rituals.

What is the sacred aspect of everyday relationships between ordinary people?

Once we get past the emotional reaction to the idea that Jesus might have been sexual, other questions arise. What would a sexual relationship look like between two very spiritually aware people like Jesus and Mary Magdalene? That seems to be a more pressing question than the nature of *hieros gamos* in ancient cultures. What is the sacred aspect of everyday relationships between ordinary people? If the success of *The Da Vinci Code* tells us anything, it tells us that for many, this may be a deeply spiritual question.

CHAPTER SIX
SYMBOLS

Dan Brown uses symbols throughout his novel to tie together various themes and plot points, particularly in relation to the Goddess and the sacred feminine. The pentacle is a five-pointed star that is the symbol for the Goddess, the five-petaled rose is the Priory symbol for Mary Magdalene, iambic pentameter has an alternating emphasis in groups of five, and so on. Many readers wonder if he has used these symbols correctly. Sometimes he does, but many of the story's symbols are part of the fiction and cannot be taken literally.

Dan Brown uses symbols...to tie together various themes and plot points...

The Pentagram or Pentacle

Robert langdon claims that the pentagram was a universal symbol for the Goddess until Christianity changed it into a symbol of evil. He explains that the pentacle became the symbol of the planet Venus because the planet traces that symbol in the sky, and as a result the Goddess Venus became connected to the symbol and to the number five.

The pentacle or pentagram is certainly an ancient symbol, but there is no evidence that it was a universal symbol for the sacred feminine, Venus, or the Goddess in general. It is true that the pentagram was sometimes associated with the planet Venus, but as we will see below, Venus and various Goddesses were more often associated with the eight-pointed star and the number eight.

The pentagram has been found on ruins in Palestine and Mesopotamia dated from roughly 4000 B.C.E. to 2700 B.C.E.[1] Some commentators theorize that the Sumerian symbol stood for the four corners of the earth plus the vault of heaven.

A five-pointed star similar to the pentagram, but not usually geometrical, has also been found in Egyptian ruins from the fourth century B.C.E. It appears to represent a star. The same symbol with a circle around it represents the underworld.

The pentagram or pentacle has had many meanings through history. It has never been the universal symbol for the Goddess or sacred feminine.

OPPOSITE PAGE *Flowers* by Jan Frans Eliaerts (1761–1848).

⊗

Aphrodite Pushing Cupid, a Roman fresco. The planet Venus was named for the Goddess of love, who was the mother of Cupid. This Goddess was sometimes associated with the pentagram or pentacle, but she was also associated with the eight-pointed star.

The pentagram symbol has been used to represent the human figure, served as Jerusalem's official seal from 300–150 B.C.E., and was connected to the Morning Star in Greek mythology, associated with Athena, the Goddess of war and wisdom.

The Morning Star aspect of Venus, Phosphoros, was also associated with Lucifer, the Bringer of Light, and this may explain why the pentagram as a symbol was later associated with witchcraft. Langdon claims that the Church intentionally changed the meaning of the pentagram from the sacred feminine to something evil, just as it changed Poseidon's trident into the devil's pitchfork and changed the wise crone's pointed hat into a witch's hat.[2]

There is little question that various pagan symbols—aspects of the Horned God of old Europe and Poseidon's trident among them—were combined in the Christian imagination to create the iconography of the devil. There is also little doubt that many Christians thought the local Gods were demonic, but there is scarce evidence of a conscious conspiracy to transform the meaning of the pentagram. The association of the pentagram with Satanism came much later than the Middle Ages and may have been initiated by Satanic practitioners, who discovered the ancient connection between the pentagram and Lucifer.

The pentagram may also have had pre-Christian meanings in European culture. A slightly elongated pentagram was the "witch's footprint" among the Celts. In Nordic countries, the pentagram was placed on the door as a sign to ward off trolls and evil. So the pentagram was not just a sign of evil, but also a magic sign used to oppose evil, which seems to contradict Langdon's theory. Today, Freemasons use the pentagram as one of several symbols for deity.

The Eight-Pointed Star

Venus remains as the Morning Star or Evening Star for eight lunar cycles, and both stars return to a given point in the sky every eight years. As a result, both the eight-pointed star and the eight-petaled flower were frequently used to symbolize the planet and various Goddesses, including Venus. The Evening Star was associated in Greek mythology with Aphrodite, the Goddess of beauty, fertility, sexuality, and peace represented by the eight-pointed star.

The eight-pointed star was also associated with Inanna, Ishtar, and Astarte in the Euphrates-Tigris region.[3] These Goddesses had a variety of powers, much like Athena and Aphrodite. They were Goddesses of love, sexuality, fertility, childbirth, as well as war. In Greek culture this symbol was associated with the love and sexuality aspect of the Goddess and not the war aspect.

Freemasonry Symbolic Structure from the Grand Lodge of Free and Accepted Masons of Japan. The water and fire triangles, represented by the compasses and square, make up an important symbol in Freemasonry.

Triangles

Brown has his characters call the triangle with its apex pointing up, the blade, and the triangle with its apex pointing down, the chalice. He also uses the symbols without the bottom line of the triangle to represent the chalice and the blade. These symbols are not listed under those names in symbol collections. They are usually called the fire triangle and the water triangle.

The water triangle, representing the pubic triangle, is one of the earliest symbols of the Goddess found on early figurines. Triangular images of the Goddess Astarte, in the form of a water triangle *(above)*, have been found dating from the sixteenth century B.C.E.[4]

The fire and water triangles were also used in European alchemy and represented not only the male and the female but all contrasting pairs, like fire and water, night and day, sun and moon. The two triangles were combined in the hexagram to symbolize opposites coming together to form a whole.

The apexes of the fire and water triangles, formed by the compasses and square and placed on a book of sacred scripture, make up one of the primary symbols of Freemasonry. In Christianity the fire triangle became the symbol of the Holy Trinity, and in modern usage the fire triangle warns of danger, while the water triangle in a circle has become the signal to stop.

The water triangle...is one of the earliest symbols of the Goddess found on early figurines.

Drawing by A. von Franckenberg in the book *Raphael oder Arzt-Engel* (1639). Hexagrams were very popular with European alchemists. In this alchemical hexagram, six, the number of days of creation, symbolizes the Opus, and the rotating motion of the Work.

The Rosy Cross from a 17th century pamphlet entitled the *Fama and Fraternity of the Meritorious Order of the Rosy Cross.* The combination of cross and roses was the symbol of the seventeenth-century German group, the Rosicrucians. It was later associated with those interested in the occult and alchemy.

The Hexagram

In the novel the hexagram symbolizes the unity of the chalice and blade. The earliest examples of the hexagram date from about 800–600 B.C.E. It was used to symbolize the Jewish kingdom and spread with the Jews as they moved in the Diaspora.[5] In the Middle Ages it was used on banners and prayer shawls in Jewish communities. During their reign of terror, the Nazis forced Jews to wear the symbol on yellow armbands, and the symbol now appears in blue on the Israeli flag. It is called the Star of David, the Shield of David, Magen David, and sometimes Solomon's Seal.

In alchemy and theosophy the hexagram was called a signet star, the star that leads to wisdom, as it led the wise men to Jesus in the New Testament. As a symbol of the joining of opposites, in the form of the fire and water triangles, the hexagram became the symbol of alchemy.

In Tibet a hexagram represents the interpenetration of Shiva and Shakti. The fire triangle represents the male energy of Shiva, and the water triangle represents the female energy of Shakti.

The Rose

Brown's characters claim that the rose is the Priory of Sion's symbol of Mary Magdalene. Since we will see overwhelming evidence in Chapter Seven that the modern Priory is a fabrication, this claim is doubtful.

The rose was often associated in Christian Europe with Mary the mother of Jesus, as in the painting *The Madonna of the Rose Bower,* not with Mary Magdalene. In fact, many flowers associated with European Goddesses were later connected to Mary the mother, the Christian replacement for all Goddesses. Flowers associated with Diana, Juno, Venus, Freya, Frigga, Bertha, and Hulda became flowers of Mary the mother; and the month of May, which was the month of Flora, the Roman Goddess of flowers and spring, became Mary's month. A month that had been associated with fertility and European fertility rites became a celebration of the Virgin.

In the seventeenth century the rose cross was associated with a German group called the Rosicrucians. Some popular writers have implied that this means that the rose was a pagan symbol and indicated a secret belief in heresy. In fact, the rose was widely used by Christians and was even the symbol of the pope in the Middle Ages.[6]

The rose, like the lotus, has been the symbol of spiritual enlightenment or spiritual wisdom. In the thirteenth-century *Romance of the Rose*, for example, the rose is associated with the feminine ideals of beauty, intelligence, purity, and grace.

The rose, like the lotus, has been the symbol of spiritual enlightenment or spiritual wisdom.

Fleur-de-lis

The authors of *Holy Blood, Holy Grail* claim that the fleur-de-lis is the symbol of the Priory, and Dan Brown appropriates that idea in his novel. The key Sophie found as a child and that Saunière leaves for her behind a painting by Leonardo da Vinci in the Louvre has the fleur de-lis on it. In *Holy Blood, Holy Grail*, the Priory is supposed to be the guardian of the Merovingian bloodline, and Clovis (481–511), a Merovingian king, is often said to be the first French king to use the fleur-de-lis as his symbol.

Legend says Mary the mother of Jesus gave Clovis a lily at his baptism. Another, less supernatural, version of the story says that Clovis was once trapped by an army of Goths. As he looked around for a way to escape, he saw lilies growing in the Rhine River, showing him where it was safe to cross. He managed to evade the army, and he took the lily as his symbol in gratitude.

Another association with the fleur-de-lis would be less appealing to the *Holy Blood, Holy Grail* authors. Their theory was that the Merovingians were the true kings of France, usurped by the Carolingians (ca. 751) with the treacherous aid of the Vatican. When Charlemagne, the most famous of the Carolingians, was crowned Holy Roman Emperor, on Christmas Day 800, the pope is said to have given him a blue banner with gold fleurs-de-lis, and this symbol continued to be a symbol of French royalty long afterward.

Iris tenax (detail) by F. H. Round. Legend says that the iris, once called a lily, saved the Merovingian king Clovis, by showing him where it was safe to cross the Rhine River. In gratitude, he made it the symbol of the monarchy.

Cathedrals were intended to inspire a sense of awe. The builders used many formerly pagan symbols, most likely with the intention of turning them into Christian symbols.

The fleur-de-lis is called the French lily, though it is what we would now call an iris. Until the nineteenth century irises were considered lilies. Saunière seems unaware of this distinction and tells Sophie the flower is a lily.

Cathedrals

Brown's novel starts soon after Robert Langdon has completed a lecture and slide show on the pagan symbolism hidden in the stones of Chartres Cathedral. The idea that pagan symbolism is somehow hidden or secret in European cathedrals is common in popular writings but is not well supported.

As we have seen in the discussions of various symbols, they tend to migrate or be adopted and take on new meaning in new cultures. The Greek philosopher Pythagoras used the pentagram as a symbol, yet few people would argue that the pentagrams on U.S. Army tanks are a hidden symbol of the Pythagorean school of mysticism and indicate that someone in the Pentagon is a secret devotee of Pythagoras. Yet that is the kind of reasoning used to argue that pagan symbols in the cathedrals indicate some hidden heresy.

The cathedral at Chartres is a good example of the use of so-called pagan symbols. This cathedral was built during the medieval renaissance that occurred in Paris from the twelfth to late thirteenth centuries, when knowledge from Europe and the Middle East had come together and fueled a religious fervor. This celebration of knowledge ended with a plague and did not arise again until 250 years later in Florence.

People from the first Crusades had brought Greek and Arabic knowledge such as mathematics, building, poetry, and philosophy back to Europe. A mixture of Arabic, Greek, and Jewish thought had also come in from Spain. For the members of the School of Chartres, all knowledge, both Christian and pagan, could be used to find and express the divine plan. They drew on the Old and New Testaments, numerology, geometry, nature, the cosmos, and more abstract concepts like divine love and the Logos or physical manifestation of the Word.[7] The formerly pagan symbolism was not usually hidden, nor was it necessarily heretical.

...its members believed that light had a very real power to transform the soul.

An important component of the school's work was the design of stained-glass windows, because its members believed that light had a very real power to transform the soul.[8] These windows included the famous rose windows, which were often dedicated to Mary the mother and frequently based on geometric design. One example *(above)*, the north rose window at Chartres, "Rose of France," was constructed according to the Fibonacci sequence.[9]

The Equal-Armed Cross

Dan Brown claims that the equal-armed cross is the peaceful cross, but little support for this theory existed before modern times. The plain equal-armed cross, found in many ancient cultures, usually represented the four seasons, four directions, four elements, or some other aspect of the physical world.[10]

Several versions of the equal-armed cross exist, but one of the most famous is the Maltese cross, which became the symbol of the Order of St. John of Jerusalem, also known as the Hospitalers. The equal-armed cross was used in the First Crusade, most commonly as a symbol for Christian warriors.

In modern times this symbol has become a peaceful one, associated with the Red Cross and medical, disaster, and wartime aid.

Jacques de Molay, the last Grand Master of the Knights Templar, is shown with the Templar cross in this 19th century engraving by Ghevauchet.

The Pope card from the Charles VI Deck. The earliest tarot cards had a female pope or papess card as well as a card of a male pope. The origin of the female pope is unclear.

The Tarot

When Sophie and her grandfather play the medieval Italian card game of tarot in the novel, Sophie's symbol is the pentacle. Langdon says to himself that the medieval card game was a way to pass on ideologies banned by the Church.

No one knows the origins of the tarot for certain. Legend says they were brought to Europe from Egypt by the Gypsies, although Gypsies have Indo-Aryan not Egyptian origins. Others believe the cards were brought from India.

Historical accounts report that the ordinary playing cards were in use in Europe by 1375. Playing cards called "triumph cards" first appeared in the 1440s in northern Italy. All the tarot cards we have from the fifteenth century are from that area. The Italian word *tarocchi*, which became the French word *tarot*, was used first around 1530.[11]

It is possible that the Italian cards were based on cards brought to Europe from the East, but the Italian cards had some clearly Christian figures, such as the pope, the female pope, and the devil. Though they were used to play a game, as regular playing cards were, they also made extensive use of symbols. Whether they passed on heresy is unknown.

JOHN ANGLICUS

There was a legend of a female pope, but there are no reliable documents to support it. According to the legend, a young woman dresses as a man to be with her lover, but so excels at her studies that she rises to the position of pope and is called John Anglicus. After reigning for a few years she suddenly gives birth to a child while walking in procession or mounting a horse. In most versions of the story she is immediately killed, but in one she is put in a nunnery. The best known version of the story is found in the writing of Martin Polonus, a thirteenth-century Dominican priest, but textual research shows that this story was inserted into his manuscript shortly after his death.[12] A copy of that information was also inserted in one copy of the early papal history *Liber Pontificalis*, but in a different hand and at the bottom of a page. Despite the clumsiness of these forgeries, the story spread successfully in the Middle Ages.[13] Copyists of

Polonus's work included the story in future drafts, and it was circulated under his authority.

The dates of the alleged reign of this female pope vary from the ninth century to the eleventh, but no evidence has been found of a gap in the papal succession that would support the claim.

MAIFREDA

The female pope of the tarot may have a different origin. In the thirteenth century a woman named Guglielma of Bohemia came to Milan and acquired a following as a preacher. When she died in 1281, her tomb became something of a shrine. Some of her followers believed that she was the Holy Spirit and would return to place a young woman from Milan, Maifreda di Pirovano, on the Vatican throne, thus ushering in a new Age of the Spirit. This idea may have been inspired by the legend of John Anglicus. In preparation for the coming event, Maifreda began to say mass and to make plans for a new college of cardinals, some or all of whom would be women. Maifreda had planned her ascension for Pentecost in 1300. Instead, the Church authorities took action and Maifreda and several of her followers were burned at the stake as heretics.

There was a legend of a female pope, but there are no reliable documents to support it.

The religious movement of Maifreda and Guglielma appeared to die with them, but Maifreda was related to the Visconti family, which commissioned the first known tarot deck some two centuries after her death. It is possible that the female pope or papess card was intended to commemorate Maifreda. This may have been some form of heresy from the Church's point of view, but it is unclear what the heretical belief was.[14]

Though the tarot was used as a game in its earliest European form, its reinterpretation by occultists in the nineteenth and twentieth centuries led to later, almost exclusive, use for some form of divination. One of the most famous writers on the tarot is Aleister Crowley, who claimed it was based on the Egyptian Book of Thoth. Others interpreted the tarot in terms of the Kabbalah and Rosicrucian symbolism. Modern designers have re-created the tarot on virtually every imaginable theme. In this process the card of the female pope became the high priestess, and the story of Maifreda that her family may have intended to preserve has been lost.

The architects of the pyramid say there are 698 panes, not 666, and that President Mitterand did not make any requests about the number of panes in the pyramid. Some French papers in the 1980s started the rumor of 666 panes and its possible esoteric meaning.

666

This is the number of glass panes Robert Langdon says are in the pyramid of the Louvre *(above)*. Langdon claims this was "at President Mitterrand's explicit demand,"[15] and notes that conspiracy theorists say this is the number of Satan.

The architects of the pyramid say there are 698 panes, not 666, and that President Mitterand did not make any requests about the number of panes in the pyramid.[16] Some French papers in the 1980s started the rumor of 666 panes and its possible esoteric meaning.

Today the number 666 is associated with Satan by both conspiracy theorists and some Evangelical Christians. In antiquity it was widely known as the number of the sun, because it is the sum of the numbers 1 through 36, the numbers making up the square of the sun. That is a square in which every line of numbers adds up to 111, and which was believed to have magical significance.

The connection of 666 with Satan comes from the Book of Revelation (Rev. 13:18). It is likely that the writer of Revelation associated the number with Satan because it was an indicator of the sun, and therefore of the Sun God Sol Invictus and the Roman soldiers' mystery religion of Mithra. The worshipers of the Sun God and Mithra were competitors of the Jesus movement in the early centuries of this era and may have appeared Satanic for that reason.

Walt Disney

The question of whether Walt Disney classics like *Snow White* are really about the lost sacred feminine is one symbologists and others could debate for a very long time. Many of the Walt Disney classics were based on European folklore and continue those cultural myths. It is probably too limiting to restrict the meaning of this folklore to the story of the lost sacred feminine alone.

A painting of the penitent Magdalene does appear in the movie *The Little Mermaid*, as Starbird and Brown claim.[17] The painting is part of the swag that Ariel has gathered from shipwrecks. Walt Disney studios may have found significance in the painting, but they could have chosen it for a more mundane reason: Ariel refers to fire, and touches a lit candle in the painting as she sings.

The Vigilant Magdalene (detail) by Georges de La Tour (1593–1652). It is difficult to know why this painting was included in the Walt Disney film about the Little Mermaid. During her song, Ariel, the mermaid, puts her hand through the flame, so the painting may have been chosen because it contained a candle.

Phi and the Fibonacci Sequence

The number phi, also called the golden number, golden ratio, and golden section, has fascinated humanity since antiquity. Brown has Langdon recall his lectures on the subject and his students' amazement at the number's appearances in nature. Langdon's star pupil pronounces it "fee," but it should be pronounced as it looks, "fi."

In professional mathematical literature this number is commonly represented by the Greek letter *tau* (τ), a designation that comes from the Greek word τομή, meaning "the cut" or "the section." At the beginning of the twentieth century, the American mathematician Mark Barr used a different designation. He called it phi

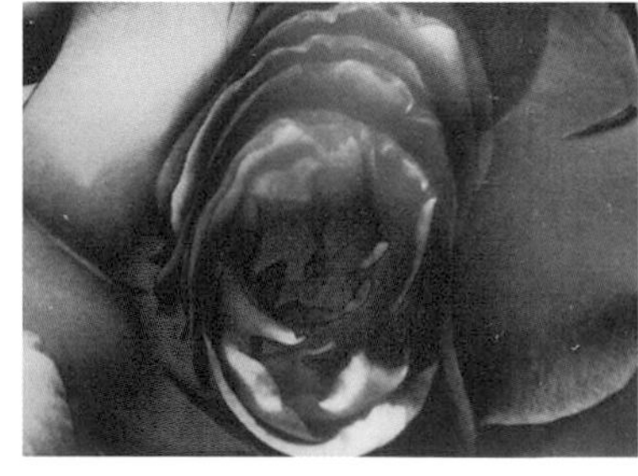

The number phi is found in many natural forms. It defines the petal arrangement of the rose.

"A certain man put a pair of rabbits in a place surrounded on all sides by a wall. How many pairs of rabbits can be produced from that pair in a year if it is supposed that every month each pair begets a new pair which from the second month on becomes productive?"

(Φ), which is the first Greek letter in the name of Phidias, the sculptor of the *Athena Parthenos* in Athens and *Zeus* in Olympia.[18]

The number phi is related to a few of the symbols Brown uses. It defines the petal arrangement of a rose, and it is the ratio of the longer to shorter sides of each of the five triangles formed by a pentagram. Some have claimed that phi was used in ancient times in the Great Pyramid and the Parthenon. We do not know who discovered phi, but it was first explained by Euclid of Alexandria circa 300 B.C.E.

FIBONACCI

The Fibonacci sequence is a series of numbers in which each is the sum of the previous two. It is related to phi, though not directly derived from it. The sequence was the result of a problem posed by a man named Leonardo of Pisa (ca. 1170–1270). The nickname *Fibonacci*, "son of good nature," was given to him centuries later and became attached to the sequence he discovered.

The mathematical problem Leonardo posed was part of a book called *Liber abaci*. In chapter XII he presented this question:

> *A certain man put a pair of rabbits in a place surrounded on all sides by a wall. How many pairs of rabbits can be produced from that pair in a year if it is supposed that every month each pair begets a new pair which from the second month on becomes productive?*[19]

Anyone who successfully calculates the answer has found the Fibonacci sequence. The connection to phi is that as you go down the sequence, the ratio of two successive numbers is alternatively greater and smaller and comes closer and closer to phi. The great German astronomer Johannes Kepler discovered this relationship in the seventeenth century. Kepler had apparently discovered the sequence on his own, without reading *Liber abaci*.[20]

THE WORK OF LEONARDO DA VINCI

There is much debate and little agreement on the extent to which Leonardo da Vinci used the divine proportion in his work. Having studied with Luca Pacioli *(above)*, a leading mathematician, and provided sixty illustrations for Pacioli's three-volume work *Divina Proportione*, he was certainly aware of it. Pacioli expressed a great interest in teaching artists about the secret of harmonic forms. As we will see in Chapter Ten, this work with Pacioli led to Leonardo's drawing of *Vitruvian Man*, a drawing that plays a central role in *The Da Vinci Code*.

Ritratto di Luca Pacioli by Jocopo de' Barbari (1591–1666). Luca Pacioli was a renowned teacher of mathematics. Leonardo da Vinci studied with him and drew illustrations for his book on the divine proportion.

PART THREE

The Holy Grail

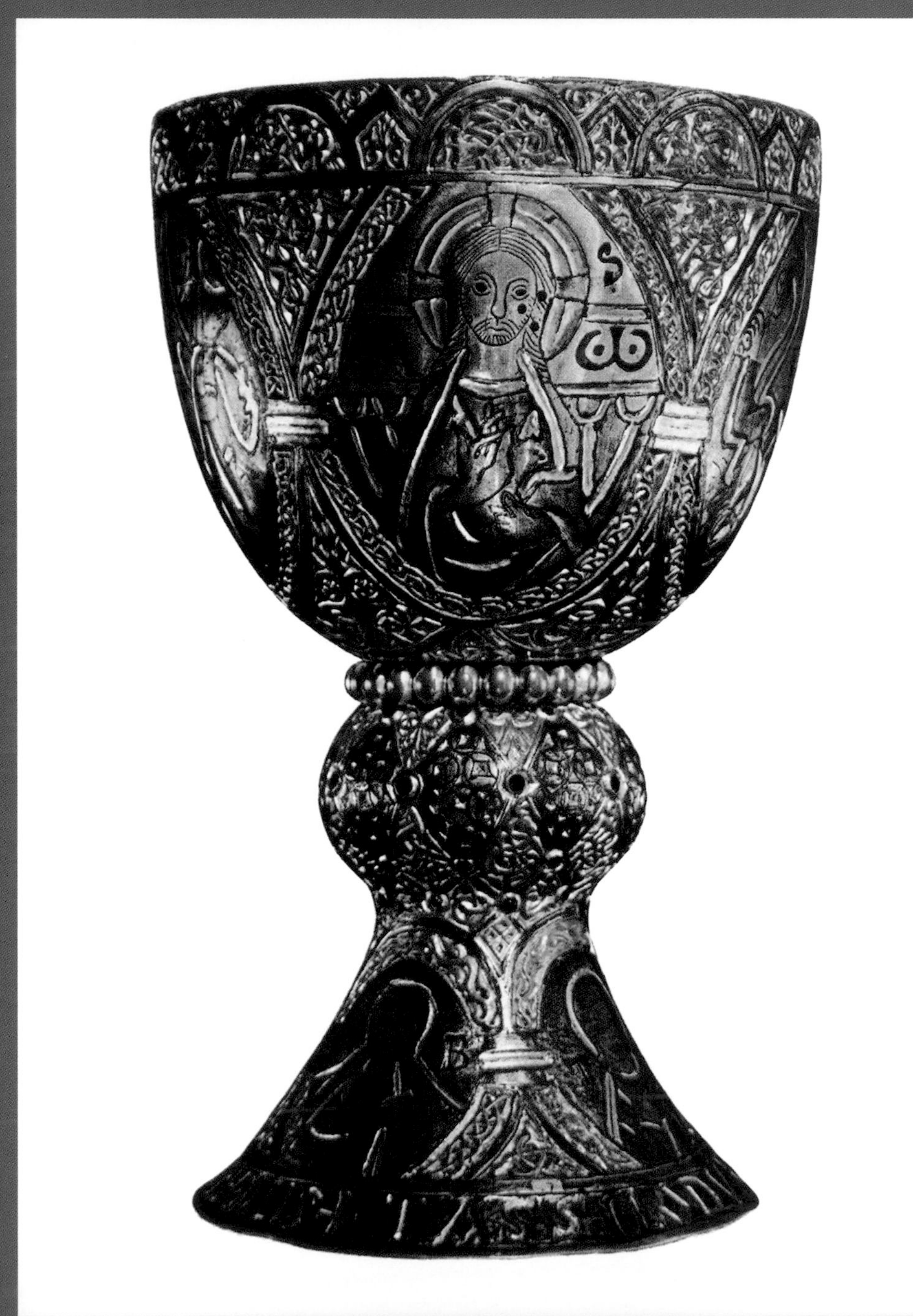

SEVEN
ORIGINS OF A GRAIL MYTH

The Grail Legend in The Da Vinci Code

The Grail myth behind Dan Brown's novel begins at the crucifixion, where Mary Magdalene is pregnant with the child of Jesus. Her friends fear for her safety and that of the child and help her to leave Palestine. She travels to France, where she gives birth to a daughter named Sarah. Sarah is an ancestor of Mérovée, who is king of the Franks some 300 years later and founder of the Merovingian Dynasty. Mérovée's modern descendants, the carriers of the bloodline of Jesus and Mary Magdalene, are named Plantard and Saint Claire.

ABOVE Godfroi de Bouillon leaves for the Crusade (15th century illustration). After participating in the First Crusade, Godfroi de Bouillon became the first king of Jerusalem. Dan Brown claims that he founded the Priory of Sion.

OPPOSITE Christ and saints adorn this 8th century chalice.

Godfroi de Bouillon, who Brown mistakenly calls a king of France, became the first king of Jerusalem after the First Crusade. According to Brown's version of the myth, Godfroi was the descendant of one of the last Merovingian kings, Dagobert II, through his son Sigisbert IV. The information of his family's history had been passed down to him, and he created a secret brotherhood called the Priory of Sion in Jerusalem to safeguard the secret and pass it on. The Priory learned of a stash of documents hidden under the ruins of the Jerusalem Temple, which they thought would confirm Godfroi's secret of a bloodline from Jesus. This was such an explosive secret that the Priory believed the Church would try to get the documents, so they formed the Knights Templar to retrieve and guard the documents.

According to Brown, after searching for nine years, the Templars found the documents and either blackmailed the Vatican for power or the Church tried to buy their silence by issuing a papal bull giving them unlimited power. By the fourteenth century the Knights had become so powerful, Pope Clement V decided to get rid of them and had the Templars in France arrested. Some Templars escaped and have continued under a variety of names, but at the time of the arrest they had already entrusted the documents found under the Temple to the Priory of Sion. Since the fourteenth century the Priory has continued to move and hide the

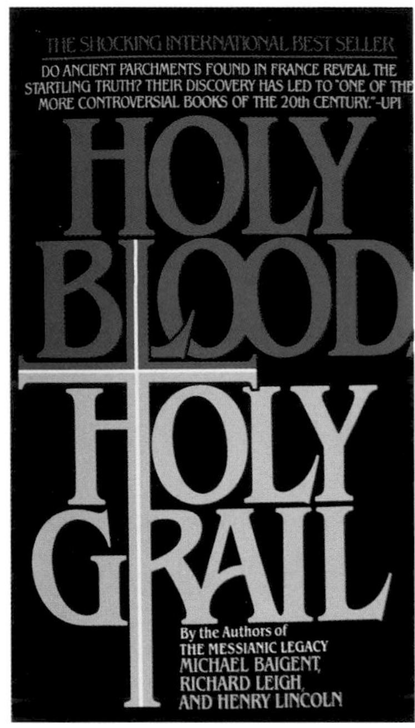

Much of the background information about the Priory of Sion and the theory that Mary Magdalene is the Grail is found in this international best-seller.

Their history of the Priory of Sion differs slightly from Dan Brown's version.

documents. At some point that is not specified, the body of Mary Magdalene became part of the hidden treasure. The documents and body have now been buried under the inverted pyramid at the Louvre in Paris.

The story of the bloodline of Jesus and Mary Magdalene is the true story behind the legend of the Holy Grail. Evidence of the conspiracy to preserve this legend is found in the work of Leonardo da Vinci, who was Grand Master of the Priory of Sion during his lifetime. Is this myth true?

Holy Blood, Holy Grail

Most of the information about the Priory of Sion appears to come from the book *Holy Blood, Holy Grail* by Michael Baigent, Richard Leigh, and Henry Lincoln. In fact, Brown is so impressed by these authors that the name of his villain in the novel, Leigh Teabing, is probably based on their names; Leigh is from Robert Leigh, and Teabing is an anagram of Baigent. Their 1982 book was an international best-seller and received both acclaim and extensive criticism.

Their history of the Priory of Sion differs slightly from Dan Brown's version. *Holy Blood, Holy Grail* claims the Priory was a continuation of an eleventh-century organization in Jerusalem called the Chevaliers de l'Ordre de Notre Dame de Sion.[1] The authors said they found evidence that such an order did exist and continued in France after the Christians were driven out of Jerusalem. The European order, however, was called the Prieuré de Sion, and there is no evidence that it was a continuation of the order in Jerusalem of a different name. In 1619 the property of the Prieuré was taken away and given to the Jesuits because the monks were no longer following their own rule, were neglecting divine service, and were failing to maintain the property.[2]

In 1956 a modern organization by the name of Prieuré de Sion was formed in France, and in the 1960s information purporting to be about that organization was placed in France's Bibliothèque Nationale. Most of the information is contained in the "Prieuré documents" written under blatantly false names and with nonexistent publishers. In some cases the writer or writers have apparently taken news stories about mysterious deaths and worked them into the Priory story,

trying to give the impression that the Priory is surrounded by intrigue. Nevertheless, these documents form the primary "evidence" to support the theories of *Holy Blood, Holy Grail*, and consequently *The Da Vinci Code*.

The authors of *Holy Blood, Holy Grail* admitted that the documents in the Bibliothèque Nationale could have been faked, but said they believed the story was true. Nonetheless, their researches led them back to one person as the source of the stories about the Priory and related legends.

Shortly after the publication of the book and the resulting publicity, Plantard was investigated by a variety of French writers. The resulting revelations were devastating, both to him personally and to the theories behind Holy Blood, Holy Grail.

Pierre Plantard

That person was Pierre Plantard, who called himself Pierre Plantard de Saint-Clair. Plantard said he was the spokesperson for the Priory of Sion and released information to the French press in 1981 claiming that he had been elected Grand Master of the Priory of Sion by 121 dignitaries who were éminences grises of high finance and international political or philosophical societies. He also claimed that he had been legally proven to be the direct descendant of the Merovingian kings.[3] In an interview with the authors of *Holy Blood, Holy Grail* shortly after this purported election, Plantard openly claimed to be the rightful king and appeared to expect the people of France to proclaim him king in a reinstated monarchy.[4]

Shortly after the publication of the book and the resulting publicity, Plantard was investigated by a variety of French writers. The resulting revelations were devastating, both to him personally and to the theories behind *Holy Blood, Holy Grail.*

THE WAR YEARS

Plantard's character was called into question when it was revealed that far from being the Resistance-supporting patriot of World War II that Baigent, Leigh, and Lincoln had represented him to be, Plantard had been an ultraconservative supporter of the Vichy regime and the Nazis during the war. In 1940 he wrote a letter to Field Marshal Pétain, the French Head of State in Vichy, under the name Varran de Vérestra. The letter urged Pétain to end "the war started by the Jews" and "put an immediate stop to this terrible 'Masonic and Jewish' conspiracy." He warned

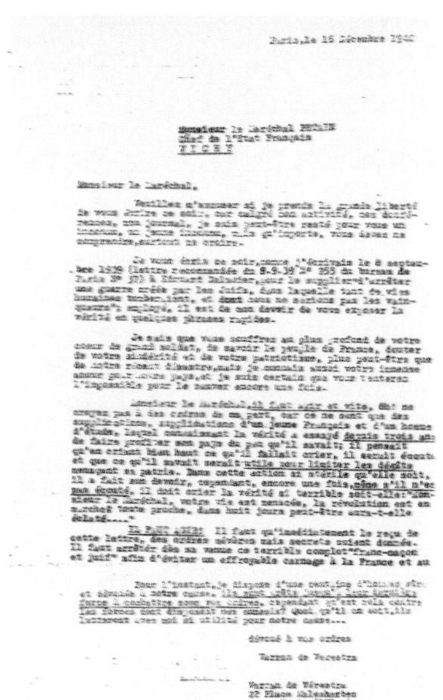

Paris, le 16 Décembre 1940

Monsieur le Maréchal PETAIN
Chef de l'Etat Français
VICHY

Monsieur le Maréchal,

[illegible]

dévoué à vos ordres

Varran de Verestra

Varran de Vérestra
22 Place Malesherbes
Paris (17ème)

TOP Field Marshal Pétain, head of the government at Vichy, France, shakes hands with Adolph Hitler, a gesture that symbolized his government's collaboration with the Nazi government of Germany.

BOTTOM Letter from Plantard, calling himself "Varran de Vérestra," to Field Marshal Pétain. The English translation is shown in the text box on the opposite page.

Pétain that a revolution was imminent, and claimed to have a hundred men under his command who would fight in response to orders from Pétain.

Pétain was sufficiently concerned by the letter to have the writer investigated. A 1941 police report revealed that the writer was Pierre Plantard, a twenty-one-year-old who lived with his mother in a two-room apartment in Paris. His father, a butler, had died in an accident and had left a small income to his wife, on which she supported herself and Pierre. In 1937 Pierre had helped to form an anti-Semitic, anti-Masonic organization of about one hundred members. Plantard boasted of having links to numerous politicians and was believed to run more or less fictitious groups in hopes of attracting government attention. The police dismissed Plantard as an unstable attention seeker.

In 1942 Plantard, then calling himself Pierre of France, formed an organization called Alpha Galates (the First Gauls), which was to support the Vichy government and to "eradicate from [the soul of the Fatherland] the dominant pathogens, the hate-filled resentments and the false dogmas such as secularism, godlessness, and the corrupt principles of the old democratic Judaeo-freemasonry." In a later statement in 1942, Plantard said, "I want Hitler's Germany to know that every obstacle to our own plans does harm to him also, for it is the resistance put up by freemasonry that is undermining German might." Plantard also indicated that his organization was a continuation of the Knights Templar.[5]

THE FIRST PRIORY OF SION

After the war and the German defeat, Plantard redefined Alpha Galates as an organization to help youth who had suffered under the Germans. A police report of the new organization revealed that Plantard had been imprisoned for four months by the Vichy government for setting up organizations and publishing various documents without permission.[6] Plantard would later portray himself as someone beaten and tortured as a Resistance fighter helping the Jews. The 1945 police report described Plantard as "an odd young man who has gone off the rails."

Within a few years, Plantard married and moved to a town called Annemasse in the Haute Savoie region of France. In 1954 he was imprisoned for six months on a conviction for fraud, though no more details are available.[7]

Paris, 16 December 1940
Field Marshal PÉTAIN
French Head of State
VICHY

Sir,

Please forgive me for taking the liberty of writing to you this evening. Despite my various commitments, my lectures and my magazine, I am perhaps still unknown to you. Just another unknown youngster, but what does that matter? You must try to understand what I am saying and, above all, to believe what I am saying.

I am writing to you this evening, just as I wrote on 8 September 1939 (by registered letter of 9.9.39 N° 255 from Paris post office N° 37) to Edouard Daladier, to beg you to 'put a stop to a war started by the Jews in which so many human lives have been lost and which we cannot hope to win'. Being myself in a reserved occupation it is my duty to reveal to you the truth in a few short phrases.

I know that, in the depths of your soldier's heart, you are suffering from the knowledge that the people of France are questioning your sincerity and your patriotism, and are suffering more perhaps from that than from the effects of our recent disaster. But I know also of your great love for our country, and I am certain that you will do everything possible to save it once more.

Sir, you must act–and quickly. Please do not think I am giving you orders: these are merely entreaties, entreaties from a young Frenchman who has studied the matter, someone who knows the truth and who has tried for three years now to use what little he knows to help his country. I believe that by crying at the top of my voice that which must be heard that I will be heard, and that what I know could be of some use in limiting the harm that threatens to befall our country. Through this action, however futile it might prove, I have made it my duty, even if I go unheard, to once again let people know the truth, no matter how terrible that truth might me: 'Sir, your life is in danger, the revolution is already underway'. You do not have much time. In just eight days it may perhaps be in full swing.

YOU MUST ACT! Immediately upon receiving this letter you must issue strict but totally confidential orders. You must put an immediate stop to this terrible 'Masonic and Jewish' conspiracy in order to save both France and the world as a whole from terrible carnage.

At present I have about a hundred reliable men under me who are devoted to our cause. They are ready to fight to the bitter end in response to your orders. But what is a hundred men when faced with the might of our enemies? Whatever the case may be, they will fight alongside me for our cause.

Varran de Verestra

Varran de Vérestra
22 Place Malesherbes
Paris 17

Pierre Plantard at the time of the second Priory of Sion. Plantard claimed to be the Grand Master of the Priory, the descendant of Jesus and Mary Magdalene, and the true king of France. He later admitted that the documents on which he based these claims were forged.

In 1956, Plantard and a few associates formed an organization called the Prieuré de Sion, the Priory of Sion, which was named after a nearby hill called Mont Sion. Its purpose was to support an opposition candidate for the local council elections, and to advocate on the issue of low-cost housing.[8] The organization was disbanded when Plantard was arrested again, this time for "détournement de mineurs," or corruption of minors. He was convicted and served another year in prison.

THE SECOND PRIORY OF SION

After 1960, Plantard revived the Priory of Sion, claiming it was created by Godfroi de Bouillon in the eleventh century. This story may have been influenced by a tale told by Roger Lhomoy, the former warden of the château of Gisors, where a treasure was supposed to have been found. When French researchers contacted the original 1956 members of the Priory, none of them knew anything about ancient origins or any of Plantard's story.[9] Around this time, Plantard met Noel Corbu, who would inspire him to launch his new career as pretender to the throne of France.

The Original Saunière

In *The Da Vinci Code*, Dan Brown's murder victim, Jaques Saunière, is the current Grand Master of the Priory of Sion. In the novel the Priory is portrayed as the ultimate Goddess cult and as an advocate for restoring the sacred feminine. It is opposed by the ultraconservative Catholic organization, Opus Dei. Ironically, Plantard, an ultraconservative Catholic, probably had more in common with Opus Dei than with Brown's idea of the Priory.

The victim in the novel is named after a nineteenth-century historical figure, Bérenger Saunière, who played a major role in Plantard's historical creations. Saunière was a conservative Royalist who opposed the Republican government of his time. He was censured for his political activity and sent to be a village priest in the remote village of Rennes-le-Château. He was eventually suspended from the priesthood for selling masses, though just before his death, his suspension was lifted and he was given the last rites. He left his estate to his housekeeper, Marie Dérarnaud, who had difficulty paying for his coffin.

In spite of this rather mundane history, a legend arose about Saunière and Rennes-le-Château. The invention of the legend was begun by Noel Corbu, who inherited Saunière's estate from Marie Dérarnaud and started a restaurant there.

Corbu's fictionalized history started an avalanche of stories about Rennes-le-Château and a series of published books. The expanded myth included stories of hidden codes, occult significance, and secret bloodlines. Several of these innovations originated with a 1967 book called *L'Or de Rennes*, allegedly by Gérard de Sède. Researcher Paul Smith claims, however, that it was written by Plantard, who allowed de Sède to rewrite it when he could not sell his version.[10] The book's biggest selling point was the reproduction of the parchments that Saunière was supposed to have found in Rennes-le-Château. The contract for the book gave a man named Philippe de Chérisey a share of profits for providing the parchments.[11] When de Sède did not honor the contract to de Chérisey's satisfaction, de Chérisey revealed in 1979 that he had falsified the parchments in a fraud with Plantard.[12] Plantard denied the charge until 1989, when he admitted that the parchments had been fabricated by de Chérisey but claimed that authentic parchments did exist. His claims that the real parchments were in a safe-deposit box in England proved to be false.

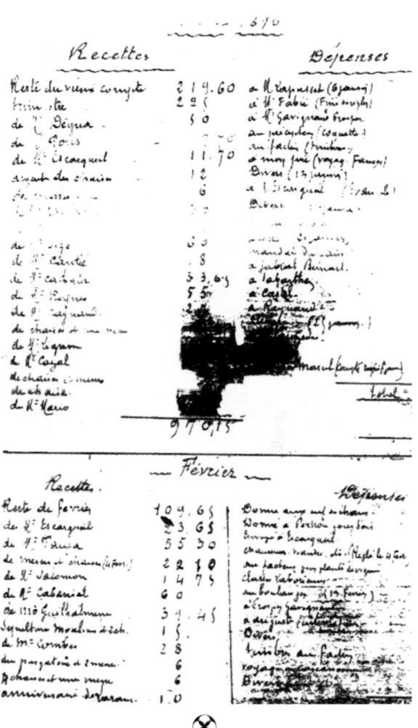

Bérenger Saunière's accounts, showing his income from the sale of masses. Later legends claimed that Saunière was very wealthy, and implied that he had been paid for occult secrets. His income can actually be explained on the basis of the widespread sale of masses, many of which he never performed.

These parchments contained a genealogical chart tracing a bloodline from Dagobert II to Pierre Plantard, mentioned Sion, and connected the painters Poussin and Teniers to the story. This information formed the primary basis for the theories behind *Holy Blood, Holy Grail.* The other evidence on which the authors of *Holy Blood, Holy Grail* claimed to rely was the material lodged in the Bibliothèque Nationale, which consisted of twentieth-century typewritten documents about genealogies, the Merovingians, poetry, and occult references. There are also newspaper clippings and drawings. These documents included a list of purported past Grand Masters of the Priory of Sion, including the name of Leonardo da Vinci.

The ultimate import of all this was to present Plantard as a pretender to the French throne and as a successor to Leonardo, Isaac Newton, Victor Hugo, and other great people of history. Plantard claimed to be the chosen leader of people of both finance and learning. On the basis of all this he marketed himself as an author, a psychic, and an authority on European occult history.

Portrait of Leonardo da Vinci, 16th century engraving by Giorgio Vasari. Leonardo da Vinci was once claimed as a former Grand Master of the fictionalized organization, the Priory of Sion. Pierre Plantard later claimed that the Priory was not founded until after the time of Leonardo, and insisted that Leonardo was never a Grand Master.

Plantard's fiction-based fame ran into difficulty after the publication of *Holy Blood, Holy Grail*, when the French researcher Jean-Luc Chaumeil unearthed information about Plantard's conviction for corruption of minors.[13] At first Plantard protested and threatened suit for defamation, but in 1984 he publicly resigned as Grand Master of the Priory of Sion.

THE THIRD PRIORY OF SION

In 1989 Plantard tried to stage a comeback as the Grand Master of the Priory, claiming that the Grand Master between the death of de Chérisey in 1985 and 1989 was Patrice Pelat, a former close friend of François Mitterand, who had just committed suicide because of a financial scandal.

Plantard claimed that the documents on which the entire theory of *Holy Blood, Holy Grail* had been based were fraudulent and created by a man named Philippe Toscan under the influence of LSD, though some of the documents and much of their contents can be linked to Plantard. Plantard also claimed the story of the Priory formed by Godfroi de Bouillon was completely false. The Priory of Sion, he said, was founded on September 19, 1738, in Rennes-le-Château by François d'Hautpoul and Jean-Paul de Nègre. Leonardo da Vinci was never a Grand Master, and the Priory was never linked to the Knights Templar.[14]

The new Priory, which Plantard proclaimed at that time, was really based, he said, on the immense energy of the Black Rock situated close to the summit of Château de Blanchefort. Plantard admitted that his claim to have the treasure of the Jerusalem Temple was a fraud, but that fraud had, he said, only been created to prevent people from digging near the Black Rock.[15] By 1990 Plantard was saying that he had never claimed to be the rightful king of France or a descendant of Jesus and that was all a hoax by the authors of *Holy Blood, Holy Grail*.[16] He was of the line of Sigisbert IV, but not the direct descendant. The direct descendant was Otto von Habsburg.[17] When contacted by Paul Smith, von Hapsburg knew nothing of this.[18]

Plantard's fabrications came back to haunt him in 1993, when an investigation was instigated into the death of Patrice Pelat and the securities scandal that precipitated his suicide. Because Plantard had claimed Pelat was a Priory Grand Master, he was called as a witness, detained, and questioned for forty-eight hours.

His house was searched, and several purported Priory documents were found that called Plantard the "true King of France." Plantard admitted that he had invented the whole story, and the investigating judge reprimanded Plantard for playing games and released him. That seemed to be the end of the game for the seventy-three-year-old Plantard, who never claimed to be connected to the Priory of Sion again. He died in 2000.

Sir Isaac Newton by Sir Godfrey Kneller (1646–1723). Isaac Newton was also named as a former Priory of Sion Grand Master, and later repudiated by Plantard.

Holy Blood, Holy Fraud?

The evidence is overwhelming that the story of the Priory of Sion and the bloodline leading to Plantard was a fabrication created by Plantard and his cohorts. The obvious question is, did the authors of *Holy Blood, Holy Grail* know Plantard's story was fraudulent before they published the book?

The story of the forged parchments had been revealed in the 1979 book *Le Trésor du Triangle d'Or*—published three years before *Holy Blood, Holy Grail*—which also contained an interview with Plantard. The authors claimed to have done extensive research for their book. If so, how could they have failed to find information about Plantard's past, his criminal convictions, and his past misrepresentations? Information about his arrest record and war history would have been easier to find than the arcane bits of history the authors claimed to have unearthed.

Did they know the truth about Plantard or did they fail to investigate him? We cannot know for certain, but no doubt their book would have been less successful if they had revealed that their theory depended on the credibility of a former Nazi supporter with a penchant for fictitious organizations, a criminal record, and a reputation for instability.

Plantard admitted that he had invented the whole story...

A Desire for Certain Knowledge

Despite all the evidence that the Priory of Sion is a fraud, many people continue to believe in it. There are Web sites that relay the history of Plantard's second version of the Priory of Sion as fact.

Despite all the evidence that the Priory of Sion is a fraud, many people continue to believe in it. There are Web sites that relay the history of Plantard's second version of the Priory of Sion as fact.[19] Why do so many of us want to believe that such an organization exists?

We may enjoy secrets, puzzles, and conspiracy theories, but we also want to know what really happened in the past. Who was Jesus? What is the truth about Goddess worship? In Dan Brown's version of the story, the Priory has all the answers to all our questions. There are thousands of pages of documents that will prove what is true.

Many of us seem to be uncomfortable with the idea that we cannot know for certain what really happened. What cannot be known as fact is often made certain by belief—not just belief about what we cannot prove, like the existence of God or the true nature of Jesus, but about alleged historical events like the birth of Jesus in Bethlehem. This desire to know can produce a willingness to believe in the improbable and sometimes in the absurd.

Even if we want there to be an organization that has preserved untainted and accurate information about Jesus, the origins of Christianity, and the Goddess, would it be likely to look like the Priory of Sion? This organization described by five men—Plantard, Baigent, Leigh, Lincoln, and Brown—is a strange vehicle for conveying the truth of the Goddess.

MALE DOMINATION

Dan Brown claims that the Priory of Sion is the protector of Mary Magdalene and "the pagan goddess worship cult."[20] The Priory list of past Grand Masters (which Plantard admitted was faked) appears on pages 326–327 of *The Da Vinci Code*. The last woman on the list of Grand Masters was Iolande de Bar, daughter of René d'Anjou, who is said to have been Grand Master from 1480 to 1483, more than 520 years ago. According to Brown, this pagan Goddess worship cult has been dominated by males for more than 500 years. The feminine is idealized, but women are not given positions of power.

In the Catholic Church, which Brown criticizes severely, Mary the mother of Jesus and women saints are honored and idealized, but women are kept out of the priesthood and the highest levels of power. In the organization Brown claims is real, the pagan Goddess is worshiped, but women have not held the highest leadership position for centuries. In Brown's fictionalized Priory, the Grand Master and all three assistants, or sénéchaux, are male. Women like Sophie's grandmother and the nun at Saint Sulpice play only supporting roles. There seems to be very little difference in the position of women between these two organizations, though Brown presents one as the defender of the sacred feminine and the other as its opponent.

In Brown's fictionalized Priory, the Grand Master and all three assistants, or sénéchaux, are male.

A MALE BLOODLINE

Another anomaly in an organization that is supposed to honor the feminine is that the bloodline documented in *Holy Blood, Holy Grail* that Plantard traced is based on male succession. This means that the royal succession passes through male children. If there are daughters, they are passed over and the succession only comes to them if there are no male heirs.

This version of the Priory of Sion may be Dan Brown's ideal group for honoring the sacred feminine, but a male-dominated group that worships the Goddess by protecting a male bloodline will not appeal to most women. As interesting as it would be to have an organization that has maintained information about women's spiritual history and honors the divine feminine, we might be thankful that this one is a fabrication.

The Tree of Jesse, 18th-century icon from the Ionian Isles, Greece. Tracing the bloodline of Jesus has fascinated people since antiquity. This icon shows Jesus as the descendant of Jesse, the father of King David. Ancient Middle Eastern genealogies were often done for political and religious purposes, and were not historically accurate. This genealogy traces Jesus' descent through the male line.

CHAPTER EIGHT
BLOODLINES AND GUARDIANS

The bloodline theory of *The Da Vinci Code* and its predecessors is based on the legend that Mary Magdalene traveled to France and raised a daughter there. Is there evidence that she actually traveled to France and lived there? We do not have any concrete evidence of what happened to Mary Magdalene after the crucifixion. From the various texts we can tell that she was extremely well known over a wide geographical area in the early years of Christianity, but we have no details about specific places where she traveled or lived. We have only legendary reports that she went to France, and those are fairly late. The earliest legends place her in Ephesus.

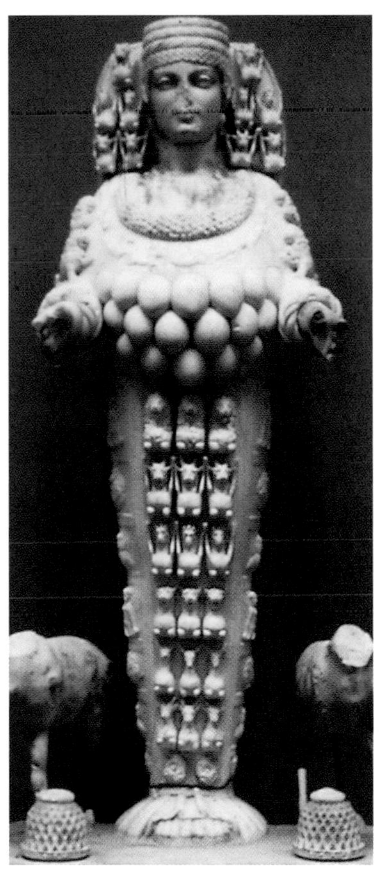

ABOVE *Artemis of Ephesus*, Roman statue from 1st century B.C.E. The Goddess Artemis was associated with bees and was often portrayed covered in honeycomb. Artemis was a major deity in Ephesus.

OPPOSITE *Mary Magdalene in Provence*, 16th century painting by an unknown Netherlandish artist.

Mary Magdalene In Ephesus

By the fifth and sixth centuries, a legend had developed that Mary Magdalene went to Ephesus, the city of Artemis and Diana, with Mary the mother of Jesus and the beloved disciple John, where she died a martyr. Ephesus is a city where Paul spent a great deal of time and where he had a dispute with people usually referred to as Gnostics.[1] We already have seen that some of the apocryphal documents praising Mary Magdalene most likely came from that area as well. That raises the possibility that Mary Magdalene traveled there, taught there, or was particularly known there for some reason. There is no proof that she lived there, however, and Mary Magdalene may have been known in the area because people she had known or taught had brought news of her there.

The legend of Mary Magdalene's travel to Ephesus was written down in the sixth century by the Frankish historian Gregory of Tours, and cited by Pope Gregory in his fateful sermon in 590 when he characterized Mary Magdalene as a prostitute. This apparently widespread and long-lasting legend was also referred to by several Byzantine historians in the tenth century. Because Mary Magdalene

Mary Magdalene's alleged tomb in Ephesus was linked to the myth of the Seven Sleepers.

and Mary of Bethany became conflated into one character, there was also a late sixth-century story that Lazarus followed his "sister" to Ephesus and became a bishop there.[2]

Mary Magdalene's alleged tomb in Ephesus was linked to the myth of the Seven Sleepers. These were seven Christian martyrs who were walled in a cave by the Roman emperor around 250 and then miraculously awoke 200 years later. Her tomb was said to be outside of their cave, a legend that must have arisen between 449, when the sleepers are supposed to have awakened, and 590, when Gregory of Tours wrote the story down. Mary Magdalene could not have been linked to the Seven Sleepers during her life, so the location of her tomb in Ephesus has no reliable historical foundation. It is more likely that a late legend of Mary Magdalene in Ephesus was linked to the already legendary cave of the Seven Sleepers. Pilgrims continued to visit the sepulcher of Mary Magdalene in Ephesus until the twelfth century.[3]

Mary Magdalene in European Myth

Bede, abbot of Jarrow (709–715), wrote a commentary on the Gospel of Luke, and conflated the biblical figures of Mary Magdalene, Mary of Bethany, and Luke's sinner into Mary Magdalene the repentant sinner, in line with Pope Gregory's portrayal of her. A ninth-century Anglo-Saxon legend reported that after Jesus ascended into Heaven, Mary Magdalene retired to the desert, where she was lifted into heaven by angels each day for spiritual sustenance.[4] This event, transferred from the Middle Eastern desert to Europe, was a popular image in European art.

The Assumption of the Magdalene by Giulio Romano (ca. 1499–1546). The legend that Mary Magdalene was carried to heaven by angels for daily sustenance was a popular theme in European art.

Mary Magdalene became a model for female asceticism in Europe in the eighth and ninth centuries, and with the legends of her asceticism in the desert, devotion to her increased. In the tenth and eleventh centuries, churches and chapels in Germany, Spain, and England were dedicated to her.[5]

Mary Magdalene in Provence

Nowhere was the devotion to Mary Magdalene so remarkable as in eleventh-century France. Between 1024 and 1049, six churches were dedicated to her. One eleventh-century French legend, contained in the chronicle of the Bishops of Cambrai, said that Mary Magdalene had died and been buried in Jerusalem, but her body had later been brought to France. At the beginning of the century another legend that Mary Magdalene had come to Provence after the crucifixion of Jesus emerged. Scholars have not been able to trace the legend to earlier times, and there is a great deal of discussion about how and why the legend arose when it did.

The story itself had many forms and accumulated parts of earlier tales. In the most widely accepted early version, Mary Magdalene arrived in Marseille by boat accompanied by Maximinus. She preached and converted the pagan prince in Marseille, while Maximinus became the first bishop of Aix.[6]

Popular stories of Mary Magdalene had long combined her with the character Mary of Bethany, making Mary Magdalene the sister of Martha and Lazarus. During this period, she was also combined with other figures like Mary of Egypt, a prostitute who reformed and went to live in the desert wearing nothing but her long hair. That may have been linked to a fifth-century tale that when the Christian Agnes was thrown naked into a brothel because she refused to marry, her hair miraculously grew and covered her.[7]

A later version of the Provence story has Mary Magdalene arriving with Martha and Lazarus. Mary preaches, Lazarus becomes the bishop of Marseille, and Martha overcomes a wicked dragon at Tarascon. By the thirteenth century, there were many versions of this legend.[8]

Mary Magdalene was said to have lived in seclusion for thirty years. In earlier versions she was contemplative, but in later versions she became a penitent sinner. By the twelfth century the location of her seclusion was identified as a large cavern east of Marseille.[9] In the Vézelay version she spent her seclusion at Sainte Balm (Holy Balm).

The story of Mary Magdalene was expanded and embellished in the thirteenth-century *Golden Legend.* There Mary crosses the sea in a rudderless boat, set

Saint Catherine of Alexandria and Saint Agnes. Agnes, clothed in her hair and accompanied with her characteristic lamb, is pictured with Catherine of Alexandria. The legend of Agnes may have been the source of the legend that Mary Magdalene lived naked in her retirement, wearing only her hair.

Mary Magdalene was said to have lived in seclusion for thirty years.

Mary Magdalene by Jose de Ribera (1591–1652). French legend claimed that Mary Magdalene retired for thirty years to a cavern at Sainte Balm.

adrift by "heathens," with Martha, Lazarus, and the three Marys. The cast of characters in this legend has grown remarkably and includes Mary's servant Sarah the Egyptian, Trophimus, Maximinus, Martial, Saturnininus, Sidonius, Eutropius, Marcellina, Cleon, and Joseph of Arimathaea.[10]

When she arrives, Mary Magdalene preaches at the temple. She makes a deal with the barren prince and princess; if they will not persecute Christians or sacrifice to pagan Gods, she will ask God to give them a child. In this role she replaces the fertility Goddesses Cybele and Ishtar. After the child is born the prince and princess go to Rome to see Peter and confirm what Mary has told them. The princess drowns on the way, and the prince leaves her body and the child on a

rock, since he cannot feed the child. When he returns two years later, he finds the child still alive, because he has been miraculously nursed by his mother's body. The prince gives thanks to Mary Magdalene for this miracle, and the princess is restored to life.

After teaching for some time, Mary Magdalene retires for thirty years to a contemplative life. Angels come down to take her to heaven each day for sustenance. The *Golden Legend* also says that Mary Magdalene was of royal birth and part of the lost tribe of Benjamin.[11]

These legends are not history and cannot be relied on as historical proof. The later thirteenth-century versions are especially suspect. They reflect the conflation of Mary Magdalene with Mary of Bethany and several others and add many embellishments. The eleventh-century story that Mary Magdalene came to France with Maximinus, as the earliest level, is the most likely to be linked to some level of historical fact. It is important to remember that we have no traces of European legends about Mary Magdalene before the eighth century, and those earliest European legends place her in the desert of the Middle East, not in Europe.

...we have no traces of European legends about Mary Magdalene before the eighth century, and those earliest European legends place her in the desert of the Middle East, not in Europe.

Changes In Europe

If the legend of Mary Magdalene's move to France is true, why did it not surface until the eleventh century? Was the legend discovered then? Europe was undergoing many changes at that time. In the seventh and eighth centuries Islamic invaders occupied the Iberian Peninsula and part of France. From 732 to 1492, Moorish Spain was the repository of knowledge from Islam, Judaism, classical Greek philosophy, and many other Eastern sources of knowledge. There was travel and the exchange of knowledge between the Moorish-occupied lands and the rest of Europe. For example, Nicolas Flamel, the West's most famous alchemist, claimed to have learned his secrets from a book he got in Spain. One of the leading Grail writers, the Bavarian knight Wolfram von Eschenbach, wrote his Grail story *Parzival* based on a story he claimed was found in Spain.

The Cathars

"Our men spared no one, irrespective of rank, sex or age, and put to the sword almost 20,000 people. After this great slaughter the whole city was despoiled and burnt, as Divine Vengeance raged marvellously."

The Cathars were an alternative Christian group that the Church condemned as heretics. The Church's antagonism toward them was based in part on the Cathars' criticism of corruption in the Church. The Cathars rejected the financial greed and corruption that gripped much of the Church at that time. Their ministers, who were both women and men, lived in poverty, and the groups worshiped out of doors whenever possible to avoid vast expenditures for churches. Their beliefs appear to have been Gnostic in character, but few texts survive.

The Cathar influence was centered in the Languedoc, where they were not the majority but had a great deal of influence. They often had the protection of rulers who remained independent of the Church. The culture of the Languedoc was rich, and there was open exchange with the Moorish culture that occupied part of the area. This contact may have given the Cathars access to texts from the East.

In the early thirteenth century, the Church under Pope Innocent III began a war against the Cathars and their supporters, which it called the Albigensian Crusade.[12] This war consisted of a pattern of systematic genocide that took place over a period of many years. In the documentation of that campaign we find descriptions of horrors committed by the Church's troops, including gloating accounts of the slaughter of everyone—men, women, children, babes in arms, and the elderly.

> *Our men spared no one, irrespective of rank, sex or age, and put to the sword almost 20,000 people. After this great slaughter the whole city was despoiled and burnt, as Divine Vengeance raged marvellously.*[13]

Orthodox Christians who would not turn on their Cathar neighbors and relatives were also killed. When the city of Béziers was attacked in 1205, the townspeople stuck together against the invaders. As the Church troops broke through the walls, the people ran to the church of Mary Magdalene for sanctuary, but the invaders disregarded the right of sanctuary and slaughtered them.

Crusaders expelling Cathars from Carcassonne, a 14th century illumination by the Boucicaut Master and Workshop. Both Cathars and their orthodox Christian supporters were killed by the Church's troops when they refused to renounce their faith or their support for religious choice. The Church's representatives described the slaughter of thousands with relish.

The chroniclers emphasized that this slaughter took place on the feast day of Mary Magdalene. "Oh supreme justice of Providence!"[14] This was appropriate, the chroniclers said, because the Cathars had asserted that Mary Magdalene was the concubine of Jesus Christ.[15] If this was true—and it would have been a strange thing for the attackers to invent—then the Cathars may have had documents similar to the *Gospel of Philip*.

We know that the apocryphal texts were in wide circulation in Gaul in the second century, because the Christian writer Irenaeus complained about them.[16] Did the texts survive for 900 years, or did new texts come into Europe from the Islamic East, where some copies may still have been in circulation? We can only guess what texts the Cathars might have had.

It is possible that the teachings of the Cathars about Mary Magdalene, including the teaching that she was the concubine or perhaps wife of Jesus, may have

A troubadour performing at a courtly dinner.

...the troubadours continued to carry a new message of romantic love, chivalry, honor, courage, and loyalty...

helped to stir up interest in her in the eleventh century and may have given rise to legends about her. It is also possible that some account of Mary Magdalene's journey to France had been preserved in the East and made its way to Europe through the Moors to the Cathars or by some other path. This is pure speculation, of course. The only historical evidence we have is that the Cathars believed there was a sexual relationship between Mary Magdalene and Jesus.

The culture of the Languedoc, where the Cathars flourished, also gave rise to the troubadours. The area of the Languedoc was named after its language. It was the language of oc, meaning that *oc* was the word for "yes." The *langue d'oc* was considered more beautiful than the *langue d'oïl* of the north, and was a favorite for poetry and song. The troubadours appear to have been strongly influenced by Islamic love poetry.

After the destruction of the Cathars and their culture, the troubadours continued to carry a new message of romantic love, chivalry, honor, courage, and loyalty to the rest of Europe, a message that would transform the society. Did Cathar beliefs about Mary Magdalene play a role in this? We do not know, but the speculation raises interesting questions.

In about 1170, the wonderfully outrageous Eleanor of Aquitaine celebrated the ideal of courtly love in her court at Poitiers. She ran into some difficulty with a failed attempt to overthrow her husband, King Henry II of England, and was imprisoned until his death fifteen years later. The work of chivalry was carried on by her daughter, Marie, Countess of Champagne. Marie was the patron of Chrétien de Troyes, the writer of the first Grail romance. So we see that the Cathars not only possessed information about Mary Magdalene that other groups did not have,[17] but influenced the culture of chivalry and the formation of the Grail romances.

The Body of Mary Magdalene

In Dan Brown's version of the Grail, one of the secret possessions of the Priory is the body of Mary Magdalene. We can only assume that it has been miraculously preserved for almost two millennia. Brown does not say where this body came from, but many through the centuries have claimed to possess Mary Magdalene's body.

The search for the body of Mary Magdalene was an important part of the legend in France. We have already seen the earlier legend that she was buried at Ephesus, and in the ninth century the Emperor Leo VI claimed to have translated or moved her body from Ephesus to Constantinople, where she was buried beside Lazarus. We also saw the eleventh-century legend that she was buried in Jerusalem and then translated to France. A thirteenth-century claim placed her body in Rome, minus the head.[18]

In France, the primary early claim for the body was at Vézelay, where a church was begun in 1096. The inspiration for this claim seems to have come from a monk named Geoffrey, who became abbot in 1037. Up until his time, the patrons of the abbey in Vézelay were Mary the mother of Jesus, Peter, Paul, and the Roman martyrs Andeux and Pontian. After Geoffrey had spent six months in the pope's entourage, Leo IX issued a bull in 1050 making Mary Magdalene the head patron of the abbey. By the decree of Pope Stephen IX in 1058, she became the only patron.[19]

Mary Magdalene's usurpation as patron was based on the claim that her body was in Vézelay, and the various legends about her travel to France began to lead to the conclusion that her body had been taken to Vézelay. Thousands flocked to the church there, and it became one of the most popular pilgrimage sites in the world. Vézelay was on the road to Compostela in Spain, which claimed to have the body of James the apostle, and this was an extremely successful pilgrims' route. The pilgrims brought great financial success to both the abbey and the surrounding area.[20]

Many miracles were attributed to Mary Magdalene at Vézelay. She was known for freeing prisoners, who came to lay their chains before her altar. Legend says that so much metal was brought that Geoffrey was able to build a

Cave of the Seven Sleepers in Ephesus. A sarcophagus, similar to the one shown here, was identified as that of Mary Magdalene. Her supposed tomb here was a place of pilgrimage for centuries.

The church at Vézelay dedicated to Mary Magdalene. At the height of the church's popularity, many miracles were attributed to Mary Magdalene here.

The crypt under the Church at Vézelay where the abbey claimed to keep the body of Mary Magdalene.

railing around the altar. Mary Magdalene was also given credit for raising knights killed in battle from the dead. Ordinary people came to her, because as a repentant sinner she would have compassion for them and their sins.[21]

In time, perhaps because of jealousy about the success of the abbey, doubts were raised about the authenticity of the body. At first the abbey made excuses not to show it, but in 1265 they staged a showing of a body with large amounts of hair.[22] The abbey then invited the king, Louis IV, to validate their possession. He came and cut up the body, giving small pieces to his entourage, leaving the abbey an arm, a jawbone, and three teeth, and taking the rest for himself.[23]

This sacrifice by the abbey was ultimately not successful, because a few years later the church of St. Maximin in Provence announced that they had discovered the body of Mary Magdalene in the marble tomb of St. Sidonious. They claimed that there was a piece of parchment describing how the body was moved in the eighth century to protect it from the Saracens (Moors). A substitute body was left to fool the Saracens, and that was the body that was taken to Vézelay. Conveniently, the parchment dissolved into dust when it was touched and could not be examined. Modern scholars have proved this parchment a forgery, because the dating system it used placed the Moors in Spain several years before they actually arrived.[24]

By the end of the thirteenth century there were at least five bodies of Mary Magdalene and many arms and smaller pieces claimed by various churches or individuals. A celebration is still held at St. Maximin each July in which her head, covered in gold, is paraded through the streets.

Bloodlines

Dan Brown takes his theories about the bloodlines of Jesus and Mary Magdalene straight from Pierre Plantard's claim to be their descendant. Robert Langdon tells Sophie that all the descendants are named Plantard or Saint-Clair.[25] Plantard's claims were based on the falsified parchments that he said had been found at Rennes-le-Château but that he later admitted were forged. (See Chapter Seven.) The title "de Saint-Clair" that Plantard used was an assumed name like the names Varran de Vérestra and Pierre of France that he had used in earlier years. As we have seen, he later claimed that he had never said he was descended from Jesus and Mary Magdalene.[26]

For his story Brown also uses the same bloodlines theory as *Holy Blood, Holy Grail*, which claims that the bloodline of Jesus and Mary Magdalene was merged with the Merovingian royal line. This theory is based first of all on a legend that the known founder of that line, Merovée, had two fathers, one of whom was an aquatic creature from across the sea who had had sex with or raped his mother while she was swimming. From this, and nothing more, the authors surmised that Jesus, symbolized by a fish, was the ancestor.[27]

The bloodline theory is also based on a legend that those with Merovingian royal blood had a sacred, miraculous, and divine nature. This nature was attributed to their long hair, and the *Holy Blood, Holy Grail* writers theorized that this was like the Nazorites of the Old Testament, who included Samson and Jesus' brother James, and possibly Jesus himself. No citation or proof was offered for this theory.[28]

There is a glaring anomaly in this argument. The legend that the Merovingians had sacred, miraculous, and divine nature is in conflict with Baigent, Leigh, and Lincoln's theory, with which Dan Brown agreed, that Jesus was a human prophet and not divine. If Jesus was a human prophet without divine power, why would his descendants have divine power? If the bloodline was started, as they claim, by the child or children of Mary Magdalene, who knew the true nature of Jesus, why would such a legend ever be connected to him? If Jesus *was* divine, would that divinity be passed in his bloodline?

There is no evidence connecting Jesus to Samson or to legends that would attribute his power to his long hair. It is possible that the Merovingian legend was connected to the biblical story of Samson that may have been in circulation in Gaul from the first century, when Jewish communities settled there with their scriptures. It is even more likely that the Merovingian legend had no connection to Jewish or Christian legend at all.

The *Holy Blood, Holy Grail* authors' next argument for tracing the Merovingian bloodline to Jesus is that some of the Merovingians had Jewish names and they included one section of Judaic law in their legal code.[29] The

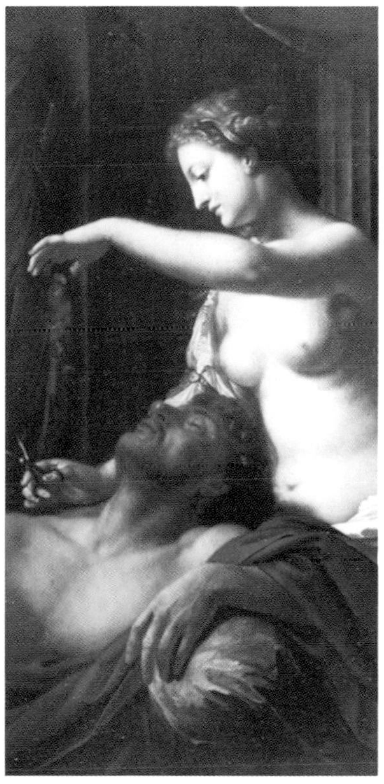

Samson and Delilah by Adrien van der Werff (ca. 1635–1672). The authors of *Holy Blood, Holy Grail* tried to connect Jesus to the story of Samson in the Old Testament. Samson got his strength from his hair, and the Merovingian magician kings had long hair that was believed to be the source of their magic and power.

authors admit that the Merovingians had a good relationship with the Jewish community in Gaul and sometimes intermarried, but they still claim to be surprised to find Jewish influence. There is little question that there was a Jewish community in Gaul, possibly even before the Diaspora in 135 C.E. Because of this, we cannot conclude that references to Jews are references to the family of Jesus, as these authors seem to do.

No reliable connection can be traced between Jesus and Mary Magdalene or their descendants and the Merovingian bloodline or the eighth-century Jewish monarch.

The *Holy Blood, Holy Grail* authors try one more argument to tie the bloodline of the Merovingians to Jesus and Mary Magdalene. In the eighth century the forerunners of the Carolingians were trying to drive the Moors out of Narbonne and may have made a deal with the Jewish inhabitants that they could have their own kingdom or princedom if they betrayed their Islamic allies. Apparently they did betray their allies, and someone who later took the name Theodoric was installed as king of the Jews. No one knows who he was, though records indicate that he came from Baghdad, where his family had lived since the Babylonian captivity.[30]

In an enormous stretch, the *Holy Blood, Holy Grail* authors try to twist that into a possible connection with Jesus. "It is also possible, however, that the 'exilarch' from Baghdad was not Theodoric. It is possible that the 'exilarch' came from Baghdad to consecrate Theodoric and subsequent records confused the two."[31] There is nothing but speculation, and possibly wishful thinking, to support this theory.

No reliable connection can be traced between Jesus and Mary Magdalene or their descendants and the Merovingian bloodline or the eighth-century Jewish monarch. Even if it would be possible to trace a bloodline through such a long period of time, we do not currently have the information to do so.

WHY A BLOODLINE?

The evidence that there is a surviving bloodline of Jesus and Mary Magdalene is virtually nonexistent. We have no proof that Jesus and Mary Magdalene were married or were sexual partners. Even if the *Gospel of Philip* meant to say that they were sexual partners, and even if that was historically accurate, there is no historically reliable evidence that they had children. If they did have children, there is no reliable information that Mary Magdalene traveled to Europe with them or

any way to identify who they or their descendants were. We have seen that a marriage and children were possible, but we have no proof that either actually happened. This is one of the things we cannot know for certain without more information.

Pierre Plantard created a fictitious bloodline that led from Jesus to himself, as part of his grandiose promotion of himself. The authors of *Holy Blood, Holy Grail* did their best to come up with some proof to support that genealogy, but the results were flimsy at best. Nevertheless, many people have believed and continue to want to believe that the bloodline of Jesus and Mary Magdalene exists.

What is the appeal of such a bloodline? Is it possible that the descendants of Jesus are seen as special beings who can save us from ourselves, like the returning king in *The Lord of the Rings*? That king is special and has the blood of an ancient race. He has the power to lead the people to defeat the evil Sauron. Would the descendants of Jesus be like messiahs who would lead us to victory over evil?

Of course, hero tales like *The Lord of the Rings* are symbolic stories about inner growth. To look for an outer savior in this situation, for a bloodline that will bring truth and salvation, may be a misunderstanding. The success of *Holy Blood, Holy Grail*, and now *The Da Vinci Code*, allows us to look at this question and ask ourselves what we are looking for in this legend of a bloodline.

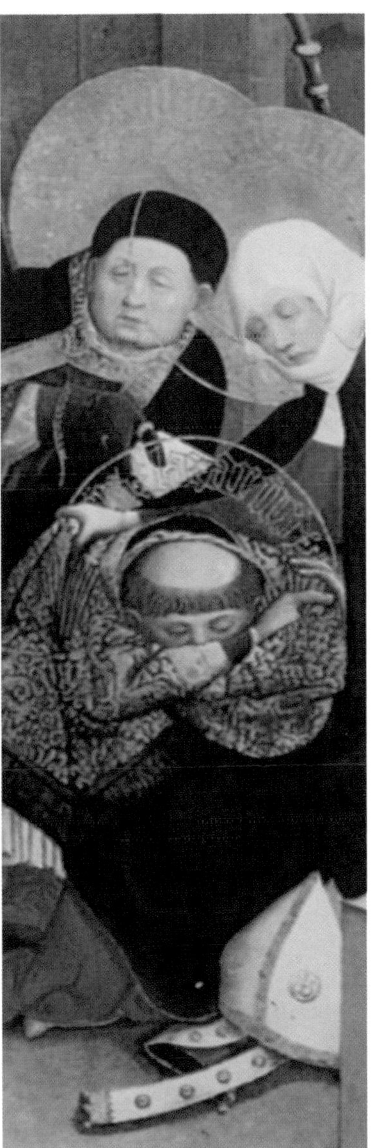

The Magdalene Altarpiece (detail) by Lucas Moser of Weil (1432). Martha, Lazarus, and Maximinus after they landed at Marseilles. In later versions of the French legend of Mary Magdalene, Martha and Lazarus join her and Maximinus, Mary's servant Sarah, and several others on their ship to France.

THE DAUGHTER

In Dan Brown's version of this story, Mary Magdalene gives birth to a daughter named Sarah. Is there some source for this information?

The first part of the story probably comes from a claim made in *Holy Blood, Holy Grail* that documents from the Montgomery family—later said to be destroyed in a fire—were copied in the nineteenth century. One alleged nineteenth-century document tells the story of Jesus, son of Joseph, who was married to Mary of Bethany. She was arrested in a revolt against Rome but was freed because she was pregnant. She went to Gaul, where she gave birth to a daughter. She was the priestess of a female cult.[32] We have no idea if this document was authentic. If it was authentic, it would only prove that there was a nineteenth-century legend about Mary of Bethany, not Mary Magdalene, as the wife of Jesus.

William Clermont Defending Acre by Dominique Louis Papety (1815–1849). The Templars defended Acre in 1291.

The chapel of the Templar fortress of Tomar in Portugal. Many Templar churches, including the Temple Church in London, were circular.

Margaret Starbird gave the daughter a name by using the thirteenth-century version of the *Golden Legend*, which says that Mary Magdalene was accompanied to France by her servant Sarah the Egyptian. Starbird theorized that the girl was called "the Egyptian" because she was born in Egypt, but that she was really the daughter of Jesus and Mary Magdalene.[33] Brown probably used this information to create the fictional story of the daughter named Sarah.

The Knights Templar

In many stories, the Knights Templar are the guardians of the Grail or of some great secret. In Brown's story they guard the documents and body of Mary Magdalene for less than a century before they give them back to the Priory for safekeeping. They play a major role in finding the treasure and probably getting it to Europe where the Priory could guard it.

What do we really know about the Knights Templar? Unfortunately, we do not know much. They were condemned by the Church in the fourteenth century, and their work was destroyed. Most of the information we have about them is from excavation of their preceptories, or monasteries, and from obviously biased Inquisition documents. The Templars have long appealed to romantic imaginations, so there is a lot of legend to be sorted out from the few facts we know.

The Knights Templar were formed around 1119 in Jerusalem after the First Crusade,[34] and they appear to have had an interest in accumulating knowledge. Many believe they collected manuscripts on subjects disturbing to orthodox Christians such as astrology, alchemy, sacred geometry, numerology, and astronomy—all subjects studied in the Islamic culture of the time. There is also a widespread belief that the Templars excavated under the Temple in Jerusalem. Some reports say that they were housed in the wing of the palace that was built over the original Temple. Other reports say they were allowed to keep their horses in a cavern under the Temple.[35]

One of the scrolls found at Qumran at the Dead Sea, the Copper Scroll—actually incised on thin sheets of copper—lists various caches of buried treasure, and that has fueled speculation that the Templars found a treasure of some

The Templars have long appealed to romantic imaginations, so there is a lot of legend to be sorted out from the few facts we know.

Crusaders by Birney Lettick (1919–1986). It was common for the Crusaders to dig for relics and treasure. Many claimed to have dreamed of the location of a relic. Here a young man named Peter Bartholomew discovers a lance head under the Church of St. Peter in Antioch. He claimed that a vision had revealed this as the lance that pierced the side of Jesus on the cross. The Knights Templar might have made similar excavations.

sort under the Temple.[36] Excavations had been conducted in Jerusalem since the time of Constantine's mother, Helena, so it is not unreasonable to think that the Templars would have excavated around the Temple, but we have no real evidence that they did. It is also quite possible that they acquired some apocryphal documents, similar to the ones found at Nag Hammadi or the ones the Cathars may have had. Documents like those would have been shocking to most European Christians of their time.

Jacques de Molay, the last Grand Master of the Knights Templar, and the preceptor of Normandy were roasted to death over a slow fire. Molay called upon Pope Clement V and King Phillipe IV of France to join him in death within a year. They both died, which added greatly to the belief in the power of the Templars.

Many have speculated why the Templar success was so phenomenal. The Templars skyrocketed to fame and fortune, and by 1139 Pope Innocent III declared them above the authority of civil rulers and religious hierarchies. They became a law unto themselves. The popular theory endorsed by Dan Brown is that the Templars discovered some secret and threatened to reveal it unless the Vatican gave them power.

There is another possible explanation for their success. As both religious ascetics and chivalrous knights, they embodied the ideal of their time, an ideal people were embracing with remarkable fervor. Many wealthy men rushed to join, transferring all their estates to the order. The Templars had able members who knew how to manage wealth, and they soon became involved in European finance.[37] Wealth brought more wealth. Their members came from powerful families and had valuable connections, allowing them to obtain favors. The pope may have wished to keep the loyalty of such a valuable fighting force all for himself. All of these reasons might account for the success of the Templars, without the possession of any treasure or the discovery of any devastating secret.

In 1307, most, but not all, of the Templars in France were arrested.

The Christian control of the Holy Land was short-lived and the Templars found themselves back in Europe without a real purpose. Without wars to fight, they became more involved in finance and diplomacy. Some governments, including that of Philippe IV of France, became deeply indebted to the order. Dan Brown blames the demise of the Templars on Pope Clement V, but historians agree that the blame rests primarily on Philippe, who wanted out of his debts and probably wanted to take possession of the Templar treasury.[38] In 1307, most, but not all, of the Templars in France were arrested. Legend says that the Templars were warned ahead of time and some escaped with their Paris treasury and library. At least we know that no treasure was listed in

Inquisition documents. The Templar fleet also disappeared from the shores of northern France.

Several Templars in France and other places in Europe were tortured and confessed under torture or threat of torture to an array of heresies.[39] The last Grand Master of the Templars, Jacques de Molay, confessed under torture and then recanted. Because of this, he and the preceptor of Normandy were roasted to death over a slow fire. As he went to his death, legend says that Molay called on Clement and Phillipe to join him before the throne of God within a year to account for their actions.[40] Clement was dead within a month, and Phillipe within a year, creating great awe of the power of the Templars. More cynical commentators have suggested that surviving Templars or their friends took revenge and helped the deaths of Clement and Phillipe along, but the story has done much for the mythical reputation of the Templars.

Templars were not treated so harshly in some other European countries as in France, and there is no doubt that a substantial number survived. If they really did have an explosive secret that they were using to blackmail the Vatican, it makes sense that they would have revealed it when the Vatican disbanded the order and allowed the king of France to murder many of its members. No such revelation occurred. There have been many claims that the "secret" of the Templars has been passed down to other organizations. Plantard's claim for the Priory of Sion is one in a long line of claimants to treasure and secret knowledge.

The Knights Templar appeared in some Grail stories as guardians of the Grail, but we have no historical evidence that they guarded a bloodline or any other secret. There are stories that they possessed powerful relics, which might have been enough to link them to Grail stories. The Templars participated in the thirteenth-century sacking of the Eastern Christian city of Constantinople, in the so-called Fourth Crusade. The crusaders joined the Venetian invasion of Constantinople in order to raise funds for another attack on the Holy Land, and that invasion was so lucrative that the crusade to the Holy Land was abandoned. The Eastern Church had many relics that were stolen by the crusaders, and the Templars were believed to have possession of several, including the Shroud of Turin. Possession of such relics could easily have given rise to legends of mysterious power.

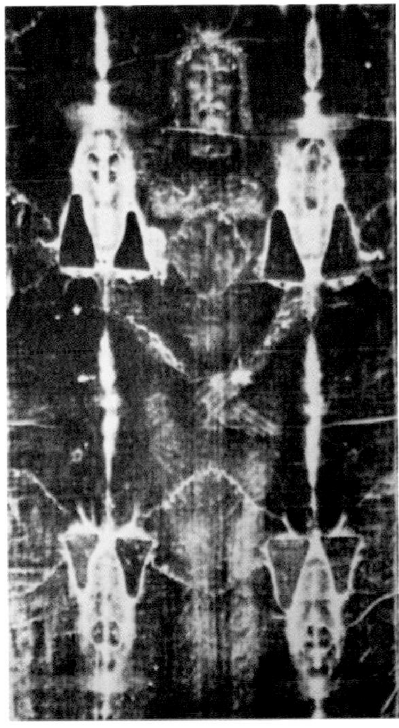

The Shroud of Turin is believed by many to be the shroud used to cover the body of Jesus for burial and to contain the imprint of his face and body. The Templars may have possessed it at one time, which might have added to their power and prestige.

CHAPTER NINE
GRAIL LEGENDS

The book *Holy Blood, Holy Grail*, claims that the Holy Grail is two different things: It is the bloodline of Jesus and it is Mary Magdalene who was the chalice that caught the blood of Jesus. Brown's characters say that the Priory knows the "true nature of the Grail."[1] In his account, the Grail is both a collection of documents—"thousands of ancient documents as scientific evidence that the New Testament is false testimony"[2]—and the body of Mary Magdalene as a relic.

The Chalice of Antioch (4th–5th century). This chalice was once thought to be the Holy Grail.

Nature of the Grail

Langdon and Teabing talk about the "true nature of the Grail," but it is very likely that the Grail has been a different thing to different people and that the Grail legends have been used to convey a variety of ideas. Even the Grail itself has been a different object in these stories. Many people have come to think of the Grail as a cup or chalice that was used to catch the blood of Jesus, but that was only one version of the Grail. In the original story, the "Graal" referred to in the story was not a cup but a platter or serving dish. Other versions of the tale portray the Grail as the dish from which Jesus ate the Passover lamb at the Last Supper; the chalice of the first sacrament; the cup in which Mary Magdalene or Joseph of Arimathea caught the blood of Jesus as he hung on the cross, was taken down from the cross, or appeared in a vision; a salver containing a man's head swimming in blood (as in the story of John the Baptist); a carved head of Jesus; the emerald that fell from Lucifer's crown as he plummeted to Hell; a stone cup brought down from Heaven by neutral angels in the battle between God and Lucifer; and a beatific vision. Modern writers have attributed many meanings to the Grail. For example, mystery writer Deborah Crombie has portrayed the Grail in fiction as a state of being that is achieved in part from listening to a twelve-part chant brought to England by Joseph of Arimathea and sung by the monks of Glastonbury.[3]

ABOVE *Salome with the Head of John the Baptist* by Andrea Solarioca (1460–1524). A head of John the Baptist was one version of the Holy Grail, and at least two heads kept as relics were believed to be his.

OPPOSITE PAGE *The Damsel of the Sanct Grael* by Dante Rossetti (1828–1882).

Grail Bearer by Arthur Rackham (1867–1939). In the early versions of the Grail legends the Grail was carried by a luminous maiden. In more Christianized versions of the story, it was carried by saints or angels.

History of the Grail Legends

LE CONTE DEL GRAAL

Most of the early Grail legends were written between 1190 and 1240.[4] The first was Chrétien de Troyes's tale *Le Conte del Graal*, which contains many Welsh and Celtic elements. The story itself is similar to a purely Welsh tale called *Peredur*. There is little doubt that *Peredur* is the older story and forms part of the basis for Chrétien's version. There are also elements of the Celtic tale of Kulhwah and Olwen that dates almost a century earlier than Chrétien's tale.[5]

Chrétien's tale follows the development of a naive boy named Perceval who has the opportunity to free the Grail king and his land from enchantment but fails to ask the right question. Unfortunately, Chrétien died before finishing the tale, and we do not know if Perceval or another knight, Gawain, eventually frees the Grail king. Several continuations were written with different endings.

Some commentators believe that two of the women in this story, the Grail maiden and the Loathly Damsel, are two aspects of the Sovranty of Ireland, who was a Goddess who appeared both as a beautiful young woman and as an ugly hag.[6] There are also possible elements from a Celtic tale of Erris, an enchanted isle with a castle that became visible once every seven years, when the king came to the mainland. If a person meeting him asked the right question, the king would tell the person where heaps of gold were located, and the enchantment of the king and the island would be removed.

The Fisher King in Chrétien's story resembles the Welsh character Bran the Blessed. Chrétien's Fisher King is wounded in the thigh (which may mean genitals) or leg with a javelin, and Bran is called "The Pierced Thigh." The horn of Bran provides unlimited food and drink for people, as does the Grail that is in the Fisher King's keeping. Chrétien's Grail also resembles several magical cauldrons of Celtic tales. These cauldrons could provide food and drink, though they would sometimes only do so for the worthy, and they could also bring the dead back to life if the bodies of the dead were dipped into the cauldron.

The focus of Celtic tales is on the virility of the king, which is essential in order to provide sovereignty over the land. The king's sexual virility is necessary to guarantee the fertility of the land and the safety of the people. Some of the ancient

Celtic rituals for crowning the king required him to demonstrate his sexual virility before he was crowned. The land, seen as female, was the mate of the king.

If Chrétien's Fisher King is actually wounded in his genitals, as many believe, and is impotent, then the land will suffer. In this story we find that not only is the king in great pain, but the land is laid waste and the maidens will be left without protection unless the king is healed.

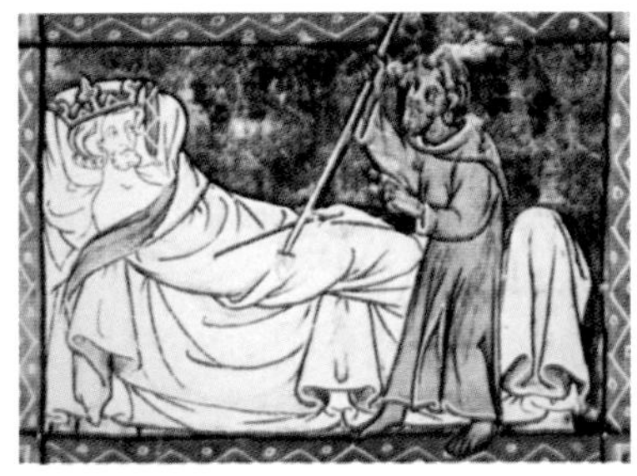

The Fisher King Pierced in the Thigh, a 14th century manuscript illustration from *Le Roman du Saint Graal*. The Fisher King of grail legend was pierced in the thigh, just like the Celtic hero Bran the Blessed.

PARZIVAL

The next major variation of the legend is found in *Parzival*, a poem of rhymed couplets written in 1220 by the Bavarian knight Wolfram von Eschenbach. Wolfram admitted that he used some of the same story as Chrétien, but complained that Chrétien got part of it wrong. Wolfram claimed he got his information from a master named Kyot in Provence, who got the story from an Arabic manuscript found in Moorish Spain. The original had been written by a "heathen Jew" about 1,200 years before the birth of Jesus.

Though many suspect that Kyot was a fictitious character, this version of the story does have several elements related to Islamic culture that are not found in the other stories. There are traces of Arabic astrology, Islamic love poetry, alchemical symbolism, and Jewish esoterica, all of which would have been related to the Moorish culture of the time. There is also a reference to some Templar knights who are waiting for the *Madhi*, an Islamic form of messiah. Parzival's father served a Saracen (Islamic) leader in Baghdad and fathered a son with an Arab woman. That son, named Feirefitz, is a mixed racial child who is both black and white.

The king's sexual virility is necessary to guarantee the fertility of the land and the safety of the people.

This tale is complete, and Parzival is definitely the one who releases the Grail king from the enchantment, with the help of his brother Feirefitz. They come together after a battle where they are evenly matched and then discover they are brothers.

The Grail in this story is a stone cup brought down from heaven by angels who are neutral in the battle between God and Lucifer, who in Islamic legend was cast out of heaven because he refused to bow down to Adam. The Grail is carried by the queen, who had the right to tend it because she guarded her chastity and shunned deceit.

How Sir Galahad, Sir Bors and Sir Percival Were Fed with the Sanc Grael; But Sir Percival's Sister Died by the Way by Dante Gabriel Rossetti (1828–1882). Galahad achieves the Grail.

This version of the Grail legend can probably best be described as a metaphysical tale. It has elements of Christian, Jewish, and Islamic mysticism, as well as the basic story of the Welsh legend. Wolfram apparently had great admiration for the Knights Templar, even traveling to visit them. It is no surprise that he gave them a significant place in his tale.

LE MORT D'ARTHUR

Probably the best-known version of this tale is one called *Le Mort D'Arthur.* This was a translation into English and a revision of earlier French texts by Sir Thomas Malory, done in 1470. By that time, the story of the Grail had become a thoroughly Christian tale, though a somewhat heretical one. In that version priests and religious hermits played a much bigger role. They interpreted the events of the

story according to Christian doctrine, and sin was couched in terms of sexuality. The most important thing about Galahad, one of the knights who achieved the Grail, was that he had never had sex. It did not matter that he killed quite a few people before the end of the story.

The story of the Grail was no longer a story about sovereignty of the land. It was a tale about mystical union and repentance of sin. Chrétien's Perceval and Wolfram's Parzival were very flawed youths who went on journeys of growth and development. Malory's Galahad was a Christ figure who cast out demons and saved souls from fire. He was good—the greatest knight in the world—from the very beginning. Percivale (Malory's spelling) and Bors, the secondary achievers of Malory's Grail, are the flawed human figures who must be saved by the grace of God.

Not only is this no longer a Celtic tale but the Celtic "old law" is equated with the devil on more than one occasion. The devil often appears in the form of a seductive woman. Only the law of Christianity is good. Women play a lesser role in this story than in Chrétien's or Wolfram's. The Grail is no longer carried by a woman but is usually held by Joseph of Arimathea, while the other maidens in the Grail procession have been replaced by angels.

This is not orthodox Christianity, however. Galahad's search for mystical union takes place outside the Church and is in the form of visions, which were suspect in the Church. Percivale's sister is also a Christ figure, who dies to save another and whose body gives off an aura of sweetness. Those around her are fed on manna from heaven. She seems to have no need to achieve the Grail. The main Christian apostle who is the source of authority for this story is Joseph of Arimathea, who some legends say brought the Grail cup to England after the crucifixion. Galahad is a Christlike figure because he is a descendant of Joseph.

Percivale's sister is also a Christ figure, who dies to save another and whose body gives off an aura of sweetness. Those around her are fed on manna from heaven.

Crucifixion, a 12th century icon. In this icon, the blood of Jesus on the cross pours into a bottle suspended in the air in front of a weeping woman, posssibly Mary Magdalene. This is the kind of bottle Mary Magdalene is often pictured holding.

The Round Table of Pentecost, 12th century French illustration. The legend of King Arthur may have been based on a fifth-century leader of the Britons.

Sources of the Grail Legend

There are historical accounts about people and artifacts that could have been used by the Grail writers in creating their stories. A review of them may help us understand what those writers believed the Grail to be.

All of the Grail legends take place during the time of King Arthur, usually in Britain. The Romans conquered Britain in the first century C.E. and gradually turned much of the administration over to the Britons, who became Roman citizens. This island would later become an outpost of the Roman Empire where an important treasure might be taken for safety.

THE MARIAN CHALICE

In 327 Empress Helena, the mother of Constantine, was in Jerusalem excavating for holy sites.[7] She claimed to discover the true cross and the burial place of Jesus.[8] In the excavated tomb she discovered a cup that she believed to be the Marian Chalice, named after Mary Magdalene. A legend of the time said that Mary Magdalene had collected the blood of Jesus in the cup he had used at the Last Supper, and Empress Helena believed this was the cup she had found. The story of Mary catching the blood of Jesus is very similar to another legend that has survived in the Eastern Orthodox tradition. In that story, a woman standing at the foot of the cross, usually Mary Magdalene, is holding a basket of eggs, which are stained red by the blood of Jesus, another explanation of why Easter eggs in many Eastern traditions are red.

The chalice Helena discovered was taken from Jerusalem to Rome, where it remained until the Visigoths threatened to invade Rome in 410. The fifth-century historian Olympiodorus wrote that the Marian Chalice was taken away for protection, and legend has consistently held that it was taken to Britain. Britain would have been the part of the Empire farthest away from the invading Visigoths, so the legend may well be true. This chalice could easily have been in Britain in what many believe to be Arthur's time as the British leader, some eighty years later.

There are varying accounts about what the Marian Chalice actually was. Some say it was a small stone drinking vessel, some say that it was a larger silver

cup, and others claim that the original cup was incorporated by the Romans into a vessel with gold and jewels.

KING ARTHUR

Around 420 a Briton named Vortigern formed the kingdom of Powys in western Britain and was succeeded by his son Britu, who did not have the support of the people. When the Picts threatened from the north, Britu brought in Angles and Saxons from northern Germany to serve as mercenaries, a move he lived to regret. The Angles and Saxons rebelled, established their own kingdom of Kent, and within a few years took control of eastern Britain. Britu was deposed and died impoverished.

Battles between the Britons and the Angles and Saxons continued for about forty years, until the Battle of Badon in 493, when the Angles and Saxons were defeated for a time by a king known as "the bear." In Welsh "the bear" is "Yr arth," reversed it becomes "arth-ur." Many believe that this king was the legendary King Arthur. "The bear" was his title or fighting name; his real name was Owain Ddantagwyn.[9]

Owain appears to have been overthrown by his nephew Maglocunus, just as the mythical Arthur was overthrown by his nephew Mordred. Maglocunus was known as the dragon, a name that also comes up in the medieval legends, where Uther Pendragon is Arthur's father. Gildas records that a nearby area was ruled by Maglocunus's cousin, Cynddylan (or Cuneglasus), who was possibly the son of Owain, our Arthur.[10]

Enthusiastic researchers have traced the line from Cynddylan (d. 658) to the baron Payn Peveril,[11] who married into the family in 854. Could this Peveril be the Percival of Chrétain's story? If so, the bloodline in this story, the Grail family, is the bloodline of Arthur, not the bloodline of Jesus. In Malory's tale it is the bloodline of Joseph of Arimathea.

...the bloodline in this story, the Grail family, is the bloodline of Arthur, not the bloodline of Jesus. In Malory's tale it is the bloodline of Joseph of Arimathea.

By the late seventh century the Britons had been defeated by the Angles and Saxons and many of them fled to Brittany, taking their tales and legends with them. In this way, the tales of King Arthur became part of the repertoire of the storytellers and troubadours of France. The story of King Arthur was known as the *Matter of Britain*.

Several of the later Grail legends, such as Malory's, portray Joseph of Arimathea as the keeper of the Grail.

Joseph of Arimathea, icon by a monk of the Brotherhood of St. Seraphim of Sarov in England. Joseph of Arimathea, who legend says brought the Grail to England, stands under the shadow of Glastonbury Tor, where he is said to have built a shrine for the Grail.

Joseph of Arimathea

Several of the later Grail legends, such as Malory's, portray Joseph of Arimathea as the keeper of the Grail. In the Bible, Joseph is the person who convinces Pilate to give him the body of Jesus to bury. In the Grail stories Jesus appears to him and gives him the cup from the Last Supper that caught his blood after the crucifixion. This vision gives Joseph of Arimathea authority, and his bloodline has the ability to achieve the Grail.

Prior to the fourth century, there were legends that Joseph of Arimathea came to Britain after the crucifixion. Joseph surfaces again in an apocryphal text of medieval date called the *Gospel of Nicodemus* (*Evangelium Nicodemi*). The original was written in Greek and the earliest parts may date to the fourth century, but we do not know if the story about Joseph of Arimathea was early or late. The text was translated into Latin and widely circulated in the Middle Ages. In this story, Joseph is imprisoned by Jewish leaders who are angry because he and Nicodemus had defended Jesus and buried him. On the Sunday after the crucifixion, the leaders are amazed to find that Joseph has returned home. Joseph tells them that the risen Jesus appeared to him and released him from prison. There is no mention of a cup or the blood of Jesus in this story.[12]

Joseph next appears in the first anonymous continuation of Chrétien's legend, circa 1180. In that story Joseph has a golden vessel he calls the Grail, and he places blood from the crucified Jesus in it and burns candles and prays before it every day. He is seen doing this and is imprisoned. When the prison magically releases him, he, his sister, and his friends are banished. They sail to England where they establish a community; the Grail guardians are descended from this community. Joseph has a horn and when he blows it, the Grail serves them all abundantly, like the cauldrons of Celtic legend and the Celtic magical horn of plenty.[13]

The legend of Joseph is developed further in Robert de Borron's poem, *Joseph d'Arimathie*, written around 1200. In that version of the story, Pilate gives Joseph the cup Jesus used at the Last Supper, and Joseph uses it to collect blood from the body of Jesus. He is then taken and imprisoned without the cup, but the risen Jesus brings it to him in a vision and tells Joseph that he will have the guardianship of it and that there will be three successor guardians. Joseph and a few others, including his sister and her husband Bron (Bran), establish a community in England. They have difficulties until a voice from the vessel tells Joseph that some of the company are guilty of lust. The group is told to reenact the Last Supper, with Joseph taking the place of Jesus. Those who are lustful are unable to sit down, and they leave. The seat of Judas must remain empty until the grandson of Bron can fill it. The Grail guardians in this story are descended from Joseph's sister and the Celtic hero Bran the Blessed.[14]

The Ardagh Chalice from 5th century Ireland. The Grail was often believed to be a Christian chalice like this one.

Joseph tells them that the risen Jesus appeared to him and released him from prison. There is no mention of a cup or the blood of Jesus in this story.

Josephus, son of Joseph of Arimathea, 14th century manuscript illustration. Several Grail legends gave Joseph of Arimathea children, including two sons and a daughter.

EVOLUTION OF A LEGEND

We have seen that the fourth-century levels of these myths identify Mary Magdalene as the one who gathered the blood of Jesus in a vessel and preserved it. This is also reflected in a thirteenth-century record of a relic that was believed to be a phial containing the blood of Jesus and the spikenard (fragrant ointment) of Mary Magdalene.[15] In both canonical and apocryphal texts, Mary Magdalene is most often portrayed as the first witness to the risen Jesus and one of his leading disciples.

. . .Joseph of Arimathea takes her place and is portrayed as the first recipient of a vision of Jesus.

In the medieval legend of Nicodemus, one of the Jewish leaders friendly with Jesus, Joseph of Arimathea takes her place and is portrayed as the first recipient of a vision of Jesus. He tells the Jewish leaders that Jesus appeared to him at midnight on the Sabbath, the first moment of the resurrection. In the twelfth-century anonymous ending to Chrétien's story, Joseph is the one who placed the blood of Jesus in a vessel and becomes the guardian of that vessel.

Brown, and others who think Mary Magdalene is the Grail, claim that Joseph is portrayed as the guardian of the Grail because he was the guardian of Mary. We have seen that late versions of the Provence legend portray Joseph as one of the people who accompanies her to France, but most of the legends about Joseph and the Grail say nothing about a trip to France. They have Joseph take the blood of Jesus directly to England, where the knights of the Round Table can later go in quest of it.

If it exists, the cup that caught the blood of Jesus is most likely the Marian Chalice, the cup identified in the earliest level of legend. The bloodline of guardians would be the people to whom the chalice was entrusted when it was taken to Britain.

Mary Magdalene and the Grail

Was the physical body of Mary Magdalene the chalice that caught the blood of Jesus? The Eastern Christian legend of Mary Magdalene holding a basket of eggs under the cross certainly reminds us of fertility. As appealing as that theory is, however, it is inconsistent with important aspects of the Grail legends. If the Grail story is about Mary Magdalene and her bloodline, why does the story involve King Arthur? We have no legend that Mary Magdalene was miraculously in Britain hundreds of years after her lifetime, that her body was taken there, or that her bloodline can be traced there in the fifth century, so what is the connection between Mary Magdalene and King Arthur's court? Is it not more likely that the Grail was an artifact connected in some way to Arthur's England?

Pewter ambulla or pilgrim flask from Jerusalem (ca. 600). A flask with the image of two women approaching the empty tomb with Jesus watching them. These flasks were used to hold oil that had been made holy by touching a relic like the bones of a martyr.

RELICS

The time of the Grail legends was a time of great reverence for relics. People went on pilgrimages to visit them, and relics were big business for the churches and abbeys that held them. While the official view was that relics were conduits for miracles of God, many people, including religious officials, probably thought of them as magical objects that could give protection and bring luck, wealth, healing, and spiritual transformation. It is hard for us to imagine the fervor with which people of those times regarded relics.[16]

The descriptions of the Grail in various stories almost certainly relate to famous relics. One version of the Grail is a head of Jesus said to have been carved by Nicodemus. This relates to the *Volto Santo*, a carved image of Jesus on the cross that has been housed in the Lucca Cathedral in Tuscany since the twelfth century. This figure was believed to be the only true likeness of Jesus and to have been carved by Nicodemus from his memory of Jesus. The carving attracted pilgrims from all over Europe in the Middle Ages. Several heads of John the Baptist were also claimed as relics, as well as several cups from the Last Supper. Another Grail was an emerald, and this may have been a reference to the *Sacro Cantino*, a relic stolen in the sack of Caesarea in 1101 that was carried to Genoa and is still in the cathedral there. This relic is a green glass dish, about forty centimeters across, that

Bronze reliquary cross (ca. 11th–12th century). This reliquary would hold a relic, such as a piece of the true cross or a fragment of a saint's body.

Mary Magdalene by Anthony Frederick Augustus Sandys (1829–1904). Mary Magdalene is holding a spice jar similar to the one the gospels say she took to the tomb of Jesus to anoint his body.

was once believed to be made of emerald and to have been the gift of the Queen of Sheba to Solomon.

These stories are strong indications that the writers of the Grail legends thought they were talking about a physical relic and not just about an allegory of Mary as a chalice. We know that Mary Magdalene is the one portrayed as catching the blood of Jesus in the earliest level of myth and that legend says the cup believed to be the one she used was taken to Britain and was there at the time of the historical King Arthur. Though Joseph of Arimathea had usurped her position by the time the later Grail stories were written, the most likely physical artifact is still the Marian Chalice.

THE MARIAN CHALICE IN SHROPSHIRE

Graham Phillips, a British researcher who thinks the original Grail was the *Gospel of Thomas*, has found what he believes to be the Marian Chalice in Shropshire, England.[17] Shropshire may have been the location of Powys, the kingdom of the historical Arthur (Owain). Phillips has traced the descendants of Payne Peveril to his great-grandson Sir Fulk FitzWaryn. A thirteenth-century ballad claims that the Grail was kept at FitzWaryn's castle in Shropshire. After his death, legend says that it was passed to Alberbury Priory, and his descendant Robert Vernon reclaimed it in the late sixteenth century. The story says that a surviving member of the family hid it in a statue, and a clue to its location was left in a stained glass window in a parish church in Shropshire. The window showed the Grail being held by a disciple, with an eagle overhead. There was a stone statue of an eagle in a nearby grotto, but it had been vandalized and there was no cup hidden there.

Phillips searched historical records and found that a man named Walter Langham had discovered a cup while he was repairing the grotto in the early 1900s. Phillips contacted Langham's descendants, who had the old cup stored with junk in the attic. When Phillips had the cup analyzed by the British Museum, it turned out to be a first-century Roman spice jar, like the one Mary Magdalene is said to be carrying to the tomb of Jesus in the various gospel stories. As the Romans settled in Britain in the first century, there may have been many spice jars available, but special significance was given to this one for a long period of time. At the very least we can say that a first-century spice jar seems to have been preserved and passed down for centuries by a British family.

When Philips announced he had found the Grail, there were some interesting reactions. The first was from a man named Rocco Zingaro, who claimed to be the Grand Master of a group descended from the Knights Templar—similar to Plantard's Priory of Sion—and he claimed that their organization was the keeper of the Grail. Not to be outdone, several European churches claimed possession of the Grail, and the dispute became so heated that they appealed to the Vatican. On September 6, 1995, Pope John Paul II announced that the true Grail was in Valencia Cathedral. The cup there is one claimed to be the cup of the Last Supper, but not the Marian Chalice.[18]

Glass dishes dated to the beginning of the Common Era. The dish to the left is a drinking bowl, and the one to the right is a cup. The cup Jesus drank from at the Last Supper may have been similar to these.

A MODIFIED LEGEND

The story of the Marian Chalice is somewhat consistent with the Grail story of *The Da Vinci Code*. Mary Magdalene, as the most intimate disciple of Jesus, caught his blood and preserved it in a cup. Because that cup contained the actual blood of Jesus, and perhaps also because of the early prestige of Mary Magdalene and her later prestige in eleventh-century France, that cup was considered the most powerful and most holy relic in Christendom. In the fifth century, the cup was taken to Britain where it was lost or hidden. King Arthur and his knights, perhaps desiring to use the power of the cup to drive the Angles and Saxons out of Britain, went in search of it, and that search became part of the tales that Britons brought to France a few centuries later.

We cannot prove that Mary Magdalene was the chalice, but it is very likely that the cup that inspired several versions of the Grail story, a relic thought to have the power of a Celtic magic cauldron, was her cup. Just as Peter came to usurp Mary as the leading disciple of Jesus or his most insightful companion, Joseph of Arimathea replaced her in the story of the Marian Chalice. In that sense, we can say that the story of the forgotten Magdalene has been repeated.

169

PART FOUR

Leonardo da Vinci

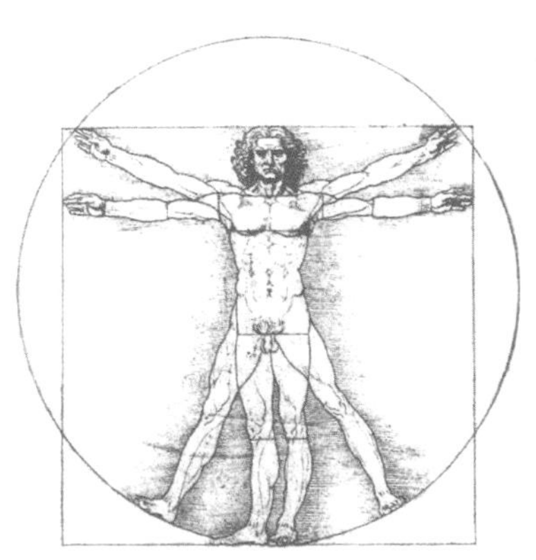

TEN
LEONARDO

The first thing to address about Dan Brown and Leonardo da Vinci is that Leonardo is not known as "Da Vinci," though Brown has most of the characters throughout his book call him that. The "da Vinci" in his name means "of Vinci" the town with which he is identified. Art historians and experts call him Leonardo, so the experts, and many not so expert, cringe when Dan Brown calls him Da Vinci over and over again.

Names aside, who was Leonardo? His shadow hovers over the novel from first page to last. His art and inventions provide the clues or the basis for clues left by the murder victim, and he is the repository of the "truth" that underlies the mystery behind the murder mystery. His art provides clues to the true nature of Christianity.

According to Brown, Leonardo was a past Grand Master of the Priory of Sion who received the secret information from the Priory that had been passed on from the eleventh century. Robert Langdon says Leonardo had a "fascination for goddess iconology, paganism, feminine deities, and contempt for the Church"[1] and was a "well-documented devotee of the ancient ways of the goddess."[2]

The town of Vinci, where Leonardo grew up and from which he got his name. His name, Leonardo da Vinci, means Leonardo of Vinci. "Da Vinci" is not a surname.

OPPOSITE PAGE *Self Portrait of the Artist as an Old Man* by Leonardo da Vinci (1452–1519).

Leonardo and an Underground Stream

BROWN'S THEORY

We have seen in Chapter Seven that there is no reliable evidence that the Priory of Sion ever existed as a secret organization and as the protector of documents or relics discovered in Jerusalem. Was Leonardo involved in some other secret organization that was part of an underground stream of esoteric knowledge? We have no real evidence that he was.

Most of Brown's assertions about Leonardo are based on the representations of Lynn Picknett and Clive Prince in two of their books, particularly *The Templar Revelation*,[3] which Teabing cites as a source.[4] These authors claim that Leonardo was a prankster and a devotee of Mary Magdalene. Picknett and Prince also claim that Leonardo was a devotee of John the Baptist, whom he believed to be the true Messiah, and was hostile toward Jesus and the Church.

For the French royalty, he created a mechanical lion that took a few steps and then its chest opened to reveal lilies—no doubt the iris of the fleur-de-lis.

The Prankster

Leonardo's reputation as a prankster arises from incidents supposed to have happened in his youth and old age. Much of the information comes from the work of Giorgio Vasari, who was too young to have known Leonardo and wrote from secondary sources that may or may not have been accurate. Many believe that Vasari enhanced stories he heard and is not a reliable source.

Vasari's first story about Leonardo is that when he was young, he painted a shield with the likeness of a monster made up of parts of other animals, like lizards, crickets, snakes, butterflies, and bats. He supposedly used dead animals as his models but took so much time painting that the animals rotted. He was so intent on his painting that he did not notice the smell. This is a disquieting image of Leonardo, a young man who was obsessed and squalid, but much of that may be due to Vasari's literary imagination.[5]

The other stories relate to Leonardo in his later years. It is said that he found a strange-looking lizard and made wings out of other lizard scales and glued them onto it, adding horns and a beard. He then tamed the lizard and carried it around in a box to surprise and frighten people. According to another portrayal he had animal intestines dried and cleaned so that they were very thin, then attached them to bellows in the next room and would inflate them when guests were present, forcing people to back up against the wall in shock.[6]

Leonardo also put on theatrical exhibitions in his later years, and he seemed to have a great deal of fun with them. For the French royalty, he created a mechanical lion that took a few steps and then its chest opened to reveal lilies[7]—no doubt the iris of the fleur-de-lis. All of this reveals both a sense of fun and a willingness to use his creativity to tease, play, and entertain.

This does not, however, mean that Leonardo was a prankster in all his work and that we should look for tricks and hidden secrets everywhere. In his treatises on painting and his various writings, it would appear that Leonardo also had a serious side. There is every indication that he took his work very seriously, working and reworking his paintings. One report says that he sometimes stayed on the scaffold for *The Last Supper* from morning to night, repainting to get something just right.[8]

Leonardo and John the Baptist

Picknett and Prince's theory that Leonardo believed John the Baptist was the true Messiah is mostly based on the history of the two paintings, both called *The Virgin of the Rocks* (also *The Madonna of the Rocks*). The original painting was commissioned by the Confraternity of the Immaculate Conception, a group of Franciscan monks (not nuns as Brown says).[9]

The name of the group is significant because it commemorates the Franciscan success in having the Church accept the doctrine of the Immaculate Conception, which is that Mary the mother of Jesus was conceived without sin (though it is often misunderstood as applying to Jesus). Pope Sixtus IV accepted the doctrine and established the feast of the Immaculate Conception in 1476. The Confraternity wanted a painting that would reflect what they saw as Mary's pure nature.[10]

Picknett and Prince's theory that Leonardo believed John the Baptist was the true Messiah is mostly based on the history of the two paintings both called The Virgin of the Rocks.

ABOVE *Saint John the Baptist* by Leonardo da Vinci.

The Virgin of the Rocks by Leonardo da Vinci. This is the first version of the paintings that was sold to an anonymous purchaser for one hundred ducats. There is no direct evidence that the Franciscan Confraternity rejected it.

Another Franciscan theory that had less support was that of the Blessed João Mendes da Silva, also called Amadeus of Portugal. His book, *Apocalypsis Nova*, portrayed Mary the mother of Jesus as the incarnation of Wisdom or Sophia, and presented Mary and John the Baptist as the true protagonists of the New Testament.[11]

Some commentators see the influence of this theory in the paintings of *The Virgin of the Rocks*, where the baby John and Mary are the focus of the painting. In the first version *(left)*, which is now in the Louvre in Paris, the archangel Uriel points at John and glances toward the viewer. The primary evidence for the idea that Leonardo was portraying João Mendes's doctrine in this painting is that Leonardo may have owned *Apocalypsis Nova*. He made a manuscript note about a book called "libro dell'Amadio" (the book of Amadio).[12] It appears, however, that there were several books about or by someone called Amadio, and scholars have a long list of alternative possibilities.[13]

We do not know whether Leonardo was even aware of João Mendes's ideas about Mary the mother or John. If Leonardo did not own the Franciscan's book, it is possible that he painted the panel according to the requests of Franciscans who agreed with João Mendes or who expressed similar ideas. It is also possible that the painting was not intended to have the heretical or semi-heretical meaning some viewers see in it today.

The first panel was never delivered to the Confraternity.

The first panel was never delivered to the Confraternity. Brown, along with many commentators, assumes that this was because the iconography of the work was unacceptable to them. The real reason may have been more prosaic. Sometime before 1494 Leonardo filed a petition asking for more money from the Confraternity, saying that someone else had offered one hundred ducats for the painting. Apparently, the dispute was resolved when the painting was sold to the unidentified party and Leonardo started another version.[14]

The second version of the painting *(shown on next page)* which is now in the National Gallery in London, is somewhat different. The angel is not pointing or glancing at the viewer and the figures have traditional halos, though these may have been added later. By the time this second painting was begun, Leonardo was busy with a large equestrian monument to Francesco Sforza and was beginning his plans for *The Last Supper*. X-ray examination of the second version of *The Virgin of the Rocks* shows that others in Leonardo's workshop did part of the work.

Though the second version of the painting is different from the first, there is no proof that this is because the Confraternity considered the first heretical, as popular writers argue. There are several possible explanations. The Confraternity apparently allowed Leonardo to sell the first version, so they may have objected to it; or they may have preferred to wait for another version instead of paying more money for the first. It is interesting to note that both versions of the painting have John the Baptist and Mary as the focus, so the emphasis on those figures was acceptable to the purchasers and may have been at their request.

There is very little reason to believe that Leonardo agreed with the ideas of *Apocalypsis Nova*, even if he had read it. There is even less reason to assume that he viewed Mary the mother of Jesus literally as a pagan Goddess of Wisdom, though we know that he was familiar with the Greek portrayal of Wisdom as Sophia. It is unlikely that João Mendes believed in some idea of a pagan Goddess either, yet the tenuous information linking Leonardo to him is the only information that would link the artist to Goddess worship. Also, João Mendes had replaced Mary Magdalene as the representation of Wisdom that we saw in *Pistis Sophia* with Mary the mother of Jesus. If Leonardo was as much a supporter of Mary Magdalene as Brown's characters claim, he would not have approved of this interpretation.

The Virgin of the Rocks by Leonardo da Vinci. Some of the work on this second version was done by others in Leonardo's workshop. This version was delivered to the Franciscans.

Leonardo the Heretic

The idea that Leonardo was a heretic comes from Vasari, who wrote:

> *Leonardo was of such a heretical frame of mind that he did not adhere to any kind of religion, believing that it is perhaps better to be a philosopher than a Christian.*[15]

This claim is quickly contradicted in the second edition of the book nineteen years later, when Leonardo is portrayed as returning to his faith:

> *He desired to occupy himself with the truths of the Catholic faith and the holy Christian religion. Then having confessed and shown his penitence with much lamentation, he devoutly took the sacrament.*[16]

Both versions of the painting have John the Baptist and Mary as the focus.

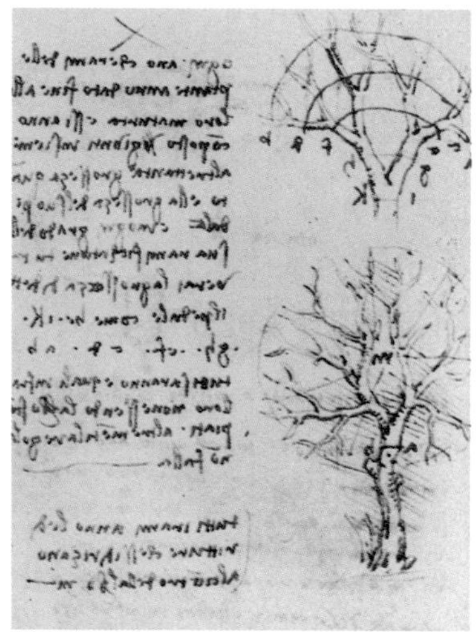

Cross Section of Branches by Leonardo da Vinci. Leonardo theorized that the quantity of sap in each branch was in proportion to its cross section.

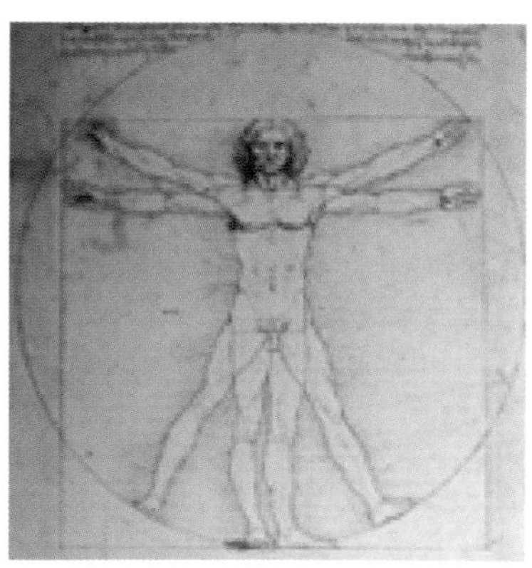

Vitruvian Man by Leonardo da Vinci. This drawing is part of Leonardo's study of proportions of the human body.

The truth may well be somewhere in between. Leonardo was very likely a heretic by the standards of his day, but we need to keep in mind that it was much easier to be a heretic in his time than in ours. We know that he dissected dead bodies, an accepted practice in modern medical schools but a major sacrilege in his time. Leonardo also thought the earth revolved around the sun instead of the reverse, as the Church held, a heresy for which Galileo was condemned. Leonardo came very close to the theory of evolution, an idea not likely to endear him to the religious authorities of his time.

It is fairly clear, however, that Leonardo was more of a naturalist than a philosopher.[17] He studied the functions of the human body, drew the first accurate diagram of the human heart, studied proportions in nature, the arrangement of leaves, the movement of water. He drew the most accurate maps of his time and imagined paddle-wheel boats, helicopters, diving suits, and people talking to each other over a long distance. He obviously did not allow religious attitudes to interfere with his studies, basing his conclusions on his observations, not on the teachings of the Church. This alone was probably enough to support Vasari's description of him. There is no evidence that Leonardo had theological differences with the Church over issues like the roles of John the Baptist and Mary Magdalene.

Renaissance Studies

There is also no evidence that Leonardo belonged to any secret societies, though he was interested in the new knowledge that was the rage of the Renaissance. Much of the "new" thought was actually ancient, preserved in the East when the West was experiencing its "dark age" of intolerance. Leonardo was particularly interested in divine geometry and the significance of geometry in nature.[18] This explains his interest in the Roman Vitruvius and his drawing called *Vitruvian Man* that Brown's murder victim imitates on the Louvre floor.

That drawing was part of Leonardo's effort to study the mathematical proportions of the human body. He reached conclusions such as, "When a man kneels down he will diminish by a quarter of his height. When a man kneels with his hands to his breast, the navel will be the midpoint of his height and similarly the points of his elbows."[19]

Leonardo believed that geometry was the basis for the design of all organic forms, and he studied the human body, plants, and water vortices. Though the Church eventually suppressed many ideas that Leonardo and his compatriots investigated in the new quest for scientific knowledge that marked the Renaissance, we have no evidence that Leonardo himself was involved in any problems or theological conflicts with the Church. In fact, Leonardo lived at Belvedere Palace in the Vatican at Pope Leo X's invitation from 1513–1516, until he retired to France where he received a pension from the king, Francis I.[20]

Secrecy

Brown and others portray Leonardo as secretive, and he is supposed to be the inventor of the fictional "cryptex" that hides the clues to the Grail in the novel. Though Leonardo's notebooks are full of drawings of inventions that he never built, he did not invent a cryptex. Sophie's grandfather in the book enjoyed building the cryptex and other models of Leonardo's inventions, as many people in real life have done using Leonardo's sketches and diagrams.

Much of the claim that Leonardo was secretive is based on his habit of writing in mirror image. There has been much debate about whether he did this to keep his writing secret, because it was an easy way to write left-handed, or both. Leonardo wrote all his notes from right to left, put short words together and divided long ones, and left out punctuation, accents, and paragraphs. This may have simply been the quickest way for him to record his flow of thoughts, or it may have been because he did not want others to read his notes.[21]

Leonardo often talked of organizing and publishing his notes, but he may have also wanted to hide some of his activities, like the dissection of dead bodies. When he died, Leonardo left several thousand pages of loose notes to his pupil Francesco Melzi without any instructions for secrecy. Melzi distributed some of them and preserved others, but he had no apparent interest in using them. The pages were later organized and published as notebooks.

Sample of Leonardo's writing. Leonardo wrote all his notes from right to left. This technique may have been more comfortable for a left-handed writer, but he might also have wanted to preserve the secrecy of his notes.

Much of the claim that Leonard was secretive is based on his habit of writing in mirror image.

Leonardo took [Salai] in at about age ten and recorded his peccadilloes, describing him as "thievish, lying, obstinate, greedy."

Profile of Salai by Leonardo da Vinci. Most experts identify this figure as Salai, Leonardo's servant and friend, who many also believe was his homosexual lover.

Homosexuality

Was Leonardo homosexual as Langdon asserts? He may have been, but we do not know for sure. Homosexuality was a punishable offense in his time, so it is not something he would have advertised. He was accused of homosexuality as a young man in Florence when a message was placed in the *tamburo*, a box where anonymous or signed accusations could be placed. This message accused a young man of being a homosexual prostitute and named Leonardo and three others as his customers. The matter went to court

two times, but no one came forward with evidence and all of those accused were acquitted.

Leonardo also had close relationships with men, particularly with a peasant boy he adopted as a servant and a pupil named Gian Giacomo Caprotti da Oreno, nicknamed Salai, or "little Satan." Leonardo took him in at about age ten and recorded his peccadilloes, describing him as "thievish, lying, obstinate, greedy."[22]

When Salai grew up, Leonardo continued to support him, loaned him money for his sister's dowry, and left him money when he died. He taught Salai to paint and retouched some of his work. Both their contemporaries and modern commentators have assumed that they had a homosexual relationship. At least one commentator believes that Leonardo was bisexual because of this comment on his feelings about drawing female genitalia: "There immediately arose in me two feelings—fear and desire—fear of the menacing, dark cavity, and desire to see if there was anything miraculous within."[23]

Whether he was homosexual, heterosexual, bisexual, or asexual, there is no reason to assume that Leonardo's sexual orientation influenced his work in any stereotypical way. Many commentators have made assumptions about what Leonardo painted because they believed he was a homosexual, but they never assume that other painters work in a certain way because they are heterosexuals. Most of what is attributed to Leonardo's presumed homosexuality is due to stereotypical thinking. One of the most extreme examples is the explanation given by Picknett and Prince for why Leonardo was interested in Mary Magdalene:

Whether he was homosexual, heterosexual, bisexual, or asexual, there is no reason to assume that Leonardo's sexual orientation influenced his work in any stereotypical way.

> *He may have been a homosexual, but that has never stood in the way of men's adoration of the Feminine Principle—often quite the reverse. Gay icons are classically strong and colourful women who have had traumatic lives—just like Mary Magdalene and Isis herself.*[24]

Leonardo's work was that of a great man, whatever his sexual orientation. We cannot make reliable conclusions about his intentions based on stereotypes.

The person sitting by the right hand of Jesus in this painting looks feminine, and Picknett, Prince, and Brown claim the figure is Mary Magdalene.

The Last Supper

Dan Brown's characters make claims about hidden meaning in Leonardo's painting *The Last Supper*, which appear to be taken almost word for word from *The Templar Revelation*[25] by Lynn Picknett and Clive Prince.

THE FEMININE FIGURE

The person sitting by the right hand of Jesus in this painting looks feminine, and Picknett, Prince, and Brown claim the figure is Mary Magdalene. Teabing says that this figure has the "suggestion of breasts," which proves she is female. She is also said to be wearing the reverse colors of Jesus, which is presumed to be significant.

Brown's characters call *The Last Supper* a fresco, but it is not, and the distinction is important in this case. A fresco is done with water-based paints on wet plaster. Like watercolor painting, fresco painting is a technique that must be done quickly and cannot be reworked. Fast painting was not Leonardo's style, so he developed what he thought would be a new technique, sealing the wall so that he could use some oil-based paint and varnish. Unfortunately, not all of Leonardo's

Leonardo's *The Last Supper* after the most recent restoration. That restoration removed as much of the overpainting of previous restorers as possible.

ideas worked, and this was one of his failures. The wall remained damp and the painting, completed around 1497, began to deteriorate quickly. By 1642 one observer said that the work was rendered almost useless,[26] and by 1722 another observer said that all the figures on the right-hand of Jesus had been entirely defaced with mold and damp.[27] Over the years several efforts have been made to restore the painting, which placed clumsy brushwork on top of Leonardo's masterpiece. The most recent restoration removed as much of the previous ones as possible, but only small patches of paint are left on the clothing of the figure at the right-hand of Jesus, and the painting is much too damaged to discover anything as subtle as the suggestion of breasts.

The feminine figure is wearing a blue robe, but so are four others at the table, and the robes of a few others seem to be closer to the color of Jesus' cloak. Two of the other figures are also wearing reddish cloaks, and Philip's is the closest in color to Jesus' robe. Given that so many of the figures are wearing similar colors, it is difficult to attribute too much significance to them. Jesus and the figure next to him are wearing their cloaks in the same way, perhaps because they are the only two calm people at the table.

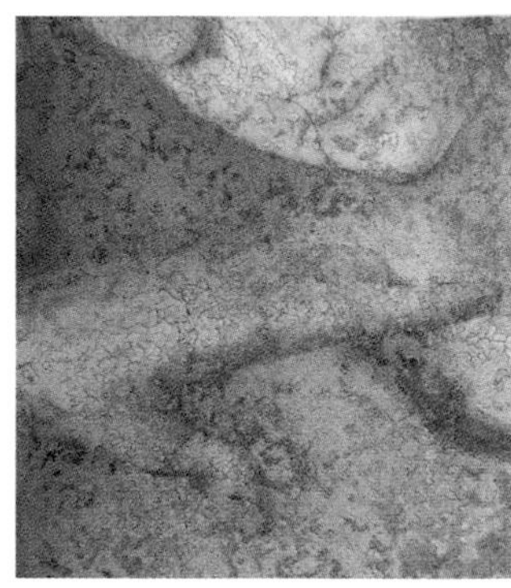

A close-up of the figure at the right hand of Jesus shows that the painting is damaged and much of the paint on the body is missing. Any suggestion of breasts is likely due to damage caused by mold and damp.

Figure Study (Accademia, Venice). In this study the figure next to Jesus is in the traditional pose of the apostle John. At the time of his studies, Leonardo apparently intended to portray John, not Mary Magdalene, in the painting.

Is this feminine figure Mary Magdalene? The figure certainly appears feminine by twenty-first-century ideas about gender, but this is a fifteenth-century painting. The femininity of the figure has been reflected in many copies of the painting done over many years, but no one in the past has thought the figure was a woman. There are several reasons to think that it is not.

The first is that Leonardo did some studies for the painting, and in them this figure appears to be male. The painting depicts the moment of the Last Supper when Jesus announces that one of them will betray him. The Gospel of John says that the disciple Jesus loved—whom legend has named John—was reclining next to him during the supper (John 13:23). In the culture of first-century Palestine, this meant reclining on a couch, since they believed that it was bad for digestion for food to fall directly from the mouth to the stomach. In fifteenth-century Europe, the reclining beloved disciple was often depicted as leaning forward on the table.

There are several reasons to think the figure is not a woman.

In a very rough sketch for *The Last Supper* now in the Royal Collection at Windsor Castle, Leonardo has the figure of the beloved disciple facedown on the table, which would indicate that Leonardo was sketching the beloved disciple, known as John, not Mary Magdalene. In Leonardo's study in red chalk now at the Accademia in Venice, the figure is facedown again with its head on folded arms. This figure and the one in the rough sketch both look male. Leonardo labels the apostles in the chalk study without labeling the figure next to Jesus, but this may have been because the reclining figure was so well known as John that there was no need to label him. Judas, seated in his traditional position across from Jesus, is not labeled either.

When Leonardo completed his painting he made changes from these studies. He moved Judas from the other side of the table and had the figure next to Jesus sit upright. He also gave this figure a feminine face, but does this mean he thought the figure was a woman? There is another possible explanation.

Leonardo repeatedly taught that the faces of people in a painting should reflect their characters.[28] There is a story that he spent two hours a day for a year combing the worst part of Milan looking for a model for Judas, and a humorous anecdote that he threatened to use the Prior of the monastery as the model if he did not stop nagging him to get on with the work.[29] We can theorize, then, that

Leonardo made the face feminine because that conveyed something essential about the character of the figure.

Leonardo also paid a great deal of attention to gestures in this painting. In his notes he considered several possibilities for gestures.[30] The figure next to Jesus is the only one besides him who is calm and relaxed. This is another indication of Leonardo's ideas about the character of this figure. A character who, like Jesus, calmly accepts the will of God that Jesus will suffer and die is somewhat angelic in nature, and that is where we can look for models for this figure.

Leonardo painted several angels. Gabriel brings the news to Mary in *The Annunciation* and Uriel cares for the infant John in the two versions of *The Virgin of the Rocks*. Though these are male archangels, both of these figures are definitely feminine in Leonardo's portrayal of them. Leonardo may have thought of angels as androgynous, because many Christian writers had argued that Adam and Eve were androgynous in Eden before the Fall.[31] He may also have thought of goodness as a feminine trait. Whatever the reason, a man with angelic traits, such as the most beloved disciple of Jesus, would very likely have been portrayed with feminine features like the figure in *The Last Supper*.

If the figure *is* a woman, as the popular writers argue, it would not prove that Leonardo thought Mary Magdalene was the Holy Grail, as Teabing claims. On the other hand, it would be very strange for Leonardo to replace the traditional figure of John with a woman. If he did so, the most likely conclusion would be that Leonardo thought the beloved disciple was a woman, even though the figure is clearly male in the Gospel of John.

It is worth noting that only longtime bias in biblical studies makes us think that the idea of a woman at the Last Supper would be shocking or heretical. There is nothing in the New Testament accounts that says only men were present at the Last Supper. Most accounts say that disciples and the twelve were there, not that only the twelve were there.[32] To have a woman *instead* of one of the twelve males listed in the New Testament, though, would be a revision of the text.

There is no evidence, aside from the femininity of the figure, that the person sitting at the right hand of Jesus is a woman. There is good reason to think that the figure is the beloved disciple, called John, who Leonardo conceived of as a young man with angelic qualities.

Leonardo painted male angels with very feminine faces. Several of them were more feminine than the figure from *The Last Supper*, yet they were all male. Leonardo may have intended to show that the figure sitting on the right hand of Jesus had somewhat angelic qualities.

TOP Uriel, *The Virgin of the Rocks* (detail). BOTTOM Angel in *The Baptism* (detail) by Andrea del Verrocchio (1435–1488) and Leonardo da Vinci.

This section of the painting shows Peter holding a knife in his right hand and leaning toward the figure next to Jesus. According to Leonardo's notes, Peter is leaning over to speak into the ear of the feminine-looking figure. The notes identify that figure as male.

AN ARM AND A KNIFE

Behind the back of Judas, a hand holds a knife. The hand would appear to be Peter's hand turned back, but the painting is clumsy and awkward, not at all up to Leonardo's standard of anatomical excellence. Because of this sloppiness theories have arisen that the hand with a knife is not Peter's, but the hand of a disembodied arm.

A more likely explanation is that the awkward drawing of the arm is the product of the restorers. We have a study of the arm of Peter by Leonardo that shows the angle of the arm and the bend of the wrist, which though very rough is not as strange or cardboard-looking as the efforts of the restorers. It is most likely that the hand holding the knife was painted by Leonardo as Peter's hand.

Study for the right arm of Peter (Windsor Royal Library inv. 12546). This study makes it clear that Leonardo originally painted the arm of Peter holding the knife. Later restorers may have damaged the painting.

This leaves us with the question of why Peter is holding a knife. In his early notes on the painting, Leonardo listed possible gestures for the apostles, including this: "Another speaks into his neighbor's ear and he, as he listens to him, turns towards him to lend an ear, while he holds a knife in one hand, and in the other the loaf half cut through by the knife."[33] It is significant that Leonardo identifies the listener as male, since the listener in the final painting is the feminine figure next to Jesus. In the final painting Peter leans toward the John figure and speaks in his ear. John leans over to hear, while it is Peter who holds a knife in one hand. Instead of holding bread in the other, he gestures in front of the John figure, perhaps pointing toward Jesus.

Some commentators assume that the knife symbolizes the sword Peter will draw on the people who come to arrest Jesus, but that is just speculation. Others assume that Peter is telling John to ask Jesus who will betray him. Peter is often portrayed in the New Testament as a hothead, so the knife may indicate his anger and potential violence toward whoever is going to betray Jesus. Picknett and Prince and Brown's characters Langdon and Teabing assume that the figure next to Jesus is Mary Magdalene and that Peter is menacing her with his gesture. They also assume that the arm with a knife is disembodied and threatening her.

While we know that Peter was sometimes portrayed in apocryphal texts as the enemy of Mary Magdalene, that is not likely to have been Leonardo's meaning in this painting. Popular theories about the painting are based on the assumption that Leonardo was the Grand Master of the Priory of Sion and keeper of the secret of the Grail. Since Pierre Plantard has admitted that there was no Priory of Sion at the time of Leonardo, and since a great deal of evidence indicates that the idea of the Priory was a fraud by Plantard, there is no reason to look for hidden Grail images in Leonardo's paintings.

We have Leonardo's study for the hand with a knife and his notes about a character holding a knife. The notes indicate that the knife had no special significance. Despite theories to the contrary, *The Last Supper* is very likely what it appears to be, a brilliant and dynamic portrayal of a legendary moment in the New Testament.

While we know that Peter was sometimes portrayed... as the enemy of Mary Magdalene, that is not likely to have been Leonardo's meaning in this painting.

The Mona Lisa

In his novel, Brown is the latest in a long line of commentators who have tried to explain why the Mona Lisa is smiling her enigmatic smile. Robert Langdon claims that she is reflecting on a word play on the name of the painting. A short review of the history of the painting reveals that Leonardo did not name it, so the woman in the painting is not amused by the name.

The *Mona Lisa* is unsigned and undated but universally attributed to Leonardo, and he had it in his possession until his death. If the painting was commissioned as a portrait, it was never delivered. After Leonardo's death, the painting was purchased by Francis I of France, reportedly for 4,000 gold crowns.

Leonardo left no information about the subject of this painting, and so the game of naming the model and explaining the smile has gone on for over five centuries. In the years after Leonardo's death, the French royal catalog called the painting *Courtisane au Voile de Gaze* (*A Courtesan in a Gauze Veil*). About thirty years after Leonardo's death, Vasari wrote his biography of Leonardo in which he described a painting of Mona Lisa del Giocondo, the wife of a wealthy Florentine, that he said was then in the possession of the King of France. In describing the portrait of Mona Lisa, Vasari raved about the eyelashes and eyebrows, but the *Mona Lisa* has neither eyelashes nor eyebrows. Because Vasari never actually saw the portrait of Francesco del Giocondo's wife, some art experts think he was describing another painting, and others believe that he had the right painting but confused details in his notes.[34]

In 1625 Cassiano del Pozzo, who had read Vasari, saw the *Mona Lisa* at Fontainebleau, and identified it as the portrait of Mona Lisa del Giocondo.[35] The identification stuck, and the painting has been known since as the *Mona Lisa* or *La Gioconda* in Italian (*La Joconde* in French), but the acceptance of the name has in no way settled the question of the subject's identity.

In the early twentieth century, the art historian Adolfo Venturi argued that the model for the painting was Constanza d'Avalos, duchess of Francavilla. There is evidence that Leonardo did paint a portrait of the duchess, in which she was portrayed as a widow under a dark veil.[36] Other suggested sitters for the *Mona Lisa* are Isabelle of Aragon and Isabella d'Este. Some have suggested that there was no sitter, that

ABOVE *Isabella d'Este* by Leonardo da Vinci. There are several similarities between *The Mona Lisa* and this portrait of Isabella d'Este. Some believe that she was the sitter for both.

OPPOSITE PAGE *Mona Lisa* by Leonardo da Vinci. Two issues have long been debated about this painting: Who is the sitter and why is she smiling? Dan Brown presents another in a long list of explanations for her smile and a possible identification of the sitter.

The game of naming the model and explaining the smile has gone on for over five centuries.

Self Portrait by Leonardo da Vinci. This drawing is believed to be a self-portrait of Leonardo. The arrangement and proportions of the features are very similar to the *Mona Lisa*, leading some to theorize that the *Mona Lisa* is a self-portrait.

The painting may also be of an imaginary woman...

Leonardo simply painted his ideal woman. Others have suggested that the painting is of a man in disguise, possibly one of his young male models.

The last suggestion has led to the theory that the *Mona Lisa* may be a self-portrait. Lillian Schwartz, a computer graphics expert, digitalized the *Mona Lisa* and Leonardo's 1514 self-portrait drawing, and concluded that the facial points correspond exactly. She reported this process in her book, *The Computer Artist's Handbook*.[37] The chin in Leonardo's drawing is not visible and his nose is wider than the nose of the *Mona Lisa*, but the forehead, eyes, nose length, and distance from nose to mouth align remarkably. On the other hand, the similarities of facial features and hairstyle with Isabella d'Este are also remarkable.

When the *Mona Lisa* was x-rayed, many changes and revisions were shown in several layers. Was this because Leonardo reworked the painting so many times, or was it because he painted his own or some other image underneath? The painting may also be of an imaginary woman, or of a combination of women, which might account for the alterations.

THE SMILE

As we saw, Langdon claims that the *Mona Lisa* smile is explained by the joke of her name, Mona Lisa, which he asserts is really an anagram of the divine union of masculine and feminine as represented by the God Amon and the Goddess Isis, once known as L'Isa: Amon Lisa. Langdon claims that the double entendres and playful allusions have been documented in most art history tomes.[38]

While it is true that art history tomes have speculated about the painting and about Leonardo's affection for it, they have not attributed the name to a sacred union of Amon and Isis. As we have seen, Leonardo did not identify the painting as the Mona Lisa; that was an attribution that did not take place until over a century after Leonardo's death. So whatever the explanation of the smile, it is not because of a joke about the name of the painting.

Many have offered explanations of the smile. Vasari wrote that the painting of Mona Lisa del Giocondo had a smile more divine than human, because Leonardo employed singers, musicians, and jesters to entertain her.[39] Sigmund Freud thought Leonardo's tendency to paint such smiles was because of some memory, probably of his mother in childhood[40] A creative explanation has been

offered more recently by an Italian doctor, Filippo Surano. Surano believes that the model for the painting suffered from bruxism, an unconscious habit of grinding the teeth when asleep or under mental stress. He believes that the tedium of long sittings caused the lady to grind her teeth, producing an other-worldly smile.[41]

In fact, the *Mona Lisa* smile is not unique in Leonardo's paintings. He painted and drew similar subtle and ironic smiles on other characters as well: Saint Anne and Mary in his cartoon and painting *Virgin and Child with Saint Anne*, Leda in *Leda and the Swan* (available only in copies), and Saint John in *St. John the Baptist*. The smile was so common in Leonardo's paintings that the style was given the name Leonardesque.

ANDROGYNY

One of Dan Brown's themes is that androgyny is a remedy for the loss of the sacred feminine, and he attributes this intention to Leonardo. As we have seen, Christian writers like Jerome believed that androgyny was the natural state of humanity before sin, and Leonardo may have agreed with that. Some people perceive the *Mona Lisa* as somewhat masculine, and given Leonardo's attachment to this painting, it may portray his ideal of beauty. Whether he thought it was androgynous, we cannot know.

The sly smile of the Mona Lisa is not unique in Leonardo's work. Several characters in his paintings have similar smiles.

TOP *Mona Lisa* (detail).
MIDDLE *Saint John the Baptist* (detail).
BOTTOM Mary in *The Virgin and Child with Saint Anne and John the Baptist* (detail).

All by Leonardo da Vinci.

Are There Secrets in Leonardo's Work?

Dan Brown was careful to say that we do not know what Leonardo intended or that "clues" in his work are meaningful. Robert Langdon thinks to himself, "Maybe Da Vinci's plethora of tantalizing clues was nothing but an empty promise left behind to frustrate the curious and bring a smirk to the face of his knowing Mona Lisa."[42] It is more likely that Leonardo's work is functioning as a modern Rorschach test in which we see clues to whatever theory attracts us. Leonardo's mystique as the creative genius and true Renaissance man is so tantalizing that it is hard to resist, but it is good to keep in mind that this idea, like Rorschach results, may reflect our unconscious, not truth or history.

PART FIVE

Modern Times

ELEVEN
THE MODERN CHURCH

The ancient Church provides the background of *The Da Vinci Code*, but the murder mystery is intricately tied up with the interior workings of the modern Roman Catholic Church. In Brown's fictional time frame the current pope, Pope John Paul II, has died and has been replaced by a more liberal thinker who is disturbed by the practices of Opus Dei, an ultraconservative group. The new pope has withdrawn the special status of Opus Dei and is repaying money they had donated in the past. The implication is that Opus Dei had obtained its special status through a form of bribery, and with the withdrawal of the status, the money is being repaid.

...does Brown accurately depict a member of Opus Dei?

Opus Dei

In the novel the primary killer, though not the ultimate villain, is an Opus Dei "monk" named Silas, who wears a cilice, or belt with sharp points, around his thigh and whips himself to do penance for murder. Aside from the murder aspect, does Brown accurately depict a member of Opus Dei? Opus Dei does not think so, but many of its detractors do.

Opus Dei, which means "the work of God," was founded on October 2, 1928, by a Spanish priest named Josemariá Escrivá de Balaguer y Albas. In 1943 Escrivá founded the Priestly Society of the Holy Cross so that priests could be ordained in connection to Opus Dei, and from 1946 until his death in 1975, he lived in Rome and ran Opus Dei, or the Work, with iron control, demanding absolute obedience from those below him. In 1968 Escrivá petitioned for and was given the title Marques de Peralta,[1] an action consistent with his concern that members of Opus Dei have prestige and high status.

Opus Dei has approximately 80,000 members from more than eighty countries worldwide, with only about 1,800 priests. The majority of members are "lay"

ABOVE Josemariá Escrivá de Balaguer y Albas, the founder of Opus Dei.

OPPOSITE PAGE *Sixtus IV Nominates Platina Prefect of the Vatican Library* by Melozzo da Forli (1438–1494).

The New York headquarters of Opus Dei is estimated to have cost from $42 million to $54 million. This seventeen-story building is located on the corner of Lexington and E. 34th Street, at 243 Lexington Avenue. Like all Opus Dei residences, it has separate entrances for men and women.

members, or at least Opus Dei describes them that way. The largest group is called supernumeraries, married people who live and work as laypeople, but contribute a portion of their income to Opus Dei. Though Escrivá claimed he was sanctifying the state of marriage, his statements make it clear that he considered the married state inferior to the celibate.[2] The rest of Opus Dei members are known as numeraries, who are not laypeople in any ordinary sense of the word. They take vows of celibacy, poverty, and very strict obedience. They normally live in Opus Dei residences and every aspect of their lives is severely controlled, including their reading material and parts of their work.

The character Silas would have been a numerary, not a monk, who lived in the new Opus Dei residence in New York.

The character Silas would have been a numerary, not a monk, who lived in the new Opus Dei residence in New York. The cost of this residence varies in different reports, but it is only one of many houses, mansions, and other properties owned by Opus Dei. In all of them, men and women numeraries are strictly separated, coming in contact as little as possible.

By the end of the novel we see that neither Silas nor the head of Opus Dei are evil men, though they have been duped because of the leader's desire for power, prestige, and control. There is no doubt that in reality the majority of the members of Opus Dei are sincerely devout people seeking deeper spirituality in a world too often given over to shallow materialism. They are not alone in this search.

There are some aspects of Opus Dei, however, that many find disturbing, including others within the Roman Catholic Church. In the novel, the nun who is the caretaker of Saint Sulpice expresses her concern about and dislike of Opus Dei. Hers is a sentiment undoubtedly shared by many. Opus Dei does not listen to such criticism, however, because Escrivá characterized those who criticized him or Opus Dei as literally devils.[3]

The Teachings of Escrivá

Escrivá has been called conservative, ultraconservative, and traditional, but the most accurate description of his thought would be medieval, in a literal sense. His views on human nature, sin, the body, sexuality, women, obedience, coercion, suffering, and salvation are in surprising agreement with medieval Spanish Christianity. The conflict of those views with modern thought has led to secrecy within the organization and charges of dishonesty and wrongdoing. Most of the criticisms of Opus Dei—secrecy, an unhealthy emphasis on suffering, a belief that self-inflicted pain is pleasing to God, fear of sexuality, and the repression of women—are all aspects of the medieval aristocratic Spanish culture that Escrivá so admired.

Escrivá himself was much less than straightforward in public about what his teachings actually were. He said in interviews that women were equal to men,[4] but secretly ordered female numeraries to sleep on boards covered with a sheet. Men slept on mattresses, but women, Escrivá said, were more sensual[5] and so apparently needed this extra physical discomfort. If married men strayed, Escrivá blamed their wives for not being more attractive and attentive:

> *I am not afraid to say that women are responsible for eighty per cent of the infidelities of their husbands because they do not know how to win them each day and take loving and considerate care of them.*[6]

He explained to a group of Brazilian women what that meant:

> *When your husband comes back from work, from his job, from his professional tasks, don't let him find you in a temper. Do yourself up, look pretty and, as the years go by, decorate the façade even more, as they do with old buildings. He'll be so grateful to you.*[7]

In the constitutions he drafted in 1950, Escrivá assigned the women's section of Opus Dei traditionally female work, but this was changed after his death. He also

SUFFERING

No ideal becomes a reality without sacrifice. Deny yourself. It's so beautiful to be a victim!

The Way #175

The joy of us poor humans, even when it has a supernatural motive, always leaves an aftertaste of bitterness. What did you expect? Here below, suffering is the salt of our life.

The Way #203

Let us bless pain. Love pain. Sanctify pain...Glorify pain!

The Way #208

War! "War has a supernatural purpose" you tell me "that the world is unaware of: the war has been for us..."

War is the greatest obstacle to the easy way. But we shall, in the end, have to love it, as the religious should love his disciplines.

The Way #311

Quotations from Josemariá Escrivá de Balaguer y Albas will appear throughout this section in shaded text boxes.

CORPOREAL MORTIFICATION

To defend his purity, Saint Francis of Assisi rolled in the snow, Saint Benedict threw himself into a thorn bush, Saint Bernard plunged into an icy pond....You...what have you done?

The Way #143

Where there is no mortification there is no virtue.

The Way #180

THE BODY

The body should be given a little less than its due. If not, it turns traitor.

The Way #196

Tell your body: I prefer to keep you in slavery than be myself your slave.

The Way #214

Treat your body with charity, but with no more charity than one would show towards a treacherous enemy.

The Way #226

If you know that your body is your enemy, and an enemy of God's glory, since it is an enemy of your sanctification, why do you treat it so softly?

The Way #227

insisted that women in the home had the full responsibility for housework. These were common views in that period, but Escrivá claimed to be rejecting them while following them more stringently than others. Women in Opus Dei hold more traditional and restricted roles than in any other part of the Catholic Church.

This kind of inconsistency carried into other areas. Escrivá claimed that he valued personal freedom and that members of Opus Dei could form their own opinions on subjects in the same manner as other Catholics.[8] In practice, reports too numerous to be disregarded tell how Opus Dei members have been reprimanded and threatened with expulsion for simple matters like choosing their own friends, associating with a former Opus Dei member, or confessing to or even talking to a non-Opus Dei priest.[9] Anyone who is expelled from Opus Dei is ostracized by the community and refused sacraments like confession by Opus Dei priests. There are repeated stories of numeraries and priests who have been imprisoned, repeatedly interrogated, and otherwise subjected to what Escrivá called "holy coercion," purportedly for their own good.[10]

One story is told of how Escrivá himself ordered that a female numerary be beaten, and he gave detailed instructions on how to do it: lift her skirt, pull down her panties, and whack her until she talked. She was being punished for carrying letters to the post for another numerary who was being held incommunicado at Escrivá's orders.[11]

Escrivá spoke about the importance of people, particularly married couples, curbing their tempers and treating each other with respect.[12] There are numerous reports that Escrivá himself had frequent red-faced tantrums in which he screamed at various people, from Opus Dei members to employees.[13] He called people names like scum, devil, and sleazy, and called women whores and sows. Alberto Moncada, formerly associated with Opus Dei University, summed Escrivá's character up this way: Escrivá "is charming, pleasant, and persuasive when one is on his side. He is intolerant, intractable, and crude when his standards are not accepted."[14] Opus Dei members were told it was a special favor to be on the receiving end of his abuse or "correction."[15]

Escrivá also spoke about the problem of poverty and criticized others for not working to alleviate it[16], yet Opus Dei has no charitable work. Its numeraries live and work in mansions,[17] and it uses its extensive resources for recruitment and expansion. Opus Dei workers refer to the charity of "not giving."[18]

CORPOREAL MORTIFICATION

One of the most controversial practices of Opus Dei is the practice of corporeal mortification. This might include minor things like forgoing sugar in one's coffee, but it also includes use of the cilice and the discipline, common instruments of self-torture in medieval Spanish Christianity.

Dan Brown describes the cilice as a belt that Silas tightens around his thigh. It is actually a chain with barbs that dig into the flesh. Opus Dei numeraries are required to wear it at least two hours a day except on Sundays and holy days, and sometimes also during certain activities, like teaching class.[19]

The discipline is a whip made of rope tied in knots. Numeraries are to give themselves thirty-three strokes on the buttocks privately each Saturday. They are directed to deliver the strokes with energy and vigor,[20] and can obtain permission to whip themselves more or wear the cilice for longer periods of time. Former members claim that such permission is freely given and Opus Dei members are proudly told that Escrivá used the discipline with such enthusiasm that he splattered the bathroom walls with blood.[21] This is clearly presented as the ideal to be emulated.

Opus Dei defends the practice by referring to the medieval practices of several saints, including Francis of Assisi and Teresa of Avila. Most of the Church has abolished such practices in the understanding that for many people, these practices can degenerate into masochism and psychological pathology. Teresa of Avila often warned about the dangers of excessive penance and required that penance be done in public in her convents. For Opus Dei members, these practices represent true religious zeal.

The belief underlying the use of the cilice and the discipline is that the human body is a temptation toward evil, particularly sexuality, which must be disciplined and defeated. Sainthood, which Opus Dei members seek, depends on overcoming the desires of the body. As we have seen, Escrivá shared the medieval view that the body has a stronger hold on women and so they must discipline it more strenuously. These views are in such conflict with modern understandings of psychology and sexuality that it is not surprising Opus Dei has wanted these practices kept quiet.

The Rapture of Saint Teresa by Gianlorenzo Bernini (1598–1680). Teresa of Avila was admired by Opus Dei for her physical penance. Though she was said to wear a cilice on her wrist at times, Teresa wrote often about the dangers of excessive corporeal mortification.

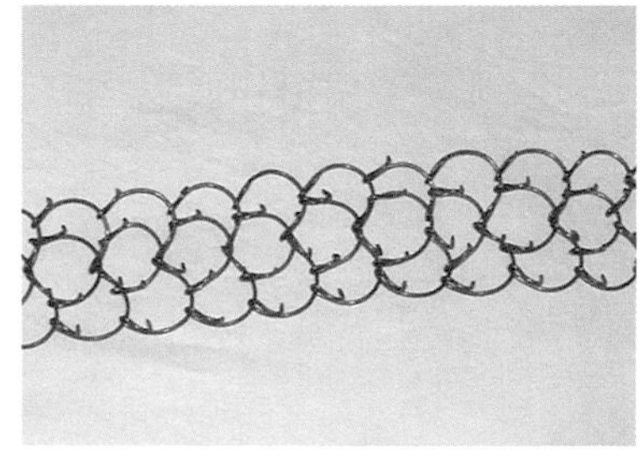

The cilice, or barbed chain, is worn around the thigh by Opus Dei numeraries for at least two hours a day. Permission can be obtained to wear it longer. In the novel, Silas wore it for a longer period to do penance for murder.

Saint Francis Embracing Poverty by Giotto di Bondone (ca. 1267–1337). Medieval saints emphasized the importance of poverty and ascetic practices. Francis is admired by Opus Dei for throwing himself into a snowbank to avoid sexual thoughts.

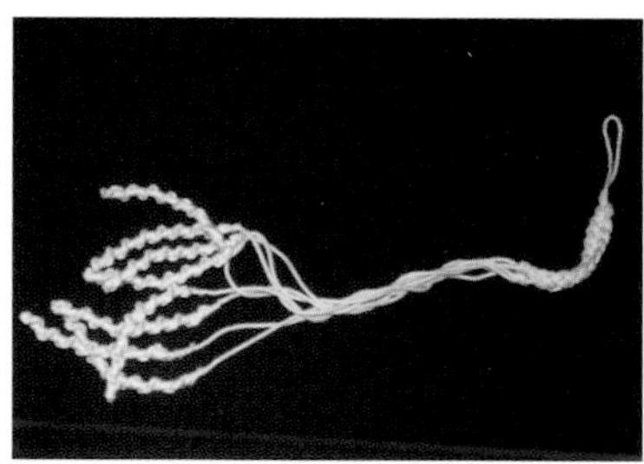

Though numeraries are required to give themselves 33 strokes per week with the discipline, they can ask to do more. They are told that Escrivá splattered the bathroom walls with blood using his, and are at least indirectly encouraged to follow his example.

OBEDIENCE

In the novel, Silas follows orders to kill four men and then kills a nun out of his own fury. This has highlighted controversies about approaches to obedience in Opus Dei. This is not to say that Opus Dei members would commit murder, of course, but a significant number of former members or children of members have complained that Opus Dei members have less freedom than members of most other groups and certainly less than other Catholics.

Opus Dei continues to maintain a list of forbidden books, a practice long abandoned by the Catholic Church. The list forbids the works of Kierkegaard, Spinoza, Sartre, Kant, Hegel, Nietzsche, Heidegger, John Stuart Mill, and William James,[22] and, no doubt, *The Da Vinci Code*. Opus Dei members are told to check with Opus Dei superiors before reading or buying books.

Opus Dei numeraries are expected to give unquestioning obedience to their supervisors, even if they are ordered to do what they find abhorrent, a level of obedience that is no longer required of most nuns or priests. Some religious orders have reached the conclusion that requiring this kind of obedience creates a situation asking for abuse or error on the part of well-meaning but less than competent superiors.

OPUS DEI AND WOMEN

Opus Dei emphasizes that it believes in equality for women, and its Web site speaks of "authentic feminism." On closer examination, Opus Dei implies that the only real problem is the women's inferiority complexes. The authentic feminism of Opus Dei involves not only a rejection of pornography, abortion, and divorce (apparently equally offensive), but also an acceptance of the belief that God created men and women for different purposes. There is no way around this divine intention:

> *Our Lord, infinitely just and infinitely wise, created man and woman with distinct missions both capable of being sanctified. To try to change that order is of no avail. We are witnessing how it only leads to greater alienation and misunderstanding of our humanity.*[23]

Christ and the Woman Taken in Adultery (detail) by Lucas Cranach the Younger (1515–1586). The woman taken in adultery in the Gospel of John symbolized the way women were often regarded in the early Church. Escrivá agreed with the belief of early Church Fathers that women are more sensual than men and need more extreme practices.

The Opus Dei approach to the equality of women, then, is a variety of separate but equal. In fact, Opus Dei is effectively divided into two organizations—male and female—with separate administration and organization. There are even separate magazines for men and women.

Women numeraries now sleep on boards on top of mattresses instead of on boards alone. Opus Dei still teaches that women are more sensual than men, with the implication that God created them that way. Women are sometimes required to act as servants, cleaning, cooking, and doing laundry for the male numeraries, but the men are never required to do these services for women. This is in line with Escrivá's machismo ideas. During his lifetime women were not allowed to wear pants; in fact, women numeraries were not allowed until 1993. Women were also forbidden to smoke but men were encouraged, because smoking was a sign of masculinity.[24]

Women numeraries now sleep on boards on top of mattresses instead of on boards alone.

Women with professional abilities or prestige are encouraged to pursue education and careers, and women are not relegated to traditional caretaker or housekeeping roles. Nevertheless, women are always considered essentially different from men. Opus Dei members enforce their understanding of those differences in all the community's activities.

HOLY COERCION

If our Lord wanted to force strangers to come to his banquet, how much more will he want you to use holy coercion with those who are your brothers...this most beautiful coercion of charity far from taking away your brother's freedom, will delicately help him to use it well.

Cronica, vi, 1969

WOMEN

If you want to give yourselves to God in the world, more important than being learned (women don't need to be learned: it's enough if they are discreet), you must be spiritual, closely united to Our Lord through prayer: you must wear an invisible cloak that will cover each and every one of your senses and difficulties: praying and praying; atoning, atoning and atoning.

The Way #946

SELF-DEPRECATION

Your worst enemy is yourself.

The Way #225

Secrecy

One of the most common criticisms of Opus Dei is that secrecy is widely practiced by the group, and this appears to be true. Opus Dei does not circulate its constitutions, even to its members,[25] though constitutions are readily available in most religious orders. The magazines for both men and women are also secret. The only copies available for examination are the ones made secretly by a former male numerary before he left Opus Dei.[26] Members are strongly discouraged from contact with people outside of Opus Dei, particularly other Catholic priests.[27]

The biggest controversy is about recruitment, often of students, without telling them they are being recruited for Opus Dei. New recruits are often encouraged to keep their membership secret, even from their families.[28] In 1981 Cardinal Hume, Archbishop of Westminster, issued a list of restrictions for Opus Dei because of complaints about their recruitment practices and other activities. They were not to accept commitments from children under eighteen, they were to encourage young people to discuss the decision to join Opus Dei with their parents, they were to allow people to join or leave without undue influence and to allow them to choose their own advisors (including advisors outside of Opus Dei), and Opus Dei should openly identify its activities. The next year Pope John Paul II removed Opus Dei from the supervision of bishops, and there are reports that all the activities forbidden by the Cardinal continue.

Opus Dei is accused of hiding much of its activities, including fund-raising activities, by acting under other names. It has many affiliated nonprofit organizations, but Opus Dei is said to deny that organizations run by its members and under its direct or indirect control are Opus Dei organizations. Some of those organizations named by a former Opus Dei member are the Association for Educational Development in San Francisco, the Woodlawn Foundation in Chicago, the Clover Foundation, and the Association for Cultural Interchange.[29]

Conflicts with the Church

Opus Dei is under the protection of Pope John Paul II, who made it a personal prelature to the Vatican in 1982, in spite of strong opposition.[30] Popes Paul VI and John XXIII had refused the status. This is the status that the fictional new pope withdraws in the novel. The current pope, though personally popular with many people, is himself much more conservative than much of the Church. He has been repeatedly in conflict with liberal and moderate factions.

One conflict involves Opus Dei's attitude toward the rest of the Church. Opus Dei members are not forbidden to see priests who are not in Opus Dei, but they are told they are not welcome in the Work if they do.[31] Open prohibition would violate Church rules, but in practice both lay members and priests are punished if they associate with outside people.[32] People within the Work are considered superior to the rest of the Church. Escrivá has called them "the predilect of God" and has compared his own work to that of Jesus, "… as Jesus received his doctrine from the Father, so my doctrine is not mine but comes from God and so not a jot or tittle shall ever be changed."[33]

Escrivá has been quoted as saying that it would be better for an Opus Dei member to die without the last rites than to receive them from a Jesuit.[34] He did not hesitate to characterize the rest of the Church as evil:

> *As I have not ceased to warn you, the evil comes from within [the Church] and from very high up. There is an authentic rottenness, and at times it seems as if the Mystical Body of Christ were a corpse in decomposition, that it stinks… Ask forgiveness, my children, for these contemptible actions which are made possible in the Church and from above, corrupting souls almost from infancy.*[35]

This quote, as well as the quote about the divine origin and infallibility of his ideas, appeared in the secret magazine for male numeraries and helps to explain the secrecy of these publications. Many members of the Church would not appreciate these comments.

Pope John Paul II with Escrivá's successor, Alvaro del Portillo. Pope John Paul II has long been an enthusiastic supporter of Opus Dei.

[Escrivá] did not hesitate to characterize the rest of the Church as evil…

Despite controversy and opposition, Pope John Paul II declared Escrivá a saint in 2002.

Fast Track to Sainthood

Despite all the controversy surrounding Escrivá, Pope John Paul II put him on what is called the fast track to sainthood. The process of considering someone for beatification, the first step to sainthood, cannot begin for five years after that person's death, unless the pope waives the waiting period. This was done in Escrivá's case and he was beatified in 1992 and named a saint in 2002.

Several former members of Opus Dei tried to testify in opposition to the beatification and canonization processes, but most were not allowed to do so. Two women members were accused of lesbianism by Opus Dei officials and rejected as unfit for testimony by Spanish Church officials. There is no evidence that the women were lesbians, but they independently reported that they had been threatened with disgrace by Escrivá himself if they dared to speak against Opus Dei.[36] Former members wrote letters to the pope that were also ignored.[37]

One person who was allowed to testify in opposition to the beatification, Alberto Moncada, told National Public Radio that the panel members did not even listen to his testimony but sat drinking cognac and whiskey and refused to look at him.[38]

Escrivá was the 468th person to be declared a saint during the tenure of John Paul II. The pope may be determined to have conservative people he admires canonized quickly before his death, possibly because he fears that a new pope, like the fictional pope in *The Da Vinci Code*, would not share his view of their sanctity.

Escrivá was the 468th person to be declared a saint during the tenure of John Paul II.

The Church and Science

In the novel, when the fictional head of Opus Dei, Bishop Manuel Aringarosa, is called to the Vatican to be told that the Opus Dei status as a personal prelature of the pope is being revoked, he is called to Castel Gandolfo in the Alban Hills outside of Rome. We are told that this is the location of the Vatican observatory and astronomy library.

The idea of the Church as a sponsor of astronomical studies sounds strange to those who remember Galileo Galilei, one of the first scientists to base his astronomical theories on observation and the use of telescopes. In 1633, Galileo was condemned by the Inquisition for arguing that the earth revolved around the sun and spent the last eight years of his life under house arrest. The Church's scientific and epistemological section of the Pontifical Commission recently spent thirteen years studying the Galileo case and finally concluded in 1992 that the Church had been in error—no surprise to the rest of the world, who had reached that conclusion centuries ago.[39]

The Church's interest in an observatory began a century before the Galileo trial, when Pope Gregory XIII wanted the calendar corrected. He had an observation tower built in Rome with a meridian line and a metal plate on the floor that could be used to track the seasons of the year, demonstrating that the old calendar was in error.

Castel Gandolfo was originally built by the man who would become Pope Urban VIII, the pope who persecuted Galileo. It has been the pope's summer residence since Urban's tenure in the sixteenth century but became the observatory as well in 1933, when the lights of Rome became bright enough to interfere with observation.

The headquarters of the Vatican observatory remain at Castel Gandolfo, where the pope's collection of 1,000 meteorites and a library of 24,000 books, including rare works of Copernicus and Kepler, are stored. Since 1989, most of the observation has been done with the Vatican Advanced Technology Telescope (VATT) at the Mount Graham International Observatory in Arizona. Ten Jesuit astronomers staff the program.

Galileo Before the Holy Office by J. N. Robert-Fleury (1797–1890). Galileo defended his finding that the earth orbits around the sun and is not the center of the universe, but he was still convicted of heresy. He was subjected to house arrest for the remainder of his life.

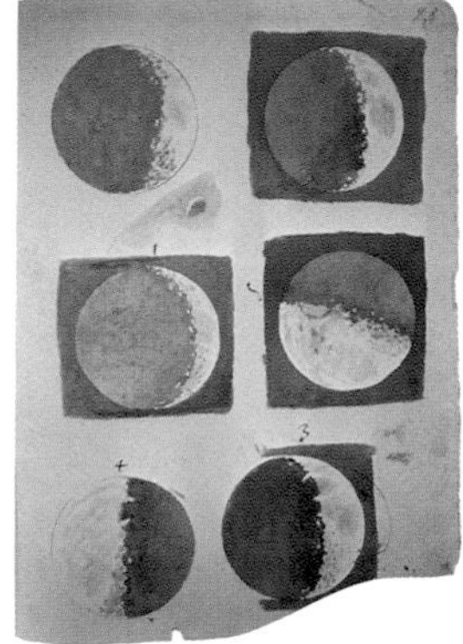

These drawings by Galileo represent the beginning of the science of astronomy, which the Church now continues.

The Vatican contains many treasures, but no outsider knows for sure what treasures are to be found in the Secret Vatican Archives.

...the entire contents of the pre-eighth-century archives have disappeared...

Crux Gemmata

In *The Da Vinci Code*, we wonder for a while if the police detective, Captain Bezu Fache, is in league with Opus Dei. The main reason we wonder this is that he is wearing a *crux gemmata*, or cross with thirteen jewels. Fache, it turns out, is not part of Opus Dei and the *crux gemmata* has no particular symbolic meaning beyond representing Jesus and the twelve apostles.

Secret Vatican Archives

The Secret Vatican Archives are mentioned in the novel, though they play a much larger role in Brown's earlier book, *Angels & Demons*. These archives sound like something out of a conspiracy theory, but there really is a collection called the Secret Vatican Archives. They were removed from the Vatican Library in the seventeenth century at the direction of Pope Pius IV and were closed to anyone outside the Vatican until the nineteenth century. Documents up to 1922 are now available to accredited scholars, but users of the collection cannot browse, and the catalog, which is incomplete, is very large. No one, with the possible exception of the archive staff, knows just what the collection contains. It is primarily made up of centuries of records of acts taken by the Papal See. It contains documents such as Henry VIII's request to annul his marriage to Katharine of Aragon and letters from Michelangelo.

Probably the most interesting point in relation to *The Da Vinci Code* is the Vatican's claim that the entire contents of the pre-eighth-century archives have disappeared with no record of what happened to them. Those archives contained the earliest records of the Church, including information about early "heresies." In other words, they may have been the most complete records of alternative forms of early Christianity, and those records were apparently destroyed or hidden by someone in the Church sometime after the eighth century.

The modern Roman Catholic Church no longer calls Mary Magdalene a prostitute. It has removed the title "Penitent" from the mass for her feast day.

The Modern Church and Mary Magdalene

The modern Roman Catholic Church no longer calls Mary Magdalene a prostitute. It has removed the title "Penitent" from the mass for her feast day. Her feast day is no longer celebrated on the same day as Mary of Bethany and Luke's sinner, and the story of Luke's sinner is no longer read as part of the mass on that day. In making these changes, the Church admitted it had been mistaken. Mary's vision of the risen Jesus at the tomb, however, is still read mid-week rather than celebrated on Easter Sunday and she is not yet recognized as an important person in the early community or a woman with any special relationship with Jesus.

Noli Me Tangere, 16th century icon. Though she is no longer considered a prostitute, Mary Magdalene is given no special role in the modern Church. Even the New Testament portrayal of her as the first witness to the risen Jesus gives her no special status.

TWELVE
FOLLOWING THE CODE

Several characters in *The Da Vinci Code* follow clues left by one of the murder victims, Jacques Saunière. These clues are intended to lead his granddaughter to the secret of the Holy Grail. The road takes them from Paris to the countryside of France to London to Scotland and back to Paris. We will go on the road with the Code and visit some of the most interesting locations along the way.

The Ritz Hotel, Paris. This 19th-century hotel is known for its elegance and luxury.

Paris

THE RITZ

Robert Langdon is sleeping at the Hotel Ritz when he is awakened by the police and summoned to a murder scene. The Ritz has been a Paris institution since it was opened in 1898 and is associated with luxury and class. The hotel is the home of the Escoffier cooking school, the Hemingway Bar, and the Athenian swimming pool. Suites are named after some of the most famous guests: Coco Chanel, the Prince of Wales, and Elton John.

THE LOUVRE

Langdon is taken to the Louvre, where Saunière's body is sprawled in the Denon Wing, in the position of Leonardo's *Vitruvian Man*. The Denon Wing houses the collection of Italian paintings, including those used by Saunière to leave clues for Sophie and Langdon. The *Mona Lisa* is located in Salle 3 and *The Virgin of the Rocks* is in Salle 5.

The Louvre was a medieval fortress and palace for the kings of France before the French Republic turned it into a museum in 1793. It has become one of the leading museums in the world, and is home to several of the great works of Leonardo da Vinci. In the courtyard Langdon passes the pyramid, a two-level complex of shops, reception areas, and exhibition space. The architect I.M. Pei

OPPOSITE AND ABOVE The new pyramid entrance to the Louvre.

St. Sulpice, the location of the brass meridian strip and obelisk used to mark the solstices and equinoxes. Silas is sent here on a false trail of the Grail.

Stained-glass window in St. Sulpice.

designed this unique pyramid as the new entrance to the Louvre. Completed in 1989, the pyramid is every bit as controversial as Langdon indicates, mixing uneasily with the traditional architecture of other parts of the museum.

SAINT SULPICE

While Langdon is being interrogated at the Louvre, Silas is on his way to the church of Saint Sulpice, where Saunière has told him he will find the Grail. This seventeenth-century church is best known as the place where the Marquis de Sade and Charles Baudelaire were baptized and Victor Hugo was married. It was begun in 1646 and built in stops and starts for many years. The church was built over an older church, but there is little evidence that it was built over a pagan chapel as Brown claims. It is possible, of course, that the site was originally the site of a temple. Churches were often built on holy ground to usurp the power and authority of past religions.

Saint Sulpice was built on the meridian established in Paris in 1672 that is now called the Rose Line. To take full advantage of this, the church has a brass meridian strip running from a plaque in the south to an obelisk in the north, which was used to calculate the exact date of Easter and the summer and fall equinoxes. A ray of sun coming through a spot in the upper window of the south transept hits the plaque on the summer solstice, the obelisk on the winter solstice, and behind the communion table during the equinoxes.

This calendaring system is not an indication of anything occult; it is simply the way that the seasons of the year were measured in past centuries. We have seen that the first Vatican observatory used a similar arrangement to measure the seasons and there is an obelisk in front of Saint Peter's in Rome for the same purpose. Keeping careful track of the ecclesiastical calendar was very important to the Church.

Most people visit the church to see its two wonderful Delacroix frescoes, *Jacob Wrestling with the Angel* and *Heliodorus Driven from the Temple*, and the church's remarkable organ. Saint Sulpice has an additional meaning for careful readers of *Holy Blood, Holy Grail*, because the original Saunière allegedly traveled there to obtain secrets of the occult.

DEPOSITORY BANK OF ZURICH

Sophie and Langdon escape the Louvre and follow the clues to the Depository Bank of Zurich. Does the bank exist? No. This is one of Dan Brown's fictional locations.

Does the bank exist? No. This is one of Dan Brown's fictional locations.

CHÂTEAU VILLETTE

When the bank manager tries to take the box with the clues to the Grail from Sophie and Langdon, they steal the bank truck and head for the home of Sir Leigh Teabing, a friend of Langdon's and an expert on the Grail.

Teabing lives in the Château Villette, an estate about thirty minutes outside of Paris. This is a 240-acre estate built in the seventeenth century for the Count of Aufflay, ambassador to Venice for Louis XIV. The estate was known as La Petite Versailles because of its beautiful gardens. Now it is a vacation rental for the very wealthy, renting for 6,500 euros a day, with a one-week minimum stay. It is not open to the public.

London

TEMPLE CHURCH

To escape the French police who are pursuing them, Sophie and Langdon fly with Teabing to London. On the plane they open one level of the cryptex they retrieved from Sophie's grandfather's bank vault. The clue sends them to a tomb in London. Teabing claims that the tomb is at the Temple Church.

This was the church on the grounds of the English headquarters of the Knights Templar, hence the name "Temple." Built in the twelfth century, it is one of the few surviving examples of a round church. When the Templars were dissolved in the fourteenth century, the property was given to the order of the Knights Hospitaller. The Hospitallers in turn rented the property to two colleges of barristers, known as the Inner and Middle Temples and also as the two Inns of Court. When Henry VIII broke with the Catholic Church, he took the property of religious groups for the crown, including the Temple grounds, but continued the lease to the Inns. Near the end of the sixteenth century, the Inns petitioned for a more permanent arrangement,

The effigies of knights located inside the Temple Church, London, are not tombs. Teabing misled Langdon and Sophie to entice them there.

The lake and aerial view of a section of St. James's Park.

The ceremony of the Changing of the Guard takes place each morning at Horse Guards Parade, the area where Teabing directed his chauffeur.

and King James I granted them the use of the property in perpetuity on the condition that they maintain the church.

ST. JAMES'S PARK

As the characters discover that there are no tombs in the Temple Church, Teabing's chauffeur pretends to kidnap Silas and Teabing. Once in the car, Teabing directs the chauffeur to drop Silas off at an Opus Dei house and to take him to St. James's Park.

St. James's, one of London's oldest parks, is bordered by three palaces. The oldest palace bordering the park is Westminster Palace. This is the home of the two houses of Parliament, the House of Commons and the House of Lords, and also of the much beloved Big Ben clock tower.

St. James's Palace was built by Henry VIII in 1532 and was the home of the British monarchs until Victoria moved to a new home on another side of the park. Buckingham Palace, home of the present Queen, was originally built in the eighteenth century as a townhouse for John Sheffield, the Duke of Buckingham, and was known as Buckingham House. George III bought the house in 1762 and George IV began the renovations that would turn it into a palace. Victoria, crowned in 1837, was the first monarch to live there.

The park itself has a large lake with an island that is home to several varieties of ducks, gulls, swans, and pelicans. The first birds were donated by the London Ornithological Society in 1837. Several fountains play on the lake. The rest of the park has avenues of trees and lawns and a children's playground. Deck chairs are available in warm weather and band concerts are given two times a day in the summer months. This park has been open to the public since the seventeenth century.

Teabing instructs the chauffeur to park at Horse Guards Parade. This is London's largest paved open space, located at the east end of the park. It was originally the end of a canal that was filled in by the first Hanoverian monarchs. The remaining canal later became the lake. The ceremony known as the Changing of the Guard takes place at Horse Guards Parade at 11 am Monday through Saturday and at 10 am on Sunday. Teabing arrives much earlier and is able to murder his chauffeur without interruption.

KING'S COLLEGE

When Sophie and Langdon realize that the tomb they are seeking is not at the Temple Church, they head for the Research Institute in Systematic Theology at King's College. In the novel this is a high-tech computerized research center. In reality, the institute is primarily a group of scholars who meet, discuss topics of interest, and host conferences. There is no computerized database.

King's College, one of the two oldest and largest colleges of the University of London, is located in several different historic sites in central London. The founding campus is on the Strand, next to Somerset House.

Pope's actual role was to write the epitaph...

WESTMINSTER ABBEY

Sophie and Langdon conclude that the tomb they are looking for is the tomb of Isaac Newton at Westminster Abbey. Westminster plays an important role in British life, since it is the place where monarchs are crowned and most are buried, along with the very famous.

Newton died in 1727 and was buried in Westminster Abbey, but his tomb was not built until 1731. Though Sophie and Langdon think Newton was buried by Alexander Pope, Pope's actual role was to write the epitaph:

Nature and Nature's Laws lay hid in Night.
God said, Let Newton be! And All was Light.

Newton's tomb's stonework is carved with representations of a telescope, furnace, prism, earth and other planets, the sun, mathematical numbers, and books labeled *Chronology*, *Optica*, *Divinity*, and *Phil. Princ. Math.* There is also a Latin inscription proclaiming: "Mortals! Rejoice at so great an ornament to the human race!" There is, however, no apple, since the story that Newton discovered gravity when an apple fell on his head is most likely apocryphal.

The tomb that Langdon and Sophie were seeking was the tomb of Isaac Newton at Westminster Abbey. This is also the burial place of many former British monarchs.

Many believe that the Knights Templar, shown in this 19th century engraving escorting pilgrims to Jerusalem, went to Scotland to join forces with Robert Bruce when the order was disbanded.

Scotland

ROSSLYN

Having finally solved both riddles of the cryptex and witnessed the arrest of Teabing, Sophie and Langdon set out on the last part of their search for the Grail at Rosslyn Chapel in Scotland outside Edinburgh. The chapel is located outside the town of Roslin, which legend says was built to house the masons and freemasons that the builder of the chapel imported from the Continent.

Rosslyn is famous for its alleged connection to the Knights Templar and the Freemasons.

Rosslyn is famous for its alleged connection to the Knights Templar and the Freemasons. When the Templars in France were arrested in 1307, some are said to have escaped with the order's treasury and records and the Templar fleet. They apparently traveled to northern France and sailed to some safe harbor. There is no historical record of what that safe harbor might have been, but legend says that they sailed up the coast of Ireland, where they had holdings, and then on to Scotland.

This legend is quite plausible. The Templars had several properties along the coast of Ireland and Robert Bruce, the king of Scotland, was no friend to the pope. Bruce had been excommunicated for killing his leading rival to the throne in a church. He would not have done the Vatican's dirty work for it, nor would he have been likely to turn away any potential soldiers he could use in his battles against the English.

Templars were not arrested in England until a considerable time after the arrests in France. All the Templars in England who wanted to escape had ample opportunity, and some went north to Scotland. Scholars are fairly certain some Templars remained there.

In 1314 Bruce won a major battle against the English at Bannockburn, which allowed him to take full control of Scotland. His victory was a surprise and has led to many theories, including the one that says he won because of the assistance of the Knights Templar. There is no historical proof of this, but it is certainly possible.

Rosslyn Chapel was begun in 1446, long after the death of Bruce and any Templars who may have settled in Scotland. It was built by Sir William Sinclair (Saint-Clair), the descendant of another Sir William who had been close to Bruce. The chapel was intended as a part of a larger church, but after forty years of construction, Sir William's son refused to continue the project.

The popular theory is that the second Sir William had inherited the treasury that the Templars brought to Scotland and built Rosslyn to hide it. There is no evidence of this, but this legend ties in to the legend of the origins of Freemasonry. Freemasons were originally the stonemasons who worked with a softer chalky stone called freestone: freestone masons became known as freemasons. They were skilled artisans who did intricate carving, and there is no place in Scotland with more examples of their art than Rosslyn.

Sometime in the seventeenth century, close to two centuries after Rosslyn was built and more than three centuries after the Templars would have arrived, the freemasons of the workers' guild were replaced by the Freemasons, a speculative organization seeking spiritual advancement and, perhaps, occult knowledge. The Sinclair family was involved in the formation of this brotherhood and has continued to be involved in Scottish Freemasonry. Because Freemasonry has at times claimed to be a continuation of the Knights Templar, the Sinclair family has long been connected with the Templars in legend. There is no direct historical evidence that the Freemasons are in any way related to the Knights Templar; the large gaps of time would make it very unlikely. Nevertheless, it is not surprising that Rosslyn has been put forth as the hiding place of the Templar secrets and the Grail.

The inside of Rosslyn is decorated by intricate carvings done by freestone masons, also called freemasons.

The organization of Freemasons was based in some way on the guild organization of builders. The exact connection between masons and Freemasons is unknown.

Arago plaque next to the Comédie Française. The Arago medallions mark the Paris Rose Line, which runs through the Paris observatory. The 135 medallions, designed by Netherlands artist Jean Dibbets, were placed in 1995. They are named after François Arago (1786–1833), an astronomer and political figure.

Return to Paris

THE ROSE LINE

Langdon learns from Sophie's grandmother that though the Grail was once located at Rosslyn, it has been moved to a new secret location. Still puzzling over the last clues to the Grail's whereabouts, Langdon returns to Paris and goes back to visit the Louvre. As he walks along he sees bronze medallions embedded in the ground at his feet.

These are the Arago medallions, located next to the Comédie Française across from the Louvre. The bronze plaques mark a meridian known as both the Arago line and as the Paris Rose Line. The Paris observatory was built over this north/south line in 1672. At that time France was interested in promoting the importance of this meridian as a way of extending France's maritime power and international trade.

The 135 medallions marking this line were designed by Netherlands artist Jean Dibbets and placed along the Rose Line in 1995. They contain the name Arago with an N for *Nord* above and an S for *Sud* below. The line is named after François Arago (1786–1833), a well-known astronomer and political figure.

Langdon thinks of the line as the world's first prime meridian, but that is not true. A meridian is any line that circles the globe and runs directly through the north and south poles, so there are millions of them. The prime meridian is a completely arbitrary choice of a line to number 0 degrees longitude; other meridians are counted from there. Before an international prime meridian was established in 1884, there was little agreement on how to number the meridians. The French used the Paris line as prime meridian, but there is little evidence that others did. There were earlier prime meridians; the Greek Ptolemy placed it in the Canary Islands as early as the second century.

In 1884 Greenwich, England, became the international prime meridian. A big factor in this decision was the location of the international date line at 180 degrees longitude. This line was established where it does not pass over inhabited land, since it would be very difficult if Wednesday was one block away from Thursday. The Greenwich prime meridian established a 180-degree longitude—located mostly in the Pacific Ocean—that requires the least zigging and zagging for the date line. Though the French appear to have been offended by this choice (they did not ratify the new line for more than twenty years), the selection of Greenwich for the prime meridian was very practical.

La Pyramide Inversée at the Louvre. In Brown's novel this is where the murder victim, Saunière, has buried the Holy Grail: a stash of documents and the body of Mary Magdalene.

La Pyramide Inversée

Langdon realizes that a clue he thought referred to the village of Roslin is really a reference to the Paris Rose Line. He then understands that the rest of the clue refers to the inverted pyramid in the new Louvre center.

La pyramide inversée is one of the most innovative skylights in existence. This inverted pyramid of glass brings natural light to the new underground areas of the Louvre complex. In crowded Paris, if the Louvre wanted to expand it had to go up or down, and this lighting design for the new underground areas is remarkable. At night the inverted pyramid is lit by many small lights and acts as a very large chandelier.

The apex of the inverted pyramid comes down over the point of a small pyramid on the floor. These are Brown's chalice and blade. Believing that this is the location of the Holy Grail, Langdon falls to his knees.

Believing that this is the location of the Holy Grail, Langdon falls to his knees.

REFLECTIONS

The remarkable success of *The Da Vinci Code* has many people asking, "What is the appeal?" If we look at other popular books and movies over the past few years, we begin to see a trend. There have been several huge or remarkable successes in book sales and movies: the *Harry Potter* book series; the *Left Behind* book series, a fictionalized story of the end-of-time prophecy from the Book of Revelation; the movie series of *The Lord of the Rings*; and the very different movie *The Passion of the Christ*, the story of the crucifixion of Jesus.

Two of these successes, the *Left Behind* series and *The Passion of the Christ*, are overtly Christian. J.R.R. Tolkien, author of *The Lord of the Rings*, was a devout Catholic, but his story is metaphorical rather than openly Christian. *Harry Potter* is not about religion, though some Christians have condemned the series because they equate witchcraft with Satanism. Among these, *The Da Vinci Code* is alone in opposing aspects of Christianity. Yet all these popular works share themes which indicate an appeal based on fulfilling needs that are experienced by Christians and non-Christians alike.

ABOVE *The Riders of the Sidhe* by John Duncan (1866–1945). The elven folk were often the wise ones in European mythology, as they are in *The Lord of the Rings*.

OPPOSITE PAGE *She Shall Be Called Woman* by George Frederick Watts (1817–1904).

Themes in Modern Myths

...Ernest Becker wrote that humans have what he called an urge to cosmic heroism...

THE HERO

Pulitzer prize–winning author Ernest Becker wrote that humans have what he called an urge to cosmic heroism, a need to contribute to cosmic life in a way that goes beyond the self and transcends the necessity of death. He theorized that if no positive heroism is available, people will find negative heroism, such as the viciously destructive heroics of Hitler's Germany.[1] Teenagers with no opportunity for heroism might join gangs, race cars, use drugs, or prove themselves in some other self-destructive way. Adults will do the same, but to potentially more damaging effect. They may provoke and promote war and other

Illumination from *The History of William of Tyre* (13th century). The crusaders committed unspeakable atrocities against Jews, Muslims, and, eventually, Eastern Christians, yet they were hailed as heroes in their time.

"How Sir Launcelot slew the knight Sir Peris de Forest Savage that did distress ladies, damosels, and gentlewomen." Illustration by Arthur Rackham (1867–1939). The knight who saves damsels in distress is a popular image of the hero.

destructive activities to provide themselves with an opportunity to feel like heroes, even if only vicariously.

Historically, heroism has been a magnet for many seeking something more from life, from the Crusades to the Knights Templar to a celibate lifestyle; people have been eager to make sacrifices for a greater good. The characters in the recently popular tales have an opportunity for heroism that we rarely find in the modern world. Harry Potter and his friends fight Lord Voldemort and his evil assistants; the *Left Behind* characters fight the agent of Satan in the form of the Antichrist; the fellowship of the ring proves itself in many different ways in the fight against Sauron and his evil allies; Jesus proves himself in his selfless acceptance of death in *The Passion of the Christ*; and leading characters in *The Da Vinci Code* risk their lives and liberty to save the secret of the Grail.

In all these scenarios, good and evil are clearly delineated. There is generally very little doubt who the good guys and who the bad guys are. The characters do not have to deal with the kind of ambiguities we meet every day. The only doubt relates to which ordinary people will become heroes. Two of the stories are controversial, *The Passion of the Christ* and *The Da Vinci Code*, to the extent that they make first-century Jews and early Christians the bad guys of the piece. Fictional bad guys like Sauron and Lord Voldemort are clearly less controversial.

Do we like these hero tales partly because they allow us to be vicarious heroes, fighting to save Middle-earth or the sacred feminine? Do they fill a need in our own lives to take risks and make sacrifices for something beyond ourselves? If so, then they may be helping prevent us from seeking some negative form of heroism. Hero tales might have less appeal in a society where people have more opportunity for direct and positive heroism in our everyday lives.

WISE MEN AND WOMEN

Another theme shared by these stories is the portrayal of wise people who can answer our questions and show us the way. In a society where leaders are neither trusted nor highly respected by many, it is certainly appealing to have a wise person to guide us.

Joseph Campbell identifies this as a common mythical theme.[2]

Harry Potter has Dumbledore to guide him; the *Left Behind* characters have the converted Jewish teacher Tsion Ben-Judah; the fellowship of the ring has Gandalf, the wizard, and Elrond and Galadriel, the elf leaders; Jesus has God the Father, whose will he knows; and for Sophie and Langdon, Leonardo da Vinci plays the role of a wise man who left messages to guide them. Additionally, they can rely on members of the Priory of Sion, who possess all the factual knowledge about early Christianity.

LEFT *The Druids: Bringing in the Mistletoe* by George Henry (1858–1943) and Edward Hornel (1864–1933). The druids were guides and wise people in Celtic mythology.

In a time of uncertainty and danger—which includes all of history—the appeal of a savior who is clearly good is very strong.

EXTERNAL SAVIORS

Several of these stories have external saviors who save the characters or humanity from evil. Dumbledore tends to step in to save Harry after Harry has heroically risked everything to stop Voldemort. The people left behind in the Rapture only have to hold out for the return of the Messiah, who will defeat Satan. The king who returns after the defeat of Sauron will bring safety and prosperity to all who submit to him. Jesus, by his death, is the savior of humanity, and the bloodline of Jesus and Mary Magdalene holds out some kind of hope for inspired leadership or a tangible presence of Jesus and Mary Magdalene in the modern world.

In a time of uncertainty and danger—which includes all of history—the appeal of a savior who is clearly good is very strong. We see in ourselves a mixture of good and evil, of consciousness and unconsciousness. Our political systems are such that they do not attract the most wise among us to participate, so we see very flawed people in positions of leadership. It is very consoling to think a truly good leader will appear to show us the way.

The Arming and Departure of the Knights (tapestry) by E. Burne-Jones (1833–1898) and William (1834–1896). The myth of the quest for the Holy Grail has been one of the most powerful and enduring in Western culture.

"...myth is the secret opening through which the inexhaustible energies of the cosmos pour into human cultural manifestation."

The Purpose of Myth

For Joseph Campbell all myths are really one and fulfill an essential need:

> *Throughout the inhabited world, in all times and under every circumstance, the myths of man have flourished; and they have been the living inspiration of whatever else may have appeared out of the activities of the human body and mind. It would not be too much to say that myth is the secret opening through which the inexhaustible energies of the cosmos pour into human cultural manifestation. Religions, philosophies, arts, the social forms of primitive and historic man, prime discoveries in science and technology, the very dreams that blister sleep, boil up from the basic, magic ring of myth.*[3]

The popularity of modern myths indicates a yearning for this connection to the "inexhaustible energies of the cosmos." The controversy surrounding *The Da Vinci Code* raises questions about the way we understand myth.

THE METAPHOR

According to Campbell, myths are by definition symbolic, a metaphor for life, and deal with the fantastic and unreal.[4] Myths are about the psyche, not about history. In our modern, scientifically oriented world, we have tended to undervalue this role of myth.

Becker believed that the psychological tension created by the differences in the two dimensions of human life—body and spirit—creates a form of madness that needs a relief in personal heroism.[5] Campbell believed that myth was so essential to the psyche that if we did not have a sufficient element of myth in our culture, we would manufacture myths in our dreams.[6] Yet in our materialistic world, we tend toward literalism. We examine a story for historical truth, and if it is not historical, dismiss it as "just a myth." Myth has come to mean "false story," instead of an essential and valuable metaphor that teaches us the art of living fully.

The Da Vinci Code deals with Christian legend, and Christian legend has traditionally been taken literally. The disobedience of Adam and Eve, the virgin birth of Jesus, the divinity of Jesus, and his father-son relationship with God, are all taken literally as historical events.

The literal understanding of some of these stories has led to cultural problems. The belief that Eve was responsible for all sin and all human suffering because she tempted Adam to eat the forbidden fruit has been used to justify the subordination and mistreatment of women and to support the argument that women are weaker and more carnal than men. Consequently, the spiritual development of women has been undermined and undervalued for two millennia.

Adam and Eve by Lucas Cranach (1472–1553). A literal interpretation of this myth has led to a portrayal of women as temptresses of men.

Ernest Becker presents a pattern of human development that can be applied to this story and that conveys a metaphorical, not external or historical, meaning.[7] The story of Adam and Eve is the story of every human, who as a child sees the world through the eyes of wonder and innocence. As the child is acculturated in a society, it is cast out of the garden of innocence and spontaneity into the world of repression, modesty, work, and responsibility. The story of Adam and Eve is the story of a virtually universal human experience. Each child yearns to join the adult world of the parents, and in doing so loses the garden of innocence.

The story of Adam and Eve is the story of a virtually universal human experience.

The literal interpretation of the story of the virgin birth of Jesus has led to the idea that virginity is pure, and though sexuality may not always be sin, it is always impure. We know this because God chose to be born without the "taint" of sex. Virginity is of the spirit, sexuality is of the body, and the spirit is always superior to the body. This idea has also led to the view that the ideal woman is mother and virgin, while the natural process of sexuality and childbirth has been devalued.

The story of a virgin birth is so common across cultures that it is archetypical in character. Joseph Campbell gives it a metaphorical meaning that changes the effect. He says that the virgin birth is the internal rebirth of the spirit from the level of the heart. Using the model of the seven chakras or energy centers in the body, the first three chakras are about the body and the physical world. They concern food and elimination, sexuality, and power. The

Shakyamuni Buddha, detail from a 17th century tangka, probably by Choying Gyatso. Buddhist legend says that Shakyamuni was conceived when his mother dreamed that a white elephant entered her side while she was sleeping. Though his mother, Maya, was not a virgin, the conception was virginal, and so legend says the Buddha too was born in a virgin birth.

fourth chakara, the heart, is the midpoint between the lower and the upper, between the physical and the spiritual, which exists in each of us. This is the place where we give birth to the spiritual self.[8] In this interpretation, the myth of virgin birth is not a condemnation of sexuality but a map to higher consciousness and the integration of body and spirit. People of high consciousness have been born from a virgin birth, a birth into spirit. Attis, Mithras, Jesus, and Buddha, among many others, are said to have been born from virgin births.

By understanding these stories as metaphors, we gain a guide for our lives. We have too often interpreted them to limit and condemn humanity, and have been left with external restrictions, not internal guides.

INTERNAL VS. EXTERNAL

The purpose of myths as psychological tales is not to recount history or events that really happened in physical space and time. The purpose is to provide a guide to dealing with the internal tensions we experience on life's path and to point us beyond. Real truth cannot be spoken because it is beyond the limitations of language and intellect. Lao-tzu's *Tao te Ching* begins with a statement that is translated many ways but means the Tao that can be spoken or written is not the essential or true Tao. Christianity too teaches that truth is ineffable, unknowable.

The mystic Osho once said that myths are like guideposts. If you see a sign pointing toward Delhi, you can take the sign apart and analyze it, and you will not find any Delhi in it. It is simply pointing the way.[9] Myths do not contain truth, but point the way to the experience of it.

If we understand myths as internal rather than external, we interpret the urge for heroism differently. We do not need to seek it in war, violence, or extreme practices. We can use legends and myths as guideposts pointing toward some experience that cannot be explained or told, a journey of mystery in which we will face many dangers and have the opportunity to meet our inner wise persons, become heroes, and discover the savior within. In this model, even if the savior is Jesus, we meet him inside.

Questions Raised

Some Christian commentators have characterized Dan Brown's novel as an attack on Christianity, and some of Brown's arguments, such as that Jesus was not divine and that the New Testament is a fraud, certainly strike at the core of Christianity. On another level, the novel addresses issues that affect our entire society. Because Christianity has had such a major effect on the development of thought in Euro-American culture, some of our societal problems can be traced to ideas in Christianity. Attitudes about women, sexuality, marriage, motherhood, work, and our relationship to the environment have all been deeply affected by Christian interpretations.

In a sense, Brown's novel creates a myth that balances out distortions that have arisen in our culture and that can be traced back to interpretations that arose in Christian thought.

...some of our societal problems can be traced to ideas in Christianity.

THE NATURE OF SEXUALITY

One of the most controversial issues brought up by the novel is the question of the sexuality of Jesus. The idea that Jesus was married and sexual seems to be more upsetting to many people than the idea that he was not divine. The view that divinity and sexuality are separate has had a widespread effect in Christian culture. Sex is seen as base and impure.

This idea is in conflict with our psychological notions that sexuality is natural and part of the natural good. We hear that sexuality is healthy and beneficial on the one hand, and subtly that it is impure on the other. This conflict is bound to create psychological tension, and, in fact, we see many sexually related psychological problems in our culture.

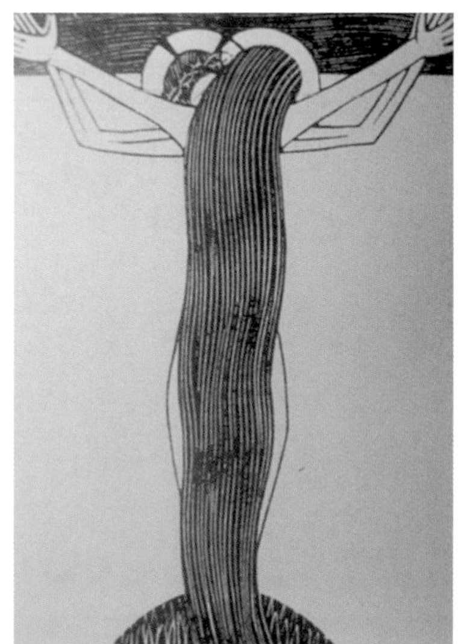

The Nuptials of God by Eric Gill (1882–1940). Sexual portrayals of Jesus disturb many people, but the image persists in fiction and art.

THE SACRED IN RELATIONSHIP

If sexuality is not sacred and marriage is inferior to celibacy, we cannot expect to have healthy sexual relationships. Though our modern society superficially rejects the preference for celibacy, the idea that Jesus or even religious leaders are sexual is often distressing. This schizophrenic cultural approach to sexuality has resulted in the loss of the idea of the sacred in sexual relationships.

The Three Marys at Calvary by Domenico Morelli (1826–1901). Every gospel in the New Testament reports that the women were loyal and courageous and stood by Jesus when the men ran away, but Christianity has traditionally considered women too weak to lead or teach.

If Jesus, the most idealized man in this culture, was sexual and loved a woman, this would radically challenge cultural views about relationships and sex.

THE NATURE OF WOMEN

The teachings of early Christianity characterized women as inferior to men—created out of man, the first to sin, the downfall of man, and spiritually inferior. For two millennia the story of the mission of Jesus has been presented as the story of Jesus teaching men, while a few women took care of them all. Men were the ones who understood Jesus and inherited his spirit. His teachings for centuries were passed down through an all-male hierarchy.

Recent studies, indicated in the novel, reveal that this is not an accurate picture. Early Christians portrayed Mary Magdalene and other women as leading disciples of Jesus, and Mary Magdalene was frequently presented as the one who understood him best. This can have an enormous impact on the way women are seen in this culture, and the way they see themselves. If people believed Jesus recognized women as equal to and sometimes superior to men, the relationship between men and women would change dramatically. Men would no longer be the only spiritual guides, the only ones capable of spirituality, the only mentors and interpreters of the meaning of scripture and doctrine.

This has resulted in the perception that only males are created in the image of God...

THE GODDESS

Though learned theologians would probably say that the Christian God is neither male nor female but beyond gender, there is no doubt that God has been presented as male in the writings and art of Christianity. This has resulted in the perception that only males are created in the image of God, while females emerge from Adam's rib and are not reflections of God. We have seen that Mary the mother of Jesus replaced the Goddess in Christianity by assuming many of the roles of the Goddess such as virgin, mother, protector, nature Goddess, and Queen of Heaven. She did not portray the sexual, lover aspect of the Goddess, and she had power only as an intercessor with God.

The aspect of the lover was played out mythically by Mary Magdalene, who searched for the body of her "lover" after his death. She became the lover in the

Magdalene in the Grotto by Jules-Joseph Lefebvre (1836–1912). Mary Magdalene has been associated with sexuality, and was called a prostitute by the Western Church as a result. She is sometimes portrayed in Venus-like poses in European art.

Song of Songs, who searched for her beloved. When, in addition to this, she is presented as the most spiritually advanced disciple, the spiritual consort of Jesus, the one who knew him best, she personifies several aspects of Goddess that have been missing from the traditional Christian portrayal.

The idea that women do not reflect divinity, that they are not as spiritually ideal as men, has done great psychological damage in this culture. The success of Dan Brown's novel tells us there is a hunger for another portrayal of our cultural history that corrects this distortion. Dan Brown's story captures the imagination, because it presents an alternative myth in which women are equally divine in nature.

[Mary Magdalene] became the lover in the Song of Songs, who searched for her beloved.

THE SEARCH FOR CERTAINTY

As much as we yearn for certainty, we live lives of uncertainty and insecurity. We say that the only things we can be sure of are death and taxes, and know at some level that this is true. We believe that if we have certainty, we will have security. If we only knew for sure, we could control our lives and guarantee safety and happiness. Yet certainty remains a thing of myth.

The mystics of various religious traditions use different words, but they agree that the first step to spiritual growth is the release of desire for certainty and

Saint Magdalene Reading after Correggio (ca. 1775–1825). A bloodline left by Mary Magdalene and Jesus might be a source of saviors for the modern world.

control. The first step is to admit we do not know, and from there a different kind of knowing emerges. This is not the knowing of the intellect that is subject to doubt, but an inner knowing.

Myths present a wise man or woman, metaphorically an inner man or woman, who knows the truth and can guide us. If we see myth as an internal journey, the search for certainty changes from a search for information on the outside to a search on the inside. In the end of Brown's novel, we discover that the guardians are not going to give people certain knowledge. People must find that for themselves.

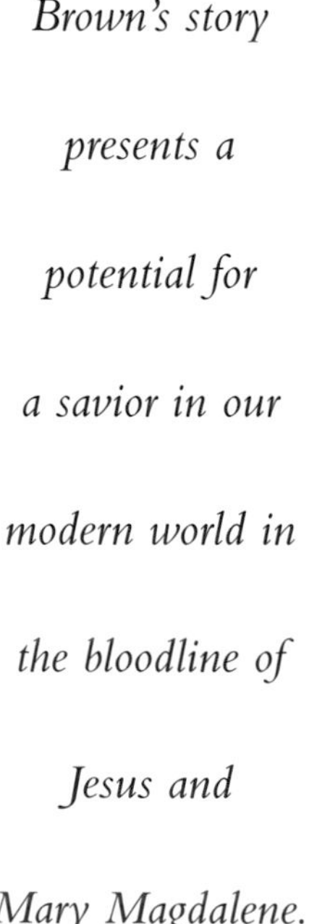

Brown's story presents a potential for a savior in our modern world in the bloodline of Jesus and Mary Magdalene.

SAVIORS

Brown's story presents a potential for a savior in our modern world in the bloodline of Jesus and Mary Magdalene. He does not elaborate on what that bloodline really means, though we know that Pierre Plantard used the idea to justify a kingship. The bloodline is a royal bloodline, which confers a right to rule. The discovery of the bloodline means the return of the ancient king.

Throughout human history leaders have been seriously flawed, whether they were governmental or religious leaders, or both. This creates a sense of insecurity and disquietude. People yearn for a truly good leader and love stories like the return of Jesus as Messiah who will rule a good world for 1,000 years—that is security. The modern bloodline of Jesus is another variation on that idea.

If we look at this as a metaphor, the search for a savior is no longer external. A mythical savior is the inner savior, the bloodline within.

Going Beyond The Da Vinci Code

The success of this novel has highlighted many important issues, and the next step is to know how to move beyond it. One online writer, an Episcopal priest, tells how he organized a community meeting about *The Da Vinci Code* and was amazed when 600 people showed up on a Wednesday night. One person stood up and said, "We are here tonight because we are searching."[10] How do we continue the search from here?

We can see that we need myths for our modern world that act as guideposts for us to resolve psychological tensions, move to a heroic place within ourselves, and allow us to be positive heroes in our everyday lives. We also need myths that can balance cultural distortions that have caused pain to so many people. *The Da Vinci Code* is having an impact because it begins that process. It gives us an alternative myth.

It is unlikely that Brown's myth will have the long-term effect of providing a myth for our time or balancing our culture. For that we need something more. Joseph Campbell recommends something entirely new:

> *As Professor Arnold J. Toynbee indicates in his six-volume study of the laws of the rise and disintegration of civilizations, schism in the soul, schism in the body social, will not be resolved by any scheme of return to the good old days (archaism), or by programs guaranteed to render an ideal projected future (futurism), or even by the most realistic, hardheaded work to weld together again the deteriorating elements. Only birth can conquer death—the birth, not of the old thing again, but of something new. Within the soul, within the body social, there must be—if we are to experience long survival—a continuous "reoccurrence of birth"* (palingenesia) *to nullify the unremitting recurrences of death.*[11]

Brown's novel and other modern myths tell us that we need a new mythological guide that is relevant to our needs. We can continue to seek it in fiction or go beyond fiction to create a functional myth for our time.

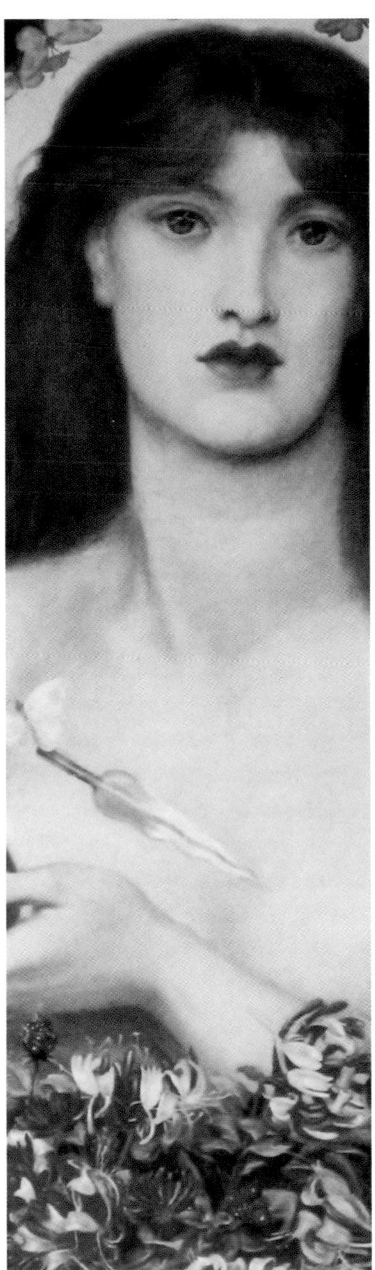

Venus Verticordia by Dante Gabriel Rossetti (1828–1882). Do the old myths still serve us, or should we give birth to something entirely new?

Endnotes

INTRODUCTION

1. Laurie Goodstein, "Defenders of Christianity Rebut 'The Da Vinci Code'," *New York Times*, 27 April 2004.

2. Dan Brown, *The Da Vinci Code* (New York: Doubleday, 2003), 1.

3. Ibid., 163, 217, 255.

4. Ibid., 163.

CHAPTER ONE: WAS JESUS MARRIED?

1. *Living on the Edge*, "The Bible vs. The Da Vinci Code," http://crosswalk.com/community/newsletters/popup.asp; Catholic Answers, "Cracking The Da Vinci Code," http://www.catholic.com/. Conservative theologian Darrell Bock claims that the vast majority of both liberal and conservative theologians believe Jesus was not married. See Darrell L. Bock, *Breaking The Da Vinci Code: Answers to the Questions Everybody's Asking* (Nashville, Tenn.: Nelson Books, 2004), 33.

2. E. P. Sanders, *The Historical Figure of Jesus* (London: Penguin, 1993), 54.

3. Ibid., 87.

4. Ibid., 85-86.

5. Pliny the Elder, *Natural History* 5.15.73, cited in Peter Brown, *The Body and Society: Men, Women and Sexual Renunciation in Early Christianity* (New York: Columbia University Press, 1988), 38.

6. P. Brown, *Body and Society*, 38.

7. "Birth Control," http://catholic.com/library/Birth_Control.asp.

8. P. Brown, *Body and Society*, 39.

9. See also Matthew 11:18-19. All citations from the Bible, unless otherwise indicated, are from *The Holy Bible: Containing the Old and New Testament*, New Revised Standard Version (Grand Rapids, Mich.: Zondervan Publishing House, 1989).

10. Elaine Pagels, *Adam, Eve, and the Serpent* (New York: Random House, 1989), 14.

11. See also Mark 12:18-27.

12. Flavius Josephus, *Antiquities* 18.1.16-17, William Whiston, trans., http://www.ccel.org/j/josephus/works/JOSEPHUS.HTM; Flavius Josephus, *The Wars of the Jews* 2.8.165, William Whiston, trans.http://www.sacredtexts.com/jud/jos phus/#woj.

13. Stephen M. Miller and Robert V. Huber, *The Bible: A History: The Making and Impact of the Bible* (Intercourse, Pa.: Good Books, 2004), 90.

14. The Jesus Seminar has done its own translation of the five gospels called the Scholars' Version. Robert W. Funk, Roy W. Hoover, and the Jesus Seminar, *The Five Gospels: The Search for the Authentic Words of Jesus* (New York: Macmillan, 1993), *xiii-xviii*.

15. Ibid., 220.

16. Ibid., 220-21.

17. Ignatius, *Letter to Polycarp* 5.2, cited in P. Brown, *Body and Society*, 41.

18. Geza Vermes, *Jesus the Jew* (Philadelphia: Fortress Press, 1981), 99-102.

19. James M. Robinson, ed., *The Nag Hammadi Library in English* (San Francisco: Harper & Row, 1988), 145.

20. Antti Marjanen, *The Women Jesus Loved: Mary Magdalene in the Nag Hammadi Library and Related Documents* (Leiden: E.J. Brill, 1996), 149-51.

21. Ibid., 151.

22. Ibid., 153-54.

23. Ibid.,154.

24. Ibid.

25. Ibid.

26. *Nag Hammadi Library*, 148.

27. Marjanen, *Women Jesus Loved*, 154.

28. John Dominic Crossan, *The Historical Jesus: The Life of a Mediterranean Jewish Peasant* (San Francisco: HarperSanFrancisco, 1992), 431; Funk, *Five Gospels*, 544.

29. Sanders, *Historical Figure*, 19, 87.

30. P. Brown, *Body and Society*, 43.

CHAPTER TWO: MARY MAGDALENE IN THE NEW TESTAMENT

1. It is customary to capitalize the word God only when it is referring to the male Christian, Jewish, or Islamic concept of one God or persons in the trinity. All references to Gods in other traditions or to any aspect of a Goddess are generally lowercase. Since this style reflects a strong bias in favor of Christianity and its related traditions and to the concept of a male God, all references to Gods and Goddesses outside of quotes are treated alike and capitalized in this work.

2. Bernadette J. Brooten, "Jewish Women's History in the Roman Period: A Task for Christian Theology," *Harvard Theological Review* 79:1-3 (1986) 22-30; Tal Ilan, "Women's Studies and Jewish Studies—When and Where Do They Meet?" *Jewish Studies Quarterly* 3:2 (1995), 162-173; Mayer I. Gruger, "The Status of Women in Ancient Judaism" in Jacob Neusner, ed., *Judaism in Late Antiquity*, Part 3, vol. 2 (Leiden and New York: E.J. Brill, 1995).

3. Tamar Frankiel, *The Voice of Sarah: Feminine Spirituality and Traditional Judaism* (San Francisco: Harper, 1990), 38.

4. Ibid., 42.

5. See Romans 16:3,7; 1 Corinthians 16:19.

6. Pagels, *Adam, Eve, and the Serpent*, 24-25.

7. Bernadette J. Brooten, *Women Leaders in the Ancient Synagogue* (Chico, Calif.: Scholars Press, 1982), 5-99.

8. Ibid., 6; see also Mary R. Thompson, *Mary of Magdala: Apostle and Leader* (New York: Paulist, 1995), 85.

9. Ibid., 103-138.

10. James B. Pritchard, ed., *The Times Atlas of the Bible: The Land, Events, and People of the World's Most Famous Book* (New York: Crescent Books, 1987), 163.

11. Thompson, *Apostle and Leader*, 25-26.

12. Jane Schaberg, "Luke," in Carol A. Newsom and Sharon H. Ringe, eds., *The Women's Bible Commentary* (Louisville, Ky.: Westminster, 1992), 290.

13. Elizabeth Schüssler Fiorenza, *In Memory of Her: A Feminist Theological Reconstruction of Christian Origins* (New York: Crossroad, 1983), 275; Schaberg, "Luke," 275; Ann Graham Brock, *Mary*

Magdalene, the First Apostle: The Struggle for Authority (Cambridge, Mass.: Harvard Theological Studies, 2003), 36-38.

14. See also Matthew 26:6-13.

15. Schaberg, "Luke," 288.

16. Schüssler Fiorenza, *In Memory of Her*, 21-35, 161; Schaberg, "Luke," 288-289; Graham Brock, *First Apostle*, 38.

17. See Morna D. Hooker, "Mark, The Gospel According to," in Bruce M. Metzger and Michael D. Coogan, eds., *The Oxford Companion to the Bible* (New York and Oxford: Oxford University Press, 1993), 492-496.

18. David Tresemer and Laura-Lea Cannon, "Preface: Who Is Mary Magdalene?" in Jean-Yves Leloup, *The Gospel of Mary* (Rochester, Vt.: Inner Traditions International, 2002), *xvii*.

19. Tal Ilan, "Notes on the Distribution of Jewish Women's Names in Palestine in the Second Temple and Mishnaic Periods," *Journal of Jewish Studies* 40 (1989), 191.

20. See Thompson, *Apostle and Leader*, 116-117.

21. Susan Haskins, *Mary Magdalene: Myth and Metaphor* (New York: Harcourt Brace & Co., 1993), 250-251.

22. Margaret Starbird, *The Woman with the Alabaster Jar: Mary Magdalene and the Holy Grail* (Rochester, Vt.: Bear & Co., 1993), 29.

23. Lynn Picknett and Clive Prince, *The Templar Revelation: Secret Guardians of the True Identity of Christ* (New York: Simon & Schuster, 1997), 245-264.

24. Starbird, *Woman with the Alabaster Jar*, 50-52.

25. Thompson, *Apostle and Leader*, 26-27.

CHAPTER THREE: OTHER VIEWS OF MARY MAGDALENE

1. Interview with Elaine Pagels, "What Was Lost Is Found: A Wider View of Christianity and Its Roots" in Dan Burstein, ed., *Secrets of the Code: The Unauthorized Guide to the Mysteries Behind The Da Vinci Code* (New York: CDS Books, 2004), 103.

2. Ibid., 103-104.

3. Karen L. King, *The Gospel of Mary of Magdala: Jesus and the First Woman Apostle* (Santa Rosa, Calif.: Polebridge Press, 2003), 155.

4. Marjanen, *Women Jesus Loved*, 37 n. 22.

5. Ibid., 171.

6. Introduction in *Nag Hammadi Library*, 22.

7. Coptic Christianity was the form of Christianity established in Egypt in the first century, which legend says was founded by the apostle Mark. The documents of the early Coptic Church were in the Coptic language.

8. Elaine Pagels, *The Gnostic Gospels* (New York: Random House, 1989), xxiv.

9. Ibid., xix.

10. Stevan L. Davies, *The Gospel of Thomas and Christian Wisdom* (New York: The Seabury Press, 1983), 3:146-147.

11. Marjanen, *Women Jesus Loved*, 38.

12. Ibid., 40-41.

13. Ibid., 98.

14. King, *Gospel of Mary*, 96-118.

15. Ibid., 7-12.

16. Ibid., 11.

17. Some writers, including Haskins, *Myth and Metaphor*, 13, use the translation "men," instead of "human beings." Human being is the correct translation, Marjanen, *Women Jesus Loved*, 51.

18. *Papyrus Berolinenses*, known as the Berlin Codex.

19. King, *Gospel of Mary*, 177-178.

20. Valentinian Christianity was based on the teachings of Valentinius (ca. 100-175), an Egyptian who studied in Alexandria and became a Neoplatonic philosopher and teacher. When he went to Rome, he became involved with the Church and taught an allegorical interpretation of Christian Scriptures to a select secret group. Salvation was achieved through a gnosis of God. Valentinius's teachings were expanded by his students.

21. Marjanen, *Women Jesus Loved*, 147.

22. Ibid., 147-149.

23. Ibid., 171.

24. Ibid., 170-188.

25. Ibid., 59-63.

26. King, *Gospel of Mary*, 145.

27. Marjanen, *Women Jesus Loved*, 77 n. 9.

28. Ibid., 123 n. 6.

29. *Nag Hammadi Library*, 26.

30. King, *Gospel of Mary*, 143.

31. Thompson, *Apostle and Leader*, 116-117.

32. According to Acts, Christianity was introduced into Ethiopia in the first century by the apostle Philip (Acts 8:26-40).

33. Pagels, *Gnostic Gospels*; Marjanen, *Women Jesus Loved*; Graham Brock, *First Apostle*.

34. Graham Brock, *First Apostle*, 104.

CHAPTER FOUR: EVOLUTION OF THE EARLY CHURCH

1. E. Glenn Hinson, *The Early Church: Origins to the Dawn of the Middle Ages* (Nashville, Tenn.: Abingdon Press, 1996), 42-43.

2. Thompson, *Apostle and Leader*, 110.

3. Hinson, *Early Church*, 23-25.

4. Sibyls were women with the gift of prophecy, who were present throughout much of the ancient world. The Sibyl who prophesied for Rome was the Greek Sibyl at Cumaean.

5. Marvin W. Meyer, *The Ancient Mysteries: A Source Book: Sacred Texts of the Mystery Religions of the Ancient Mediterranean* (Philadelphia: University of Pennsylvania Press, 1999).

6. James George Fraser, *The Golden Bough* (New York: Macmillan, 1923). http://pantheon.org/articles/a/attis.html; homepage.mac.com/cparada/GML/Attis.html.

7. See http://www.ctio.noao.edu/instrument/ir_instruments/osiris2soar/tale.html; http://sobek.Colorado.edu/LAB/GODS/osiris.html; http://members.aol.com/egyptart/osi.html;

www.pantheon.org/articles/o/osiris.html.

8. Tertullian, *De Praescriptione Haereticorum*, 40 (Tübingen: J.C.B. Mohr, 1910), 3.

9. Justin Martyr, *Dialogue with Trypho*, 70, A. Lukyn Williams, trans. (London: Macmillan, 1930), 148-150.

10. Hinson, *Early Church*, 200.

11. Richard J. Baukham, "2 Peter," in *The Oxford Companion to the Bible*, 586-588.

12. Hinson, *Early Church*, 25-27.

13. D. Brown, *Da Vinci Code*, 231.

14. Albert Bates Lord, *The Singer of Tales* (New York: Atheneum, 1968), 9-10. Originally published as *Harvard Studies in Comparative Literature*, 24 (Cambridge, Mass.: Harvard University Press, 1960).

15. Funk, *Five Gospels*, 27-29. See the extensive discussion of oral traditions in John Dominic Crossan, *The Birth of Christianity: Discovering What Happened in the Years Immediately After the Execution of Jesus* (San Francisco: HarperSanFrancisco, 1989), 49-84.

16. Nicholas Thomas Wright, *The New Testament and the People of God* (Minneapolis: Fortress Press, 1992), 423.

17. Sanders, *Historical Figure*, 5.

18. Ibid., 64-65.

19. Crossan, *Historical Jesus*, 430; Funk, *Five Gospels*, 544.

20. Funk, *Five Gospels*, 10.

21. Ibid.

22. Emanuel Tov, "Manuscripts: Hebrew Bible," in *The Oxford Companion to the Bible*, 486-488.

23. Gerd Teissen and Annette Merz, *The Historical Jesus: A Comprehensive Guide* (Minneapolis: Fortress Press, 1998), 47.

24. Helmut Koester, *Ancient Christian Gospels: Their History and Development* (London: SCM Press; Philadelphia: Trinity Press International, 1990), 296.

25. "Letter of Clement of Alexandria on Secret Mark," Morton Smith, trans., http://earlychristianwritings.com/text/secretmark.html.

26. Ibid.

27. Robert P. Gordon, "Translations: Ancient Languages" in *The Oxford Companion to the Bible*, 753.

28. Robert G. Bratcher, "Translations: English Language" in *The Oxford Companion to the Bible*, 758-763.

29. Funk, *Five Gospels*, 8-9.

30. Ibid., 9.

31. Pagels, *Gnostic Gospels*, xviii-xix, 17; Hinson, *Early Church*, 183-185; Miller and Huber, *The Bible: A History*, 96.

32. Pagels, *Gnostic Gospels*, xviii-xix.

33. Miller and Huber, *The Bible: A History*, 96.

34. Ibid., 94-95.

35. Hinson, *Early Church*, 199, 203-206.

36. Ibid., 197.

37. Ibid., 200.

38. Ibid., 233-236.

39. The majority view is that the scrolls concern a group called the Essenes, who most scholars believe was a separate group from the disciples of Jesus. One academic writer believes the Dead Sea Scrolls are related to Christianity, but his work has not been accepted by other scholars. See Robert Eisenman, *The Dead Sea Scrolls and the First Christians* (Shaftsbury, Dorset: Element, 1996).

CHAPTER FIVE: THE GODDESS AND SEXUALITY

1. James Mellaart, *Çatal Hüyük* (New York: Thames and Hudson, 1967), 32, illus. 15, 16.

2. Merlin Stone, *When God Was a Woman* (New York: Dial Press, 1976), xviii.

3. Robert Graves and Raphael Patai, *Hebrew Myths* (New York: Doubleday, 1914), 31.

4. Ibid. 80; Stone, *When God Was a Woman*, 62-69.

5. Stone, *When God Was a Woman, xvii-xviii.*

6. Tikva Frymer-Kensky, *In the Wake of the Goddess* (New York: Macmillan, 1992), 156.

7. Ibid., 159.

8. Stone, *When God Was a Woman*, 203.

9. Ibid., 200.

10. Riane Eisler, *The Chalice and the Blade: Our History, Our Future* (San Francisco: Harper and Row, 1987), 88-89.

11. Graves and Patai, *Hebrew Myths*, 78.

12. Ibid.

13. Pagels, *Adam, Eve, and the Serpent*, 27.

14. P. Brown, *Body and Society*, 86.

15. Jerome, *Letters*, 22,18, http://www.newadvent.org/fathers/3001.htm.

16. Pagels, *Adam, Eve, and the Serpent*, 110-113.

17. Ibid., 91-97.

18. Jerome, *Against Jovinianus*, 1,7, Philip Schaff and Henry Wace, eds., http://www.ccel.org/fathers/NPNF2-06/treatise/jovinan1.htm; Augustine, *De Bono Coniugali*, 34 in *Saint Augustine: Treatises on Marriage and Other Subjects*, Charles T. Wilcox, et al. trans. (New York: Fathers of the Church, Inc, 1955), 50-51.

19. Pagels, *Adam, Eve, and the Serpent*, 29.

20. Tertullian, *De Culta Feminarum*, I, 12, quoted in Pagels, *Adam, Eve, and the Serpent*, 62-63.

21. Augustine, *Opus Imperfectum* 4,40, quoted in Pagels, *Adam, Eve, and the Serpent*, 133.

22. Haskins, *Myth and Metaphor*, 65.

23. Carl G. Liungman, *Dictionary of Symbols* (New York: W.W. Norton & Co., 1991), 290.

24. D. Brown, *Da Vinci Code*, 308.

25. A. T. Mann and Jane Lyle, *Sacred Sexuality* http://istartemple.org/sacredIshtar.html.

26. D. Brown, *Da Vinci Code*, 311.

27. See, http://se.msnusers.com/miriamangeldancer/hildegardavbingen.msnw.

28. *Nag Hammadi Library*, 151-152.

29. Picknett and Prince, *Templar Revelation*, 256-264; Starbird, *Woman with the Alabaster Jar*, 35-47.

CHAPTER SIX: SYMBOLS

1. Liungman, *Dictionary of Symbols*, 298.

2. D. Brown, *Da Vinci Code*, 37.

3. Liungman, *Dictionary of Symbols*, 335-337.

4. Miranda Bruce-Mitford, *Illustrated Book of Signs & Symbols* (New York: DK Pub., Inc., 1996) 71.

5. Liungman, *Dictionary of Symbols*, 300.

6. James Underwood Crockett, *Roses* (New York: Time-Life books, 1971), 76.

7. Painton Cowen, *Rose Windows* (San Francisco: Chronicle Books, 1979), 14.

8. Ibid., 18.

9. Ibid., 22.

10. Liungman, *Dictionary of Symbols*, 138-139.

11. D. J. McAdam, "History of Tarot Cards," http://www.tarot-decks.com/tarotarticle.htm.

12. Rosemary and Darrol Pard, "The Female Pope: The Mystery of Pope Joan," http://www.users.global.net.co.uk/~pardos/PopeJoanHome.html.

13. Ibid.

14. Ibid.

15. D. Brown, *The Da Vinci Code*, 21.

16. David A. Shugarts, "The Plot Holes and Intriguing Details of *The Da Vinci Code*," in *Secrets of the Code* (New York: CDS Books, 2004), 259.

17. Starbird, *Woman with the Alabaster Jar*, 174-176.

18. Mario Livio, *The Golden Ratio: The Story of Phi, The World's Most Astonishing Number* (New York: Broadway Books, 2002), 5.

19. Ibid., 96.

20. Ibid., 101.

CHAPTER SEVEN: ORIGINS OF A GRAIL MYTH

1. Michael Baigent, Richard Leigh, and Henry Lincoln, *Holy Blood, Holy Grail* (New York: Dell, 1983), 113.

2. Ibid., 165.

3. Ibid., 214.

4. Ibid., 224-227.

5. Minutes of meeting of *Alpha Galates* dated December 27, 1942, http://priory-of-sion.com/psp/id86.html.

6. Police report dated May 1954, http://priory-of sion.com/psp/id172.html.

7. Paul Smith, "Pierre Plantard's Judicial Archives and Criminal Convictions," http://priory-of-sion.com/psp/id30.html.

8. Paul Smith, "Pierre Plantard Profile" (1956) http://priory-of-sion.com/psp/id84.html.

9. Paul Smith, http://priory-of-sion.com/psp/id78.html.

10. Paul Smith, "Pierre Plantard and the Priory of Sion Chronology" (1967), http://priory-of-sion.com/psp/id22.html.

11. Ibid. (1967).

12. Ibid. (1984).

13. Jean-Luc Chaumeil put the authors of *Holy Blood, Holy Grail* in contact with Plantard. Did he know about the convictions at that time?

14. Noel Pinot, "An Interview with Pierre Plantard," *Vaincre* (April 1989), http://priory-of-sion.com/psp/id132.html.

15. Smith, "Plantard Chronology" (1987) http://priory-of-sion.com/psp/id22.html .

16. Pierre Plantard, "The Merovingian Myth," *Vaincre* (April 11, 1990), http://priory-of-sion.com/psp/id22.html.

17. Ibid.

18. "Letter from Otto Von Hapsburg about Bérenger Saunière" (1983), http://priory-of-sion.com/psp/id44.html.

19. See http://orobtempli.org/priory-of-sion.html; http://freemasonrywatch.org/prioryof-sion.html.

20. D. Brown, *The Da Vinci Code*, 113.

CHAPTER EIGHT: BLOODLINES AND GUARDIANS

1. Haskins, *Myth and Metaphor*, 106.

2. Ibid., 106-108.

3. Ibid., 107-108.

4. Ibid., 110.

5. Ibid., 112.

6. Ibid., 121.

7. Ibid., 120.

8. Ibid., 121-122.

9. Ibid., 120.

10. Ibid., 122.

11. Ibid., 157.

12. Cathars were sometimes called Albigensians because of their presence in and around the city of Albi in the Languedoc.

13. William of Puylaurens, *The Chronicle of William of Puylaurens: The Albigensians and Its Aftermath*, W.A. and M.D. Sibly, trans. (Rochester, N.Y.: Boydell Press, 2003), 128.

14. Pascal Guébin and Henri Maisonneuve, *Histoire Albigeoise* (Paris: Librairie Philosophique J. Vrin, 1951), 41.

15. Ibid.

16. Pagels, *Adam, Eve, and the Serpent*, 60-61.

17. We do not know if this information was historically accurate, but it was believed by the Cathars and possibly the writers of the *Gospel of Philip*.

18. Haskins, *Myth and Metaphor*, 108.

19. Ibid., 114-115.

20. Ibid., 98.

21. Ibid., 116.

22. Ibid., 124-125.

23. Ibid., 124-126.

24. Ibid., 127-131.

25. D. Brown, *Da Vinci Code*, 260.

26. Plantard, "The Merovingian Myth," http://priory-of-sion.com/psp/id22.html (1990).

27. Baigent, *Holy Blood, Holy Grail*, 235, 387.

28. Ibid., 387-388.

29. Ibid., 388-389.

30. Ibid., 393.

31. Ibid.

32. Picknett and Prince, *Templar Revelation*, 50-51.

33. Starbird, *Woman with the Alabaster Jar*, 60-61.

34. Piers Paul Read, *The Templars* (New York: St. Martin's Press, 2000), 91-92.

35. Ibid., 131.

36. Ibid., 304-306.

37. Ibid., 107-109.

38. Ibid., 269-270.

39. Ibid., 279-280, 291.

40. Ibid., 299-300.

CHAPTER NINE: GRAIL LEGENDS

1. D. Brown, *Da Vinci Code*, 162.

2. Ibid., 341.

3. Deborah Crombie, *A Finer End* (New York: Bantam Books, 2001).

4. Roger Sherman Loomis, *The Grail: From Celtic Myth to Christian Symbols* (New York: Columbia University Press, 1963), 3-4.

5. Ibid., 16-17.

6. Ibid., 49-52.

7. Jan Willem Drijvers, *Helena Augusta: The Mother of Constantine the Great and the Legends of her Finding of the True Cross* (Leiden and New York: E.J. Brill, 1993), 63.

8. Ibid., 79.

9. We know about this king called "the bear" from the work of the ninth-century Welsh monk Nennius, *Historia Brittonum*, as well as from the sixth-century monk Gildas, who wrote of the bear and the bear's stronghold in *De Excidio Conquestu Britannae*. Many scholars do not consider Gildas and Nennius as reliable sources, but they are the best we have.

10. Tim Carrington, "Shropshire's Secrets," http://shropshire-promotions.co.uk/shropshire%20Secrets/SS-5.html.

11. Ibid.

12. Malcolm Godwin, *The Holy Grail: Its Origins, Secrets and Meaning Revealed* (New York: Barnes & Noble, 1998), 86.

13. Ibid., 87.

14. Ibid., 88.

15. Haskins, *Myth and Metaphor*, 102.

16. "Relics came to assume such an important part in Christian life that the Second Council of Nicaea of 787 fulminated against those who despised them, and ruled that churches could not be consecrated without them." Haskins, *Myth and Metaphor,*103.

17. Graham Phillips, *The Chalice of Magdalene: The Search for the Cup That Held the Blood of Christ* (Rochester, Vt.: Bear & Co., 2004), 183, 199–214.

18. Britannia Internet Magazine, "*The Marian Chalice: The Holy Grail?*" http://britannia.com/history/Arthur/marian.html.

CHAPTER TEN: LEONARDO

1. D. Brown, *Da Vinci Code*, 113.

2. Ibid., 96.

3. Lynn Picknett and Clyde Prince, *Turin Shroud—In Whose Image?* (London: Bloomsbury, 1994).

4. D. Brown, *Da Vinci Code*, 253.

5. A. Richard Turner, *Inventing Leonardo* (New York: Alfred A. Knopf, 1993), 65-66.

6. Ibid., 66-67.

7. Margaret Cooper, *The Inventions of Leonardo* (New York: Macmillan, 1965), 33; Patrice Boussel, *Leonardo Da Vinci* (New York: Konecy & Konecy, 1986-1992), 16.

8. Roger Whiting, *Leonardo: A Portrait of the Renaissance Man* (New York: Knickerbocker Press, 1992), 60.

9. Pietro C. Marani, *Leonardo Da Vinci: The Complete Paintings* (New York: Harry N. Abrams, 2000), 124.

10. Ibid., 138.

11. Ibid., 139.

12. Ibid.

13. Ibid, 153, n. 36.

14. Ibid., 136-137.

15. Boussel, *Leonardo*, 16.

16. Ibid.

17. Turner, *Inventing Leonardo*, 180.

18. Whiting, *Portrait*, 133.

19. Ibid.

20. Boussel, *Leonardo*, 16.

21. Jean Paul Richter, *The Notebooks of Leonardo Da Vinci: Compiled and Edited from the Original Manuscripts* (New York: Dover Publications, 1976), 1:xiv.

22. Boussel, *Leonardo*, 12.

23. Whiting, *Portrait*, 18.

24. Picknett and Prince, *Templar Revelation*, 165.

25. Ibid., 20-22.

26. Francesco Scanelli writing in 1642. Turner, *Inventing Leonardo*, 69-70.

27. The Richardsons from England. Ibid.

28. Whiting, *Portrait*, 57.

29. Ibid., 57-58.

30. Turner, *Inventing Leonardo*, 152-153.

31. Roy McMullen, *Mona Lisa: The Picture and the Myth* (Boston: Houghton Mifflin Co., 1975), 84.

32. See Matthew 26:17-35; Mark 14:12-31; Luke 22:7-23; John 13:1-30.

33. Turner, *Inventing Leonardo*, 153.

34. Marani, *Complete Paintings*, 187.

35. Ibid.

36. McMullen, *Mona Lisa*, 43.

37. Lillian Schwartz, *The Computer Artist's Handbook* (New York: W. W. Norton & Co. Inc., 1992), 273.

38. Whiting, *Portrait*, 54-55.

39. Boussel, *Leonardo*, 6.

40. Slobodan Prvanoic, "Mona Lisa—Ineffable Smile of Quantum Mechanics," http://arxiv.org/abs/physics/0302089.

41. D. Brown, *Da Vinci Code*, 170.

CHAPTER ELEVEN: THE MODERN CHURCH

1. Michael Walsh, *Opus Dei: An Investigation into the Secret Society Struggling for Power Within the Roman Catholic Church* (San Francisco: HarperSanFrancisco, 1992), 14.

2. Maria Del Carmen Tapia, *Beyond the Threshold: A Life in Opus Dei* (New York: Continuum, 1997), 219.

3. Ibid., 125; National Public Radio Weekend Edition, October 6, 2002, interview with Alberto Moncada.

4. *Conversations with Mgr. Escrivá de Balaguer* (Dublin: Scepter Books, 1969), 25.

5. Tapia, *Beyond the Threshold*, 45.

6. *Conversations*, 128.

7. Walsh, *Opus Dei*, 194.

8. *Conversations*, 42-43.

9. Walsh, *Opus Dei*, 115.

10. Ibid., 169; Tapia, *Beyond the Threshold*, 258.

11. Tapia, *Beyond the Threshold*, 270.

12. *Conversations*, 117, 129.

13. Tapia, *Beyond the Threshold*, 121-122, 270-271, 310-311.

14. Ibid., 311.

15. Ibid., 122.

16. *Conversations*, 133-134.

17. Anna Morales, "This Apple Guiltlessly Falls Far From the Tree: Recollections of a Supernumerary's Daughter," http://odan.org. Escrivá ate the best food on expensive dishes and silver, Walsh, *Opus Dei*, 194.

18. Tapia, *Beyond the Threshold*, 87; Walsh, *Opus Dei*, 108.

19. Tapia, *Beyond the Threshold*, 55.

20. Ibid., 34, 55.

21. "Corporal Mortification in Opus Dei," http://odan.org.

22. Walsh, *Opus Dei*, 123.

23. *Conversations*, 101-103; Javier Echevarria, "Authentic Feminism," http://opusdei.com/art.php?w=32&p=8096.

24. Tapia, *Beyond the Threshold*, 38.

25. Walsh, *Opus Dei*, 8-9, 120.

26. John Roche, "The Inner World of Opus Dei," http://odan.org.

27. Walsh, *Opus Dei*, 115, 119-120.

28. Ibid., 121; Tapia, *Beyond the Threshold*, 103.

29. Tapia, *Beyond the Threshold*, 205-206.

30. Walsh, *Opus Dei*, 73-74.

31. Ibid., 114-115.

32. Ibid., 173; Tapia, *Beyond the Threshold*, 36-37; Morales, odan.org.

33. "Excerpts from *Cronica*, Opus Dei's Secret, Internal Magazine," ODAN newsletter vol. 10, no. 4 (2000), http://odan.org.

34. Tapia, *Beyond the Threshold*, 37.

35. Walsh, *Opus Dei*, 116.

36. Tapia, *Beyond the Threshold*, 276-277, 296.

37. Ibid., 353-359; "Letter to the Pope," http://odan.org.

38. NPR Evening Edition, October 6, 2002.

39. See http://www.space.com/php/popup/promo/freeupdate/noad_freeupdate_011002.php.

REFLECTIONS

1. Ernest Becker, *The Denial of Death* (New York: Free Press Paperbacks, 1997), 5-6.

2. Joseph Campbell, *The Hero with a Thousand Faces* (Princeton, N.J.: Princeton University Press, 1968), 9.

3. Campbell, *Hero*, 3.

4. Ibid., 29.

5. Becker, *Denial of Death*, 29.

6. Campbell, *Hero*, 12.

7. Becker, *Denial of Death*, 64.

8. Joseph Campbell, Program 5, "Love and the Goddess," in *Joseph Campbell and the Power of Myth* [Video recording] (New York: Mystic Fire Video, 1988).

9. Osho, *The Mustard Seed: Commentaries on the Fifth Gospel of Saint Thomas* (Cologne: Rebel Publishing House, 1975), 17.

10. John W. Sewell, "The Da Vinci Phenomenon," http://www.explorefaith.org/daVinci/1.html#sewell.

11. Campbell, *Hero*, 16.

Bibliography

Augustine. *De Bono Coniugali; De Sancta Virgintat.* Translated by P .G. Walsh. New York: Oxford Press, 2001.

———. *Opus Imperfectum* 4,40, cited in Elaine Pagels. *Adam, Eve, and the Serpent.* New York: Random House, 1989.

Baigent, Michael, Richard Leigh, and Henry Lincoln. *Holy Blood, Holy Grail.* New York: Dell, 1983.

Baukham, Richard J. "2 Peter." In *The Oxford Companion to the Bible.*

Becker, Ernest. *The Denial of Death.* New York: Free Press Paperbacks, 1997.

Bock, Darrell L. *Breaking The Da Vinci Code: Answers to the Questions Everybody's Asking.* Nashville, Tenn.: Nelson Books, 2004.

Boussel, Patrice. *Leonardo Da Vinci.* New York: Konecy & Konecy, 1986-1992.

Bratcher, Robert G. "Translations: English Language." In *The Oxford Companion to the Bible.* New York: Oxford University Press, 1993.

Brooten, Bernadette J. "Jewish Women's History in the Roman Period: A Task for Christian Theology." *Harvard Theological Review* (1986).

———. *Women Leaders in the Ancient Synagogue.* Chico, Calif.: Scholars Press, 1982.

Brown, Dan. *The Da Vinci Code.* New York: Doubleday, 2003.

Brown, Peter. *The Body and Society: Men, Women and Sexual Renunciation in Early Christianity.* New York: Columbia University Press, 1988.

Bruce-Mitford, Miranda. *Illustrated Book of Signs & Symbols.* New York: DK Pub., Inc., 1996.

Burstein, Dan, ed. *Secrets of the Code: The Unauthorized Guide to the Mysteries Behind The Da Vinci Code.* New York: CDS Books, 2004.

Campbell, Joseph. *The Hero with a Thousand Faces.* Princeton, N.J.: Princeton University Press, 1968.

———. Program 5, "Love and the Goddess." In *Joseph Campbell and the Power of Myth* [Video record ing]. New York: Mystic Fire Video, 1988.

Conversations with Mgr. Escrivá de Balaguer. Dublin: Scepter Books, 1969.

Cooper, Margaret. *The Inventions of Leonardo.* New York: Macmillan, 1965.

Cowen, Painton. *Rose Windows.* San Francisco: Chronicle Books, 1979.

Crockett, James Underwood. *Roses.* New York: Time-Life Books, 1971.

Crombie, Deborah. *A Finer End.* New York: Bantam Books, 2001.

Crossan, John Dominic. *The Birth of Christianity: Discovering What Happened in the Years Immediately After the Execution of Jesus.* San Francisco: HarperSanFrancisco, 1989.

———. *The Historical Jesus: The Life of a Mediterranean Jewish Peasant.* San Francisco: HarperSanFrancisco, 1992.

Davies, Stevan L. *The Gospel of Thomas and Christian Wisdom.* New York: The Seabury Press, 1983.

Drijvers, Jan Willem. *Helena Augusta: The Mother of Constantine the Great and the Legends of her Finding of the True Cross.* Leiden and New York: E.J. Brill, 1993.

Eisenman, Robert. *The Dead Sea Scrolls and the First Christians.* Shaftsbury: Element, 1996.

Eisler, Riane. *The Chalice and the Blade: Our History, Our Future.* San Francisco: Harper and Row, 1987.

Frankiel, Tamar. *The Voice of Sarah: Feminine Spirituality and Traditional Judaism.* San Francisco: Harper, 1990.

Fraser, James George. *The Golden Bough*. New York: Macmillan, 1923.

Frymer-Kensky, Tikva. *In the Wake of the Goddess*. New York: Macmillan, 1992.

Funk, Robert W., Roy W. Hoover, and the Jesus Seminar. *The Five Gospels: The Search for the Authentic Words of Jesus*. New York: Macmillan, 1993.

Godwin, Malcolm. *The Holy Grail. Its Origins, Secrets and Meaning Revealed*. New York: Barnes & Noble, 1998.

Goodstein, Laurie. "Defenders of Christianity Rebut 'The Da Vinci Code.'" *New York Times*, 27 April 2004.

Gordon, Robert P. "Translations: Ancient Languages." In *The Oxford Companion to the Bible*. New York: Oxford University Press, 1993.

Graham Brock, Ann. *Mary Magdalene, the First Apostle: The Struggle for Authority*. Cambridge, Mass.: Harvard Theological Studies, 2003.

Graves, Robert and Raphael Patai. *Hebrew Myths*. New York: Doubleday, 1914.

Gruger, Mayer I. "The Status of Women in Ancient Judaism." In Jacob Neusner, ed., *Judaism in Late Antiquity*, Part 3, vol. 2. Leiden and New York: E.J. Brill, 1995.

Guébin, Pascal and Henri Maisonneuve. *Histoire Albigeoise*. Paris: Librairie Philosophique J. Vrin, 1951.

Haskins, Susan. *Mary Magdalene: Myth and Metaphor*. New York: Harcourt Brace & Co., 1993.

Hinson, E. Glenn. *The Early Church: Origins to the Dawn of the Middle Ages*. Nashville, Tenn.: Abingdon Press, 1996.

Holy Bible: Containing the Old and New Testament, New Revised Standard Version. Grand Rapids, Mich.: Zondervan Publishing House, 1989.

Hooker, Morna D. "Mark, The Gospel According to." In *The Oxford Companion to the Bible*. New York: Oxford University Press, 1993.

Ignatius. *Letter to Polycarp* 5.2. cited in Peter Brown, *The Body and Society*.

Ilan, Tal. "Notes on the Distribution of Jewish Women's Names in Palestine in the Second Temple and Mishnaic Periods." *Journal of Jewish Studies*, 1989.

———." Women's Studies and Jewish Studies—When and Where do They Meet?" *Jewish Studies Quarterly* 3:2 (1995).

Josephus, Flavius. *The Wars of the Jews*. Translated by William Whiston. New York: E.P. Dutton, 1920.

Josephus. *Antiquities*.

Justin Martyr. *Dialogue with Trypho*. Translated by A. Lukyn Williams. London: Macmillan, 1930.

King, Karen L. *The Gospel of Mary of Magdala: Jesus and the First Woman Apostle*. Santa Rosa, Calif.: Polebridge Press, 2003.

Koester, Helmut. *Ancient Christian Gospels: Their History and Development*. London: SCM Press; Philadelphia: Trinity Press International, 1990.

Leloup, Jean-Yves. *The Gospel of Mary*. Rochester, Vt..: Inner Traditions International, 2002.

Liungman, Carl G. *Dictionary of Symbols*. New York and London: W.W. Norton & Co., 1991.

Livio, Mario. *The Golden Ratio: The Story of Phi, The World's Most Astonishing Number*. New York: Broadway Books, 2002.

Loomis, Roger Sherman. *The Grail: From Celtic Myth to Christian Symbols*. New York: Columbia University Press, 1963.

Lord, Albert Bates. *The Singer of Tales*. New York: Atheneum, 1968. Originally published as *Harvard Studies in Comparative Literature*, 24. Cambridge, Mass.: Harvard University Press, 1960.

McMullen, Roy. *Mona Lisa: The Picture and the Myth*. Boston: Houghton Mifflin Co., 1975.

Marani, Pietro C. *Leonardo Da Vinci: The Complete Paintings*. New York: Harry N. Abrams, 2000.

Marjanen, Antti. *The Women Jesus Loved: Mary Magdalene in the Nag Hammadi Library and Related Documents*. Leiden, New York, Köln: E. J. Brill, 1996.

Matthews, John. *The Grail: Quest for the Eternal*. New York: Crossroad, 1981.

Mellaart, James. *Çatal Hüyük*. New York: Thames and Hudson, 1967.

Metzger, Bruce M., and Michael D. Coogan, editors. *The Oxford Companion to the Bible*. New York and Oxford: Oxford University Press, 1993.

Meyer, Marvin W. *The Ancient Mysteries: A Source Book: Sacred Texts of the Mystery Religions of the Ancient Mediterranean*. Philadelphia: University of Pennsylvania Press, 1999.

Miller, Stephen M. and Robert V. Huber. *The Bible: A History: The Making and Impact of the Bible*. Intercourse, Pa.: Good Books, 2004.

National Public Radio Weekend Edition. Interview with Alberto Moncada, October 6, 2002.

Osho. *The Mustard Seed: Commentaries on the Fifth Gospel of Saint Thomas*. Cologne: Rebel Publishing House, 1975.

Pagels, Elaine. *Adam, Eve, and the Serpent*. New York: Random House, 1989.

———. *The Gnostic Gospels*. New York: Random House, 1989.

———."What Was Lost Is Found: A Wider View of Christianity and Its Roots." Interview in Dan Burstein, ed., *Secrets of the Code: The Unauthorized Guide to the Mysteries Behind The Da Vinci Code*. New York: CDS Books, 2004.

Phillips, Graham. *The Chalice of Magdalene: The Search for the Cup That Held the Blood of Christ*. Rochester, Vt.: Bear & Co., 2004.

Picknett, Lynn and Clive Prince. *The Templar Revelation: Secret Guardians of the True Identity of Christ*. New York: Simon & Schuster, 1997.

———. *Turin Shroud—In Whose Image?* London: Bloomsbury, 1994.

Pliny. *Natural History*, cited in Peter Brown. *The Body and Society*.

Pritchard, James B., ed. *The Times Atlas of the Bible: The Land, Events, and People of the World's Most Famous Book*. New York: Crescent Books, 1987.

Read, Piers Paul. *The Templars*. New York: St. Martin's Press, 2000.

Richter, Jean Paul. *The Notebooks of Leonardo Da Vinci: Compiled and Edited from the Original Manuscripts*. New York: Dover Publications, 1976.

Robinson, James M., ed. *The Nag Hammadi Library in English*. San Francisco: Harper & Row, 1988.

Sanders, E. P. *The Historical Figure of Jesus*. London: Penguin, 1993.

Schaberg, Jane. "Luke." In Carol A. Newsom and Sharon H. Ringe, eds., *The Women's Bible Commentary*. Louisville, Ky.: Westminster, 1992.

Schüssler Fiorenza, Elizabeth. *In Memory of Her: A Feminist Theological Reconstruction of Christian Origins*. New York: Crossroad, 1983.

Schwartz, Lillian. *The Computer Artist's Handbook*. New York: W. W. Norton & Co. Inc., 1992.

Shugarts, David A. "The Plot Holes and Intriguing Details of *The Da Vinci Code*." In *Secrets of the Code: The Unauthorized Guide to the Mysteries Behind The Da Vinci Code*. New York: CDS Books, 2004.

Starbird, Margaret. *The Woman with the Alabaster Jar: Mary Magdalene and the Holy Grail.* Rochester, Vt.: Bear & Co., 1993.

Stone, Merlin. *When God Was a Woman.* New York: Dial Press, 1976.

Tapia, Maria Del Carmen. *Beyond the Threshold: A Life in Opus Dei.* New York: Continuum, 1997.

Teissen, Gerd and Annette Merz. *The Historical Jesus: A Comprehensive Guide.* Minneapolis: Fortress Press, 1998.

Tertullian. *De Culta Feminarum*, I, 12, quoted in Elaine Pagels. *Adam, Eve, and the Serpent.*

———. *De Praescriptione Haereticorum.* Tübingen: J.C.B. Mohr, 1910.

Thompson, Mary R. *Mary of Magdala: Apostle and Leader.* New York and Mahway, N.J.: Paulist, 1995.

Tov, Emanuel. "Manuscripts: Hebrew Bible." In *The Oxford Companion to the Bible.* New York: Oxford University Press, 1993.

Tresemer, David and Laura-Lea Cannon. "Preface: Who Is Mary Magdalene?" In Jean-Yves Leloup, *The Gospel of Mary.*

Turner, A. Richard. *Inventing Leonardo.* New York: Alfred A. Knopf, 1993.

Vermes, Geza. *Jesus the Jew.* Philadelphia: Fortress Press, 1981.

Walsh, Michael. *Opus Dei: An Investigation into the Secret Society Struggling for Power Within the Roman Catholic Church.* San Francisco: HarperSanFrancisco, 1992.

Whiting, Roger. *Leonardo: A Portrait of the Renaissance Man.* New York: Knickerbocker Press, 1992.

William of Puylaurens. *The Chronicle of William of Puylaurens: The Albigensians and Its Aftermath.* Translated by W.A. and M.D. Sibly. Rochester, N.Y.: Boydill Press, 2003.

Wright, Nicholas Thomas. *The New Testament and the People of God.* Minneapolis: Fortress Press, 1992.

Websites

http://arxiv.org/abs/physics/0302089

http://britannia.com/history/Arthur/marian.html

http://catholic.com/library/Birth_Control.asp

http://earlychristianwritings.com/text/secretmark.html

http://explorefaith.org/daVinci/1.html#sewell

http://freemasonrywatch.org/prioryofsion.html

http://istartemple.org/sacredIshtar.html

http://members.aol.com/egyptart/osi.html

http://odan.org

http://opusdei.com/art.php?w=328p=8096

http://orobtempli.org/priory-of-sion.html

http://pantheon.org/articles/a/attis.html; homepage.mac.com/cparada/GML/Attis.html

http://priory-of-sion.com

http://shropshire-promotions.co.uk/shropshire%20Secrets/SS-5.html

http://sobek.Colorado.edu/LAB/GODS/osiris.html; members.aol.com/egyptart/osi.html pantheon.org/articles/o/osiris.html

http://www.ccel.org/fathers/NPNF2-06/treatise/jovinan1.htm

http://www.ccel.org/j/josephus/works/JOSEPHUS.HTM

http://www.ctio.noao.edu/instrument/ir_instruments/osiris2soar/tale.html

http://www.newadvent.org/fathers.3001.htm

http://www.sacred-texts.com/jud/josephus/#woj

http://www.space.com/php/popup/promo/freeupdate/noad_freeupdate_011002.php

http://www.tarot-decks.com/tarotarticle.htm

http://www.users.global.net.co.uk/~pardos/PopeJoanHome.html

From the Author

This project was the joint effort of many wonderful people, and I would like to thank those who made it possible.

At *Barnes & Noble*, I want to give a special thanks to Jeanette Limondjian who visualized and believed in the project and in us, to Rachel Federman for her insight, patience, and careful editing, and to Peter Norton for his artistic input.

At *The Book Laboratory*, a thanks goes to Philip Dunn, without whom the project would not have been possible, Manuela Roosevelt, Jeannine Jourdan, Amy Ray, Anila Manning, Barbara Patterson, and, most of all, Priya Hemenway, whose patience and perseverance have been an inspiration to us all.

I also want to thank the wonderful librarians who have been so helpful with the research for this book. Thanks goes to the Fairfax branch of the Marin Public Library and to the staff of the Graduate Theological Union library, particularly to Mary Moore at the San Anselmo branch.

I extend a special thanks to one of my professors at the Graduate Theological Union, Ingrid Kitzberger, who through her class "Jesus and Women," taught me to read the Bible with new eyes.

Finally I want to thank all my friends who have supported and encouraged me when things got difficult. I couldn't have done it without any of you.

—*Sangeet Duchane*

Art Acknowledgements

INTRODUCTION

6: Manchester City Art Galleries, Manchester, England.

CHAPTER ONE

12: Uffizi Gallery, Florence;13: Musee Conde, Chantilly; 14t: Bibliothèque Nationale, Paris; 14b: Convent of San Marco, Florence; 15: Convent of San Marco, Florence; 16: Chora Church, Istanbul; 17: AKG, London; 19: Palazzo Pitti, Florence; 20t: National Gallery, London; 20b: AKG, London; 21: Mary Evans Picture Library; 23: Convent of San Marco, Florence; 24: The Art Archive; 25: Convent of San Marco, Florence; 26: San Francesco, Arezzo, Italy; 27: Uffizi Gallery, Florence; 28: Musée Rodin, Paris; 29: Bibliothèque Nationale, Paris.

CHAPTER TWO

30: Hermitage, St. Petersburg; 32: National Library, Paris; 33t: Victoria & Albert Museum, London; 33b: Thyssen-Bornemisza Collection, Lugano, Italy; 34: Pompeii, Italy; 35: Prieure Museum, France; 36: Convent of San Marco, Florence; 37: Icon Museum, Recklinghausen, Germany; 38: Municipal Library, Besancon, France; 39: Portinari Salviati Palace, Florence; 40: Pierpont Morgan Library, New York; 41: Pierpont Morgan Library, New York; 42: National Gallery, London; 43: St. Godehard Church, Hildesheim, Germany; 44: National Gallery, Prague; 47: National Gallery, London; 48: Central Library, Lucerne, Switzerland; 49: Birmingham Museum and Art Gallery, Birmingham.

CHAPTER THREE

50: Holy Transfiguration Monastery, Brookline, MA; 53: Birmingham Museum and Art Gallery, Birmingham; 54: Israel Department of Antiquities and Museums, Jerusalem; 55t: Vatican Museums, Vatican City, Rome; 55b: Museo de Santa Cruz, Toledo, Spain; 56: Staatliche Museum, Berlin; 58: Mary Evans Picture Library; 60: *Book of Wonders* by David Jors, 16th century; 61: Brancacci Chapel, Santa Maria del Carmine, Florence, Italy; 63: Museo del Prado, Madrid; 64: Castle de Wijenburgh, Echteld, Netherlands; 65: Cathedral of the Annunciation, Moscow; 66: National Gallery of Art, Washington, D.C.

CHAPTER FOUR

68: Galleria degli Uffizi, Florence; 69: Kunsthistorisches Museum, Vienna; 70: Lower Saxony Museum, Hannover; 71: Museo di San Marco, Florence; 72: Capitoline Museum, Rome; 73t: Sistine Chapel, Vatican City; 73b: Musée d'Unterlinden, Colmar, France; 74: Kunsthistorisches Museum, Vienna, Austria; 75: Israel Department of Antiquities and Museums, Jerusalem; 76: Paul Saivets; 77: Convent of San Marco, Florence; 79: Sistine Chapel, Vatican, Rome; 80: The Wallace Collection, Manchester; 81t: Bridgeman Art Library; 81b: Pierpont Morgan Library, New York; 82: Convent of San Marco, Florence, Italy; 83: Pinacoteca, Vatican Museums, Vatican City; 84: Museo del Prado, Madrid; 85: Monastery of St. Nicholas, Moscow; 86: British Museum, London; 88: Santa Croce, Florence; 89: Aghiosminas, Heraklia, Crete; 90: Tretyakov Gallery, Moscow; 91: Monastery of St. Catherine, Sinai.

CHAPTER FIVE

94: Palazzo Pitti, Florence; 95t: Natural History Museum, London; 95b: Ice Age Art exhibition catalog by Alexander Marshack; 96: Zev Radovan, Jerusalem; 97: Mary Evans Picture Library; 98t: Musée du Louvre, Paris; 98b: Zev Radovan, Jerusalem; 99: Rijksmuseum, Amsterdam; 100t: Uffizi Gallery, Florence; 100b: Vatican Museums, Rome; 101: Giovanni Dagli Orti; 102: Vatican Museums, Rome; 104: National Gallery, London; 105: British Museum, London; 107: Bibliothèque Nationale, Paris; 108: Mary Evans Picture Library.

CHAPTER SIX

110: Private Collection; 112: Pitti, Palatine Gallery; 113: Grand Lodge of Free & Accepted Masons of Japan, Tokyo; 114t: Universitatsbibliothek Heidelberg; 114b: Hannah Firmin; 115: F.H. Round; 116: Bruce Dale; 117: Mary Evans Picture Library, London; 120: Matthew Weinreb; 121t: Musée du Louvre, Paris; 121b: Scarlet Berner; 123: Museo e Gallerie Nazionali di Capodimonte, Naples.

CHAPTER SEVEN

126: Stiftsbibliothek in Kremsmunster; 127: Bibliothèque Municipale, Amiens; 134: Private Collection ; 135: Farleigh House, Hampshire, England; 137: Bridgeman Art Library.

CHAPTER EIGHT

138: National Gallery, London; 139: Jean Edelstein; 140: National Gallery, London; 141: Jean-Loup Charmet; 142: Museo del Prado, Madrid; 145: British Library, London; 147b: Dorling Kindersley; 149: National Gallery, Prague; 151: Parish church, Tiefenbronn; 152t: Chateau de Versailles, France; 152b: Mary Evans Picture Library, London; 153: Birney Lettick; 154: British Library London; 155: Cathedral of St. John the Baptist, Turin, Italy.

CHAPTER NINE

156: Private Collection ; 157t: Metropolitan Museum of Art; 157b: Kunsthistorisches Museum, Vienna; 158: Arthur Rackham; 159: British Library, London; 160: Tate Gallery, London England; 162t: Schatzkammer, Munich; 162b: Bibliothèque Nationale, Paris; 164: Private Collection; 166: Bibliothèque de l'Arsenal, Paris; 167t: Dumbarton Oaks, Washington, D.C.; 167b: Caesarea Museum, Caesarea; 168: Delaware Art Museum; 169: Israel Department of Antiquities and Museums, Jerusalem.

CHAPTER TEN

172: Royal Liberty, Windsor, England; 173: Erich Lessing; 175: Musée du Louvre, Paris; 176: Musée du Louvre, Paris, France; 177: National Gallery, London; 178t: Institute de France, Paris; 178b: Galleria dell' Accademia, Venice; 179: British Museum, London; 182: Santa Maria della Grazie in Milan, Italy; 184: Accademia, Venice; 185t: Musée du Louvre, Paris; 185b: Galleria degli Uffizi, Florence; 187: Windsor Castle, Royal Library, London; 188: Musée du Louvre, Paris; 189: Musée du Louvre, Paris; 190: Bibliothèque Reale, Turin.

CHAPTER ELEVEN

194: Pinacoteca, Vatican Museums, Vatican City, Rome; 199: Santa Maria della Vittoria, Rome; 200: Scala Istituto Fotografico Editoriale, Florence; 201: Roudnice Lobkowicz Collection, Nelahozeves Castle, Czech Republic; 205t: Musée du Louvre, Paris; 205b: Biblioteca Nazionale Centrale, Florence; 207: Angela Heuser.

CHAPTER TWELVE

208: Diede von Schawen; 209b: Richard L'Anson; 210t: Robert Harding Picture Library ; 210b: Dorling Kindersley; 211: Mary Evans Picture Library, London; 212b: Patrick Thurston; 214: Bridgeman Art Library; 215b: British Library, London; 216: David Henry, www.davidphenry.com; 217: David Henry, www.davidphenry.com.

REFLECTIONS

218: Tate Gallery, London; 219: Dundee Art Gallery, Scottland; 220t: Bibliothèque Nationale, Paris; 220b: Arthur Rackham; 221: George Henry and EA Hornel; 222: Birmingham Museum and Art Gallery, England; 223: Tate Gallery, London; 224: Shelly & Donald Rubin Collection; 225: Eric Gill; 226: Napoli, Museo di San Martino; 227: Musee de l'Ermitage, St. Petersbourg; 228: Collection of the New York Historical Society; 229: Russell-Cotes Art Gallery and Museum, East Cliff, Bournemouth, England.

Index

K–8

6·11

Pam Allyn's Best Books for Boys

How to Engage Boys in Reading in Ways That Will Change Their Lives

SCHOLASTIC

New York • Toronto • London • Auckland • Sydney
Mexico City • New Delhi • Hong Kong • Buenos Aires

For Jim

And for Cindy and Lou Allyn,

who raised a boy whose love of reading was the reason
I fell in love with him in the first place

Cover Designer: Maria Lilja
Acquiring Editor: Lois Bridges
Copy/Production Editor: Danny Miller
Interior Designer: Sarah Morrow

Printed in the U.S.A.
ISBN: 978-0-545-20455-2

1 2 3 4 5 6 7 8 9 10 23 17 16 15 14 13 12 11

Table of Contents

Acknowledgments

Thanks to Jen Estrada for her brilliance and sparkle with children and adults. Her luminous companionship along these pathways to our vision for global literacy has been indispensable. Her contributions are vital and indispensable to this book.

Thanks to Flynn Berry, lovely and wise, who graces these pages with her care and who graces my life with her spirit.

Lois Bridges, my inspiration, my beloved friend, you are all about every child, and you believe in the power of words. You make us all believe in the goodness of the world.

Thank you to all my wonderful colleagues at LitLife and LitWorld, and to Lisa DiMona for your care for all our words. Your commitment to children and to the purpose of this work is extraordinary. Thank you as always to our dream guy, Danny Miller, who champions the words, the work, the life of every child as he makes every sentence shine. And a special thanks to Rebekah Coleman whose blessings are many, on and off the page.

Much appreciation to everyone at Scholastic: Maria Lilja, Sarah Morrow, Virginia Dooley, Eileen Hillebrand, and Patrick Daley. From the smallest details to the biggest vision, you all, each and every one of you, are a beacon of light for what teachers and children most hope for and love most. I love being part of the Scholastic community and I celebrate the credo! Thank you, Dick Robinson, for your child-centered vision.

Thanks to Jeannie Blaustein and Peter Bokor, and Lauren and Paul Blum, miraculous friends who cause miracles to happen.

Thank you to Sue Meigs, whose love for the boys of Children's Village is beyond compare, and who is my dear friend and lifelong partner in the passion that is our shared vision of Books for Boys. And to Joanne Levine, Nancy Kliot and Nicole Clark for your leadership of our LitWorld reading initiative FLY, which helps so many boys learn, word by word, that they, too, can construct meaning on the page.

Thanks to Elizabeth Fernandez, who has been my forever compatriot in this journey of friendship, teaching, and the lives of boys as readers.

Thanks to Jeremy Kohomban, wise and inspiring mentor and dear friend, and the amazing team at Children's Village, including Candy Fitts, Erica Mason, Linda Stutz, and Tonyna McGhee for all you do for the boys.

Thanks to Sandy and Shelly Mallah for your extraordinary devotion, professionally and personally, to the boys of Children's Village and for making a safe haven for these precious boys both inside and outside the classroom.

My parents started me off at a very young age by introducing me to Children's Village and taught me the gifts the boys have brought to our lives. They were the first contributors to the glimmering sparkle that became Books for Boys. My husband, Jim, and I have the best girls of all time, Katie and Charlotte. Thank you, my dearest young women for your time and love for the boys and for your wisdom and inner beauty. Katie and Charlotte have spent many years at Children's Village with me reading to and with the best boys in the world. Much gratitude to these girls and these boys whom I love so much, always and always.

Walking Between the Towers

When I first met Whalon, he was sitting at the far back seat in his classroom with his head down on the desk.

And then Whalon and I had our first conversation. He was seventeen and had been in and out of foster care his whole life. On that day, I read him a Langston Hughes poem. *Down on Lenox Avenue the other night By the pale dull pallor of an old gaslight.* He smiled. His face was beautiful, and oh so young. He said: "That reminds me of a song I like to sing. That song reminds me of my mother." When I looked up from my reading, he was crying. I met Whalon ten years ago when, supported by extraordinary volunteers, I started Books for Boys, a program to bring books to the boys who were part of New York City's foster care program. Books for Boys began simply, with cardboard boxes of donated books, but it ultimately became transforming for me. I immersed myself in the world of boys and reading. I saw hundreds of children enter the program completely alienated from reading, feeling it was not something that belonged to them.

These boys had been almost systematically excluded from the culture of literacy. But as the years have unfolded, and I launched my national initiative LitLife and eventually my global initiative LitWorld, both designed to improve and enhance the reading experience in school for children of all ages and in all different kinds of settings and schools—rural, suburban and urban, public, charter and private—I learned that on a wider level, at every socioeconomic level, a similar phenomenon affects boys across the country and even across the world. The question is: Why are over 300,000 boys dropping out of high school each year? Why are 93 percent of young people in our prison system young men? Why do illiteracy rates correlate with the risk of a jail sentence later in adolescence, making it twice as likely for nonreaders to be incarcerated? And even in our highest performing schools, parents and teachers worry that the boys are the ones who seem less likely to want to read on their own or outside of school. The 2010 Kids and Family Reading Report sponsored by Scholastic reports that "only 39 percent of boys say reading books for fun is extremely or very important versus 62 percent of girls."

My work alongside teachers in schools across the country and the globe has taught me that simple changes in what we provide for boys and how we talk with them about the choices they make as readers can and will have profound impact on the outcomes we want for all readers.

Simply put, in many cases we are not giving boys the books they want to read. We are not giving them enough time to read them. This book advocates what boys of all ages tell me: we must give them choices in their reading lives and make the classroom an opportunity for readers at different levels and with a variety of reading interests to thrive.

The author Eudora Welty said: "All serious daring starts from within." I think we don't share this wise advice often enough with boys. They are made to feel as if all daring comes from taking a physical risk. Delving into a new book or exploring an idea through a reading journey is also a way of expressing one's sense of daring and building one's sense of self.

In the great picture book and true story by Mordicai Gerstein, *The Man Who Walked Between the Towers*, the performance artist Philippe Petit practices for years to walk on a tightrope wire between the two World Trade Towers. "He looked not at the towers but at the space between them and thought, what a wonderful place to stretch a rope."

Reading can feel as risky as walking a tightrope even if it doesn't look nearly as daring. It can be so public in the classroom that a boy who wants to hide his vulnerability might prefer resistance to failing in front of his peers. This book is about fortifying our teaching so that our boys see the space between the towers and say, "What a wonderful place to stretch a rope."

In this book, I will share with you the critical elements for helping boys build confidence, feel like contributing members of a reading world, and stretch the rope so that they can make progress in leaps and bounds.

And I will share with you my top reading lists for your boys, organized according to the themes boys themselves have told us they like best.

Let's cultivate a culture of literacy that is welcoming for boys. Being a reader comes with behavioral expectations that often feel exclusionary. Let's change those expectations:

let's value not just what boys want to read, but also where and how. There are concrete ways to make the act of reading appealing to boys. We can show the many reasons why people read: To laugh. To discover. To research, wonder, and imagine. We can help a boy find his own particular areas of interest, those ideas or topics or stories that capture his attention fully and draw him into books. We can create a reading environment that is tailored to him, whether that means through solitude or companionship, active playful reading or reading during quiet times on car trips or on a train. Boys are often drawn to reading for purpose, and all too often reading can seem intimidating in its vast open-endedness. We can create clubs and collaborations; opportunities to share ideas and thinking and titles. We can give reading a shape with which all boys can identify.

All of us, but it seems boys especially, are taught to dislike what we cannot do easily. To avoid that trap, let us balance challenge and comfort. Giving boys books at a variety of levels helps them to build a sturdy foundation so they feel safe in trying more challenging ones. It is also essential to value each book in and of itself, not just as a stepping stone to more challenging ones. Simple books are so often the most cherished. The brilliant author David Foster Wallace once said, "The truth is I don't think I've ever found anything as purely moving as the end of *The Velveteen Rabbit* when I first read it." We must be careful not to dismiss "easy" books, but instead, to celebrate and affirm boys' reading.

Again, as boys themselves have indicated, there is one wonderfully simple, essential way to make reading appealing to them: book choice. I will share a list of books I think are just amazing because I have seen them open the doors to literacy and to lifelong reading enjoyment for hundreds of boys. It is my intention for us to put them where boys can find them so we can create reading environments brimming with books that appeal to all readers.

At times, as I talk about boys and girls, this book may appear to veer into stereotype. While my goal is to avoid generalities, at the same time, I have seen differences in the way many boys and girls learn, differences we cannot ignore. True equality both in the school environment and in the workplace will come when we can embrace differences and affirm them, celebrate them, and move past them. By bringing this conversation into our homes and classrooms, we will also benefit the girls in our lives by exposing them to a more varied approach to learning and to the text choices they are all being offered in the classroom. Just as Title IX changed the landscape of girls' sports, we need a Title IX for the classroom to equalize the gender opportunities for all and ensure that boys and girls receive equitable treatment regarding how they are perceived as readers. Girls may love spiders but may have trouble finding the "just right" book because there isn't enough nonfiction in the classroom. Let this book prompt you to revisit your classroom offerings for all your students, not just the boys. Similarly, your boys may want to read books on ballet or fashion, and other interesting nonfiction topics. Make sure your classroom libraries reflect a wide diversity of topics, but also of genre. I hope this book will help us move in those directions.

The author Alfred Tatum, in his important writing about boys, has campaigned to help boys build a "reading lineage." I find this a very powerful call to action: that we as teachers help our boys see themselves as building a reading history for themselves. But I must caution that adults have not valued nearly enough what boys already love to read. I can't tell you how many boys and men will say to me that they "don't read" when in fact they are reading CONSTANTLY. We have to help our students to identify their own reading history as a lineage worth celebrating.

I am thinking of Sammy, age 8. He just loved the Bailey School Kids books. They were the first books he'd ever read that he felt success with. They are simple and straightforward, silly and fun. The language is direct and uncomplicated. He loved them. After he had read them all straight through (a breakthrough experience for him), he happened upon an anthology of those very same books. He excitedly showed his teacher, who said: "Sammy, you've already read these books! Choose something else." His face fell. I gently encouraged the teacher to allow Sammy to take that anthology as his reading choice. He was so proud he had read those books, and to have them in a thick anthology so he could carry around a big book would have meant so much to him. Additionally, rereading is a good thing for a struggling reader. One more sweep through the Bailey School Kids and Sammy would be an infinitely stronger reader! Luckily, the teacher was receptive to my perspective, and she handed that collection over to Sammy!

Later, she reported to me that Sammy was beaming for days carrying that heavy volume around! He was decidedly pleased with his special book and especially pleased that he wouldn't be intimidated by the length of pages or numbers of words . . . because he knew them well!

Every boy has a unique reading life and needs support in creating one. Let this book help you strengthen your own knowledge about boys and reading.

For many children, reading is a journey that requires a measure of courage and risk taking. It is also one of the most deeply satisfying and pleasurable of all human endeavors and inarguably one of the most profoundly useful. My mission is to help all children achieve not only functional literacy but transformational literacy, the kind of literacy that will allow them to learn something new every day, connect to all people everywhere, and to invent new ideas that could change the world. And in this process, they just may learn, through reading, how to be the kind of person they want to become.

Part 1

Why the Focus on Books for Boys?

It seems like every day there is a new article or study about how boys are failing or underperforming academically. But for those of us working with boys on a daily basis, this isn't news. Why is this happening?

One reason is our own preconceptions about boys and reading. Many people hold onto the notion that reading is a quiet, solitary activity involving a single person alone with a book or other printed text. That definition is too narrow to include many boys and ignores the changing landscape of words and text in the new millennium. We need to value the kinds of reading boys and girls are doing. Video and computer games, sports pages, magazines, comic books, and graphic novels all have countless words and opportunities for boys to practice and strengthen their reading skills.

In order to navigate successfully from a home page to various subpages, we need strong reading skills as well as the ability to focus on certain information over others and parse out the material relevant to our purposes. Even text messages have a place in the spectrum of literacy. They force us to convey meaning concisely, encouraging careful word choice. Being successful in this kind of literacy is valuable, increasingly so in the modern, interconnected world.

Let's take a closer look at the classroom. When children are learning to read, they are often asked to read aloud in front of their peers. For some, this is an intensely unpleasant experience. Their shortcomings and struggles feel magnified in the moment they are exposed to their peers. The stress of that experience can create a negative emotional reaction to reading that continues into adulthood, making reading a hated activity removed from how that person sees himself in a world where literacy is increasingly becoming a currency of its own. As David Von Drehle put it in a *Time Magazine* article, "In an economy increasingly geared toward processing information, an inability to read becomes an inability to earn." We must make the classroom an absolutely safe place for boys to read. Reading should not mean just reading aloud or reading in a round robin. Reading should mean reading as it is meant to be: independent reading that suits the boy at the level he is at, where he can make his own choices as to what he is going to read, and where he can choose books he loves; or reading in clubs and partnerships, where boys can talk about and laugh about and explore the books they read, together.

Research on Boys' School Success

There are so many statistics available on boys and school success. It can be daunting to put them together in a way that tells a story about how our boys are doing with reading. By streamlining these facts, we can see how we might improve the way we approach literacy for boys.

The Center on Educational Policy released a report in March 2010 titled, *Are There Differences in Achievement Between Boys and Girls?* The report revealed that in reading, girls outperformed boys in 2008 at the elementary, middle, and high school levels in every state where data could be collected. In some states, these gaps exceeded ten percentage points. The CEP asserts that based on this report a clear achievement gap exists, with higher percentages of girls than boys reaching basic, proficient, and advanced levels. The CEP feels that this is cause for concern and, based on the conversations I have had with teachers, parents, and caregivers who struggle to help the boys in their lives and classrooms achieve, I think we are all in agreement.

The standardized NAEP test, known as the nation's report card, indicates that by their senior year of high school, boys have fallen nearly 20 points behind their female peers in reading. According to an article by Peg Tyre published in *Newsweek* in 2005, 80 percent of high-school dropouts are boys and less than 45 percent of students enrolled in college are young men. A study by the National Endowment for the Arts showed that by 12th grade, boys score an average of 13 points lower than girls on reading proficiency tests. It is becoming the norm that fewer boys than girls take the SAT, apply to college, and earn college degrees.

These disparities begin in elementary school, where behaviors associated with the normal developmental phases of boys are sometimes misread as disorders. Boys are more than twice as likely than girls to be diagnosed with learning disabilities. In elementary school, boys are also twice as likely to be placed in special education classes than girls. Harvard psychologist William Pollack says, "More boys than girls are in special education classes. More boys than girls are prescribed mood-managing drugs. This suggests that today's schools are built for girls, and boys are becoming misfits."

This conception of boys is what is most concerning. It is not only the poor test scores that are so disturbing, but what they mean for the learning lives of our boys over time. Boys often report they don't like school, aren't passionate about learning or their education, and don't see themselves as readers or writers. The MetLife Survey of the American Teacher series reported in March 2010 that boys are more likely than girls to do just enough work to get by in school and boys are less likely than girls to be confident that they will achieve their goals for the future. Many boys are becoming disconnected from the classroom experience. One theory is that the increased emphasis on assessment and standardization in educational policy has created classrooms that no longer allow for the unique ways that boys learn. Anthony Rao, a noted behavioral psychologist, points out that most boys learn best with hands-on manipulation of objects and visual representations of concepts. Former U.S. Assistant Secretary of Elementary and Secondary Education Susan Neuman concurs, calling the recent CEP study a rallying cry for our boys' struggle. Neuman suggests that schools are not meeting the needs of young boys because of a curriculum that does not reflect their interests and classroom management that does not tolerate their learning styles.

The climate of educational policy has encouraged teachers to narrow their teaching and school administrators to narrow the options for curriculum innovation. This is all to the detriment of our boys. The focus on testing in academic learning has left less time for choice and more demand for conformity. What will help our boys become active learners and self-identified readers is a return to creative innovation and choice in the classroom. Let's pay attention to the way our children learn best, at home, at school, and in the world. Let's embrace their unique learning styles and let them inspire us to inform our teaching. Let's give our children options that intrigue them and tap into their natural curiosity. Together we can help every child feel empowered in the classroom and become engaged learners and readers throughout their lives.

Part 2

R-E-A-D, and Your Questions Answered

Reading helps boys connect their experiences with others' and begin to build a sense of the world. But how, exactly, can we make sure boys know that reading is for them? We want boys to feel that reading belongs to them. We want them to go at it with joy. How can we encourage them to read without turning it into an obligation? The READ model presents four essential elements to crafting a reading life: *Ritual, Environment, Access,* and *Dialogue*. Once these are in place, the stage is set for a lifelong love of reading.

R—Ritual

Rituals are the comforting, familiar routines and processes of our everyday lives. Rituals can help our children deal with big changes, like the end of one school year and the start of another. Rituals give life a sense of continuity.

Rituals around reading cultivate a love of books and language in even the youngest children. Begin each school day with a read aloud or independent reading time. We can create new rituals for resistant or struggling readers, no matter their age. We can begin now. It is never too late. Many boys come to our reading programs emergently literate at the ages of sixteen and seventeen. Even then, I begin the way I would with any younger child: with the read aloud and with simple texts that I read and reread each day I see them.

The first time I read *Where the Wild Things Are* to a boy named Daniel, a teenager, he said to me: "That's the first time anyone's ever done that for me before." In the classroom, be sure that your read alouds are not restricted to narratives or picture book stories but also include poetry and nonfiction, excerpts from funny sections of Web sites and magazines. Let the rituals we create show our students that we advocate for a varied and rich reading life, with all the different genres that brings.

E—Environment

Allow for spontaneity and whimsy often in a boy's reading life, perhaps from carrying a book to recess or clustering with a group of friends around a computer screen. At the same time, it is also essential to create a firmly identified physical space that is conducive to reading. Devoting a space to reading emphasizes its importance. Create a classroom library that is rich with variety in genre and also inventive in placement of print. Create baskets of books that the children in your classroom can create themselves, with themes and categories you might never have thought of on your own. When I ask boys and girls to create their own labels for categories of books, I am often enchanted and surprised by their responses. Everything from "worlds we've never seen" to "questions we have about life and nature" to "ugly pets" makes me smile and gets the boys over to those baskets more frequently.

Comfort is a key element in planning a reading environment, although we are not all comfortable with the same things. Some boys prefer to read standing up. In one friend's home, her nine-year-old son had devised what he called his reading counter. He used an upturned music stand anchored at a living room window. Shifting from leg to leg, he would read book after book, a basket of new reads and favorites within arm's reach. Occasionally he would stare out the window, a key element in his design. He told me that he loved to look out at his street and imagine the worlds and people that were in the stories he read.

Celebrate every boy's uniqueness by asking what matters most to him about his reading place. Then work together to create an area that suits him best. Consider lighting, any other (potentially competing) amusements in the area, temperature, noise, and whatever else matters. Lighting can be a bigger factor for children than for adults. Some prefer soft lamps, while others prefer to read in bright sunlight. You can organize your classroom in new and innovative ways based on the input of your students. Take a strong interest in what their thoughts are about how best to create a reading environment. Let them write about it independently, asking them: "How could we design this space so as to encourage you to be the most comfortable reader you can be?" (Younger children can draw their responses). For some boys, silence is essential, while for others soft music is welcome. Have your students share with you their favorite music they play at home. Bring this music into independent reading time either by having students use earphones or by sharing the music with the class, and have your students join you in the discovery question: "Is this music helping us read longer and stronger?" If you allow a boy to make the space his own, he will enjoy and use it. As he grows both physically and as a reader, his tastes and needs will shift. Honor this growth by asking him to reevaluate his reading environment from time to time. Help him make his reading space grow as his reading self grows. Even if you have a large and crowded classroom, you can meet the needs of all your students by having them join you in this inquiry and having them notice their own differences and similarities from each other. Have them record their changing reading preferences throughout the year in their readers' notebooks or on sticky notes you post together on a wall in the classroom. (You might create a title or banner, such as: "Our Changing Reading Lives.") Let the sense of a changing self as reader be a strong impetus for the boys in your classroom to become more reflective and more empowered in how they fashion a reading environment that will really work for them and will honor their friends' needs as well.

A—Access

Surround boys with books and all kinds of text. Keep books in places that allow for spontaneous reading. Baskets of books, boys' own stories, as well as magazines should be easily accessible. Don't forget about newspapers, instruction manuals, and even baseball cards, iPads, computers. Easy access to them all should be highly valued in your rooms, and where, when, and how students access them should also make sense.

Access is about not just having a lot of books, but having the right ones. The best way to do this is to pay close attention to what boys say they like. Instead of trying to make a boy interested in certain books, boys (and girls) should have access to a wide variety of different genres, authors, and stories. Check your collection; there should be at least 30 percent nonfiction books, 30 percent poetry, and 40 percent fiction. There should be books written by both men and women. There should be books on topics ranging from fashion to sharks. Access is also about levels. Boys who are struggling readers in eighth grade need to be offered access to books that are truly at their reading levels. If they are reading at an emergent level, and you want them to be familiar with great fiction that is mandatory or suggested reading for older boys, you can read it aloud to them. For their independent reading, they need books at their independent reading levels—and they need not to be embarrassed to read them.

I once entered a classroom and saw a very unhappy eight-year-old boy reading Junie B. Jones. He looked miserable. Now, I love Junie B. Jones, but this reader did not look happy about this situation. I asked him what was going on, and he said: "Because this is my level, I always have to read this same book, and I don't want to read books about girls! I don't even want to read a book with chapters in it!" My heart broke for him. If his library had been stocked with books at every level in every genre, his choices would have been greater, and he would have been hooked. He knew exactly what wasn't working. The problem was no one was asking him what choices he would have made for himself as a reader.

D—Dialogue

Dialogue is key to cultivating a love of books and reading in all children, especially those who are resistant to making reading a part of their own identity. Active, thoughtful dialogue makes the reading experience social and interactive. It can take a variety of forms: between two people, in small or large groups, with pen pals or a book club. Genuine, open communication is a treasure between teacher and student. Literature gives us all an opportunity to think about the world that we live in and react to it in a deeply personal way. Talking to boys about their reactions to a text creates moments for boys to express their feelings in ways that feel safe and nonthreatening.

Pay attention to the quirky things boys say about the books and stories they read. What do they notice? Who do they identify with in the story? Celebrate their unique perspectives by asking questions that only they can answer. You could ask, "How do you feel about that?" or "What would you have done if you were that character?" It is fascinating to explore these avenues of thought with boys of any age. Their ideas will often surprise you and it is such a wonderful way to learn more about every child. These conversations are also an opportunity for you to share a part of yourself with boys. Dialogue around literature can be a way to share values, impart wisdom, open up about life experiences, and explore our beliefs and hopes.

Recently, I held panel discussions on the subject of boys and reading for boys in schools around the country. I asked them what criteria they used to judge their success as readers. They all said: "How many words or pages we could read!" Let's not underestimate the fun of talking about how much we've read or how many minutes we were able to read yesterday. I also asked the boys: "How do you select books?" They shocked the audience when they all agreed they tend to steer clear of "those books with medals," instead choosing books with "weird covers," and "definitely dragons," and "some kind of great art on the front." These are topics worthy of discussion; your open inquiry with your students will enable them to tell the truth as readers and for you to then stock the reading environment with the kinds of texts that will compel them to get to school early.

Questions and Answers

1. What should reading look like?

Let's take a critical look at the ways we are affirming how and where people read. For example, my husband prefers to read at the kitchen table. He likes to read in an upright position, usually poring over a biography or history. I, on the other hand, like to lounge on the couch. And I prefer to read fiction. The optimal environment would be a place that meets both our needs, a non-judging environment where how we read and what we read are supported. But it's clear enough to me that as teachers and parents we become very rigid and narrow about what we think reading "looks like" and what doesn't. Let's become more flexible and more open in complimenting readers who stand when they read, or switch positions routinely, or like to read with music. Our environments must be flexible and fluid enough so that all readers find a welcome place, not just physically but also emotionally.

2. How can we make boys more comfortable with reading?

The most important thing is to foster a sense of belonging. One way to do this is to choose authors and characters with whom boys identify. A boy who loves the American

Northwest might feel a kinship with Jack London. A boy who is always getting into trouble will, no doubt, appreciate Calvin, of *Calvin and Hobbes*. We must be sure to include male protagonists both in the picture books we select as well as the chapter books featured in our classrooms and in our homes. Often, though not always, boys gravitate more towards boy characters, just as girls tend to gravitate towards girls. This is obviously not a hard and fast rule, and if one of your male students is reading a lot of books with female protagonists and vice versa, this is wonderful! We must make a boy who wants very much to read *Angelina Ballerina* feel as comfortable doing so as a girl who makes that choice. A sense of belonging does not have to fall along gender lines. We don't want to limit what children read, but instead strive to stock our classroom libraries with an expansive awareness and acceptance of the books all children will love. We must serve as reading role models for our boys, whether we are male or female, and make them comfortable with the choices they make or the levels at which they read. As teachers, we tend to read chapter books to older students even though we may have many struggling readers in our rooms. Model that you love Dr. Seuss and Shel Silverstein, two authors who appeal to early readers and also are ironic and brilliant enough to appeal to older boys, by reading those texts aloud to your students. Showing you value books even when they are short and sweet will help your boys feel more of a sense of belonging in the room, no matter what they have selected to read. Tell how E. B. White and J. K. Rowling chose not to use their first names so that both boys and girls would feel comfortable picking up their books and how in this era we can really honor them by making it acceptable and comfortable for boys and girls to read what they want without any fear of being made fun of for their choice.

3. What should boys read?

I have received many emails and inquiries from parents and teachers who say: "My son/student is not reading." And when I ask boys what they are reading, they will often say "Nothing." But when I dig deeper, and ask the child to tell me more specific details, I find out that the child is actually reading a LOT. One of my students was recently telling me he is literally obsessed with graphic novels about history. He shared with me that his parents think of them as "comics," but as he said to me: "They are just cooler ways of telling really serious stories." When we think of "reading," many of us think about chapter books, which is kind of ironic as it's really not what we are mostly reading out there in the work world (unless we are lucky enough to be a book editor!). We think of reading as turning pages under trees, and moments lost in the world of fiction.

Even when I ask adults about their reading lives as children, I am struck by the frequency with which men will say to me: "Oh, I hated to read!" and then minutes later will report: "Well, I read lots of MAD magazines and comics, and I read war histories and *Boy's Life*!" But they don't think they read very much then. This seeming contradiction arises from their sense that what I consider "reading" doesn't match with what they recall doing, and loving to do. In fact, I believe the reading they describe is precisely the sort of reading that will help our children learn to read powerfully well in the digital age.

The truth is that our lives are full of print coming to us in a variety of ways. Those very habits and behaviors that we may not value as "reading" are precisely how we are reading most of the time as adults. Rereading, browsing, skimming, and jumping around are all valuable reading strategies and have the power to build lifelong readers. Valuable reading includes:

- Video/computer games
- Sports page/magazines
- Comic books/graphic novels
- Text messages
- Web sites
- Blogs

4. Does reading online count?

Technology is changing the landscape of literacy by the day. We live in exciting times. I personally and professionally value the screen as much as I value the printed page, the book I hold in my hands. We will not lose the power of reading because it appears to us on a screen. We give boys too much grief for spending so much time on their computers, texting, playing games. In fact, there are opportunities for reading development here. The irony is that the classroom devalues these experiences, which is also not great for girls who may not be as influenced by their peers outside the classroom to experiment with them. And because the classroom devalues these experiences, boys are made to feel as if they are "not reading." On the Internet, the child browses, rereads, jumps around, and reads in different order (not just linearly). At work, even at home, we are constantly doing the same thing: seeking and storing knowledge by browsing, rereading, jumping around, and reading out of order. We need to rename how we define reading, both for the sake of the boys in our lives and for the girls, too.

5. Do you have to be alone while reading?

We often insist that reading is quiet and solitary. We encourage boys to take a book and find a quiet place, or go to their rooms. For both boys and girls, this can be problematic. Children are extremely social as readers. We read to them (hopefully); they read and talk with one another (hopefully). But what happens is that as soon as they can read on their own, we usher them away, to the land of reading in isolation. This isolation can make reading unappealing, lonely, and boring for many children, especially those who love to be surrounded by people and action. Even the classroom can feel very isolated during reading time. I want to advocate for a far more collaborative, social view of reading. There is no question that some reading involves independence and solitude. I crave that for myself each and every day. But the reading environment has to suit both the social and the reflective. Being a reader does not always mean being alone. Each boy will have his own ideas about what makes a reading environment perfect. Whether it's by blogging about his favorite books so others can see what he is reading and recommending or hanging up his favorite recommendations in the classroom, the main thing is to support that idea of social reading and interacting. One year, I started a boys reading club. I asked the boys what their favorite part of the club was and they said it was the months we celebrated poetry, where they could read poems aloud to each other while munching on pizza during lunch. It was companionable and cozy, collegial and contented.

6. When should I stop reading aloud?

Never! Continue reading aloud to boys for as long as you can. We put a lot of pressure on our boys to do everything on their own. As soon as they can read independently, we forsake the read aloud. It inspires conversation and is a warm and nurturing way to introduce them to harder text or to genres they might not read on their own. Make reading an interactive experience. Take turns reading pages. Read the same book together; download them together on your iPhones or iPads. Make sure your read alouds represent a wide range of genre and interest. The read aloud is a great opportunity to introduce boys to books that are societally more acceptable for girls to pick up (books with girls on the cover or a girl protagonist). We also want to make it more possible for boys to see other genres valued, too. Read aloud from a great Seymour Simon book on animals and watch your students' faces light up!

Recently I asked a group of boys what their favorite reading memories were (they were six years old). Almost universally, each reported time alone with a parent, especially a father, reading aloud to him at the end of the day. While we can't recreate that in the classroom, we can create cozy environments for reading aloud, and invite adult men into the school environment to read their own favorite books or stories or articles.

7. How does school affect boys as readers?

Schools have not always been that helpful in supporting boys as readers. The testing mania and the idea in our culture that learning is symbolized by children sitting quietly in their seats has been, in some cases, defeating for active boys. Another big problem is the emphasis in the upper elementary and middle grades on the whole-class novel. The whole-class novel has been pretty successful in convincing boys NOT to read. The whole-class novel is the single most deadly bullet aimed directly at a boy's impulse to read. The teacher selects a book for the entire class that is about something a boy doesn't have that much interest in, or it's about a twelve-year-old girl. Also, because the novel becomes the teaching tool, the emphasis is on reading comprehension strategies and retelling of plot lines and we end up moving way too slowly through just one book; the entire journey becomes answering questions at the end of a chapter instead of the glory of reading fast and furiously, through a book one cannot put down.

We really don't let our students read often enough. As teachers we find a thousand other ways to keep our students busy. We give out activities; we talk to them about "comprehension strategies." For goodness sake, people! Please, just let your boys read! It is important. I have actually pleaded with teachers to give their students reserved, protected time to read every day, and they have said to me, over and over: "We don't have time." But there is nothing more important than creating time and space for engaged, independent reading.

Absorption is one key quality I believe is missing from our instruction. We jump from skill to skill, activity to activity. Let's create a sanctuary around the independent reading time so that boys can dig in, discover, wander and explore.

The fabulous book *Einstein Never Used Flash Cards: How Our Children Really Learn—and Why They Need to Play More and Memorize Less* by Kathy Hirsh-Pasek makes a compelling case for changing the structure of early education. Successful completion of worksheets and flash cards is nothing compared to the creative learning accomplished through play. Let's align reading more with play. Let's think of it more as a joy, as one of the delights of being human, than as a task. Let boys read and let them read what they like.

8. What if the boys get distracted?

Do your best to remove things that might distract boys from investing in their reading. Put a sign on your door or desk saying "Now is independent reading time," and let students know you are asking that no one approach unless it's an emergency. Ask your principal to commit to times during each day when no announcements are made over the loudspeaker and use those times for independent reading. Make sure the seating in the room is conducive to those students who need the absence of distraction. I know we all love collaborative learning, but those desks facing each other? They are not always the best for independent reading time. Who wants to be staring at someone every time he has to do his work? Let your students turn their chairs around or, even better, let them find more comfortable spots around the room to read. Create take-home bags for your students for their independent reading selections. Send a note to parents explaining that you want to ensure sacred time for reading at home and ask that space and time and quiet be created for boys at home to read independently. Mention that you are experimenting with the role music can play in the students' sustained attention to reading, so if he has his earphones in that might be fine as long as you both feel he is able to concentrate. Help your students create their take-home, independent-reading bags by including both books at their levels and also books for browsing.

9. What if the boys are highly active and don't love to sit still to read?

Make reading part of active lifestyles. Take nature guidebooks out on walks. Relate novels boys are reading to the lives they live by having them record their own experiences in reading notebooks, along with art and doodles. Some boys might read a chapter and then act it out for the class. Let boys' reading spill over into all the corners of their lives.

All children sometimes need room just to move. Harness a boy's kinetic energy in reading, instead of tamping it down. Let boys act out scenes from books; let them stand up and move around, taking short breaks during reading. Some schools now have desks at which students stand instead of sit—this alone could revolutionize a classroom.

Our classrooms are all too often failing to engage boys. Still, we place the blame for this squarely on the boys themselves. According to the Centers for Disease Control, 11 percent of boys aged 4–17 have been diagnosed with ADHD, as opposed to only 4.4 percent of females. Studies found 6.2 percent of boys are on medication for ADHD, compared to 2.4 percent of females ("Mental Health in the United States: Prevalence of Diagnosis and Medication Treatment for Attention-Deficit/Hyperactivity Disorder—United States, 2003," US Centers for Disease Control *http://www.cdc.gov/mmwr/preview/ mmwrhtml/mm 5434a2.htm*). Certainly many of those boys have a disorder for which medication is incredibly helpful. But are we confident that all of them do? Or do we, in our classrooms, only accept a narrow range of behaviors we deem "normal" and, therefore, suitable for school?

The problem is not that boys are "too active," the problem is that our classrooms do not allow them to be themselves. One of the authors of *Raising Cain*, Michael Thompson, says, "Too often, the behavior of girls is the gold standard. Boys are simply treated as defective girls" (Tyre, *The Trouble with Boys*, Crown: 2008). Energy and verve are, of course, good qualities, and there are ways to support and encourage them in the classroom. Poetry books and one-act plays, as well as books with strong character voices are ideal for acting out and for doing mini-plays in book clubs. Encourage your students to think outside the box in these ways as often as possible.

Also remember to compliment your students for time spent reading. Start with small increments and build the time up each and every day. Let them see that you are so proud of them for reading and that the minutes they read on their own are really important to you.

10. How do we know if a book will appeal to boys?

The best way to know what boys like is to ask and really listen. Tailor book choices to boys' interests and give them options that are at their reading level, as well as some that are slightly above and below. The ones that are slightly below reading level will build confidence and allow them to relax with a book that they can go through as quickly or slowly as they like. The ones that are slightly above reading level should be on subjects or by authors they truly love, motivating them to push themselves as readers and thinkers. Give them a variety of these in their take-home, independent-reading bags and in their independent reading baskets in school so there is always a choice and always room to change one's mind.

The Web site *surveymonkey.com* is my favorite tool du jour for the classroom, and for my own children, my best tool is the dining room table. I want to know about my children's and my students' reading lives, and here's what I ask:

- What gets you excited to read?
- What keeps you reading? Is it:
- Book cover art
- White space between paragraphs and chapters (One of the reasons I believe *The Invention of Hugo Cabret* is so successful is because of its ingenious and appealing use of white space; don't underestimate it.)
- Short text/chapters (magazines, newspapers, snippets)
- Genre (Action/Adventure, Mystery, Humor, Sports, Nonfiction, Graphic Novels, Fantasy, Manuals, Internet Reading)
- Peer recommendations
- Male characters
- Male authors
- Series books
- Art in the books themselves (Visual literacy is really important, and you can talk a lot with your boys about art in books; don't ignore it.)
- Getting to the end—finishing the book, i.e., it's short enough to get through fast, or long enough to make you feel like you've climbed Mount Kilimanjaro

11. How can I choose books that build reading confidence in boys?

We must encourage environments that offer a variety of reading levels without judgment. Even those of us adults who read fluently have to have some down time with a celebrity magazine or a fun Web site, like Facebook or YouTube, which is easy on the eyes. I had a student who started each reading time by reading the same, simple book about racecars. After reading it, he would then move on to other, more challenging books. The racecar book was the first book he had learned to read on his own, and the ritual of rereading it, as he put it, "got him all pumped up" to read his other books. The level is the key thing. If our boys are interested in a particular topic, then the book may be a bit more challenging than what they might ordinarily read, but he is going to be more likely to want to browse like mad. We must allow our boys to read above their levels. This obsession and fixation on reading "at one's level" is fine in certain circumstances, but there are plenty of times that our boys want to peruse a topic and can glean a great deal just by browsing, especially if they are deeply interested in something.

12. How can I build stamina in boys' reading lives without frustration?

Support "quick reads." Books shouldn't have to take weeks to read for a child to have a successful reading experience. Value the brevity of a good text, a comic strip, a short story. Change lengths of time for independent reading, allow for stretches, allow multiple texts as part of one independent reading session—mix it up. Ask your boys to experiment with how much they can read in a given time period. Start with small increments of time (five to ten minutes) and see if they can build up every day. Give incentives for increased time. Use a timer to support "quick reads." Read alongside boys with the timer set and don't judge the time by pages read, instead celebrate the minutes with eyes on text.

13. What kinds of goals and outcomes encourage reading in boys?

Tap into what motivates your boys in other areas of life. At Back to School Night, ask parents deeper questions about their boys. What do they like to do in their free time? What worries them? What is their preferred form of play? If being able to share knowledge is a motivator, let your student teach you something from what he's read. If he's reflective, be sure to encourage him not just to answer questions in his reading response notebook but to also dig deeper into his perspective in writing. Create fun and exciting goals, not all of which have to do with reading comprehension but may have to do with reading stamina. The boys may want to see how fast they can read in a number of minutes. They may like to see if they can read in many different genres by the end of the week. They need to know there is a purpose for goal setting. Tell them: if you practice reading fast, this will help you build stamina. If you read lots of different kinds of texts this week, you learn how different people tell the same ideas in different ways.

14. Are reading mentors important?

Reading role models are key in helping boys integrate reading into their sense of self. Often, boys who don't see themselves as readers are taught by women and end up reading books written by women that feature female protagonists. It can be difficult for boys to connect reading to their ideas about themselves and masculinity without a male figure in their lives who encourages them and reads himself.

Create ways for boys to see men reading; if you are a man reading this book, find boys to talk with and engage with about reading. Talk about men who read and what they read; have male teachers/leaders come to read to students; where possible, encourage both parents to be more "visible" readers at home. Encourage men to come visit your classroom who have varied reading passions; let the boys see a strong grown man read a simple picture book or a tender story about a fear of going to sleep.

15. How can book clubs help?

Form an all-boy book club within a class. The club's book choices and activities can be tailored to the interests and preferences that set your boys apart from the girls in their lives. The conversations that boys have about the books they read together will bring new depth to their understanding of the text and also allow them the experience of hearing and responding to opinions that differ from their own.

If possible, see if you can encourage father-son book clubs. (Uncles, older brothers, family friends can also fill the bill.) By taking part in a father-son book club, boys are exposed to males who care about them and who have a love of books and reading. They can aspire to read as fluently as their dad or with the stamina of their uncle or with the depth of understanding that a male neighbor shows. This experience can be truly life-changing. As a teacher, you can promote this idea to parents (and grandparents) via a newsletter with some good book recommendations.

16. How can I celebrate and affirm boys' achievements in reading?

This isn't just a boy thing, of course, it's a human thing, but celebration is critical and often forgotten. Be sure to notice not just the numbers of books read, but also the minutes spent reading. Every minute does count. Take Fridays to revel in the amount the boys have read. Remember that the key here is words absorbed, not necessarily books read. So if boys have absorbed thousands of words that week, whether it's on the screen or anywhere else (including the back of the cereal box), this is good news and ought to be celebrated. I can't tell you how many classrooms I've been in where I see boys slogging through long text with no kind word, no compliment for the sheer stamina it takes to read.

Create opportunities for clubs, both coed and single sex, so boys can explore their own reading interests and discussions. Discuss books online, on a Web site or your own blog. One great example is *voicethread.com*, a site where you can post a book title and ask your students to respond. What's great about *voicethread.com* is that you can encourage your boys to respond in ways that aren't just about words. They can create art to go with a text or even write and record a song.

Find moments to praise time spent browsing, affirm text selections, and compliment rereading. Create public records of reading growth and show all your support for the completion of personal goals. Ask your students at the beginning of the year, and then again several times throughout the year, to set and reflect upon their personal reading goals and to devise ways to determine if they have achieved them. Engage in healthy competition by having Reading Battles. Have Readathons to raise money to benefit a nonprofit, and create community acknowledgement of success and steps forward through bulletin board announcements. Ask boys what they gain from reading, and celebrate the wonder of being able to slip into new worlds.

17. Why are boys so drawn to graphic novels?

I think it's easier for boys to feel successful with text that is balanced masterfully with drawings. (Also, I think we haven't done a great job exposing our GIRLS to graphic novels. They may very well love them, too!) Make an effort to find out more about graphic novels and to learn the historical background of many of our most famous comics. They are often really subversive and political. Graphic text has always been a tool for the greatest challengers of our times to make important and powerful statements about society. Superman and other superheroes were saying something important about the state of the culture, and the artists were drawing on their own sense of social justice to write and draw these stories. The graphic design helps boys to stay focused on the stories behind the pictures and to be fully engaged with the text. We are missing a lot if we don't take time to read graphic novels with our boys and to talk deeply about the meaning and power of many of these titles. Additionally, graphic novels are a great support for a struggling reader who is thinking at very high levels in spite of this struggle. They don't look "babyish" but they are giving lots of support through the pictures for reading comprehension. Allow boys to revel in these books for all these reasons. Include them in your discussions, in class and at home, about theme, character and plot. Graphic novels can be instructive tools for teaching humor. They can be sly, clever, and brilliant.

Also, there are many versions of classic texts written as graphic novels, which give much needed support to boys in the upper grades who might need help with more complex texts.

18. How can you get boys to read outside of the usual environment and routine?

Ask your boys to describe times when reading has felt good for them. Don't dismiss their descriptions of the sports pages, or an art drawing book, or a great Web site, or a manual for how to build a castle. Embrace all these examples as part and parcel of an authentic, inspired reading life. Be sure to compliment them when you see them carrying a book around, or skimming a Web site or reading a book online. Capture the moments with a cheer and a prize of some kind when you see your boys reading or get reports from home that they've read over the weekend, or in the car, or in some surprising place—a tree fort in the backyard or at their cousin's sleepover. Have them share their favorite reading places when they come into school on Monday morning. Let the sheer fact that they chose to read be cause for celebration.

19. Many children seem to like to read more than one book at a time but may not be "finishers." Do you consider this a problem and, if so, do you have any suggestions for dealing with this issue?

It's not a problem if the books they are reading can be enjoyed without being finished. However, if you notice boys not finishing a novel or a mystery, then this may be a red flag that the book is too difficult. If a boy has a stack of nonfiction texts: science, biography, etc., and is poring over them, this should be encouraged. Some of the time, though, when a reader is not finishing a text, there is a good reason. It is not capturing his interest, or it is just too hard. He may not want to admit to you or anyone else that the book is too hard for him. Find gentle, dignifying ways to extricate him from this book and move him down a level, carefully and privately. Let him know that sometimes you get "stuck" in books, too, and that this is a great opportunity to pick up another one that will feel like a "smooth" read. Have in your hand a few examples of books that might be a "better fit" for him. Compare reading to trying on sneakers: sneakers should fit just right for a good long run; they should be solid and secure. A book and a reader are a lot like a sneaker and a foot. Ask your boys to let you know: "Does this book feel like a good fit?" "Will this be a smooth read for you?"

However, I also want to be sure you are offering your boys a wide variety of texts, from nonfiction to poetry, both of which are more amenable to browsing than a longer chapter book. Browsing—rereading and reading through different sorts of books—is a sign of a strong reader, and should be encouraged.

20. How do you promote reading for pleasure vs. learning to read, or reading for information, with sticky notes, text-to-self connections, etc.?

We've overdone the sticky-note musings, the forced connections, the strategy work. The best way to promote reading for pleasure is to LET KIDS READ. Reading deeply is more valuable than constantly being drawn back to a task. However, when used thoughtfully and intentionally, these sticky notes and connection strategies can be extremely helpful to the growing reader. Saying to your reader: "Mark the page you want to talk about with someone with a sticky note" is a good strategy for encouraging that student to see himself as a reader in community with others. Saying to your reader: "Is there a place in this text that reminded you of something in your life?" is a powerful statement indeed and can lead to amazing whole-group, whole-class, whole-family conversations. Done every day, through every reading lesson, though, your boys may start to stare blankly out the window! Make sure your number one priority is EYES ON TEXT. Make sure each and every day you are giving your boy readers ample opportunity to read and that minutes spent reading is really minutes spent reading and not mostly you talking about the reading.

21. How do you feel about "light" books, such as *Captain Underpants*?

I LOVE these books. They have been radically helpful in getting boys to read. As in eating, we have to offer our children a balanced diet. Don't underestimate the power of these books. They help our boys build stamina and independence. I am deeply grateful to authors who have created the kinds of books that our younger boys can't put down and our older boys can read and enjoy without feeling too babyish. Sometimes our boys will get "stuck" in a level, though. They find these books extremely comforting and nonthreatening. You may begin to notice this, and at a certain point you can nudge your boys out of this category with a good suggestion for another book that resembles *Captain Underpants* but is a notch up levelwise. *Bone*, for example, or other graphic novels, such as *Diary of a Wimpy Kid,* take the love of art and print and move it up to the next reading level.

22. How do you teach a child to juggle all of the books being thrown at him, e.g., the classroom book, the library book, and the book for home reading? How can they learn to manage a reading life that's enjoyable and not overwhelming?

This is the teacher's job: to pare down the child's reading life into something manageable and fun. If he is getting that many different kinds of reading to do all in one day, there is something not being managed well in the classroom system. He'd be very happy to create a more simplified reading life, but he needs his teacher's permission to do so. All of the above books should be one and the same, or there should be a short stack of books that our boys are perusing systematically, not randomly. There should be little difference between reading for school and reading for fun: we want boys to approach all their books with curiosity and excitement. Creating a "book stack" or a "book baggie" for our boys is one good way to do this. They may have a few browsing books in there, as well as a longer chapter book. As your boys' reading mentor, you should review the contents of the bag or stack on a weekly basis and help your boys refresh their stacks regularly. The stack should reflect a variety in the boy's reading life, but not chaos.

23. We know that reading aloud to the child is vitally important—how do you feel about the child reading aloud to an adult?

I am only open to this if the child is really excited to do it and if the adult manages the time wisely, so that it doesn't begin to feel like a burden. You don't want the child to feel like he's being tested or embarrassed. If it's wonderful fun, with teacher and child sharing character voices and taking turns reading pages, then sure. If it's for you to assess the child as a reader, you'd be better off having him read one quick sentence or two to see how smoothly he reads, and then asking questions about what he is reading independently. Ask: *What have you read lately that you love? What are you reading now that is feeling great for you?* This will give you more helpful information than having your student read aloud for long periods of time.

24. How do we get our boys interested in so-called "girl" books, like *Anne of Green Gables* or *The Midwife's Apprentice*?

Teachers ask if there are tricks to make *Anne of Green Gables* or *Little Women* appealing to boys. Boys are sometimes less likely to want to read books by women about girls.

You can read these books aloud to your boys to demonstrate your own enthusiasm. Also, it's important to relieve your boys of the feeling that it's not "cool" to read these books. My own husband cried the first time he heard *Anne of Green Gables*, at the age of 40, while we listened to the book on tape with our daughters. He said, "Why didn't I ever get to read this as a kid?" We put a lot of pressure on our boys to read "like men." Let's give them a chance to explore all aspects of themselves and acknowledge that books are a great place for those explorations. It may be that they avoid books about girls because it's hard to read those in public and feel okay about it. Male teachers can model enjoyment of books with both male and female characters, and women should be sensitive to these issues and be sure boys feel they can select those books, too.

Part 3

Pam Allyn's Best Picks for Boys:

A Thoughtfully Annotated List

This list is annotated so you will have a richer understanding of what the readings are all about and can make a confident decision as to which ones would be just right for your boys. It has been created through years of research—not research in a lab, but research in the classroom, where I ask boys over and over: *What do you like best?*

For certain books, a special "Talk About It" section offers a guide for discussing key ideas from the reading. These are recommendations for talking points, but are certainly not the only possibilities for cultivating book discussion. They are meant to be guides and inspiration, with the hope that you will create your own great conversations as you listen deeply to the boys in your class and follow your own instincts.

In this section, I have labeled each book with a code to help you in determining which ones might be best for your boys. You will see that each book is marked with one of the following initials:

E = Emerging

D = Developing

M = Maturing

Note: There are also several titles that fall somewhere between levels. These books may be labeled E →**D** (for Emerging to Developing) or D →**M** (Developing to Maturing).

- *Dex: The Heart of a Hero* by Caralyn Buehner (HarperCollins, 2007)
- *Eliot Jones, Midnight Superhero* by Anne Cottringer (Tiger Tales, 2009)
- *The Incredible Dash* by R. H. Disney (RH/Disney, 2004)
- *SuperHero ABC* by Bob McLeod (HarperCollins, 2008)
- *Superhero School* by Aaron Reynolds (Bloomsbury, 2009)
- *Traction Man Is Here!* by Mini Grey (Knopf, 2005)
- *Traction Man Meets Turbo Dog* by Mini Grey (Knopf, 2008)

Tsunami! **by Kimiko Kajikawa, illustrated by Ed Young (Philomel, 2009) E**

Striking collages made from textured paper materials illustrate the story of Ojiisan, a wealthy man who lives high above a village. His view affords him early warning of an impending tsunami, and he must immediately warn the villagers below of the coming danger.

For Developing Readers

Airman **by Eoin Colfer (Hyperion Books for Children, 2009) D**

Conor Broekhart's birth in a hot-air balloon sets the course of his destiny in this 19th-century adventure from the author of the acclaimed Artemis Fowl series. Knighted as a teenager for a valorous act that put him in the good graces of King Nicholas, Conor lives a charmed life on the Saltee Islands off the coast of Ireland. But when the traitorous Marshall Bonvilain murders Nicholas and casts the blame on Conor, the young hero must find a way to escape prison and convince his parents, and the future queen, of his innocence.

Benjamin Franklinstein Lives! **by Matthew McElligott and Larry Tuxbury (G.P. Putnam's Sons, 2010) D**

Victor Godwin considers himself to be an orderly and practical kid. He wears the same type of outfit everyday to maintain efficiency and calculates the exact time the bus comes so he will never be late. Victor's whole world gets turned upside down when he meets the new tenant in his building: Benjamin Franklin! Apparently Benjamin Franklin has been in suspended animation for the past 200 years and has suddenly woken up. Victor must help Benjamin Franklin maintain energy and adjust to modern life all while also trying to win first place at the science fair.

Captain Nobody by Dean Pitchford (Puffin, 2010) D

When Halloween rolls around, ten-year-old Newt Newman has a lot on his mind. His big brother, Chris, a high school football star, is in a coma after taking a hit in the Big Game. With busy parents and a famous brother, Newt's used to taking care of himself, so when JJ and Cecil swing by, determined to drag him out, he puts together a last-minute superhero costume. The story centers on Newt's growing confidence under the cover of the persona of Captain Nobody, an unlikely hero who acts on behalf of strangers in need. As he comes into his own, Newt will have to confront the reality of his brother's condition—and figure out how Captain Nobody can help save the day.

The Danger Box by Blue Balliet (Scholastic, 2010) D

Zoomy is a twelve-year-old boy with a different way of viewing the world. He lives with his grandparents, but one day, his father returns to their home with a box he has stolen. Inside the box there is only an old notebook wrapped in a blanket. Zoomy falls in love with the notebook, sensing a kindred spirit in its owner, and tries to discover its origins, as a mysterious man tries secretly to reclaim the notebook for himself. Balliet inspires young readers to think about why the box is so dangerous and what their own "danger boxes" might be.

Frindle by Andrew Clements (Aladdin, 1998) D

Nicholas is bored by the fifth grade and looking for ways to keep things interesting. By making up a new word for a pen, he sparks a controversy at school. If you like this book, check out other books by Andrew Clements:

- *The Janitor's Boy* (Aladdin, 2001)
- *The Last Holiday Concert* (Atheneum, 2006)
- *The Landry News* (Atheneum, 2000)
- *Lost and Found* (Atheneum, 2008)
- *Lunch Money* (Atheneum, 2007)
- *No Talking* (Atheneum, 2007)
- *The Report Card* (Atheneum, 2005)
- *The School Story* (Atheneum, 2002)
- *A Week in the Woods* (Atheneum, 2004)

The Gollywhopper Games by Jody Feldman, illustrated by Victoria Jamieson (Greenwillow Books, 2009) D

This is it—Gil Goodson's chance to change his life. If he can win the Gollywhopper Games at the Golly Toy and Game Company, Gil's dad promises that they can move to a new town and finally escape the notoriety that has tarnished the family name since The Incident. It's not going to be easy. The Games require skill, intelligence, and athleticism, and there's the little matter of it all being filmed for national television. Will Gil be able to come out a champion?

Homer Price by Robert McCloskey (Puffin, 2005) D

Hailing from Centerburg, Ohio, Homer Price is a small-town boy whose hobby is fixing old, discarded radios. Homer goes to school without complaint and even helps his parents run their business. Of course, he likes to mix it up sometimes by taking in wild skunks and manning rogue doughnut machines! A classic since the 1940s.

Leepike Ridge by N. D. Wilson (Yearling, 2008) D

While rafting, eleven-year-old Tom is swept into an underwater world of caves carved into the mountain he has lived on all his life. As he tries to escape a watery grave, Tom finds the remains of others who never made it out, a man who has been trapped in the caves for three years, and a mystery that will have readers turning pages as quickly as they can read them.

Leviathan by Scott Westerfeld, illustrated by Keith Thompson (Simon Pulse, 2009) D

A novel that imagines a fantastical alternate future from the roots of World War I history, *Leviathan* describes a world at ideological odds. The Austro-Hungarians and Germans, known here as the Clankers, depend on mechanical technology. Across the divide, the British Darwinists have integrated the discovery of a new species into their weaponry. Their most remarkable feat comes in the form of a self-contained living ecosystem, the Leviathan airship. Some of the prejudices of 1914 society remain intact. Readers will learn that Deryn Sharp, an uncommonly skilled pilot serving on the Leviathan, must hide the fact that she is a woman in order to keep her job. When the gigantic ship crashes in Switzerland, Deryn meets the renegade Prince Aleksander, who is on the run from his homeland since the assassination of his parents. Together they embark on a worldwide adventure.

Lost Island Smugglers: A Sam Cooper Adventure by Max Elliot Anderson (Port Yonder Press, 2010) D

The first in a new series by Max Elliot Anderson, Sam Cooper's adventure at sea is filled with twists and turns boys won't see coming! Sam moves to a new place because of his father's job as a research biologist. Sam quickly makes friends with Tony and Tyler, and the three learn to scuba dive at Tony's father's boat rental shop. The boys decide to take a boat out, without permission, while Tony's father is out of town. Their fun sailing trip goes terribly wrong when a storm comes up and they get stranded on Lost Island. Filled with mystery, danger, and a good deal of suspense, boys won't be able to put down this first installment in the Sam Cooper Adventure series.

The Neil Flambé Capers series by Kevin Sylvester (Key Porter Books) D

Neil Flambé is a teen chef with a keen sense of smell. Inspector Nakamura uses Neil to help him solve cases. In the first book of the series, *Neil Flambé and the Marco Polo Murders*, chefs across town have been murdered, and Neil must rise to the challenge of unraveling the mystery. He uses his keen sense of smell and the journal of Marco Polo to help discover who is responsible for the crimes.

Nicholas and the Gang by Rebe Goscinny and Jean Jacques Sempe (Phaidon Press, 2007) D

Nicholas is a fun-loving and mischievous little boy growing up in France. He and his friends are always finding exciting things to do, like walking around on their hands, doing magic tricks, or going on camping trips. This collection of short stories takes us through the daily adventures of this group of creative and entertaining boys. Whether they are creating secret codes or coping with jealousy, at the end of the story they are still the best of friends. For more stories about Nicholas, read *Nicholas, Nicholas Again, Nicholas on Vacation,* or *Nicholas in Trouble*.

Talk About It:

Use *Nicholas and the Gang* to talk about the exciting or funny things that happen in everyday life.

In "Going Camping," Nicholas and his friends have a lot of fun pretending to go camping in a vacant lot near their homes.

- Have you ever pretended you were in a faraway place?
- What kinds of things help you to pretend when you're playing?

In "The Secret Code," Nicholas and his friends make up a code so that they don't get in trouble for talking in class.

- Have you ever created a secret code or your own way of communicating with your friends?
- Can you think of a reason people might need secret codes in special situations?
- If you could create a special new way of communicating with people, what would it be?

No Such Thing as Dragons by Philip Reeve (Scholastic Press, 2010) D

Nine-year-old Ansel is a silent boy sold by his father to Brock, a reputed dragon hunger. Brock is quite happy for the companionship, but admits to Ansel that he is a fraud. Dragons do not really exist; Brock simply carries around a skull that looks like it belongs to a dragon and convinces townspeople that they need him to keep them safe. Much to Brock and Ansel's surprise, a real dragon does turn up, and they must find a way to survive and save everyone from its clutches!

One Small Step by P. B. Kerr (McElderry Books, 2009) D

Scott MacLeod has been flying ever since his dad, a flight instructor for Vietnam War jet pilots, began letting him occasionally take the wheel during training sessions. When an accident during a training flight forces Scott to land his father's jet, he catches the attention of NASA officials and is recruited to be the first person to accompany chimpanzees on a space mission. Scott's adventures on Earth and in space will thrill readers who are fascinated with space exploration.

The Secret Science Alliance and the Copycat Crook by Eleanor Davis (Bloomsbury USA Children's Books, 2009) D

Julian Calendar has big plans to start fresh at his new school and leave behind his nerdy reputation. Instead, he meets Ben and Greta, two other super-smart kids who enjoy science just as much as he does! Together they form the Secret Science Alliance and set to work on a book of blueprints filled with inventive creations. Things aren't all fun and games, though. The evil Dr. Stringer intends to rob a museum. This graphic novel by Eleanor Davis is packed with imaginative details and narrative twists.

A Series of Unfortunate Events series by Lemony Snicket (HarperCollins) D

Violet, Klaus, and Sunny Baudelaire are three well-behaved and well-mannered children who have run into a spell of bad luck. In *The Bad Beginning* (Book 1), the children discover that their parents have perished in a terrible fire that also destroyed their home. Using their unique talents, the resourceful Baudelaire children must continually dodge the plots of their distant relative, the despicable Count Olaf, as he tries to steal what remains of their family fortune.

In *The Reptile Room* (Book 2), the three young Baudelaires find themselves with a new guardian, Dr. Montgomery Montgomery. Although the doctor is a good man, misfortune lurks around every corner.

Talk About It:

Use *A Series of Unfortunate Events* to talk about how to be resilient in the face of adversity and to seek your inner strength.

In *The Bad Beginning*, Violet's talent for inventing, Klaus's talent for researching, and Sunny's talent for biting all help the children save themselves from Count Olaf.

- Have you ever solved a problem using a special skill or talent that is important to you?

In *The Reptile Room*, the Baudelaire children feel like no one is listening to them.

- Have you ever felt like you had something important to say that wasn't being acknowledged?
- How did you make yourself heard?

Steel Trapp series by Ridley Pearson (Hyperion Books for Children) D

Steven "Steel" Trapp, so named for his spectacular photographic memory, is the son of an F.B.I. agent who can't help but find danger lurking around every corner. With the help of his friend Kayleigh, Steven uncovers even the most cleverly disguised secrets and lies. In the first book in the series, *The Steel Trapp Academy*, Steven discovers that the boarding school he attends is definitely not a normal school. In the second book, *Steel Trapp: The Challenge*, Steven gets more than he bargained for when he tries to help a person in need on a train ride to Washington, D.C.

Walls Within Walls by Maureen Sherry (Katherine Tegen Books, 2010) D

The three older Smithfork kids are not pleased about having to move from Brooklyn to Manhattan when their father's video game company hits it big. While they're learning to cope with their new home, they discover that the house they've moved into on Fifth Avenue has clues hidden in the walls about a neighbor's lost fortune. The Smithfork kids begin to unravel the puzzle running through the streets of Manhattan following clue after clue. Filled with plenty of action and New York history, curious young readers will eagerly decode clue after clue along with the Smithfork children.

Warriors series by Erin Hunter (HarperCollins) D

The Warriors series tells the story of a bunch of different cats from four clans: the ThunderClan, the RiverClan, the WindClan, and the ShadowClan. In the first installment in the series, a young cat named Firepaw emerges as a hero when war breaks out among the clans. Firepaw, along with other strong characters, must struggle for survival, victory, and to restore the peace.

We Are Not Eaten by Yaks: An Accidental Adventure by C. Alexander London (Philomel, 2011) D

Oliver and Celia Navel love nothing more than television. This is unfortunate for them, because they don't have much time to sit on the couch; their parents are avid explorers who love—well—exploring. When their mother disappears while searching for the Lost Library of Alexandria, the Navel Twins find themselves caught up in a real, live adventure. Battling through Tibet, the twins take on Poison Witches, Yetis, Oracles, and even piping hot Yak's Eye Stew! They uncover an ancient conspiracy, but to find their mother, they'll need all their wits and everything they've learned on television. If you enjoy this book, be sure to look out for the rest of the Accidental Adventure series.

For Maturing Readers

Elijah of Buxton by Christopher Paul Curtis (Scholastic, 2009) M

Elijah is the first free black child born in Buxton, Ontario, a haven for runaway slaves. When a former slave makes off with a friend's savings, money intended to buy his family's freedom, Elijah transforms. He makes the courageous but dangerous choice to pursue the thief in America. Despite the hopeful future Elijah embodies, he soon encounters the horrors his community so recently escaped by fleeing across the border. Curtis employs an admirable blend of humor and suspense in the novel, while also faithfully rendering the historical conditions of the time through a child's first-person perspective.

If you like this book, you'll also like:

- *Fallen Angels* by Walter Dean Myers (Scholastic, 1988)
- *The Skin I'm In* by Sharon Flake (Paw Prints, 2008)

The Great Wide Sea **by M. H. Herlong (Viking Juvenile, 2008) M**

Ben Byron's mother has just died in a terrible car accident. In an effort to cope with the terrible loss, Ben's father decides to buy a sailboat and take Ben and his two younger brothers on an adventure to the Bahamas. Ben is angry that he must leave everyone and everything he knows, but his father is heartbroken and wants everyone to be together. Caught in the midst of a storm, Ben's father goes missing. Will Ben be able to take charge and help them all survive the treacherous Atlantic?

Hero **by Mike Lupica (Philomel, 2010) M**

Zach is an average fourteen-year-old boy who lives in New York. He loves spending his free time with his dad who is a special assistant to the President of the United States. When Zach's dad dies, he begins to feel changes within him that sharpen all his senses. Zach feels himself getting stronger and faster. Soon he discovers that his father was a superhero. With his own powers slowly growing, Zach and his best friend Kate must figure out whom they can trust.

The House of the Scorpion **by Nancy Farmer (Atheneum, 2004) M**

This futuristic novel opens in Opium, a country of poppy fields south of the United States. Using microchips, the dictator has robbed a group of workers of their identities and reduced them to drones. He raises clones in an attempt to extend his own life indefinitely. The ruler's narcissism results in Matteo Alacrán, a boy born from a harvested cell that was transplanted into the womb of a cow. With the help of a kind bodyguard, Tam Lin, Matteo escapes. Now that he is free, Matteo must find a way not only to survive, but to discover his own humanity.

The Outsiders **by S. E. Hinton (Speak, 1997) M**

Written by S. E. Hinton at the age of 16 and published in 1967 during her freshman year of college, this classic offers an accurate depiction of the social reality of teenagers at that time. At 14, Ponyboy understands the game—it's the poor "greasers," his crew, against the "socs," the privileged "socials," who look down on just about everybody. When fellow greaser Johnny steps in to protect him during a confrontation, things turn violent and set off a chain reaction that will change Ponyboy's life forever.

Talk About It:

- What are the differences between teenagers in the 1960s and teenagers today?
- Do you think there have been social changes for the better? Why or why not?

The Thief Lord **by Cornelia Funke (The Chicken House, 2002) M**

To avoid being separated after the death of their mother, Prosper and his little brother Bo decide to run away to Venice. Once there, the brothers befriend a group of young pickpockets who are led by Scipio, the Thief Lord. When a mysterious buyer asks Scipio to arrange a special heist, the boys get caught up in a surprising adventure. Meanwhile, Prosper and Bo's aunt has hired a clever but kindhearted detective to find her nephews. Boys will love the twists and turns of this action-packed story, as they wait and see what will become of this family.

If you like this book, you'll also like:

- The Underland Chronicles series by Suzanne Collins (Scholastic)

Treasure Island **by Robert Louis Stevenson (Puffin Classics, 2008) M**

Strap yourself in for an adventure on the high seas in this classic coming-of-age tale. Young Jim Hawkins survives mutiny and murderous pirates in pursuit of an elusive stash of gold. The standard division of good and evil becomes less distinct in the iconic and complex character of Captain Long John Silver, who mixes treachery with an unconventional ethical code.

Trouble **by Gary D. Schmidt (Graphia, 2010) M**

Henry Smith's father always told him that their family had lived in Blythbury-by-the-Sea for generations to avoid trouble. Their quiet life is changed forever when Henry's older brother Franklin is killed in a car accident. The driver is Chay, a Cambodian immigrant. As racial tensions reach their boiling point in Blythbury-by-the-Sea, Henry decides to climb Mount Katahdin in Maine, a trip he had planned with Franklin.

Henry's path to self-discovery intersects with Chay's on the way to the mountain, and the two boys come to better understand each other. This poignant story cleverly mixes modern social concerns with timeless themes of loss and forgiveness in alternating first-person narration.

A Whole Nother Story by Dr. Cuthbert Soup (Bloomsbury USA Children's Books, 2009) M

The Luminal Velocity Regulator might be Ethan Cheeseman's greatest invention ever. In fact, it might be the greatest invention ever—which is why spies, big business henchmen, and international governments have started to chase after the brilliant scientist. Ethan grabs his three kids, and they hit the road in this hilarious adventure, trying to elude the bad guys while searching for a new place to call home. The novel is full of witty asides, including advice on everything from how to choose a dog to time travel!

Art and Music

For Emerging Readers

Art by Patrick McDonnell (Little, Brown, 2006) E

Art is the name of the little boy in this story, and he lives up to it! Art plays with form, creating zigzags and splotches and doodles and drawings that grow in size and complexity until they threaten to swallow the miniature master. The wordplay will put a smile on a young readers face as they watch Art gain confidence in his craft and push the limits of his own creativity. In the end, Art receives the highest honor any little artist can hope for, a place on the refrigerator, "put there by Mother 'cause Mother loves Art."

The Art Lesson by Tomie dePaola (Putnam Juvenile, 1997) E

Somewhere between autobiography and fiction, Tomie dePaola shares the story of a little boy named Tommy whose passion for drawing is briefly upset when he begins school. Tommy's parents and friends have always appreciated and encouraged his creativity, but when he arrives at art class, he discovers there are rules he must follow. Tommy must use the school's crayons and not his own new box with 64 colors. He was told artists never copy other people's work, but now he must copy the picture the art teacher draws on the board. Tommy is completely disheartened and doesn't know what to do. Luckily, his teachers understand his dilemma, and they come to a compromise that makes everyone happy.

Grandma's Gift **by Eric Velasquez (Walker Books for Young Readers, 2010) E**

A little boy named Eric and his grandmother go to the Metropolitan Museum of Art and discover the work of Diego Velazquez. The small child's fascination with this newly opened world of art doesn't escape his loving grandmother's attention. As a Christmas present she gives him art supplies and suddenly a new dream has come to him. This story, based on the author's own experiences as a boy, is a testament to the incredible impact that love and care can have on the budding talents of even our youngest artists.

Ish **by Peter H. Reynolds (Candlewick, 2004) E**

A little boy named Ramon is discouraged when his older brother tells him his drawing of a vase with flowers doesn't look real. Ramon crumples up his picture and with it his previous carefree approach to his drawing. Soon he discovers that his little sister has hung up his pictures in his room. When he tells her that the vase doesn't look like a real vase, she informs him that it looks "vase-ish." With that small addition, Ramon's confidence and creativity return with gusto and he is compelled to draw pictures of things that are "tree-ish" and "silly-ish." Ramon's story is perfect for any budding artist who needs an extra boost and is sure to inspire any reader to see the world with new eyes.

If you like this book, you'll like:

- *Art Dog* by Thacher Hurd (HarperCollins, 1997)
- *The Dot* by Peter H. Reynolds (Candlewick, 2003)
- *When Pigasso Met Mootisse* by Nina Laden (Chronicle, 1998)
- *Why Is Blue Dog Blue?* by George Rodriguez (Stewart, Tabori, and Chang, 2002)

I SPY: An Alphabet in Art **by Lucy Micklethwait (Greenwillow Books, 1996) E**

On each double page of this book, the phrase "I spy with my little eye something beginning with . . . ." For each letter of the alphabet, the opposite page contains a large painting that always has an object at the forefront to match the letter. For instance, A is for apple, and the painting is René Magritte's *Son of Man* where the man in the painting has an apple where his face should be. The alphabet continues with Henri Rousseau's *Football Players,* and also includes work by Picasso, Renoir and 22 others. Boys will love declaring the object for each letter, and the paintings are sure to catch any reader's eye.

Mole Music by David McPhail (Henry Holt & Company, 1999) E

Mole leads a nice life, digging tunnels all day and unwinding in front of the TV at night, but he feels something is missing. One night he hears a man playing the violin on a television program. It is the most beautiful sound Mole has ever heard, so he decides to learn to play. Mole practices and practices and is able to make music as melodious and peaceful as the man on TV. Through the illustrations, young readers will see that Mole's music helps a young tree above his underground home flourish and draws in listeners who gather under its branches. This story's simple message of peace and fulfillment through music may just inspire a would-be musician or two.

A Mouse Called Wolf by Dick King Smith (Yearling, 1999) E

Wolfgang Amadeus Mouse, known as "Wolf," is a very tiny mouse with a very big name. Wolf, like his namesake, has an affinity for beautiful music and loves to listen to the woman who owns the house he lives in as she plays the piano. As Wolf sits and listens to Mrs. Honeybee playing, he wishes he could sing along with her. One day, Wolf opens his mouth and sings, and he realizes he has a beautiful voice. When Mrs. Honeybee falls and can't get up, Wolf uses his talent to attract attention and get her the help she needs. The clever mouse proves that being small cannot keep you from doing great things.

For Developing Readers

The Art Book for Children, Book Two by Editors of Phaidon Press (Phaidon Press, 2007) D

This book contains hundreds of large, colorful reproductions of famous works that span from the art of the Renaissance to contemporary photography, from the Americas to Asia. For each piece, questions, observations, and opinions are added in a calligraphic style that makes the words seem to form a part of the artwork and provoke deeper reflection in young readers and art enthusiasts alike. In the final section, the size, location, and date of each work is listed along with the artists' birth and death dates. This book is perfect for boys who enjoy browsing and may inspire them to stop and study a few favorite pieces for a while.

The Boys' Doodle Book: Amazing Pictures to Complete and Create by Andrew Pinder (Running Press Kids, 2008) D

This book is sure to keep your budding artists happily drawing away. With page after page of drawing prompts and beginnings, boys who love to put pen to paper already will have the freedom to let their creativity shine, while boys who are still unsure may be given the inspiration they need to try their hand. From familiar scenarios like "Draw Dr. Frankenstein's Monster" to open-ended beginnings like a picture of a boy swimming and the prompt, "What's nibbling his toes?" each turn of the page is sure to elicit laughter, thoughtfulness, and original artwork.

Dave the Potter: Artist, Poet, Slave by Laban Carrick Hill, illustrated by Bryan Collier (Little, Brown Books for Young Readers, 2010) D

Dave lived in South Carolina in the 19th century. He was a slave, but despite the hardships of his life, he was able to become a skilled artisan—one of only two potters at the time who could make a pot that held more than 20 gallons—and also a prolific poet. In each pot he crafted, Dave would inscribe short poems. Some of his poems were observations on the natural world, others reflective wonderings about his life—past, present, and future. Growing readers will feel Dave's strength and skill in the illustrations and be intrigued by the biographical information at the end. Dave's resilience and inborn talent has left a mark on the art world, just as a boy reading his story might one day.

Hip Hop Speaks to Children: A Celebration of Poetry With a Beat edited by Nikki Giovanni (Sourcebooks Jabberwocky, 2008) D

This anthology brings rhythm and beat to life, with colorful illustrations brightening each page of lyrics, and a CD included so young musicians can listen to the artists featured. Classic poets like Langston Hughes and W. E. B. Dubois are mixed with current popular artists like Kanye West and Mos Def. The result is a collection of poems and songs that will bring every listener and reader to his feet, dancing along to the words and music.

Jimi: Sounds Like a Rainbow, A Story of the Young Jimi Hendrix by Gary Golio, illustrated by Javaka Steptoe (Clarion Books, 2010) D

Young Jimi Hendrix sees music in every corner and plays in a way that brings vibrancy and joy to all who hear him. In this celebration of a legendary guitarist's youth, Jimi's story nearly leaps off of the page. From mimicking the sounds he heard on the street with a ukulele to becoming a star, the story details his love for the artistry of music and his drive to paint with sound. Jimi Hendrix's tragic death is mentioned separately in an afterword. Any boy who loves music will be captivated by Golio's rendition of Hendrix's growth to fame.

The Story of the Orchestra by Robert Levine, illustrated by Meredith Hamilton (Black Dog & Leventhal Publishers, 2000) D

This volume introduces orchestral music in a fun, charming way. In the first section, young readers are introduced to famous composers like Vivaldi and Bach. Then, the book takes curious musicians-in-the-making through the various instruments that make up an orchestra's wall of sound. The book includes a CD to help listeners understand all of the varied elements that make up orchestral music and bring the classics to young ears. Boys with a growing interest in music are sure to get lost in the details.

Storybook Art: Hands-on Art for Children in the Style of 100 Great Picture Book Authors by MaryAnn F. Kohl and Jean Potter, illustrated by Rebecca Van Slyke (Bright Ring Publishing, 2003) D

Boys can bring their favorite stories to life in a new way with this book of art projects inspired by the work of beloved children's book illustrators. With a varied array of artists from Clement Hurd of *Goodnight Moon* to Ian Falconer of *Olivia*, each project will allow boys to put their own spin on the familiar images from picture books. Any boy who is captivated by color and imagery will love the opportunity to create a work inspired by one of his favorite books.

For Maturing Readers

Click: The Ultimate Photography Guide for Generation Now by Charlie Styr, with Maria Wakem (Amphoto Books, 2009) M

Illustrated with over 150 photographs taken by young people around the world, this guidebook is perfect for boys who have taken an interest in photography or any who just happen to have a camera. The young author takes readers through basic elements of photography like composition and lighting, and then explores 27 different techniques, including how to take action shots and how to shoot at night. Readers don't need to be accomplished photographers to pick up this helpful guide, but they will definitely be ready to take their picture-taking skills to the next level when they put it down.

Deep Blues: A Musical and Cultural History of the Mississippi Delta by Robert Palmer (Penguin, 1982) M

This book is a special treat for any growing musician interested in the roots and heroes of a rich musical tradition of the United States. Palmer is deeply knowledgeable both of the form and the history of blues music and is able to put both in the context of a social movement in American history that shaped and re-shaped popular culture and the meaning of American music. From slave music considered subversive by slaveowners in the deep South to the migration of African-Americans northward, to cities like Chicago and the influence the music they brought with them had on rock and roll, Palmer paints a rich portrait of the interplay of cultures on the American music scene.

I, Juan de Pareja **by Elizabeth Borton de Treviño (Square Fish, 2008) M**

Juan de Pareja was the slave of 15th-century Spanish artist Diego Velazquez. In this fictional account of their history together, told from the slave's perspective, de Pareja shares insight into the personal and artistic life of the royal court's painter. Their relationship deepens as Velazquez helps de Pareja learn to paint and develop his skills. Despite the demands of the era, de Pareja and Velazquez become much more than master and slave and, in doing so, prove the incredible impact that art can have on life.

Inkblot: Drip, Splat and Squish Your Way to Creativity **by Margaret Peot (Boyds Mills, 2011) M**

Margaret Peot creates a whole new way to look at inkblots by turning these accidental drops on paper into inspiration for page after page of artwork. Peot weaves her own insight and learnings with tips and techniques alongside her inkblot artwork. From simple ink drawings to elaborate creations, the artist puts together a portfolio of inkblots that proves a masterpiece can be created out of any spot or splotch on a page. Boys who show an interest in the art world will be inspired by Peot's creative ingenuity and her willingness to go where the inkblot takes her.

Masterpiece **by Elise Broach, illustrated by Kelly Murphy (Square Fish, 2010) M**

This tale of friendship and adventure delves into the art world, through the eyes of the unlikeliest of artists. Marvin is a beetle whose family lives in the kitchen of a Manhattan family. When the family's son, James, receives an art kit for his 11th birthday, Marvin discovers his own artistic talents. Although they cannot talk, James and Marvin become friends, but that is just the beginning of their adventure. Marvin's artwork is assumed to be James's, and the boy is commissioned by the Metropolitan Museum of Art to forge a painting by Albrecht Dürer in order to catch an art thief. When Marvin realizes the original is still in danger, he must risk his life and rely on his new friend to make things right. Throughout the story, the art of Dürer is explored along with themes of friendship and justice. Art lovers and adventure aficionados alike will love this book.

Patakin: World Tales of Drums and Drummers by Nina Jaffe (Cricket Books, 2001) M

In this collection of ten folktales from all over the world, drumming plays a pivotal role, and the rhythm of the tale intertwines with the rhythm of the story's drum. The stories are taken from traditional folklore from Korea, legends of the Inuit people, mythology of Ireland, and the Jewish Torah. Jaffe stays true to the traditional storytelling style of each culture, while separately providing additional background material, historical notes, musical notation, and a detailed description of the specific kind of drum central to the story. For any dedicated drummer, this is a fascinating look at the way drumming is central to self-expression and sharing ideas in cultures around the world and throughout history.

Biographies and Memoirs

For Emerging Readers

Come See the Earth Turn by Lori Mortensen, illustrated by Raul Allen (Tricycle Press, 2010) E

Léon Foucault was born a sickly child in 1819. He didn't excel in academics and eventually dropped out of medical school. People did not expect him to do great things, but Foucault gave the world a great gift. He created a simple and amazing pendulum that proved that the Earth spun on an axis, and with that, Foucault changed the way everyone saw the world. This story is sure to inspire young readers with the simple truth: there is often greatness in the most unlikely of places.

An Eye for Color: The Story of Josef Albers by Natasha Wing, illustrated by Julia Breckenreid (Henry Holt and Company, 2009) E

This biography of German-born artist Josef Albers takes colorful inspiration from its subject in gouache illustrations. Beautiful art spreads accompany the story of the man who created the "Homage to the Square" series of paintings now familiar throughout the world. The text evokes Albers' fascination with the interplay of colors and the trips to Mexico that would inform his life's work.

If you like this book, you'll also like:

- *Action Jackson* by Jan Greenberg (Square Fish, 2007)
- *Henri Matisse: Drawing with Scissors* by Jane O'Connor (Grosset & Dunlap, 2002)
- *Leonardo and the Flying Boy* by Laurence Anholt (Barron's, 2007)
- *Pablo Picasso: Breaking All the Rules* by True Kelley (Grosset & Dunlap, 2002)

***I and I: Bob Marley* by Tony Medina, illustrated by Jesse Joshua Watson (Lee & Low Books, 2009) E**

This poetic tribute to Bob Marley lyrically and delightfully tells the story of his life from his birth to his tragic death. Become immersed in the beauty of Bob Marley's own poems, accompanied by Watson's vibrant illustrations, as you hear about big events and themes in Marley's life. As the life of the musical legend unfolds on each page, you might just break into song yourself!

***Neil Armstrong*: Rookie Biography series by Dana Meachen Rau (Children's Press, a division of Scholastic, Inc., 2003) E**

Neil Armstrong spent a lot of time training to become the astronaut who would one day walk on the moon. He left his footprints on the moon, and has since inspired many future astronauts to try to fill his shoes. Learn all about Neil Armstrong in this perfect read for all budding astronauts. Read this and the other books in the Rookie Biography series for a wonderful introduction to a cast of heroes.

***A River of Words: The Story of William Carlos Williams* by Jen Bryant, illustrated by Melissa Sweet (Eerdmans' Books for Young Readers, 2008) E**

When he was a boy, William Carlos Williams, then known as Willie, loved to play baseball with his friends, explore the nearby woods and fields, and write, write, write. Although Williams grew up to become a very successful doctor, he never forgot his true love, writing. Like other great writers, Williams drew inspiration from the world around him. As you read this wonderful book, search for everyday inspiration in your life; you might just find out that you are a poet, too.

***Seeker of Knowledge: The Man Who Deciphered Egyptian Hieroglyphs* by James Rumford (Sandpiper, 2003) E**

Jean-Francois Champollion promised himself when he was eleven years old that one day he would understand the secrets of Egyptian hieroglyphs. With the help of family and friends and twenty years of study and searching, Jean-Francois succeeds! This book will inspire new readers to invest themselves in the pursuit of new discoveries in the wonderful world of words.

For Developing Readers

Bad Boy: A Memoir by Walter Dean Myers (Amistad, 2002) D

As a young boy, Walter Dean Myers had a bad reputation. He didn't always get along with his teachers, but he didn't quite get along with other kids either, mostly because they made fun of his speech impediment. An aspiring writer growing up in Harlem, he sometimes lost faith in his dreams. This is the inspirational tale of how Myers learned from his mistakes and found his voice.

Talk About It:

- Have you ever gotten into trouble at school? What happened?
- If you could be anything, what would you like to be when you grow up?
- What does it mean to have faith in yourself?

The Boy Who Invented TV: The Story of Philo Farnsworth by Kathleen Krull, illustrated by Greg Couch (Knopf, 2009) D

This illustrated narrative tells how fourteen-year-old Philo Farnsworth's idea for transmitting images through the air was inspired by the open fields of Idaho where he grew up. Following Farnsworth's ingenious path to conceiving and creating one of history's greatest inventions, the book shares the young Farnsworth's early fascination with similarly groundbreaking visionaries, such as Thomas Edison and Alexander Graham Bell, and enumerates the early signs of his own scientific ability. Philo's story is a testament to the value of perseverance and the boundless promise of imagination.

If you like this book, you'll also like:

- *Darwin* by Alice B. McGinty (Houghton Mifflin, 2009)
- *The Fantastic Undersea Life of Jacques Cousteau* by Dan Yaccarino (Knopf, 2009)
- *Moonshot: The Flight of Apollo 11* by Brian Floca (Atheneum, 2009)
- *Neo Leo: The Ageless Ideas of Leonardo DaVinci* by Gene Barretta (Henry Holt & Co., 2009)

- *Now and Ben: The Modern Inventions of Benjamin Franklin* by Gene Barretta (Henry Holt & Co., 2006)
- *Odd Boy Out: Young Albert Einstein* by Don Brown (Sandpiper, 2009)
- *One Beetle Too Many: The Extraordinary Adventures of Charles Darwin* by Kathryn Lasky (Candlewick, 2009)
- *Surfer of the Century: The Life of Duke Kahanamoku* by Ellie Crowe (Lee & Low, 2007)

Childhood of Famous Americans series (Aladdin Paperbacks) D

Learn about the childhoods of many celebrated Americans in this series. Read about Teddy Roosevelt's momentous eighth birthday and his trip to Egypt in *Teddy Roosevelt: Rough Rider*; how Sacagawea found the courage to become a hero in *Sacagawea: American Pathfinder*; or the many adventures that inspired Mark Twain's great books in *Mark Twain: Young Writer*.

The Day-Glo Brothers: The True Story of Bob and Joe Switzer's Bright Ideas and Brilliant Colors **by Chris Barton, illustrated by Tony Persiani (Charlesbridge Publishing, 2009) D**

Part biography, part science lesson, this picture book chronicles the discovery of the oh-so-groovy Day-Glo colors. Brothers Bob and Joe Switzer were opposites at their cores. Bob was responsible and hardworking while Joe was always coming up with new ideas. Their collaboration led them to discover the formula for the glowing paints that would spread far and wide in modern times. The illustrations enhance the storytelling, with initially sparse splashes of color building to a final full-on explosion of Day-Glo brilliance.

The Dinosaurs of Waterhouse Hawkins **by Barbara Kerley, illustrated by Brian Selznick (Scholastic, 2009) D**

This is the extensively researched story of Victorian artist Waterhouse Hawkins, the first person to create full-sized models of dinosaurs. Whimsical illustrations accompany the unbelievable details of a life lived to gargantuan scale. Kerley and Selznick treat readers to vivid anecdotes, from the story of the New Year's Eve party Hawkins held in the shell of an iguanadon in England to Hawkins' trials with Boss Tweed, who instigated the complete destruction of Hawkins' models in Central Park. Extensive notes round out the book, facilitating further research about this remarkable man and his impressive achievements.

The Dreamer **by Pam Muñoz Ryan, illustrated by Peter Sís (Scholastic Press, 2010) D**

Pam Muñoz Ryan tells the story of Pablo Neruda, born Neftalí Reyes, a shy Chilean dreamer who succeeds despite his father's discouragement. Neftalí feels the beauty of the world around him. He can see, hear, and feel the poetry of life's simple moments. Though his father tries to hinder his dreams, he finds encouragement from his stepmother. As a young adult, Neftalí takes a pseudonym for his writing and eventually becomes a famous poet. Ryan's lilting and lovely phrasing is beautifully matched by Sís's magical illustrations, working together to create dreamlike tale of following your heart.

The Great and Only Barnum: The Tremendous, Stupendous Life of Showman P. T. Barnum **by Candace Fleming, illustrated by Ray Fenwick (Schwartz & Wade, 2009) D**

This thorough account of the life of P. T. Barnum is delivered with appropriate panache and supplemented with informative sidebars that reveal the inner workings of 19th-century entertainment. Barnum's intrinsically absorbing trajectory takes center stage, from his childhood in Connecticut to his early forays into showmanship and his apotheosis as the organizer of hugely successful circuses. Fleming does not shy away from presenting a full portrait of Barnum, including his business failings and personal faults, while also showcasing lesser-known sides of the man, including his dedication to certain charities and his closely-held religious beliefs.

Harry Houdini **by Vicki Cobb (DK Publishing, 2005) D**

How did Harry Houdini transform himself from the poor son of immigrants to the world's most famous escape artist? Born Ehrich Weiss, Houdini left the life of a factory worker to become a spectacular show-stopper. This informative and inviting biography details the life of Houdini from his humble beginnings to his days as a magician. Make sure to take time to look through the wonderful accompanying photographs.

John Brown: His Fight for Freedom **by John Hendrix (Abrams Books for Young Readers, 2009) D**

The legendary and controversial abolitionist, John Brown, comes to life on the pages of this picture book for young readers. Hendrix includes the more recent academic studies on Brown, while detailing the extraordinary risks and remarkable steps that one man took to end slavery.

Mansa Musa: The Lion of Mali by Khephra Burns, illustrated by Leo and Diane Dillon (Gulliver Books, 2001) D

When slave raiders overrun Kankan Musa's peaceful village, the life he has always known is gone forever. Revel in the remarkable journey of Musa as he journeys far to regain his freedom. With the Dillons' breathtaking drawings, Burns tells this powerful story of how a king is born.

Quiet Hero: The Ira Hayes Story by S. D. Nelson (Lee & Low Books, 2009) D

When Ira Hayes was a young boy growing up on an Indian reservation in Arizona, he had never heard of Iwo Jima and probably wouldn't have thought in his wildest dreams that some day he would be fighting there, alongside other American Marines, for everything that his country held dear. Back then, Ira was still worried about school and escaping the girls who chased him around at recess trying to kiss him. Read how Ira Hayes grows up into a quiet hero.

We Are the Ship: The Story of Negro League Baseball by Kadir Nelson (Jump at the Sun, 2008) D

The story of the Negro Baseball League is told through the eyes of a player who witnessed the miraculous rise of the league in a time of racial segregation. From its founding in the 1920s to its folding after Jackie Robinson began the integration of Major League Baseball, this is a story that will captivate young sports fans and historians alike.

For Maturing Readers

Blackfeet Indian Stories by George Bird Grinnell (General Books LLC, 2010) M

This collection of stories and memories from the experiences of Blackfeet Indians brings to life this tribe's ancient culture. The stories have been passed down through oral storytelling through the generations, and are documented by George Bird Grinnell in a style faithful to the original "authors." Each story sheds light on the beliefs and practices of the Blackfeet people, and the stories are all short enough to be read in one sitting. This book is perfect for boys who are building their reading stamina and may be intrigued by American Indian culture.

Bloody Times: The Funeral of Abraham Lincoln and the Manhunt for Jefferson Davis by James L. Swanson (Collins, 2010) M

In this adaptation of his adult novel *Blood Crimes*, James Swanson writes about the death of Abraham Lincoln and the fall of the Confederacy president, Jefferson Davis, as a murder mystery. While Lincoln's death is often discussed in depth in American History classrooms, the manhunt for Jefferson Davis, the conspiracy theories on the Confederacy's involvement in the assassination, and the public mourning for a martyr and hero makes *Bloody Times* a fresh, fascinating take on this moment in the nation's collective past. As the journeys of Lincoln and Davis across the nation are woven together, one in a casket and the other as a fugitive, this breathless pageturner is sure to inspire new questions and conversations about the events leading up to and immediately following the end of the American Civil War.

East Side Dreams by Art Rodriguez (Dream House Press, 1999) M

This autobiography recounts the youth of Art Rodriguez as he grows up around crime and violence in San Jose, California. Rodriguez's story is not merely a cautionary tale of the tragedy of following in the footsteps of others heading down a bad road. It is an honest account of the difficult decisions and frightening situations young people sometimes face, and how one young man eventually learned how to make the right choices for himself and found his own road to happiness. The writing style is accessible for even the most resistant reader and the tension mounts palpably as Art's fate unfolds.

Facing the Lion: Growing Up Maasai on the African Savanna by Joseph Lemasolai Lekuton (National Geographic Children's Books, 2005) M

Joseph Lemasolai Lekuton tells the story of his own epic childhood. Lekuton's accounts of the Massai's nomadic tradition and the daily struggle for survival that shaped his earliest days bring a world and culture into sharp focus for older readers. It also highlights the clear contrast between that reality and the one Lekuton is thrust into when he is accepted at an exclusive Nairobi high school and later at an American university. Lekuton's journey from village to city to faraway country will fascinate young men, and his commitment to stay true to his roots and give back to his people is sure to inspire any reader to act with honor and heart.

Leonardo Da Vinci by Kathleen Krull, illustrated by Boris Kulikov (Viking Juvenile, 2005) M

This first volume in Krull's Giants of Science series gives a richly detailed narrative of Da Vinci's life and work. This concise volume takes readers through Da Vinci's apprenticeship, learning, academic revelations and discoveries, as well as his personal life. Kulikov's occasional ink drawings add depth to key moments in Da Vinci's life. Like all of the books in the series, the text is matter of fact and manageable for more hesitant readers, yet the content of Da Vinci's life is portrayed compellingly, with an action-oriented "plot" and a nuanced personal life. Perfect for fact-oriented readers who need some extra support, the Giants of Science series also includes:

- *Albert Einstein* by Kathleen Krull, illustrated by Boris Kulikov (Viking Juvenile, 2009)
- *Isaac Newton* by Kathleen Krull, illustrated by Boris Kulikov (Viking Juvenile, 2006)

Comic Books and Graphic Novels

For Emerging Readers

Boys of Steel: The Creators of Superman by Marc Tyler Nobleman, illustrated by Ross MacDonald (Random House Children's Books, 2008) E

Who were the masterminds behind Superman? Joe Shuster and Jerry Siegel never quite fit in with their high school classmates, but they graduated to become the creators of a world-famous superhero. Learn all about how two young men invented a character that became the admiration of children and adults around the world.

Watch Me Throw the Ball: An Elephant and Piggie Book by Mo Willems (Hyperion Books for Children, 2009) E

Gerald the elephant really wants to teach Piggie the pig to throw a ball. Gerald takes his job as Piggie's teacher very seriously, but Piggie just wants to have fun. Will they be able to find a solution so that everyone wins? Read the other titles in this series to follow the adventures of the pig and the elephant.

For Developing Readers

Bone series by Jeff Smith (Scholastic) D

Jeff Smith's Bone series recounts the adventures of the three Bone cousins: Fone Bone, Phoney Bone, and Smiley Bone. In *Out of Boneville*, the first book in the series, the cousins are run out of Boneville and become separated in a massive desert. They must battle wondrous creatures before they find one another in the end at the farm of Gran'ma Ben and her granddaughter, Thorn. The story continues in *The Great Cow Race*, when the troublesome Phoney Bone tries to cheat in the race. With each new adventure in the nine-volume series, the Bone cousins face great dangers and must work together to come out safely. With the help of their friends, they begin the journey back to Boneville at the close of the final book in the series, *Crown of Horns*. If you like these books, you'll like:

- *Copper* by Kazu Kibuishi (Graphix, 2010)
- Knights of the Lunch Table series by Frank Cammuso (Graphix)
- Magic Pickle series by Scott Morse (Oni Press)

Calvin and Hobbes series by Bill Watterson (Andrews McMeel Publishing) D

Calvin and his friend Hobbes, a stuffed tiger, find themselves embroiled in whirlwind adventures throughout this series. Laugh and race to finish reading the comic strips as Calvin and Hobbes weave their way in and out of trouble. Read about a face-off against some very angry snow creatures in *Attack of the Deranged Mutant Killer Monster Snow Goons* or read about life on Mars in *Weirdoes From Another Planet.*

Little Lit: Strange Stories for Strange Kids edited by Art Spiegelman and Françoise Mouly (Joanne Cotler, 2001) D

In this hybrid picture book and comic book, Spiegelman and Mouly have collected bizarre and funny stories from well-known children's authors like Maurice Sendak, Crockett Johnson, and Ian Falconer, as well as adult writers like David Sedaris and Paul Auster. Reveling in their own quirkiness, the stories in this collection run the gamut of the unexpected, from a baby who eats everything he sees to a man who discovers he has disappeared.

If you like this book, you'll also like:

- *Coraline: The Graphic Novel* by Neil Gaiman (HarperCollins, 2002)
- *Little Lit: Folklore and Fairy Tale Funnies* edited by Art Spiegelman and Françoise Mouly (Joanne Cotler, 2000)
- *Little Lit: It Was a Dark and Silly Night* edited by Art Spiegelman and Françoise Mouly (Joanne Cotler, 2003)
- *Redwall: The Graphic Novel* by Brian Jacques (Philomel, 2007)
- *The Wolves in the Walls* by Neil Gaiman (HarperCollins, 2005)

Dragonbreath by Ursula Vernon (Dial, 2009) D

Not only can Danny the Dragonbreath not breathe fire like all dragons should, he also just got an F on a paper that he wrote about the ocean. Will a field trip to the ocean with his iguana friend Wendell help him rewrite his paper and improve his grade? The boys see amazing animals that will intrigue young readers as they follow along on Danny and Wendell's guided tour led by Danny' cousin, Edward the sea serpent.

Fat Cat of Underwhere by Bruce Hale, illustrated by Shane Hillman (HarperCollins, 2009) D

Fitz the Fat Cat loves the easy life; napping, eating and ignoring humans are some of his favorite hobbies. His indulgent existence is thrown completely on its head when Fitz is called upon to leave his life of leisure to help three kids, Zeke, Stephanie, and Hector, save the world of Underwhere. Now Fitz is doing things he never dreamed of, like battling wild animals, unraveling the mystery shrouding a strange, new man in town, and even working together with humans. Look for even more stories from the land of Underwhere, including *Pirates of Underwhere, Flyboy of Underwhere,* and *Prince of Underwhere.*

Fox Trot series by Bill Amend (Universal Press Syndicate) D

Follow the Fox family—Jason, Paige, Peter, Andy, Roger, and (who could forget?) Quincy the iguana—as they go about their daily lives. All you need to bring along is your sense of humor. From "Orlando Bloom Has Ruined Everything" to "Think iFruity," Amend's comics will keep you smiling and in touch with the latest fads in pop culture.

Garfield series by Jim Davis (Random House) D

Who doesn't love a fat cat? Sometimes his owner, Jon Arbuckle, gets a little frustrated with Garfield, but their friendship has weathered the storm over the years. One of the most syndicated comics out there, Garfield has been an American mainstay, with good reason.

Negima!: Magister Negi Magi series by Ken Akamatsu (Pugol & Amado) D

Negi Springfield is a ten-year-old wizard prodigy on a mission to become a Master Magi. Before he can achieve this goal, he first has to do something in the real world. He is ultimately assigned to teach English in Japan . . . to a class of thirty-one middle school girls! There is also the mystery of Negi's missing father, the "Thousand Master" Nagi

Springfield. Will he be able to make his class take him seriously? Will he ever find out what happened to his father? If you like this book, be sure to read the other 24 books in the series!

Richard the Lionheart: The Life of a King and Crusader by David West and Jackie Gaff (Rosen Publishing Group, 2005) D

The life of Richard the Lionheart, king, crusader, and icon of the Middle Ages, is depicted in great detail in this vibrant biography. Focusing on his struggle to regain Jerusalem during the battle of Saladin, this graphic novel traces the steps that molded Richard the Lionheart into a powerful ruler. Follow the lives of Julius Caesar, Hernan Cortez, or Spartacus through the other wonderful books in this series.

The Storm in the Barn by Matt Phelan (Candlewick, 2009) D

Told primarily through illustrations, *The Storm in the Barn* is the story of a boy determined to save his farming family from the devastating effects of a long drought in Kansas during the time of the Dust Bowl. This young boy must summon up all of his courage to fight against the Storm King, the source of the great drought.

The Toon Treasury of Classic Children's Comics edited by Art Spiegelman and Francoise Mouly, introduction by Jon Scieszka (Abrams ComicArts, 2009) D

A compilation of comics that span from the 1940s to the 1960s, this book features works by renowned comic artists that include Carl Barks, the creator of Donald Duck, and Walt Kelly, the creator of Pogo. Boys who enjoy cartoons are sure to love these animated favorites in comic book form.

For Maturing Readers

American-Born Chinese by Gene Yuen Lang (Square Fish, 2008) M

In *American-Born Chinese*, the stories of three unhappy characters converge as they deal with complex issues. There is the loner, Jin Wang, the only Asian American student in his school who desperately wants to fit in; the Monkey King, who struggles to overcome his destiny and become mortal; and finally, there is Danny, an all-American Asian kid so humiliated by his stereotypical cousin Chin-Kee that he decides to change schools. Yang creates an impressive yet accessible commentary on race, identity, and acceptance.

The Sandman series by Neil Gaiman (DC Comics) M

What would you wish for if you could have anything in the world? What would you do if you captured the King of Dreams instead of Death himself? With the King of Dreams, anything seems possible. Find out what happens when a very unusual man has just that experience, unwittingly capturing a personage of unusual powers.

If you like this book, you'll also like:

- Amulet series by Kazu Kibuishi (Graphix)
- *Artemis Fowl: The Graphic Novel* by Eoin Colfer (Hyperion, 2007)
- *The Books of Magic* by Neil Gaiman (DC Comics, 1993)
- *Edgar Allan Poe: Graphic Classics* by Edgar Allan Poe (Eureka Productions 2010)
- *Flight, Volume One* by Kazu Kibuishi (Villard, 2007)
- *I Kill Giants* by Joe Kelly (Image Comics, 2009)
- *The League of Extraordinary Gentlemen* by Alan Moore (America's Best Comics, 2002)
- *M Is for Magic* by Neil Gaiman (HarperCollins, 2008)

Satchel Paige: Striking Out Jim Crow by James Sturm and Rich Tommaso (Hyperion Books for Children, 2007) M

In graphic novel format, Sturm and Tommaso tell the compelling and incredible story of Leroy "Satchel" Paige. Beginning with his early days as a pitcher in the segregated Negro Leagues in Alabama in the 1920s, Satchel Paige's life unfolds in the face of harsh social realities. Using just a baseball, Satchel struck out racist practices and managed to become a hero among world-class athletes. Recounting almost twenty years of baseball history, Sturm and Tommaso give an overview that is engaging and full of facts for budding historians and sports enthusiasts alike.

Expeditions

For Emerging Readers

Anno's Journey by Mitsumasa Anno (Putnam Juvenile, 1997) E

In this wordless picture book, Mitsumasa Anno takes young readers on a tour of northern Europe. At the start of his journey, Anno is alone but he doesn't stay that way. As Anno travels farther and farther, he encounters more and more interesting people in a variety of new places. The illustrations grow in detail throughout the story, making each reading an opportunity to find something new and imagine side stories within the expressive scenes. Because there are no words, the youngest reader can navigate this book while still being captivated by the imagery that drives this story of discovery and curiosity.

Harold and the Purple Crayon by Crockett Johnson (HarperCollins, 1955) E

The timeless story of Harold and his crayon relates a powerful message about imagination and creativity. Harold sketches a new world around him, conjuring landscapes, buildings, and even food when he gets hungry. Watch as Harold imagines and then creates his environment, simply yet bravely drawing his world. With the help of his purple crayon, Harold teaches us that we can create our own worlds and that our imaginations can come to life if we choose to use them.

The Snowy Day by Ezra Jack Keats (Puffin, 1976) E

In Ezra Jack Keats' now-classic tale, a little boy adventures through his neighborhood, transformed overnight into a snowy wonderland. Making a game out of the footprints he leaves, creating snow angels, avoiding a snowball fight, and even trying to save a snowball for tomorrow, the little boy in Keats's story revels in the universal joy that a snow-covered landscape inspires in small children. His familiar world is brand new and the day holds all of the quiet magic of childhood.

The Story About Ping by Marjorie Flack and Kurt Wise (Grosset & Dunlap, 2000) E

Ping is a little yellow duck who lives on a boat with his very large family. Every day they are let off the boat along the Yangtze River to find "pleasant things to eat." One day, to avoid getting in trouble for being the last duck back on the boat, Ping decides to stay out and explore. But that means Ping has to spend the night on his own and in the morning his home and family are nowhere in sight. Our plucky hero's feathers aren't ruffled though. Ping sets off on the Yangtze to find his family again.

For Developing Readers

Brothers in Hope: The Story of the Lost Boys of Sudan by Mary Williams, illustrated by Gregory Christie (Lee & Low Books, 2005) D

Garang is only eight years old when war changes his life forever. His village and his family are destroyed, and he and the other children who were lucky enough to escape the devastation must now find the courage to begin a new life. They become each other's new family on a vagabond's journey which takes them everywhere from Ethiopia to Kenya before they finally find a new place to call home.

Caravan by Lawrence McKay, Jr., illustrated by Darryl Ligasan (Lee & Low Books, 2008) D

Ten-year-old Jura sets off with his father on his first caravan journey. Jura is responsible for three camels as they climb through the snow and ice along the Pamir Mountains in Afghanistan. Enjoy the breathtaking illustrations of an Afghan marketplace and the vivid descriptions of mountain life.

Talk About It:

Talk about what people in different cultures do to mark the passage of time in their lives.

- What journeys have you been on?
- Have you ever been to a ceremony or graduated from a school or a camp? How did that make you feel? Are there other ceremonies or events you can think of that mark key moments of growing up?

The Good Rainbow Road by Simon J. Ortiz, illustrated by Michael Lacapa (The University of Arizona Press, 2004) D

A terrible draught has devastated the village of Haapaahnitse and two brothers, Tsaiyah-dzehshi and Hamahshu-dzehshi, must find the courage to journey far to the west to find the Shiwana, the home of the Rain and Snow spirits. Forced to cross arid deserts and steep mountains, the brothers make their way westward.

Magic Tree House series by Mary Pope Osborne (Random House Books for Young Readers) D

When Jack and Annie first stumble upon a magical tree house, they have little idea of the history that they will make! From ancient Egypt to medieval Ireland to the era of the new American West and beyond, two kids from Pennsylvania are about to redefine experiential learning. If you enjoy this series, be sure to read the follow-up series: The Magic Tree House: Merlin Missions!

The Miraculous Journey of Edward Tulane by Kate DiCamillo, illustrated by Bagram Ibatoulline (Candlewick, 2009) D

The china rabbit, Edward Tulane, begins his journey of self-discovery when a storm tragically rips him from the hands of his owner, ten-year-old Abilene, and he falls into the vast ocean. Luckily, a loving woman soon salvages Edward from the ocean. As he makes his way back to Abilene, passing through a few loving arms, Edward learns how to appreciate inner beauty and the value of love.

Talk About It:

- Have you ever lost something that was important to you? How did you cope with your loss?
- Have you ever been lost before?
- How did it feel when you found your way again?

Odd and the Frost Giants by Neil Gaiman (HarperCollins, 2009) D

Twelve-year-old Odd can't seem to shake a recent bout of bad luck. He decides to go to a hidden cabin in the forest to get away from it all. Along the way, Odd meets some strange companions and discovers that it is his responsibility to save the City of Gods from the dangerous Frost Giants! This gripping story seamlessly infuses Norse mythology into Odd's action-packed adventure; boys won't want to put it down.

The Phantom Tollbooth by Norton Juster, illustrations by Jules Feiffer (Random House, 1961) D

Milo doesn't find anything in his life very interesting. He doesn't see the point of school. After all, when will he ever need to know the location of Ethiopia or how to add and subtract turnips? He has steeled himself for another long, boring afternoon when he receives a mysterious package from an anonymous sender complete with materials and instructions on how to build a tollbooth. Soon, Milo is speeding along foreign highways in his toy car, bound for lands unknown. He travels through the land of Expectations, through the dreadful Doldrums, visits Dictionopolis and Digitopolis, and is ultimately charged with a quest to save the princesses Rhyme and Reason and restore order to the world of Wisdom.

Three Tales of My Father's Dragon by Ruth Stiles Gannett (Random House, 1997) D

While caught up in pursuing an alley cat, Elmer Elevator instead finds a baby dragon and proceeds to rescue and befriend it. Elmer and the flying dragon become fast friends when they attempt to escape from a treacherous island using unlikely tools like lollipops and rubber bands. This inspiring friendship will stay with you long after you turn the last page on this funny and heartfelt story.

For Developing to Maturing Readers

90 Miles to Havana by Enrique Flores-Galbis (Roaring Brook Press, 2010) D →M

Based on events in his own life, Enrique Flores-Galbis shares the story of a boy's journey across an ocean and into manhood. It is 1961, and Julian and his two brothers leave Cuba with 14,000 other children in what is called "Operation Pedro Pan." The story is full of adventure and suspense as Julian is separated from his brothers in the United States and must struggle alone to find them once more. A truly likeable child at the story's start, Julian grows into a compassionate and intelligent young man. As he strives to reunite with his family, he is always willing to prolong his search to help those in need that he meets along the way. Boys will be thrilled by the action but be truly drawn in by Julian's charisma, turning the pages as fast as they can read them to be sure the hero is with his family once more at story's end.

For Maturing Readers

The Arrival by Shaun Tan (Arthur A. Levine Books, 2007) M

This wordless picture book depicts the journey of a man to a land far away from his home. The pictures evoke the emotions he experiences as he leaves his family behind and emigrates to a new country. Readers fill in the story of this man's journey with their own words, using the vibrant and powerful pictures as a guide, and experience the depth of challenges that a change can cause both within and without.

If you like this book, you'll also like:

- *The Complete Persepolis* by Marjane Satrapi (Pantheon, 2007)
- *The Lost Thing* by Shaun Tan (Lothian, 2002)
- *Memorial* by Gary Crew and Shaun Tan (Simply Read, 2004)
- *The Rabbits* by John Marsden and Shaun Tan (Simply Read, 2003)
- *The Red Tree* by Shaun Tan (Lothian, 2008)
- *The Viewer* by Gary Crew (Simply Read, 2003)

Heart of a Samurai by Margi Preus (Amulet Books 2010) M

Manjiro is a 14-year-old Japanese boy. When a storm destroys his fishing boat and casts him and four of his friends adrift at sea, they almost starve on an island before being rescued by an American whaling ship. The story is set in 1841, and the two cultures are at odds, both thinking the other barbaric and backward. Despite the prejudices and misconceptions of the time, Manjiro forms a bond with the ship's captain, has many adventures at sea, and chooses to continue his adventure with Captain Whitfield by returning to America with him as his son. This seafaring adventure tale combines action and reflection as Manjiro learns about himself and discovers a whole new world.

Neverwhere by Neil Gaiman (Harper Perennial, 2003) M

Forced into the world of London Below, Richard Mayhew must embark on a quest through the dangers and shadows of a place of forgotten things. Along the way, Richard meets companions for his journey. A girl named Door is trying to find out who sent assassins that murdered her family and why. A deceiver who calls himself the Marquis of Carabas trades services for unthinkable favors. Richard's third companion is a Hunter, and she is as mysterious as the other two. The four travelers navigate through an inspired world that will leave readers hungry for more of Gaiman's unique fiction.

The Sea of Trolls by Nancy Farmer (Simon & Schuster Children's Books, 2005) M

Nancy Farmer has created an epic quest in a world where mythology and history are entwined. Jack is a Saxon boy in a medieval village. He and his little sister, Lucy, are captured by Vikings and taken to the court of King Ivar the Boneless and his half-troll wife Frith. When Jack casts a spell that makes the queen's hair fall out, he is sent on a quest across the Sea of Trolls to find a spell that will return the queen's lovely locks. If Jack fails to find Mimir's Well, the waters of which are supposed to show him the way to put things right, Lucy will be sacrificed to Frith's patron goddess, Freya. Jack meets giant troll-bears and man-eating spiders on his journey, but he also grows into a wise, courageous, young man.

Fantasy and Imagination

For Emerging Readers

And to Think That I Saw It on Mulberry Street by Dr. Seuss (Random House, 1989) E

As Marco walks home from school, he keeps his eyes open and pays attention to all that he sees and hears. When the walk seems too quiet and calm, Marco invents wonderful things that he wishes were happening on his street. A horse and cart become a zebra and a charioteer. When even the zebra starts to seem too ordinary, Marco imagines a reindeer and a sleigh instead. As Marco's imagination takes him on a wild ride, his walk home from school becomes an adventure through crowds of giraffes and elephants and even a big brass band! Marco creates a parade for himself, and he feels sure that he has a story to tell that no one could ever beat. But when his father asks him what he saw on his way home from school, Marco decides to tell the truth. All that he saw was a little horse and a cart on Mulberry Street.

Talk About It:

Use *And to Think That I Saw It on Mulberry Street* to talk about the fun of being imaginative, as well as the importance of being honest.

- How do you use your imagination to make everyday activities seem more exciting?
- Marco creates an elaborate story to tell his father about his walk home, but in the end he decides to just tell the truth. Why do you think Marco doesn't tell his father the story he invented?
- Have you ever been tempted to give a more creative answer than the truth?

Miles to Go by Jamie Harper (Candlewick, 2010) E

Miles is a preschooler and avid driver. It is another day of school and Miles has to make sure he packs his car up, puts on his seatbelt, and cranks his key. This is the story of a young boy's adventures getting to school, zigging and zagging past his sister's tricycle and brother's truck and filling up his tank.

The Odious Ogre by Norman Juster, illustrated by Jules Feiffer (Michael di Capua Books, 2010) E

The odious ogre terrorizes the countryside and is very good at his job. All the people of the town are terrified of him until one day he meets a beautiful girl in the forest who is not afraid. This young lady is in fact very kind to him and offers him food and friendship. The ogre does everything he can to frighten her but she continues to be generous and polite. This story's playful wordplay and beautiful watercolor illustrations enhance its message of friendship and kindness with a good dose of humor.

Robot Zot! by Jon Scieszka, illustrated by David Shannon (Simon & Schuster Children's Publishing, 2009) E

The three-inch alien Robot Zot has just landed in a suburban kitchen. Now he must complete his mission to take over the world, but how? Robot Zot decides to start with the kitchen and work his way up and out. He begins conquering kitchen appliances, cell phones, televisions, and everything else in his sight. Readers won't be able to stop laughing when the "battles" begin and will love how the relentless Robot Zot is the victor in the end.

The Super Hungry Dinosaur by Martin Waddell (Dial, 2009) E

One sunny afternoon, Hal must find a way to distract the ravenous dinosaur that wanders into his backyard. Distracting a dinosaur is pretty tough work, and this particular dinosaur seems bent on devouring not only Hal but his family and dog. Luckily, our calm, clever hero is up to the challenge. Young readers will be impressed and amused by the antics that ensue as Hal outwits and captures the dinosaur. In the end, spaghetti is what everyone has for dinner.

The Way Back Home by Oliver Jeffers (Philomel, 2008) E

A boy finds an airplane in his closet and decides to fly it into outer space. While flying through space, his plane begins to sputter. Much to the boy's surprise, he is out of fuel and must perform a last minute landing on the moon! A little while later another spaceship crashes, and a Martian boy comes out. At first the two boys are afraid of each other, but it isn't long before they become friends. By working together, they are able to fix their spaceships and get back home.

Where the Wild Things Are by Maurice Sendak (HarperCollins: 1988) E

When Max is sent to his room after misbehaving, his parents have no idea that he is about to set off on a magical journey to an uncharted forest and rise to become the fearless leader of the wild things. But, when Max grows homesick and yearns to return once again to his room, he isn't sure what might be waiting for him there. Have a wild adventure with Max in this Sendak classic.

Talk About It:

Have you ever used your imagination to journey to a faraway place?

- Would you want to rule your imaginary place, like Max? Why? Why not?

- Have you ever felt lonely or homesick like Max?
- What did you do to feel better?
- Did someone help you feel better?

For Developing Readers

Airborn by Kenneth Oppel (HarperCollins, 2004) D

Fifteen-year-old Matt loves his job aboard the Aurora, a luxury craft that travels through space. When Matt's travels take him to meet a dying man who insists that he saw mysterious creatures flying over a deserted island, he will rest at nothing to discover the truth. With a little bit of help from his new friend, Kate, Matt proves the mysterious man right. An apparently deserted island is actually home to unscrupulous pirates and a previously unknown species. Will Matt and Kate be able to document the creatures and leave the island safely in spite of threats from the hostile pirates?

Atherton trilogy by Patrick Carman (Little, Brown Books for Young Readers) D

In *The House of Power*, Edgar's adventures begin with a bang—he must save his world before it collapses in on itself. As the trilogy continues, so do the threats to Atherton. Each time the great responsibility of keeping the peace falls on the shoulders of young Edgar. Growing readers will look forward to the moments when Edgar is able to summon the courage that he needs, just in the knick of time. In the end, our hero is always able to save the only home he's ever known.

Babe: The Gallant Pig by Dick King Smith, illustrated by Maggie Kneen (Knopf Books for Young Readers, 2005) D

Babe is a lovable pig whose gentleness and sense of loyalty motivates him to follow in his foster mother's footsteps and become a sheep-pig. Babe's odd talent for sheepherding, despite being a pig, saves his life and prevents Mrs. Hogget from serving him as bacon. After Babe has saved his flock from danger more than once, Farmer Hogget enters Babe into the Grand Challenge Sheepdog Trials. Babe's story shows that kindness and gentleness are more powerful than brute force. Boys will love the humorous moments of the story and how Babe is able to come out on top as an unlikely champion.

Beast Quest series by Adam Blade (Scholastic) D

When strange things start happening in Tom's village, the king suddenly calls upon this unlikely hero. Tom's village is protected by special creatures, giant beasts, but something is not right. To free the kingdom and its guardian beasts from the curses unfolding, Tom must swallow his fears and battle the Dark Wizard, Malvel. Follow Tom as his adventures continue to unfold and the mysteries begin to come clear in the Beast Quest series.

The BFG by Roald Dahl, illustrated by Quentin Blake (Puffin, 2007) D

One night, a girl named Sophie sees the BFG, short for Big Friendly Giant, putting dreams in people's ears. He snatches Sophie from her bed at the orphanage and takes her to his cave to protect the secret of the giants' existence. Though she is initially afraid she will be eaten, Sophie soon learns that the BFG is not like the other man-eating giants who eat children; he is a kind and gentle soul who wants to protect children. Unfortunately, the BFG's fellow giants are nothing like him. Sophie and the BFG devise a plan to defeat the man-eating giants and keep the world's children safe.

Children of the Lamp series by P. B. Kerr (Scholastic) D

In the first book in the series, *The Akhenaten Adventure*, twins John and Philippa Gaunt discover that they are descended from a long line of djinn. Djinn are magical spirits that live on Earth disguised in human and animal forms. They can influence the normal humans around them, for good or for evil. Suddenly, John and Philippa have the power to grant wishes, travel the globe, and make things disappear. However, your boys will realize as the series builds momentum that it is what the twins choose to do with their newfound powers that will shape their future and their destinies.

Children of the Red King: Charlie Bone series by Jenny Nimmo (Scholastic) D

Charlie Bone is just a normal boy, until he discovers that he is a descendant of the Red King. Like all of the Red King's progeny, Charlie has been endowed with magical abilities. In the first book in the series, *Midnight for Charlie Bone*, Charlie finds that he can hear the thoughts of people in photographs at the moment the picture was being taken. When he finds an old photo and hears about a missing girl, he and his friends at Bloor's Academy embark on a quest to find her. The headmaster and many of the adults in the series are mysteriously sinister characters who do everything that they can to thwart the children's altruistic quest.

Chronicles of Narnia series by C. S. Lewis (HarperCollins) D

In the most well-known story in this seven-part series, four siblings, Peter, Susan, Lucy, and Edmund, stumble upon Narnia when they are playing hide-and-seek in a wardrobe. In a land where it is always winter and never Christmas, the children meet both welcoming friends and the most diabolical of enemies. It is up to them to restore peace, with the help and guidance of the Great Lion, Aslan. Read the entire series to meet all of the inhabitants and visitors who make Narnia the magical place your boys are sure to love.

Dragon Rider by Cornelia Funke (The Chicken House, 2004) D

Firedrake, a young and brave dragon, must make the dangerous journey from the Earth's surface to the Rim of Heaven. If Firedrake doesn't succeed in reaching the Rim of Heaven, the last safe place for dragons, he risks being destroyed by his human enemies. The heroic young dragon makes many friends on his journey, but will he reach sanctuary before it is too late? This story of courage and compassion will be a favorite for boys who have a penchant for dragons and adventure.

Fablehaven series by Brandon Mull (Aladdin) D

In this gripping series, Kendra and Seth are ordinary siblings until they discover that their grandfather is the guardian of the gates of a magical community of fantastical creatures called Fablehaven. When his important task is passed on to them, the brother and sister team must rise to the occasion, though they are not quite sure what that will mean for them. Their adventures to keep Fablehaven safe from powerful forces of evil will keep readers coming back to this series again and again.

Inkheart by Cornelia Funke (The Chicken House, 2003) D

Maggie's father, Mo, has the ability to bring characters from a book to life by just reading the words aloud. Maggie and Mo revel in this gift and share a love for the books and stories that Mo brings to life. Her father's gift becomes a burden when Capricorn, a story's villain, tries to use Mo's powers for his own evil plans. The father and daughter must work together to outwit their selfish and heartless foe. Maggie and Mo's adventures continue in *Inkspell* and *Inkdeath*.

Jake Ransom and the Skull King's Shadow by James Rollins (HarperCollins, 2009) D

When Jake and his sister Kady visit the British Museum to get a closer look at the Mayan treasures that their parents discovered right before they disappeared, the two siblings accidentally fall into a portal that leads them to Calypsos, a strange world complete with dinosaurs and ancient civilizations. Now Jake, Kady, and two new friends must fight to save this secret land from destruction, and find out the whereabouts of their parents along the way.

James and the Giant Peach by Roald Dahl, illustrated by Quentin Blake (Puffin, 2007) D

After four-year-old James's parents are eaten by a rhinoceros, he goes to live with his horrible aunts, Spiker and Sponge. His luck changes for the better when a mysterious man gives him a sack of green-glowing crocodile tongues and tells James how to make a magic potion with them. On his way back home, James accidentally drops the tongues near a peach tree. So begins his adventure. With the magic tongues inside of it, the tree produces the largest peach the world has ever seen. James befriends the giant insects who live inside the center of the peach, and they accidentally set off on an adventure that carries them all far away from Spiker and Sponge and their misery.

Keys to the Kingdom series by Garth Nix (Scholastic) D

When this series begins, Arthur dreams that he is given a mysterious key. Imagine his surprise when he wakes up and discovers that not only does he still have the key, but there is suddenly a strange new house on his street. Arthur must unravel the house's mysteries while saving his city from a bizarre sleeping illness. He must avoid being caught by the mysterious and ruthless Mister Monday. Arthur's adventures continue in this gripping and clever seven-part series.

If you like this, read:

- *Abhorsen* by Garth Nix (HarperCollins, 2003)
- *The Alchemyst: The Secrets of the Immortal Nicholas Flamel* by Michael Scott (Delacorte, 2007)
- *The Black Cauldron* by Lloyd Alexander (Henry Holt & Co., 1965)
- *The Book of Three* by Lloyd Alexander (Henry Holt & Co., 1964)
- *The Castle of Llyr* by Lloyd Alexander (Henry Holt & Co., 1966)
- *Lirael* by Garth Nix (HarperCollins, 2001)
- *The Magician: The Secrets of the Immortal Nicholas Flamel* by Michael Scott (Delacorte, 2008)
- *The Necromancer: The Secrets of the Immortal Nicholas Flamel* by Michael Scott (Delacorte, 2010)

- *Sabriel* by Garth Nix (HarperCollins, 1995)
- *The Sorceress: The Secrets of the Immortal Nicholas Flamel* by Michael Scott (Delacorte, 2009)

The King in the Window by Adam Gopnik (Disney Children's Books, 2006) D

Eleven-year-old Oliver Parker, an American living in Paris, knows that with great power comes great responsibility. When Oliver discovers that he is the King of the Windows, he must find the strength to save his father from the menacing Master of Mirrors. In his adventures Oliver encounters an elderly Alice in Wonderland, Nostradamus, and other inspired characters who paint a rich and exciting backdrop for this epic battle.

The Lost Hero (Book One): The Heroes of Olympus by Rick Riordan (Hyperion Books for Children, 2010) D

This is a new series from Rick Riordan that builds on his successful Percy Jackson series. Percy Jackson and his friends are no longer at Camp Half-Blood, but a new group of demigods have arrived to uncover their own prophecy. In this first book of the series, we are introduced to Jason who has amnesia, Piper whose father has been missing for three days, and Leo who feels at home at Camp Half-Blood but doesn't understand that he and his new friends are all the sons and daughters of one human parent and one parent who is an immortal god. While familiar enough for lovers of the Percy Jackson and the Olympians series, this is a series that readers new to Camp Half-Blood can dive right into.

The Last Apprentice series by Joseph Delaney (Greenwillow Books) D

As the seventh son of a seventh son, Thomas is chosen to become the apprentice of the town Spook, who fights off evil spirits. When the Spook is away, Thomas finds that he alone must protect his country from the creatures of the dark, witches and bogarts included. Follow this eerie adventure series and learn how the last apprentice defeats even the most sinister of creatures.

Lionboy by Zizou Corder (Puffin, 2004) D

After the mysterious disappearance of his parents, Charlie finds himself on the Thames River aboard the Floating Circus ship en route to Paris. While attempting to escape an evil villain and trying to free the lonely animals aboard the ship, Charlie discovers his hidden talent for languages—he can speak to cats! This special skill aids Charlie as he tries to outwit his enemies. Follow Charlie's story as it continues in *Lionboy: The Chase* and *Lionboy: The Truth*.

Nathaniel Fludd, Beastologist series by R. L. LaFevers, illustrated by Kelly Murphy (Houghton Mifflin Books for Children) D

In the first book of this series, ten-year-old Nathaniel has learned that his parents are lost at sea and presumed to be dead. The year is 1928, and Nathaniel must go off to live with his eccentric Aunt Phil A. Fludd who is a beastologist with a pet dodo. Nathaniel was never one to seek out excitement but discovers in his new home that he comes from a family of world-renowned adventurers. Nathaniel soon finds himself on a plane to Arabia to oversee the birth of a Phoenix. When Aunt Phil is captured, Nathaniel must protect the Phoenix and save his aunt and himself! This story is filled with adventures and secrets that growing readers will delight in uncovering. The adventures continue in *The Basilisk's Lair*, Book 2 in the series.

The Neddiad by Daniel Pinkwater (Houghton Mifflin Company, 2007) D

While Neddie Wentworthstein is traveling from his old home in Chicago to his new home in Los Angeles, he meets an Indian Shaman named Melvin who entrusts him with a very precious turtle. In order to prevent the destruction of civilization, Neddie must protect the turtle from falling into the wrong hands. Join the adventure as the pair make an incredible journey, and find out if Neddie will make it safely to Los Angeles with his prized companion intact. If you enjoyed this story, be sure to read the sequel, *The Yggysey*.

'Ologies series by Dugald A. Steer (Candlewick) D

Each 'Ology book is written as a fictional travel journal complete with handwritten notes in sealed pockets, photographs, letters, and a stunning array of trivia and secret knowledge from the "expert author" in the field. These books are both interactive and highly imaginative, allowing boys to actively engage with the physical elements of the book as well as the adventures that unfold in the pages of the journal. *Dragonology, Wizardology, Pirateology,* and *Monsterology* are just a few of the many favorites for boys!

Percy Jackson and the Olympians series by Rick Riordan (Hyperion Books for Children) D

In the first book in the series, *The Lightning Thief*, Percy Jackson is living in New York City with his mean stepfather. After being kicked out of school, he discovers that he is a demigod. This means he is not an ordinary boy but half-mortal and half-Greek god! As Percy mediates a fight between Zeus and Poseidon and searches for the missing Annabeth, daughter of Athena, he gradually transforms from a jaded black sheep into a true hero. Caught between the worlds of Greek mythology and reality, Percy's adventures continue in *The Sea of Monsters* and the rest of the Percy Jackson and the Olympians series.

Peter and the Starcatchers **by Dave Barry and Ridley Pearson, illustrated by Greg Call (Disney Editions, 2004) D**

Originally planned as a three-part prequel to J. M. Barrie's version of *Peter Pan*, this book tells the story of fourteen-year-old Molly, an apprentice Starcatcher, and her friend Peter (a younger Peter Pan) on their whirlwind adventures aboard the Never Land, a ship of slaves captained by a fearsome pirate. As Starcatchers, Molly and Peter try to gain special powers by tracking down and catching bits of Starstuff before it lands on Earth. Follow Molly and Peter's adventures as they continue in the rest of the Starcatchers series. If you like this series, you'll love the Never Land series, also by Dave Barry and Ridley Pearson. It begins with *Escape from the Carnivale: A Never Land Book.*

Simon Bloom: The Gravity Keeper **by Michael Reisman (Dutton Juvenile, 2008) D**

The discovery of a magical forest in the middle of his hometown of Lawnville, New Jersey, leads Simon Bloom and his friend, Owen, on the biggest adventure of their lives. With a copy of the *Teachers Edition of Physics*, Simon and his friends have the power to use scientific formulas to control gravity. Boys will love how Simon's adventures continue in *Simon Bloom: The Octopus Effect.*

Spaceheadz **by Jon Scieszka, illustrated by Shane Prigmore (Simon & Schuster Children's Publishing, 2010) D**

Michael is the new kid in the fifth grade, and his first day goes surprisingly well. In fact, it goes too well. As it turns out, all of the new friends Michael made on his first day are not fifth graders like he is; they are aliens! These aliens came to earth in the form of children, with their leader in the form of a hamster, and they are determined to convert 3,400,001 real human children to SPHDZ. Find out what Michael decides to do with his shocking discovery in this humorous and unusual tale.

The Spiderwick Chronicles series by Holly Black and Tony DiTerlizzi (Random House) D

Mallory, Jared, and Simon Grace move to the Spiderwick estate, where they enter a realm of fantasy and mystery. The siblings encounter goblins and fairies, uncover secrets, and have remarkable adventures! Each sibling has a distinct personality, but they must combine their talents to uncover all of the secrets waiting to be found in their mansion of mystery.

Swordbird by Nancy Yi Fan (HarperCollins, 2008) D

The cardinals and the blue jays of Stone-Run Forest have been fighting for so long that they can no longer remember what started their quarrel in the first place. The fight has escalated to the point where they are stealing each other's eggs and the future of forest life is in jeopardy. The only one who can stop the madness is the legendary Swordbird. But will he make it in time? If you like this book, read the others in the series.

The Tale of Despereaux by Kate DiCamillo, illustrated by Timothy Basil Ering (Candlewick, 2006) D

In four stories, DiCamillo weaves together the lives of mice, rats, and humans who fall in love, are banished, and strive for greatness. Meet the mouse, Despereaux, his lady love, the Princess Pea, the soup-and-light-loving rat, and the not-so-smart Miggery Sow. As their destinies intertwine, each character is able to find happiness by accepting who they are. Boys will laugh with and root for little Despereaux, the mouse who never lets his size stand in his way.

Time Stops for No Mouse by Michael Hoeye (Puffin, 2007) D

Hermux Tantamoq is a mouse with many skills. Hermux can repair watches and loves to write letters. When his idol, Linka Perflinger, disappears, Hermux must use his wits and courage to solve the mystery of her whereabouts. The clever hero is able escape many dastardly traps in this larger-than-life adventure and is ultimately able to uncover the truth and win the day.

Tollins: Explosive Tales for Children by Conn Iggulden (HarperCollins, 2009) D

From the co-author of the *The Dangerous Book for Boys* comes the story of an often-antagonistic relationship between humans and fairies. Iggulden's fairies are different from any that you've encountered before—the Tollinses are much more durable than Tinkerbell! Led by an innovative "Tollinboy" named Sparkler, these tales will live up to their explosive reputation.

The Unusual Mind of Vincent Shadow **by Tim Kehoe, illustrated by Mike Wohnoutka and Guy Francis (Little, Brown Books for Young Readers, 2009) D**

Vincent Shadow definitely does not fit in. Instead of playing sports and easily making friends, Vincent has a special power that allows him to receive visions of fabulous toys. When his father remarries and Vincent must move away from his home and the secret laboratory that his mother helped him build before she died, he begins to lose his inspiration. But soon, Vincent learns of a wonderful opportunity that would allow him to put his special talent to use: a toy-invention contest. Boys won't be able to put down this celebration of the wonderful gifts within each of us.

For Developing to Maturing Readers

Animorphs series by K. A. Applegate (Scholastic) D →M

The series starts with *The Invasion*, when five teens stumble across a crashed alien spaceship whose pilot is dying. Before life leaves him, the pilot gives the friends a special gift. They become Animorphs and can turn into any animal that they touch. Jake, Rachel, Tobias, Cassie, and Marco are suddenly secret superheroes, thrust into a covert war for Planet Earth!

Harry Potter series by J. K. Rowling (Scholastic) D →M

Harry Potter is an orphan who discovers he has a magical destiny when he receives a letter of acceptance to the Hogwarts School of Witchcraft and Wizardry on his eleventh birthday. In this extraordinary new world, Harry makes his first real friends, classmates Ron and Hermione, Hogwarts Headmaster Professor Dumbledore, and Groundskeeper Hagrid. Readers will also learn spells, potions, and a new vocabulary of wizarding words. While Harry is finally starting to feel at home in this new world, evil approaches in the form of Lord Voldemort, a dark wizard trying to rise again. With this richly imagined series, Rowling changed the landscape of children's literature forever.

If you like this book, you'll like:

- Daniel X series by James Patterson (Little, Brown Books for Young Readers) M
- *The Hobbit* by J. R. R. Tolkein (Ballantine Books, 1986) M
- *Witch and Wizard* by James Patterson and Gabrielle Charbonnet (Little, Brown Books for Young Readers, 2010) M
- *Witch and Wizard: The Gift* by James Patterson and Ned Rust (Little, Brown Books for Young Readers, 2010) M

The Name of This Book Is Secret **by Pseudonymous Bosch (Little, Brown Books for Young Readers, 2008) D ->M**

The first page of this book displays an unlikely warning: DO NOT READ BEYOND THIS PAGE. The secrets contained beyond it are said to be too dangerous to share. The narrator makes a deal with the reader: He'll tell the story if the reader promises to forget everything he has heard once it's over. So begins the adventure of Cassie and Max-Earnest as they battle a secret society bent on immortality. Boys who love mysterious codes and cleverly hidden clues will love this thrilling tale.

If you like this book, you'll also like:

- *The Figure in the Shadows* by John Bellairs (Puffin, 1993)
- *The Ghost in the Mirror* by John Bellairs (Puffin, 1994)
- *The House With a Clock in Its Walls* by John Bellairs (Puffin, 1993)
- *If You're Reading This It's Too Late* by Pseudonymous Bosch (Little, Brown, 2008)
- *This Book Is Not Good for You* by Pseudonymous Bosch (Little, Brown, 2009)
- *This Isn't What It Looks Like* by Pseudonymous Bosch (Little, Brown, 2010)
- *The Tilting House* by Tom Llewellyn (Tricycle, 2010)
- *The Willoughbys* by Lois Lowry (Houghton Mifflin, 2009)

The Seems series by John Hulme and Michael Wexler (Bloomsbury USA Children's Books) D ->M

In *The Seems: The Glitch in Sleep*, the first book in the series, twelve-year-old Becker Drane works as a Fixer for The Seems, a secret universe that parallels our own universe and serves to correct the flaws in our world. Becker is assigned to fix a glitch reported to the Department of Sleep, but he quickly discovers that this may not be a standard mission. It will take all of his training and tools to fix the problem. Boys will love this series as Becker's story continues in *The Seems: The Split Second.*

Skellig **by David Almond (Random House, 1998) D ->M**

Michael was excited about moving into a new house, but that all changed when his baby sister suddenly became sick. As he struggles to cope with his sister's illness, Michael finds an unusual creature, Skellig. A cross between a man, an owl, and an angel, Skellig teaches Michael and his best friend, Mina, many lessons. Skellig shares insights about love, death, and the value of caring family and friends, while Michael and Mina grow up together.

Stardust by Neil Gaiman (HarperTeen, 2008) D →M

How do you catch a falling star? Tristran Thorn could use some advice as he sets off on a journey to do just that. The most beautiful girl in town has promised him her heart if he will bring her a star they see falling from the sky. To catch the star, Tristran journeys into the magical land of Faerie. There he meets wonderful characters with incredible talents, and a special young girl who is more than what she appears!

For Maturing Readers

Alfred Kropp series by Rick Yancey (Bloomsbury USA Children's Books) M

Begin on the path to becoming a hero with the clumsy and overgrown Alfred Kropp in *The Extraordinary Adventures of Alfred Kropp*. When Alfred's mother dies, he is sent to live with his uncle who convinces him to steal a sword from the office where he is a night watchman. The sword, Alfred discovers, is actually Excalibur, and forces for good and evil come after our unlikely hero, stopping at nothing to get their hands on it. If Alfred's first fast-paced adventure intrigues you, look for the next in the series, *Seal of Solomon: Alfred Kropp II*.

Artemis Fowl series by Eoin Colfer (Hyperion Books for Children) M

Teenage genius and criminal mastermind Artemis Fowl takes on fairies, demons, and fellow humans in this series full of fantastical folklore. In *Artemis Fowl*, the first book in the series, Artemis faces off against Captain Holly Short of the fairies in an attempt to steal gold from them. Follow each of Artemis's plots to expand his criminal network as you make your way through this suspenseful collection of whirlwind adventures.

The Book of Time trilogy by Guillaume Prevost (Arthur A. Levine Books) M

Sam's discovery of the Book of Time allows him to travel to the past. In the first book in this wildly adventurous trilogy, Sam's father has been missing for days when the Book falls into his hands. As Sam travels through time and has many adventures, he is still unable to figure out exactly how the Book works. As the first volume comes to a close, Sam receives a message from his father who is imprisoned by Dracula. The sequels will have Sam navigating ancient Greece, early Rome, and Depression-era America, all while trying to rescue his father and defeat his captor.

Chronicles of Ancient Darkness series by Michelle Paver (HarperCollins) M

Torak sets out on a journey to find the World Spirit, the only force that has the power to defeat the evil demon-bear that brutally attacked his father. When the boy and his wolfish sidekick are captured by the Raven Clan, Torak learns that he is known as the Listener. Our hero must defeat the evil Shadow, a force that is overpowering the area, by uncovering three lost artifacts. As the friends journey through their mystical world, we are swept into a fast-paced story of mystery and bravery.

Chronicles of Vladimir Tod series by Heather Brewer (Speak, an Imprint of Penguin Group) M

Follow Vlad as he tries to get through junior high and high school, be popular, get the girl he likes to notice him as more than a friend and, of course, avoid being hunted down by vampire slayers! When the series begins, Vlad is in eighth grade and his parents have died in a mysterious accident. His mother was human but his father was a vampire, and without them, Vlad must confide in his friend, Henry, and rely on his new guardian, "Aunt" Nelly, to help him figure out who he is. As Vlad discovers the extent of his powers and avoids attacks from bullies and vampire hunters alike, maturing readers will see their own struggles with finding their own identity and growing up in a world that always seems to be changing.

Cirque du Freak series by Darren Shan (Little, Brown Books for Young Readers, 2002) M

Cirque du Freak: A Living Nightmare is the first episode in a series of twelve books that documents Darren Shan's transformation from human to vampire. It all begins when Darren and his best friend Steve Leonard go to a traveling freak show and meet Mr. Crepsley and Madam Octa, a horrifically engorged spider. Steve wants to become a vampire, and Darren, who has always been fascinated by spiders, would do anything to have one like Madam Octa. Blinded by their secret aspirations, both boys become caught in the web of their new acquaintances, and their lives change forever.

Ender's Game by Orson Scott Card (Tor Science Fiction, 1994) M

Ender is a boy genius selected for Battle School, a secret school that trains children in the art of war. Unbeknownst to him, Ender is humanity's last hope in an intergalactic war against fearsome aliens. Join Ender as he discovers his own destiny, while changing the destiny of two great species. Continue the adventure with Ender in *Speaker for the Dead, Xenocide,* and *Children of the Mind,* and get acquainted with Ender's friend Bean in *Ender's Shadow, Shadow of the Hegemon, Shadow Puppets,* and *Shadow of the Giant.*

The Eyeball Collector by F. E. Higgins (Feiwel & Friends, 2009) M

Hector's determination to find the glass-eyed man who scammed his father takes him on a harrowing journey to Withypits Hall, a dark and mysterious place. On his journey, Hector meets diabolical and curious characters and is confronted with riddles and twists that will keep the reader guessing. Along the way, Hector discovers his own strength as he must rise above the ways of his enemies. If you like this story, check out other books by F. E. Higgins, including: *The Black Book of Secrets* and *The Bone Magician.*

The Gatekeepers series by Anthony Horowitz (Scholastic) M

Matt is an orphan who is forced to live with an eccentric old woman. When he teams up with four other teens to fight against the evil forces behind the Raven's Gate, the friends are swept up in a globetrotting adventure. Follow these five brave heroes as they fight their way across the world, battling evil from Hong Kong to Peru!

The Golden Compass by Philip Pullman (Knopf Books for Young Readers, 1996) M

Eleven-year-old Lyra Belaqua is an orphan living at a university in Oxford, England, with her daemon, an animal spirit that accompanies and advises its human companion. Her carefree life ends when children start disappearing from her town. Lyra decides it is up to her to save them and finds herself in a race against time to save herself, too! The mystery deepens as our heroine learns her own special role to play in the conspiracy of Dust. Discover the exciting continuation of Lyra's adventures in *The Subtle Knife* and *The Amber Spyglass.*

The Graveyard Book by Neil Gaiman (HarperCollins, 2008) M

When he is only a toddler, Bod loses his whole family in a terrible attack at the hands of the knife-wielding murderous Jack. Bod manages to escape the brutal violence and finds sanctuary in a nearby graveyard under the protection of kindly resident ghosts. Cared for as he grows up by an odd assortment of living and non-living characters, Bod learns to survive both inside and outside of the graveyard. Boys will be fascinated by Bod's adventures in his creepy new home and will feel the suspense mount as Jack continues to hunt for the young hero.

The Hunger Games by Suzanne Collins (Scholastic, 2008) M

In this dystopian novel, the United States no longer exists; it has been replaced by a country called Panem that is made up of twelve districts. Every year, two children from each district must compete in the Hunger Games, a vicious, televised competition for survival. Katniss sacrifices herself, taking her sister's place in the Games. Once inside the Games, Katniss's teammate Peeta helps her discover that she may lose something more precious than her life. Will they both be able to hold on to their humanity? This book is very intense and dark, so it's not for your boys if they are easily disturbed or too young maturity wise, but it is brilliant and unforgettable. The sequel, *Catching Fire* is even better.

Talk About It:

- Have you ever felt strongly that something in your world was unfair or wrong?
- Have you ever been responsible for someone else's well-being?

Inheritance trilogy by Christopher Paolini (Random House) M

This series begins when a boy named Eragon discovers a strange blue stone in the forest. The stone turns out to be a dragon's egg, and Eragon and his dragon Saphira become friends and allies, supporting each other in a war-torn magical world. This action-packed and engrossing story is filled with elves, magic, and an epic battle between good and evil.

The Kingdom Keepers series by Ridley Pearson (Disney Editions) M

What would you do if you were turned into a hologram projection and found yourself in the middle of Walt Disney World? Five teens are not only turned into computer-generated images of themselves, but they discover they've been brought to Disney World to protect it from an evil menace that wants to destroy the Magic Kingdom. The happiness of children all over the world depends on our heroes!

Larklight by Philip Reeve (Bloomsbury Publishing, 2008) M

What if Victorian-era Britain not only governed many colonies on earth, but also had jurisdiction over colonies in outer space? Art and his sister, Myrtle, live in Larklight, a suburb of the moon, and become caught in an action-filled adventure when giant spiders attack their home and they find themselves floating in an outer space lifeboat. A young rebel pirate rescues the siblings and the three continue the adventure together, meeting mad scientists and battling robots. If you enjoy *Larklight*, you'll love its sequel, *Starcross*.

The Lord of the Rings trilogy by J. R. R. Tolkien (Del Rey) M

The Ring of Power could rule the world, but in the wrong hands it could destroy it. In this classic series by J. R. R. Tolkien, a hobbit named Frodo Baggins is entrusted with the Ring's safekeeping. He must protect it from the power-hungry Sauron and the evil Ringwraiths who Sauron sends out to recover the Ring. In order to destroy the Ring once and for all, Frodo must leave his comfortable hobbit-hole in the Shire and go on a perilous quest with skilled companions and terrifying obstacles. Journey with Frodo as he fights to complete the task that no one else can be trusted to do.

Talk About It:

- Have you ever been tempted to do something you knew was wrong?
- Were you able to overcome your temptation like Frodo?
- What might have happened if Frodo had failed?
- Can you imagine your own perilous quest?
- What would be important enough to make you embark on such a dangerous journey?
- What might stand in your way?
- Where would you find strength and courage?
- Who would you bring with you?

Maximum Ride series by James Patterson (Little, Brown & Company) M

As the members of the Flock are only 98 percent human (and 2 percent bird), this group of children raised in a lab by evil scientists is anything but normal. Join Max, Fang, Iggy, Nudge, the Gasman, and Angel as they begin their quest to escape their cruel captors and save the world in *The Angel Experiment* (Book 1). The destiny of this special group of children becomes clearer as the story unfolds in *School's Out—Forever* (Book 2) and *Saving the World and Other Extreme Sports* (Book 3). The Flock must outmaneuver the relentless "Erasers," the part human, part wolf hunters that have orders to kill the children on sight, while they search for the truth about their origins and protect the human race.

Talk About It:

Use the Maximum Ride series to talk about feeling different and using your special traits to make a difference in the world.

- There is something very beautiful about a half human, half bird. Could you imagine yourself as half human, half bird? How would that feel?
- If you could be half human and half any animal, what would your animal be? Why?

In *The Angel Experiment*, Max and her friends must save Angel when she is captured. This feels like an impossible and scary task, but they work together to help their friend.

- Have you ever had to do something that felt too hard and a little scary, too?
- How did you find the courage to do what you needed to do?

In *School's Out—Forever*, Max and her friends find a safe place to live for a little while and are able to go to a normal school. When they are forced to leave, they discover that they have something special in one another: a family they can trust.

- Have you ever felt sad when you had to leave a place?
- Is there anyone who makes you feel at home no matter where you are?

The Navigator **by Eoin McNamee (Yearling, 2008) M**

Owen and his friends Cati and Wakeful have a special hideout in the woods, but it's not a place for fun and games. These three friends must hatch a plan to stop the Harsh, evil ice people who have gained control of a powerful time machine. This book is the first in a trilogy. The adventure continues in *City of Time: Book II* and *The Frost Child: The Final Battle of the Harsh.*

The Nine Pound Hammer **by John Claude Bemis (Random House Books for Young Readers, 2009) M**

The first book in the Clockwork Dark series introduces the fantastical adventures of twelve-year old orphan Ray Cobb. Ray escapes a train bound for the South only to discover the existence of the Ramblers, defenders of nature straight out of American folklore. Not only are the Ramblers real, Ray finds out that he himself is the son of a famous Rambler. Boys will eagerly join Ray and his new friends in their quest to protect the world from dangerous machines.

Pendragon Book One: The Merchant of Death **by D. J. MacHale (Aladdin, 2007) M**

Bobby Pendragon is just a normal boy and student in Stony Brook, Connecticut, except that he also travels through time and space by riding "flumes." In the course of his journeys, he finds himself in the medieval world of Denduron. There Bobby must free the Milago people who are enslaved by the evil Bedoowan. With the help of a new friend, Loor, Bobby becomes a brave hero. Read about more of Bobby's adventures in the rest of the Pendragon series.

Powerless **by Matthew Cody (Knopf Books for Young Readers, 2009) M**

What if you had superpowers that let you fly, become invisible, or generate electricity? The children of Noble's Green all have special super powers that allow them to help others in the community: the only catch is that these powers will only last until they turn thirteen! Upon their thirteenth birthdays, the children will not only lose their powers, they will also lose their memory of ever having had the powers. When newcomer Daniel arrives, the children set out to find the villain who is stealing their power. Will they be able to avoid becoming powerless?

The Ranger's Apprentice series by John Flanagan (Penguin Group) M

Will has always dreamed of becoming a knight, and so he is devastated when his small size makes this ambition impossible. As an alternative, he is given the task of being an apprentice to the Ranger: a job that also requires a lot of courage. The kingdom is filled with evil forces, and Will must rely on his insight and good character to protect his mentor and himself. Soon, Will discovers that size doesn't mean a lot when the most important things are at stake.

Redwall series by Brian Jacques (Puffin) M

This adventure series set in a magical animal world has sparked the imaginations of children for decades. In *Redwall*, the first of the series, a young mouse named Matthias is suddenly thrust into the quest of a lifetime when he vows to find the legendary sword of Martin the Warrior. Matthias must find the sword if he and his friends will be able to stop Cluny the Scourge, an evil one-eyed rat warlord, from conquering their home of Redwall Abbey. Matthias rises to the task and readers watch him transform from an awkward, clumsy novice into a brave new leader. Growing readers who have a hard time getting interested in a story will not be able to resist the charm, humor, action, and spirit of Jacques' inspired tale. Be sure to read all the books in the Redwall series, including *Mossflower*, *Mattimeo*, *Mariel of Redwall*, and *Salamandastron*.

Summerland **by Michael Chabon (Disney-Hyperion, 2004) M**

Ethan Feld may be the worst baseball player in the Summerlands. Though he struggles with his shortcomings as an athlete, Ethan discovers he is desperately needed to save the population of Ferishers, small creatures who bring good weather to the island. With the help of the Ferishers and his friends, Ethan conquers goblins and giants and learns how to wield a powerful ball club. Boys will love the interplay of baseball and fantasy in this action-packed adventure.

Tales From Outer Suburbia by Shaun Tan (Arthur A. Levine Books, 2009) M

Fifteen short stories are accompanied by striking illustrations in this collection of unusual narratives. Tan tells the stories of fantastic characters like the water buffalo who sits in a suburban parking lot, and Eric, a very unusual foreign exchange student. These stories will fuel your boys' imaginations, and they are sure to enjoy the action as each tale starts with ordinary events and makes them the stuff of spectacular memories.

Vampirates series by Justin Somper (Little, Brown Books for Young Readers) M

In *Vampirates: Demons of the Ocean*, twins Connor and Grace are separated in a shipwreck at sea. An adventurous crew of pirates picks up Connor, while an even more exotic ship rescues Grace. She discovers that her rescuers are the legendary Vampirates. Both brother and sister must manage to survive their rescuers' escapades. Surprises are around every corner for the stranded siblings, and more are sure to follow as their story unfolds in the rest of the series.

Z. Rex by Steve Cole (Philomel: 2009) M

While waiting for his extraordinary video game-creating father to return, Adam encounters gun-toting men and a mad dinosaur. Now thirteen-year-old Adam must fend off a terrible man-eating Z. Rex. If Adam's father does not return soon, he will have to find away to survive the unexpected onslaught on his own. As the mysterious reasons behind the attacks on Adam begin to unfold, boys will be especially intrigued by the scientific elements woven into the story's plot.

Folktales, Myths, and Tall Tales

For Emerging Readers

The Frog Prince Continued by Jon Scieszka (Penguin Group, 1994) E

"Happily ever after" doesn't quite do justice to the story of the Princess and the Frog. The truth is that the Frog is nostalgic for his happy youth in his homey pond, and the

Princess isn't exactly enchanted by the habits that have carried over from her spouse's former life. If you enjoyed *The True Story of the Three Little Pigs*, you will delight in this original rendering of another classic story.

Jin Jin the Dragon by Grace Chang, illustrated by Chong Chang (Enchanted Lion Books, 2007) E

After a thousand years of incubation, Jin Jin hatches from an egg. What type of a creature is Jin Jin? He can swim like his friend the fish, fly like his friend the eagle, and wrap around a tree like his friend the snake. But he is neither a fish nor an eagle nor a snake. With help from his many new friends and the wise Old Turtle, Jin Jin not only finds the answers to his questions, but also becomes a hero to the local farmers along the way.

Talk About It:

Scattered throughout the story, there are many Chinese characters.

- How many can you find?
- Try to draw some of the characters on a piece of paper. Cover up the translation and try to guess along with Jin Jin what each character means.

The Lion and the Mouse by Jerry Pinkney (Little, Brown Books for Young Readers, 2009) E

Retell the story anew each time you flip through the pages and find inspiration in Pinkney's beautiful and majestic illustrations of animals in the wild. This wordless book breathes new life into this classic tale of an unlikely friendship.

If you like this book, you'll also like:

- *Aesop's Fables* by Jerry Pinkney (Chronicle, 2000)
- *City Dog, Country Frog* by Mo Willems (Hyperion, 2010)
- *Fables* by Arnold Lobel (HarperCollins, 1983)
- *Flotsam* by David Wiesner (Clarion, 2006)
- *Free Fall* by David Wiesner (HarperCollins, 1991)
- *The Little Red Hen* by Jerry Pinkney (Dial, 2006)
- *Puss in Boots* by Charles Perrault and Fred Marcellino (Farrar, Straus, and Giroux, 1990)
- *Rumpelstiltskin* by Paul O. Zelinsky (Puffin, 1996)
- *The Three Pigs* by David Wiesner (Clarion, 2001)

Railroad John and the Red Rock Run by Tony Crunk, pictures by Michael Austin (Peachtree Publishers, 2006) E

Lonesome Bob just has to get to Red Rock by 2:00 PM sharp to marry Wildcat Annie. Railroad John, the reliable conductor of the famous "Sagebrush Flyer," assures Lonesome Bob and Granny Apple Fritter that he has "never been late once yet!" Unfortunately for the guitar-playing Lonesome and his muffin-making Granny, Railroad John and the "Sagebrush Flyer" run into one setback after another. This Western, written in tall-tale style, is sure to bring a smile to your face.

The True Story of the Three Little Pigs by Jon Scieszka, illustrated by Lane Smith (Puffin Books, 1989) E

Have you ever heard the *true* story of the three little pigs? Find out what really happened as told by Alexander T. Wolf, who was simply cooking a cake for his grandmother when, due to a cold and a badly built house, he is framed as a terrible villain.

Talk About It:

Use this book to inspire creative writing. Read some of your favorite fairytales or stories and write your own new endings.

- Do you think Cinderella really ends up with the prince? Were her stepsisters really as evil as we've been told?

Choose a story you have read and give it a new twist.

When Turtle Grew Feathers by Tim Tingle, illustrated by Stacey Schuett (August House Publishers, 2007) E

This wonderful trickster tale upends the well-known story of the tortoise and the hare. Imagine if instead of racing a tortoise, the hare instead raced a turkey wearing the shell of a tortoise. Find out how a wily turkey turned into a turtle in this delightful story that combines humor, rhyme, and a classic fable.

If you like this book, you'll also like:

- *Always Room for One More* by Sorche Nic Leodhas and Nonny Hogrogian (Henry Holt & Co., 1972)
- *Anansi the Spider: A Tale From the Ashanti* by Gerald McDermott (Henry Holt & Co., 1987)
- *Crazy Horse's Vision* by Joseph Bruchac (Lee & Low: 2000)
- *The Gift of the Sacred Dog* by Paul Goble (Aladdin, 1984)

- *How Jackrabbit Got His Very Long Ears* by Heather Irbinskas (Rising Moon, 1994)
- *Once a Mouse . . .* by Marcia Brown (Aladdin, 1989)
- *One Fine Day* by Nonny Hogrogian (Aladdin, 1974)
- *Star Boy* by Paul Goble (Aladdin, 1991)
- *A Story, a Story* by Gail E. Haley (Aladdin, 1988)
- *Why Mosquitoes Buzz in People's Ears* by Verna Aardema (Dial, 2008)

The Wolf's Story: What Really Happened to Little Red Riding Hood by Toby Forward, illustrated by Izhar Cohen (Candlewick Press, 2005) E

This classic fairytale is retold from a new perspective. As it turns out, the wolf was doing yard work for Little Red Riding Hood's grandmother when he saw the little girl coming with toffee as a present for her grandmother. Anticipating trouble for Grandma's dentures, he ran ahead to warn her of Red's arrival and chaos ensues. Decide for yourself whom to trust, Red or the wolf!

For Developing Readers

D'Aulaires Book of Greek Myths by Ingri and Edgar D'Aulaires (Delacorte Books for Young Readers, 1992) D

This classic volume chronicles the mythology of the gods and goddesses of Ancient Greece. Follow the mood swings of the tempestuous Greek gods and goddesses in each illustrated short story. Zeus, Athena, Hera, and all of the other gods and goddesses of ancient Greece come to life in these timeless stories of heroism, sibling rivalry, and love, adapted specifically for growing readers.

The Gods and Goddesses of Olympus by Aliki (HarperCollins:,1997) D

Long ago in an ancient land, people believed that the Olympian gods were immortal. A magical substance called *ichor* was said to flow through the veins of Zeus, Hera, Aphrodite, and the rest of a select group that had fought a hard-won battle for their golden thrones in heaven. Take a tour of Olympia and read the myths that have fascinated young and old alike for centuries.

Oh My Gods! A Look-It-Up Guide to the Gods of Mythology: A Mythlopedia by Megan E. Bryant (Scholastic, 2009) D

Have you ever wanted a book that uses a more modern approach to share the stories of the Greek gods? This book gives an informative look at Greek mythology with a fun, kid-friendly flair. All of the gods have their own profile with loads of fun facts and tidbits of information on their personality, strengths, and weaknesses, as well as their "Family, Flings, Friends and Foes." Growing readers will love learning about these fascinating personas in a layout that is simple, familiar and easy to browse. If you like this book, you'll also like others in the Mythlopedia series:

- *All in the Family, A Look-It-Up Guide to the In-Laws, Outlaws, and Offspring of Mythology: A Mythlopedia* by Steven Otfinoski (Scholastic, 2009)
- *She's All That! A Look-It-Up Guide to the Goddesses of Mythology: A Mythlopedia* by Megan E. Bryant (Scholastic, 2009)
- *What a Beast! A Look-It-Up Guide to the Monsters and Mutants of Mythology: A Mythlopedia* by Sophia Kelly (Scholastic, 2009)

A Tale Dark and Grimm **by Adam Gidwitz (Dutton Juvenile, 2010) D**

Hansel and Gretel are a prince and princess in the Kingdom of Grimm. Their parents are the King and Queen of Grimm and the other characters Hansel and Gretel come across in the story come from many lesser-known stories written by the famous folktale-tellers, the Brothers Grimm. In this version of the classic, Hansel and Gretel take charge of their own destiny, refusing to let bread crumbs and witches get the best of them.

The Tales From the Odyssey #1: One-Eyed Giant **by Mary Pope Osborne, illustrated by Troy Howell (Hyperion Books for Children, 2003) D**

In the first installment of a six-book series that translates Homer's epic poetry into a narrative for young readers, Odysseus is just beginning his long journey home after years spent at war in a distant land. He has little idea of the adventure that awaits him when his little boat brings him to a huge, one-eyed obstacle. Find out how Odysseus and his crew get past Polyphemus the giant and revel in his other adventures in all *The Tales From the Odyssey*.

Zen Shorts **by Jon J. Muth (Scholastic, 2005) D**

Jon J. Muth gently introduces the concepts of Zen and the idea of looking at the world from another perspective in this first book featuring Stillwater the panda, a new neighbor to siblings, Addy, Michael, and Karl. Each child visits their new friend and to each one Stillwater tells an enlightening story, teaching lessons of generosity, luck, and forgiveness. The illustrations vary between the world of the children, depicted in soft watercolors, and the world of the stories Stillwater tells, brought to life with black ink drawings. Muth includes an author's note, sharing more about the culture and history of Zen. Stillwater and his new friends return in *Zen Ties* (Scholastic, 2008) and *Zen Ghosts* (Scholastic, 2010), with more stories and more lessons that will make any boy stop and ponder a moment or two.

For Maturing Readers

The Adventures of Ulysses by Bernard Evslin (Scholastic, 1980) M

This adaptation of the tale of Ulysses is perfect for growing readers who are fascinated by the adventures of ancient heroes. As Ulysses journeys home after the Trojan War, he encounters many obstacles, including fierce monsters and perilous conditions, including a man-eating Cyclops and a cruel, manipulative sorceress named Circe, and each time, Ulysses must find a way to save not only himself but his crew. Boys will love this ancient adventure on the high seas, complete with gods, goddesses, mythical creatures, and a true hero.

If you like this, you'll also like:

- *Beowulf: A New Telling* by Robert Nye (Laurel Leaf, 1982)
- *Heroes, Gods, and Monsters of the Greek Myths* by Bernard Evslin (Laurel Leaf, 1984)
- *King Arthur and His Knights of the Round Table* by Roger Lancelyn Green (Puffin, 2008)
- *Tales of Ancient Egypt* by Roger Lancelyn Green (Puffin, 1996)
- *Tales of the Greek Heroes* by Roger Lancelyn Green (Puffin, 2009)

Folk Tales From Simla by Alice Elizabeth Dracott (Hippocrene Books, 1998) M

This collection of Himalayan folk tales offers a fascinating peek into the history and culture of the people of Northern India. Characters in the stories range from Rajahs and princesses to magicians and witches to enchanted animals. The fun of reading and discovering the culture behind these stories is enhanced by noticing the interesting parallels some stories draw with Western folklore. These tales provide a window into a world that may be disappearing rapidly, but can survive through the telling and reading of the cultural stories.

The Legend of Bass Reeves by Gary Paulsen (Wendy Lamb Books, 2006) M

Bass Reeves was a fugitive slave who lived among the Creek Indians for 22 years until he was freed by the Emancipation Proclamation. This telling of his story provides a unique look at life in the Old West. After becoming a cattle rancher and later a Federal Marshal in Indian Territory, Reeves shows how one man can beat the odds and bring order to the very wild West.

Square Sails and Dragons by Celia Lund (Trafford Publishing, 2006) M

This adventure at sea weaves Norse history with a compelling story of the physical and personal trials of long journey. It is Leif Ericsson's first voyage in command of a ship, but from the start it is not smooth sailing. Leif discovers a stowaway, a boy named Terje Gundersson. Luck comes to Terje when one of Leif's men is injured and he is promoted from polar bear nanny to member of the crew. The action-packed tale takes readers all around the North Sea as Leif, Terje, and the rest of the seafaring group meet a host of fascinating characters who make this period of history become as real as today.

History and Historical Fiction

For Emerging Readers

Fireboat: The Heroic Adventures of the John J. Harvey by Maira Kalman (Puffin, 2005) E

Read about the many adventures of a fireboat that came to the rescue again and again over the decades. Beginning with the boat's acts of heroism in 1931, the story reaches its climax when the fireboat is brought out of retirement on September 11, 2001 to fight the biggest and most deadly fire it had ever faced. Through the story of this fireboat, Kalman shares fascinating insight into many monumental moments in New York City's history and opens a pathway for young readers to talk about one of the biggest tragedies in modern American history.

The Great Voyages of Zheng He by Song Nan Zhang and Hao Yu Zhang (Pan Asian Publications, 2005) E

Some 600 years ago, Zheng He led 20,000 sailors in 62 treasure-laden ships. He was the Imperial Admiral and the commander of the largest navy that the world had ever seen. Zheng He embarked on an expedition to see the world and prove the greatness of the Chinese civilization. Boys will love traveling back in time and following Zheng He's fleet onto the open seas and toward new discoveries.

Here Comes the Garbage Barge! by Jonah Winter, illustrated by Red Nose Studio (Schwartz and Wade, 2010) E

In 1987 a curious thing happened. Islip, New York, didn't know what to do with its garbage, so the town decided to put it on a barge and send it south. Jonah Winter retells the tale of how Cap'm Duffy and the pile of trash his tugboat faithfully towed were turned away from port after port and finally had to make their way back to New York, a sad, smelly sight. Boys will pore over the illustrations in this humourous account, created through photographs of handmade sculptures of each scene molded out of clay, wire, and yes, real garbage.

I Feel Better With a Frog in My Throat by Carlyn Beccia (Houghton Mifflin Books for Children, 2010) E

Before there was modern medicine, people would try anything to feel better and came up with pretty interesting cures. Puppy kisses, spider webs, and skunk oil are only a few of the old-fashioned "cures" that this book shares with curious young readers. Some of these cures worked, some of them didn't, and some were just plain silly. This is a great book for young readers who have a glowing fondness for all things highly fact-oriented and a little disgusting.

John, Paul, George, & Ben by Lane Smith (Hyperion, 2006) E

What kind of people were John Hancock, Paul Revere, George Washington, and Ben Franklin? Did George Washington cut down a cherry tree or a whole orchard? What happened when Paul Revere tried to sell a woman a pair of underwear? Enjoy the fabulous cartoon drawings and the delightful silly stories about each of these founding fathers.

Pharaohs and Foot Soldiers: One Hundred Ancient Egyptian Jobs You Might Have Desired or Dreaded by Kristin Butcher, illustrated by Martha Newbigging (Annick Press, 2009) E

What kind of jobs did people in Ancient Egypt wish to have? What were the responsibilities of the jobs? Young readers can use Kristin Butcher's informative book to learn the answers to these questions and so much more about Egyptian society. Presented with lots of interesting facts and approachable cartoon-like illustrations, this book is a winning introduction to Egypt or the perfect gift for a boy already fascinated by this highly developed yet very ancient culture.

Sky Boys: How They Built the Empire State Building by Deborah Hopkinson, illustrated by James E. Ransome (Schwartz & Wade, 2006) E

How do you build something 1,250 feet tall? It takes a long time—410 days, to be exact! A boy and his father watch the "sky boys" work miracles from a window in their New York City home. Learn about a fascinating monument that taught America to hope in the darkest days of the Great Depression. Complete with beautiful pictures from a host of different perspectives, it is a subject well worth the attention.

If you like this book, you'll also like:

- *Brooklyn Bridge* by Lynn Curlee (Atheneum, 2001)
- *Empire State Building: When New York Reached for the Skies* (Wonders of the World Book) by Elizabeth Mann (Mikaya, 2006)
- *The Empire State Building* by Lisa Bullard (Lerner Classroom, 2009)
- *Liberty* by Lynn Curlee (Atheneum, 2003)
- *Lightship* by Brian Floca (Atheneum, 2007)
- *The Man Who Walked Between the Towers* by Mordicai Gerstein (Square Fish, 2007)
- *Pop's Bridge* by Eve Bunting (Harcourt, 2006)
- *Rushmore* by Lynn Curlee (Scholastic, 1999)
- *Skyscraper* by Lynn Curlee (Atheneum, 2007)
- *Twenty-One Elephants and Still Standing* by April Jones Prince (Houghton Mifflin, 2005)

So You Want to Be President? by Judith St. George, illustrated by David Small (Philomel Books, 2000) E

What does it take to be president? Some presidents have been short, others tall. One loves cabbage (well, only when it was thrown at him), others hate broccoli. One president was born in a log cabin and another was a famous actor. Delve into the unique qualities and histories of past American presidents—and discover just what it takes to be a leader.

Unite or Die: How Thirteen States Became a Nation by Jacqueline Jules, illustrated by Jef Czekaj (Charlesbridge Publishing, 2009) E

Cartoonish children act out a school play about the many problems that arose after the American Revolution in this humorous but informative text. Through speech bubbles and compelling illustrations, the stages of the process undertaken to bring unity to the thirteen states come to life.

The Wall by Eve Bunting, illustrated by Ronald Himler (Houghton Mifflin Company, 1990) E

The Vietnam War Memorial is the site of record numbers of pilgrimages every year. Some people come to visit the names of lost loved ones, while others simply come to pay their respects to those who died in the service of their country. In *The Wall*, a boy and his father come to honor the service and sacrifice of the boy's grandfather, a man who died before the boy was born. Thoughtful illustrations accompany this heartfelt and beautiful story.

For Developing Readers

The American Story: 100 True Tales From American History by Jennifer Armstrong, illustrated by Roger Roth (Knopf, 2006) D

One hundred chronological stories tell the history of the United States from its colonial days to modern times. Informative illustrations accompany each story and contain fun facts about the role that figures as varied as Carry Nation, Babe Ruth, and Maya Lin played in the history of the United States.

Baseball Saved Us by Ken Mochizuki, illustrated by Dom Lee (Lee & Low Books, 1995) D

When the American government unjustly forced thousands of Japanese Americans into internment camps after the attack on Pearl Harbor on December 7, 1941, Shorty and his father decided that something had to be done to lift the spirits of their fellow prisoners. Although they were surrounded by barbed wire and monitored by guards with guns, they constructed a baseball field. This enormous undertaking helped restore their sense of dignity and offered them a spark of hope in a sad, scary time.

The Battle of Iwo Jima: Guerrilla Warfare in the Pacific by Larry Hama, illustrated by Anthony Williams (The Rosen Publishing Group, Inc., 2007) D

How did Iwo Jima come to be known as the Island of Death? What was the experience like for the 70,000 American soldiers who struggled to gain control of the Pacific Islands? Through vivid imagery and compelling text, this graphic novel details the events of the crucial Battle of Iwo Jima.

Brothers of War by J. Marshall Martin (Boysread.org, 2008) D

J. Marshall Martin shares the story of two brothers from Kentucky who are captured by the rebel army during the Civil War. The boys find themselves fighting for survival in the Andersonville Confederate Prison, one of the largest Confederate military compounds at the time. With a compelling, action-packed plot, this book gives great insight into the impact that the Civil War had on the lives of so many young men.

Bud, Not Buddy by Christopher Paul Curtis (Laurel Leaf, 2004) D

Bud, who prefers not to be called Buddy, is a ten-year-old orphan living in Michigan during the Great Depression. Bud decides to run away from his foster home to search for Herman E. Calloway, the man he thinks is his father. With wit and the occasional philosophical musing, Bud travels to Grand Rapids to meet Calloway. The man is older and meaner than Bud had anticipated but, in the midst of one of the most dismal periods in American history, Calloway's bandmates make Bud feel like he has finally come home. Even though Calloway rejects the idea that Bud is his son, together they are finally able to uncover the mystery of Bud's origins and become a family.

Cheyenne Again by Eve Bunting, illustrated by Irving Toddy (Sandpiper, 2002) D

When Young Bull is ten years old, a white man who his people call the "Taking Man" arrives and tells him that the time has come for him to go to school. At school, he must learn many new things and give up more and more of his past. He must dress differently, eat differently, and speak differently. After trying and failing to run away, Young Bull must somehow find a way to reconcile his two worlds. Young Bull's difficult experience in the American school system is a historically truthful reflection of the experience of many of his Native American peers at the turn of the century.

The Dragon's Child: A Story of Angel Island by Laurence Yep, with Dr. Kathleen S. Yep (HarperCollins Publishers, 2008) D

"Dragon's Child" follows ten-year-old Gim Lew on his difficult journey with his father from China to America. In this suspenseful work of historical fiction, the reader is exposed to the harsh realities of the life of an immigrant in the early twentieth century.

Talk About It:

- Have you ever moved to a new place? How did you feel before you left? What was it like once you arrived?
- Was anyone in your family an immigrant? Learn about your family's history!

The Earth Dragon Awakes: The San Francisco Earthquake of 1906
by Laurence Yep (HarperCollins Publishers, 2006) D

What happens when the world falls out from under your feet? Laurence Yep's story follows the friendship of two boys, one an American kid and one a Chinese immigrant, leading up to the San Francisco Earthquake of April 18, 1906. This is a story of unlikely heroes that explores how cities and families cope with disaster and ultimately cooperate to overcome it.

Talk About It:

- Who are your best friends? How are they different from you? How are they similar?
- How do you think your city or town would handle an emergency like an earthquake?

Forge by Laurie Halse Anderson (Atheneum, 2010) D

Freed from slavery by a young girl named Isabel, herself a former slave, Curzon decides to battle the British in Saratoga and reveals the conditions of life as a soldier in the winter of 1777 to 1778. Through Laurie Halse Anderson's vivid storytelling, Curzon gives growing readers a vivid look at the desperate circumstances of life at Valley Forge. When Isabel and Curzon meet again, they are once again enslaved and must work together for their freedom. Written as a follow-up to the book *Chains*, Curzon's story can also be enjoyed independently.

George Crum and the Saratoga Chip by Gaylia Taylor, illustrated by Frank Morrison (Lee & Low Books, 2006) D

Yes, you enjoy potato chips, but do you know the story of their invention? It all began with a boy named George Crum, who preferred playing with his sister to studying at school. George grew up to discover that he loved cooking, but he also learned that he was tired of complaining customers. One day, he decided to silence everyone's complaints and made a dish no one will ever be able to forget!

I Survived . . . series by Lauren Tarshis, illustrated by Scott Dawson (Scholastic) D

With titles like *I Survived the Sinking of the Titanic, 1912* (Scholastic, 2010), *I Survived the Shark Attacks of 1916* (Scholastic, 2010) and *I Survived Hurricane Katrina, 2005* (Scholastic, 2011), these stories were written with boys in mind. This series illuminates scary and life-ending moments in history through the eyes of a young boy who survived the terrible moment.

Iron Thunder **by Avi, illustrated by C. B. Mordan (Hyperion Books, 2007) D**

It is 1862 and Tom's father has just passed away fighting for the Union Army in the Civil War. Times are tough, and though Tom is only 13, he begins working at the Brooklyn Navy Yard to help support his family. Tom is helping construct the Monitor, a huge iron clad boat, for the Union Army. He takes pride in his work and manages to escape Confederate spies by living aboard the Monitor. Told from Tom's perspective, Avi provides maps, images, and diagrams to help authenticate the feel of the history in this work of historical fiction.

The Journal of Jesse Smoke: A Cherokee Boy, The Trail of Tears, 1838 **by Joseph Bruchac (Scholastic, 2001) D**

Learn about the horrors and difficulties experienced by the Cherokee people on the Trail of Tears through the eyes of Jesse Smoke, a sixteen-year-old Cherokee boy who made the long and arduous journey West. As Jesse, his family, and his friends pack up their belongings and make their way along the path to relocation, Jesse documents the daily struggle for survival and the devastating sense of loss that accompanies their departure.

Talk About It:

Use this book to talk about the history of the Trail of Tears. Research the historical event and talk about how this event must have impacted Cherokee people of all ages.

- Jesse's family and the entire Cherokee people are forced to leave their home and begin a long, difficult journey. How would you react if you heard that your family had to move against their will?
- If you were living at that time, what do you think you would have done?
- Jesse's courage helps him survive the difficult experience. Have you ever had to use your own strength and courage to handle a hard situation?
- Have you ever chosen to write down what is happening in your life? Why?
- Was it helpful to write about your experiences?

Marching for Freedom: Walk Together Children and Don't You Grow Weary **by Elizabeth Partridge (Viking Juvenile, 2009) D**

Told by the children of the Civil Rights Era, *Marching for Freedom* is a story of determination, hope, and courage. Among other characters, you will meet ten-year old

Joanne Blackmon, who was arrested for the first time because she decided to join the march for freedom. The powerful images and compelling narrative illuminate the role that children played during this great moment in history.

If you like this book, you'll also like:

- *Bad News for Outlaws: The Remarkable Life of Bass Reeves, Deputy U.S. Marshal* by Vaunda Micheaux Nelson (Carolrhoda, 2009)
- *Freedom on the Menu: The Greensboro Sit-Ins* by Carole Boston Weatherford (Puffin, 2007)
- *Freedom Summer* by Deborah Wiles (Aladdin, 2005)
- *Henry's Freedom Box* by Ellen Levine (Scholastic, 2007)
- *Martin's Big Words: The Life of Dr. Martin Luther King, Jr.* by Doreen Rappaport (Hyperion, 2007)
- *Moses: When Harriet Tubman Led Her People to Freedom* by Carole Boston Weatherford (Hyperion, 2006)
- *Smoky Night* by Eve Bunting (Sandpiper, 1999)
- *The Watsons Go to Birmingham* by Christopher Paul Curtis (Yearling, 1997)

Mongolia: Vanishing Culture by Jan Reynolds (Lee & Low Books, 2007) D

Learn about the vanishing culture of the Mongolian nomads through the eyes of two young cousins, Dawa and Olana. Living on the grassy plains means that Dawa, Olana, and their family depend on horses for food and shelter. Follow along as Dawa and Olana receive their first horses and struggle to learn to become master horsemen like their fathers.

The Mostly True Adventures of Homer P. Figg by Rodman Philbrick (The Blue Sky Press, 2009) D

After a narrow escape from his cruel uncle Squinton, Homer races to save his brother, a boy conscripted into the U.S. army during the Civil War in place of a wealthier boy. With only his wits and a little bit of good luck, Homer must dodge many dangers to find and rescue his brother from the bloody Battle of Gettysburg. Discussing Homer's story is a great way to begin a conversation about the moral complexities of this period of American history.

Mysterious Messages: A History of Codes and Ciphers by Gary Blackwood (Dutton Juvenile, 2009) D

Travel through time and break into the history of cryptography. You will learn about the great ciphers created to provide national security for civilizations throughout the ages, from Ancient Rome to modern governments like the United States and Great Britain. Be sure not to miss factoids about the incredible masterminds who cracked even the toughest of these codes!

Pharaoh's Boat by David Weitzman (Houghton Mifflin Books for Children, 2009) D

What does it take to build a ship fit for a Pharaoh? This book has the answer. Weitzman's awe-inspiring illustrations successfully capture the excitement and hard work of the masterful Egyptian craftsmen who built the largest and strongest boat of the age. Boys will especially love the ancient style of the artwork and the diagrams labeling the various tools and weaponry of the time.

Pompeii Lost & Found by Mary Pope Osborne, illustrated by Bonnie Christensen (Alfred A. Knopf, 2006) D

What happened to Pompeii on August 24 in 79 C.E.? How was the mystery of the ancient city uncovered nearly 2,000 years later? This book describes the disappearance of this once vibrant city, the process of rediscovering it, and the information that historians have pieced together about how the people of Pompeii once lived. Make sure to linger over the incredible illustrations that show so much about the history of Pompeii.

Raleigh's Page by Alan Armstrong (Yearling, 2009) D

In this book, eleven-year-old Andrew Saintleger leaves his hometown in England to become a page to the renowned explorer Sir Walter Raleigh. In the course of his adventures in Europe and America, Andrew acts as a spy for Raleigh and even helps him to steal an important map. Pore over the numerous historical details that pepper Andrew's action-packed adventures as Raleigh's page.

Sacred Mountain: Everest by Christine Taylor-Butler (Lee & Low Books, 2009) D

With incredible photographs and richly detailed text, this book explores the deep connection between the Sherpa people and the powerful mountain. Learn about the long history of the Sherpa, and how many are desperately fighting to preserve the mountain and their culture.

The Silk Route: 7,000 Miles of History by John S. Major (Harper Collins, 1996) D

With beautiful illustrations and useful facts, this book explores the history of the Silk Road and the powerful connection that developed between China and Byzantium. Follow the stops traders made along the way and learn about the goods and ideas that were traded. Use the map at the end of the book as an additional resource.

Talk About It:

Use this book to talk about the different ways that ideas and goods are exchanged today, compared to how they were exchanged along the Silk Road. Choose one picture in the book that tells a story and try to illustrate a modern day version of a similar story.

- How did the Byzantine Empire and China exchange goods and ideas?
- How do we exchange goods and ideas today?
- Do you think there is anything we can learn from the way things were done in the past?
- Would you like to change anything about how we do things today?

Swords: An Artist's Devotion by Ben Boos (Candlewick, 2008) D

From pirates to princes, samurai to sultans, and knights to ninjas, who hasn't on occasion brought out their sword with a flourish and valiantly fought for their lives and livelihoods? A sword expert, Boos takes us on a journey through time and traces the history of the sword from the top of the hilt to the tip of the blade. Illustrations etched in loving detail will be sure to delight every aspiring swordsman.

Team Moon: How 400,000 People Landed Apollo 11 on the Moon by Catherine Thimmesh (Houghton Mifflin Books for Children, 2006) D

Apollo 11 went to the moon in 1969; many people know just that much. But it wasn't just Neil Armstrong on board. Apollo 11 carried a team of brilliant scientists, and could never have lifted off without a wide range of professions from those who designed the space suits to the people who built the spacecraft itself. The Apollo Mission united the world in a way we have rarely seen before or since, and this inspiring story is universal in theme and appeal.

Who Was . . .? series by various authors (Grosset & Dunlap) D

This series bring the lives of many historical figures and more recent celebrities to readers with accessible chapters illustrated with black and white ink drawings. From the standards like George Washington and Harriet Tubman to contemporary cultural figures like Walt Disney and The Beatles, with a few pleasant surprises like Annie Oakley and Charles Darwin, this series is a wonderful addition to any library and will be a new favorite for your fact-savvy boys!

You Wouldn't Want to Be a Mayan Soothsayer! Fortunes You'd Rather Not Tell **by Rupert Matthews, illustrated by David Antram (Children's Press, 2007) D**

Mayan soothsayers were religious leaders in their communities, telling fortunes, leading rituals, and even presiding over sacrifices! Growing readers will be a little shocked by all of the tasks and jobs a soothsayer's apprentice had to endure, including unpleasant fare and tongue piercings. One of many books in the You Wouldn't Want to . . . series, David Antram's signature illustrations will make this and all of the cultures and eras featured in these books come to life for boys. More books in the You Wouldn't Want to . . . series include:

- *You Wouldn't Want to Be a Greek Athlete! Races You'd Rather Not Run* by Michael Ford, illustrated by David Antram (Children's Press, 2004)
- *You Wouldn't Want to Be a Samurai! A Deadly Career You'd Rather Not Pursue* by Fiona MacDonald, illustrated by David Antram (Franklin Watts, 2009)
- *You Wouldn't Want to Be in Alexander the Great's Army! Miles You'd Rather Not March* by Jacqueline Morley, illustrated by David Antram (Children's Press, 2005)
- *You Wouldn't Want to Be Sick in the 16th Century! Diseases You'd Rather Not Catch* by Kathryn Senior, illustrated by David Antram (Children's Press, 2002)
- *You Wouldn't Want to Explore With Marco Polo! A Really Long Trip You'd Rather Not Take* by Jacqueline Morley, illustrated by David Antram (Franklin Watts, 2009)
- *You Wouldn't Want to Work on the Great Wall of China! Defenses You'd Rather Not Build* by Jacqueline Morley, illustrated by David Antram (Children's Press, 2006)

For Developing to Maturing Readers

Hannibal: Rome's Worst Nightmare, A Wicked History **by Philip Brooks (Franklin Watts, 2009) D →M**

The A Wicked History series illuminates infamous characters in the world's history, telling their tales from their own point of view. In *Hannibal*, readers will get to know the man called evil and diabolical by those he defeated. Readers will have a chance to decide how bad he really was and see his story in a new light. Other books in the A Wicked History series include:

- *Alexander the Great: Master of the Ancient World, A Wicked History* by Doug Wilhelm (Franklin Watts, 2009)
- *Attila the Hun: Leader of the Barbarian Hordes, A Wicked History* by Sean Price (Franklin Watts, 2009)
- *Genghis Khan: 13th Century Mongolian Tyrant, A Wicked History* by Enid A. Goldberg and Norman Itzkowitz (Franklin Watts, 2008)
- *Henry VIII: Royal Beheader, A Wicked History* by Sean Price (Franklin Watts, 2009)
- *Julius Caesar: Dictator for Life, A Wicked History* by Denise Rinaldo (Franklin Watts, 2010)
- *King George III: America's Enemy, A Wicked History* by Philip Brooks (Franklin Watts, 2009)

For Maturing Readers

Before Columbus: The Americas of 1491 by Charles C. Mann (Atheneum, 2009) M

Free of the usual stereotypes and misconceptions, Mann's portrait of life in the Americas before the arrival of Christopher Columbus is vibrant and captivating. Focusing on questions that scholars are still grappling with, Mann gives clear and concise possible answers while paving the way for readers to seek out new information and continue to learn about a culture that flourished centuries before the United States existed.

Geronimo by Joseph Bruchac (Scholastic, 2006) M

Told from the point of view of Geronimo's fictional adopted grandson, Little Foot, this novel shares insight into the man who fought fiercely for his people but eventually was forced to surrender. Little Foot tells of the Apaches forced journey from their home in modern-day Arizona, east to Florida on crowded trains. The young man's perspective gives insight into the wisdom and humanity of Geronimo. Little Foot is able to avoid being sent to the Carlisle Indian School, a place where young Indians were forced to give up their culture and traditions and many contracted deadly diseases. When Little Foot and his family arrive in Florida, there are more hardships to be faced, yet the story is lifted at times by his reflective nature and sense of humor. This in-depth analysis of a hero in his time is also a compelling, accessible story that boys will dive into headfirst.

Journey to the Bottomless Pit: The Story of Stephen Bishop and Mammoth Cave by Elizabeth Mitchell (Viking Juvenile, 2004) M

Stephen Bishop is a slave in Kentucky with an unusual job. He must explore and give tours of Mammoth Cave, a pit of underground tunnels and caverns that his master owns. While some might be fearful or unnerved by the task, Bishop delights in exploring all of the caves passageways, scaling rock walls, and mapping its secrets. Based on a true story, this account is truly a timeless tale of one young man's determination and passion for geology and adventure. Readers will get lost in the descriptions of the cave and are sure to find Bishop's hard work heroic.

If you like this book, you'll like:

- *Forty Acres and Maybe a Mule* by Harriet Gillem Robinet (Aladdin, 2000)
- *March Toward the Thunder* by Joseph Bruchac (Speak, 2009)
- *Slaves in the Family* by Edward Ball (Ballantine Books, 1998)
- *Trapped! The Story of Floyd Collins* by Robert K. Murray and Robert W. Brucker (The University Press of Kentucky, 1982)
- *Warriors Don't Cry* by Melba Pattillo Beals (Simon Pulse, 2007)

The Shakespeare Stealer by Gary Blackwood (Puffin, 2000) M

Widge is an orphan with an unusual skill: He can write in shorthand and his adventures are all thanks to that knack. When a mysterious traveler hires Widge and takes him to London, the boy is suddenly asked to transcribe full plays so other theater companies can perform them. Though he does his best to do the job he is hired for, Widge loses his notebook and must take a job at the Globe Theater to get it back. Blackwood adds in a good dose of humor, as Widge winds up having to play Ophelia in the Globe's performance before the Queen. As the mysterious traveler's identity is revealed, Widge is able to evade trouble and use his inner strength to come out on top.

White Fang by Jack London (Simon and Brown, 2010) M

This story of the Gold Rush days features an unlikely narrative voice. White Fang is half wolf, half sled dog, and his life story is filled with many hardships and tragedies before kindness and love make an appearance. He is faced with cruel owners and many threats on his life from humans and animals alike. Through it all, White Fang relies on his instincts for survival, his strength of spirit, and his incredible courage to endure and thrive. This is the sequel to *The Call of the Wild*, also by Jack London.

If you like this, you'll also like:

- *20,000 Leagues Under the Sea* by Jules Verne (Sterling, 2006)
- *The Adventures of Huckleberry Finn* by Mark Twain (Bantam Classics, 1981)
- *The Alaskan: A Novel of the North* by James Oliver Curwood (Forgotten Books, 2010)
- *Baree: The Story of a Wolf-Dog* by James Oliver Curwood (CreateSpace, 2009)
- *The Incredible Journey* by Sheila Burnford (Yearling, 1997)

How-To

For Emerging Readers

Adventures in Cartooning: How to Turn Your Doodles Into Comics by James Sturm, Andrew Arnold, and Alexis Frederick-Frost (First Second, 2009) E

Through the story of a knight determined to find some bubble gum, learn all about the art of cartooning. A humorous action story combined with cartooning lessons, this is a book you won't want to miss.

For Developing Readers

101 Amazing Card Tricks by Bob Longe (Sterling, 1993) D

Have you ever wondered what you might be able to do with just a deck of cards? In this book, boys will find 101 entertaining card tricks that they can use to dazzle audiences of all ages. With the step-by-step instructions, it is fun and easy to learn how to master these tricks in no time at all.

If you like this book, you'll also like:

- *Card Trickery* by the Editors of Klutz (Klutz, 2008)
- *The Complete Idiot's Guide to Street Magic* by Tom Ogden (Alpha, 2007)
- *Easy-to-Do Magic Tricks for Children* by Karl Fulves (Dover, 1993)
- *Kids' Magic Secrets: Simple Magic Tricks & Why They Work* by Loris Bree (Marlor Press, 2003)

- *Kids Make Magic! The Complete Guide to Becoming an Amazing Magician* by Ron Burgess (Williamson, 2003)
- *The Klutz Book of Magic* by John Cassidy (Klutz, 1989)
- *Magic for Dummies* by David Pogue (For Dummies, 1998)
- *Mark Wilson's Complete Course in Music* by Mark Anthony Wilson (Running Press, 2003)
- *Street Magic: Great Tricks and Close-Up Secrets Revealed* by Paul Zenon (Running Press, 2007)
- *Young Magician: Card Tricks* by Oliver Ho (Sterling, 2005)

The Boys' Book: How to Be the Best at Everything by Dominique Enright, Guy McDonald, and Nikalas Catlow (Scholastic, 2007) D

This wonderful, how-to book provides step-by-step tips for everything from performing a card trick to perfecting an ollie. Boys will love all of the different topics the book covers, like learning how to fly a helicopter and even surviving in space. It is sure to be a new favorite whenever your boy is looking for something to do.

Talk About It:

- What have you always wanted to know how to do?
- Which suggestions do you think are the most useful?
- Create your own how-to guide. Find a few things that you are really good at and teach someone else exactly how to do them.

The Dangerous Book for Boys by Hal Iggulden and Conn Iggulden (William Morrow, 2007) D

In the age of video games and virtual reality, who knows how to tie a reef knot anymore? What is a reef knot, anyway? Did you know that there are only 17 basic rules to soccer, known more widely around the world as football? If you want to know what the rules are, or how to tie impressive knots, it's all inside this book. Here's a book just for boys, filled with good old-fashioned fun. It's like a gigantic to-do list for any active boy and the perfect entry point text for any resistant reader who is looking for just the right book.

Diary of a Wimpy Kid: Do-It-Yourself Book by Jeff Kinney (Amulet Books, 2008) D

Middle school hero Greg Heffley returns in this great addition to the Diary of a Wimpy Kid series. Like the other books in the series, the story is told through fantastic cartoons, but in this book there is also plenty of room to add in your own information, since this time, he's telling the reader's story, too. Greg has set very important rules for his family, and readers can also add in their own rules. Prompts are designed especially for boys, like "Can you remember the grossest thing you ever ate?" Boys are sure to have a great time creating their own diary just like Greg's.

The Encyclopedia of Immaturity by the Editors of Klutz (Klutz, 2007) D

As it says on the cover, this book will teach you how to never grow up! This encyclopedia of sorts is filed with page after page of step-by-step instructions for everything from wiggling your ears to faking a sneeze to how to kick a toilet bowl plunger field goal! There are also plenty of fun quizzes, challenges, and trivia. Your boy is sure to spend hours vigilantly following this guide to staying a kid forever.

How to Write Your Life Story by Ralph Fletcher (Collins, 2007) D

For any boy who likes to tell stories and always has something to share, this book will help him channel that energy and create a great piece of writing all about himself. Fletcher dispels the myth that an autobiography can only be written at the end of a person's life and encourages young writers to share what has happened so far in their life. By providing an easy framework for the writing, Fletcher helps young writers structure their writing and also gives them guidance on how to begin, what to focus on, and how to tell their story in the most compelling way.

Make Amazing Toy and Game Gadgets by Amy Pinchuk (Maple Tree Press, 2004) D

This book, from *Popular Mechanics for Kids*, is a great resource for a hands-on kid. Pinchuk gives easy-to-read, step-by-step instructions for five projects, including making a spy camera! Each step has large illustrations that make these cool projects a breeze to complete. Pinchuk even includes a section on safety, as well as how-to tips and a "What's That?" glossary. It is the perfect companion for an afternoon indoors or many evenings of fun.

For Maturing Readers

The Boys' Book of Outdoor Survival: 101 Courageous Skills for Exploring the Dangerous Wild by Chris McNab (Amber Books Ltd., 2008) M

Do you know how to survive in the wild? Have you ever thought about what supplies you would need to bring in your pack to make it through even the worst weather? Boys can learn all they every wanted to know if they want to set out to explore the wild. From how to track wild animals to how to make your own bow and arrow, any skills a boy might need on his adventure are covered in this survival guide.

Mischief Maker's Manual by Sir John Hargrave (Grosset & Dunlap, 2009) M

This is the ultimate pranksters' guidebook. Hargrave shares a multitude of pranks for the mischievous mind, with rising levels of complexity and necessary skill. Parents and teachers shouldn't be too alarmed, though. The book begins with The Prankster's Code, encouraging boys (or anyone reading the book) to remember that a prank should be funny and entertaining for everyone involved, should leave no permanent damage, and that bullying is never okay. Boys will have a blast trying their hand at the pranks and shenanigans outlined in this manual of sorts.

Pinewood Derby Speed Secrets: Design and Build the Ultimate Car by David Meade (DK Publishing, 2006) M

From the initial plans to the last coat of paint, boys can use this book to learn all of the absolutely necessary steps for building the ultimate race car. As the secrets are revealed, boys will savor the details and pore over the diagrams while learning everything they ever wanted to know about the step-by-step process of designing and constructing a Pinewood Derby winner.

Show Off: How to Do Absolutely Everything One Step at a Time by Sarah Hines Stephens, illustrated by Bethany Mann (Candlewick, 2009) M

Whether your boy wants to learn how to sink a foul shot or tie a knot one-handed, this manual has step-by-step instructions for mastering dozens of skills boys might want. The text, diagrams, and illustrations are so clear and easy to understand, boys will have a growing list of accomplishments soon after they pick up this book. A great addition to any boy's library, this is one he won't be able to put down.

Humor

For Emerging Readers

The Boss Baby by Marla Frazee (Beach Lane Books, 2010) E

In this tongue-in-cheek picture book, a new baby is the boss of his household. Clad in a suit-like onesie, this little guy demands round-the-clock meetings and made-to-order drinks from his frazzled staff of two. The little tyrant soon works his parents into exhaustion, but the clever tot finds two words that snap everyone back to attention and get things moving again. Can you guess what those words might be? Young readers, especially older siblings, will find the premise hilarious, and the perfect timing of the text and illustrations delivers a story that's as funny as it is absolutely honest.

Click, Clack, Moo: Cows That Type by Doreen Cronin, illustrated by Betsy Lewin (Simon and Schuster Children's Publishing, 2000) E

The cows on Farmer Brown's farm find an old typewriter and decide to tell Farmer Brown what's on their minds. When Farmer Brown doesn't give them what they ask for, the cows decide to go on strike. Poor Farmer Brown doesn't know what to do, but luckily they find a compromise in the end. But just when the trouble seems to be over, the typewriter falls into the hands of the ducks. This silly story will have everyone laughing, and the repetition of the sounds of the cows typing ("Click, Clack, Moo") gives a rhythm and flow to the story that is especially fun to read aloud.

Talk About It:

Use *Click, Clack, Moo: Cows That Type* to talk about the importance of compromising so that everyone can be happy. The cows decide that they want electric blankets because the barn is cold, but Farmer Brown thinks that their idea is crazy. In the end, the cows and Farmer Brown make a deal.

- Have you ever had to compromise with someone? How did that feel?

Fox and His Friends series by Edward and James Marshall (Puffin) E

Each of the Fox books contains a few stories about Fox, a funny and witty protagonist. Readers will enjoy Fox's dry sense of humor. Though the plots are relatively simple, the stories are engrossing and thoroughly enjoyable.

Frankenstein Makes a Sandwich by Adam Rex (Harcourt Children's Books, 2006) E

This hilarious collection of stories about the lives and eating habits of scary monsters will keep you in stitches. From Frankenstein, who comes across food for a sandwich in a very unusual way, to the Phantom of the Opera, who loses his talent as a composer and must find a new career path, these stories are a new take on iconic, horror-story characters.

Hi! Fly Guy **by Tedd Arnold (Cartwheel Books, 2006) E**

Fly Guy befriends a little boy named Buzz who is looking for a pet for The Amazing Pet Show. Buzz is impressed with Fly Guy since he can say his name, "Buzz," and decides he's the perfect pet for the show. At first the judges think Fly Guy is just a pest, but he proves them wrong with a spectacular show and wins Buzz the prize! Fly Guy's adventures continue in:

- *Buzz Boy and Fly Guy* by Tedd Arnold (Cartwheel Books, 2010)
- *Fly Guy Meets Fly Girl!* by Tedd Arnold (Cartwheel Books, 2010)
- *Fly High, Fly Guy!* by Tedd Arnold (Cartwheel Books, 2008)
- *Hooray for Fly Guy!* by Tedd Arnold (Cartwheel Books, 2008)
- *I Spy Fly Guy* by Tedd Arnold (Cartwheel Books, 2009)
- *Shoo, Fly Guy!* by Tedd Arnold (Cartwheel Books, 2006)
- *Super Fly Guy* by Tedd Arnold (Cartwheel Books, 2009)
- *There Was an Old Lady Who Swallowed Fly Guy* by Tedd Arnold (Cartwheel Books, 2007)

If You Give a Moose a Muffin **by Laura Numeroff, illustrated by Felicia Bond (Laura Geringer Books, an imprint of HarperCollins Publishers, 1991) E**

This young boy finds out exactly what happens if you give a moose a muffin. First the moose wants jam to go with the muffin, then a sweater for the cold, and even a needle and thread. Where will this silly adventure of special requests end?

If you like this book, look for others in the series:

- *If You Give a Mouse a Cookie* by Laura Numeroff, illustrated by Felicia Bond (Laura Geringer Books, an imprint of HarperCollins Publishers, 1985)
- *If You Give a Pig a Pancake* by Laura Numeroff, illustrated by Felicia Bond (Laura Geringer Books, an imprint of HarperCollins Publishers, 1998)
- *If You Give a Pig a Party* by Laura Numeroff, illustrated by Felicia Bond (Laura Geringer Books, an imprint of HarperCollins Publishers, 2005)
- *If You Take a Mouse to School* by Laura Numeroff, illustrated by Felicia Bond (Laura Geringer Books, an imprint of HarperCollins Publishers, 2002)

Plato the Platypus Plumber (Part-Time) by Hazel Edwards, edited by Anna Bartlett, illustrated by John Petropoulos (IP Kidz, 2010) E

Plato is a platypus that fixes watery problems for his friends while also fixing grumpy people. Hazel Edwards shows her young readers the importance of friendship while also providing information on conservation and Australia. A delightful mix of fact and fun!

Ricky Ricotta's Mighty Robot Collection by Dav Pilkey, illustrated by Martin Ontiveros (Scholastic, 2002) E

Ricky Ricotta, a lonely tiny mouse, lives in Squeakyville with his parents. He dreads the bullies that he meets on his way to school every day; all he wants is a friend. Fortunately, adventure is just around the corner: he and his personal Mighty Robot will soon be saving the world from villains ranging from Dr. Stinky McNasty to Victor von Vulture.

Rotten Ralph series by Jack Gant, illustrated by Nicole Rubel (Sandpiper) E

Ralph isn't always the kindest cat to his owner Sara. He makes fun of her when she practices ballet and tries to stop her from going to school so that he can have her all to himself. For fans of Garfield and the Fat Cat of Underwhere comes another zany cat with a mind of his own.

Shark vs. Train by Chris Barton, illustrated by Tom Lichtenheld (Little, Brown, 2010) E

Two boys have a showdown to see whose toy is tops, the shark or the train. Who would win at high diving? Well, the shark of course, but who would win at burping or trick-or-treating or basketball? This imaginative story is filled with a variety of artfully illustrated, laugh-out-loud scenarios that will inspire some toy contests of your boy's own invention.

Smelly Locker: Silly Dilly School Songs by Alan Katz, illustrated by David Catrow (McElderry, 2010) E

"Smelly Locker" is just one of the hilarious poems about school that Katz has set to classic children's tunes, like "Frère Jacques" and "Miss Mary Mack." A fun introduction to the vast world of modern poetry, each poem is both accessible and entertaining. Katz speaks to the kid in all of us, illuminating the wonderful moments that make every day an adventure of its own.

Skeleton Hiccups by Margaret Cuyler, illustrated by S. D. Schindler (Margaret K. McElderry Books, 2002) E

Skeleton wakes up with the hiccups. He hiccups as he does all of his daily activities, like polishing his bones and playing with Ghost. Ghost tries to help Skeleton get rid of his hiccups by having him drink water upside down and eat sugar, but nothing works. Will Skeleton ever get rid of his hiccups?

Talk About It:

- Many people have funny ways to get rid of hiccups. What is the funniest method you've ever tried?
- Skeleton is finally able to get rid of his hiccups with the help of his friend. Have you ever had a problem that you couldn't solve until a friend helped you?
- How does it feel to have a friend help you solve a problem?
- Have you ever been on the other side and helped a friend solve a problem?
- How did it feel to be the one helping?

For Developing Readers

Captain Underpants series by Dav Pilkey (The Blue Sky Press) D

When best friends George and Harold invent a superhero named Captain Underpants, they decide to get serious and try to bring him to life! Captain Underpants springs into action when the friends accidentally hypnotize their principal, Dr. Benny Krupp. Hilarious adventures fill the pages of every book in this series.

The Giggler Treatment by Roddy Doyle, illustrated by Brian Ajhar (Arthur A. Levine Books, 2000) D

Mr. Mack is a biscuit tester in Ireland. He is on his way to the factory where he gets to taste his very favorites and make sure that they are still delicious. Little does he know, his perfect day is about to be interrupted by the appearance of the elf-like Gigglers. Gigglers are only around when children, dogs, and other relatively helpless creatures aren't being treated fairly. Mr. Mack is a good father and a good man. He probably doesn't deserve the Giggler Treatment, but that doesn't mean that he isn't going to get it anyway. What does he do? Find out in this silly tale.

Horrid Henry series by Francesca Simon, illustrated by Tony Ross (Sourcebooks, Inc.) D

Join Horrid Henry, his brother Perfect Peter, his neighbor and co-conspirator Moody Margaret, and other colorful characters as they wreak havoc and get into all kinds of trouble. Whether it's simply making a giant gooey mess or tricking the tooth fairy, Horrid Henry seems to do it all.

Jokelopedia: The Biggest, Best, Silliest, Dumbest Joke Book Ever by Ilana Weitzman, Eva Blank, and Rosanne Green; illustrations by Mike Wright (Workman Publishing Company, 2006) D

What did the judge say when the skunk came to testify? Odor in the court! Kids around the country sent in their best jokes to make this comprehensive jokelopedia. To give you an idea of just how complete this volume is, there are 59 elephant jokes alone—boys will love it and may be inspired to think up their own and write a brand new joke book.

Secrets of Dripping Fang series by Dan Greenburg (Harcourt Children's Books) D

The Shluffmuffins have been stuck at the (not-so) Jolly Days Orphanage forever, and they have very little reason to believe that they will ever be able to leave. They aren't exactly a catch: Cheyenne is allergic to everything, and Wally's feet stink no matter how hard he tries to keep them clean. When the Mandible ladies decide to adopt the siblings and feed them chocolate at every meal, things are too good to be true. But things aren't quite what they seem!

Wayside School series by Louis Sachar (HarperCollins) D

The Wayside School was originally supposed to be built with thirty classrooms on one level, but something went wrong and the school was instead built with one classroom on each of its thirty levels! This construction mishap sets the stage for all of the crazy and hilarious events that happen each day at Wayside School. It is hard not to laugh out loud as you turn the pages and read about these likable, wacky characters.

The Zack Files series by Dan Greenburg (Grosset and Dunlap) D

Readers will love to live vicariously through the adventures of Zack, a ten-year-old boy who often finds himself in surreal and hilarious situations. In the first book of the thirty-part series, Zack encounters a talking cat! This is only the first of many crazy scenarios Zack finds himself in as each new story unfolds.

If you like this book, you'll also like:

- How to Train Your Dragon series by Cressida Cowell (Little, Brown)
- Joey Pigza series by Jack Gantos (HarperCollins)
- *The Knights of the Kitchen Table* (Time Warp Trio series) by Jon Scieszka (Puffin, 2004)
- *Knucklehead* by Jon Scieszka (Viking Juvenile, 2008)
- *Niagara Falls, or Does It?* by Henry Winkler (Grosset & Dunlap, 2003)
- Spaceheadz series by Jon Scieszka (Simon & Schuster, 2010)
- *Squids Will Be Squids* by Jon Scieszka and Lane Smith (Puffin, 2003)
- *The Stinky Cheese Man and Other Fairly Stupid Tales* by Jon Scieszka and Lane Smith (Viking, 1992)

For Maturing Readers

Letters From a Nut by Ted L. Nancy (It Books, 2001) M

This is a collection of hilarious letters to a host of institutions and companies that will have boys rolling with laughter. From the Baseball Hall of Fame to the LA Lakers to the Ritz Carlton, Ted Nancy has questions, complaints, and surprising observations for them all. This self-proclaimed "nut" has revived letter writing and made it into a wonderful forum for humorous reflection on all of life's absurdities and the odd choices some people make.

If you like this, you'll enjoy other books by Ted L. Nancy, including:

- *All New Letters From a Nut: Includes Lunatic Email Exchanges* by Ted L. Nancy (Crown Archetype, 2010)
- *Extra Nutty! Even More Letters From a Nut* by Ted L. Nancy (St. Martin's Press, 2000)
- *Hello Junk Mail!* by Ted L. Nancy (National Lampoon Press, 2008)
- *More Letters From a Nut* by Ted L. Nancy (Bantam, 1998)

The World's Dumbest Criminals by Daniel Butler and Alan Ray (Scholastic, 2005) M

This is a humorous look at the exploits of the world's least clever criminals. Butler and Ray take readers around the world to poke fun at folks who broke the law in the most unintelligent of fashions. As their introduction states, this book teaches you three things. One, dumb crime is a universal phenomenon. Two, every nation in the world has good cops with a great sense of humor. Three, there is no right way to do a wrong thing. Boys will fall off their chairs as they learn about all of these dumb crimes around the world, and the message will ring clear that crime really never does pay.

If you like this book, you'll like:

- *Great Government Goofs! Over 350 Loopy Laws, Hilarious Screw-Ups and Acts-Idents of Congress* by Leland II. Gregory III (Dell, 1997)
- *Lonely Planet Signspotting 2: The World's Most Absurd Signs* by Doug Lansky (Lonely Planet, 2007)
- *What's the Number for 911? America's Wackiest Calls* by Leland H. Gregory III (Andrews McMeel Publishing, 2000)

Learning to Love Reading

For Emerging Readers

Biscuit series by Alyssa Capucilli, illustrated by Pat Schories (HarperCollins) E

The lovable puppy Biscuit has plenty of adventures for young readers to follow. In *Biscuit Goes to School*, Biscuit tries very hard to go to school like his friends, but he quickly learns that no dogs are allowed. Biscuit also tries everything possible to get out of taking a bath in *Biscuit Takes a Bath*. Biscuit's owner finally has to get into the bathtub, too!

Talk About It:

Use the books in this series to talk about themes ranging from going to school and taking a bath to having a new baby in the house. The joyful and light nature of these books will make talking about any subject easier and more fun.

In the book *Biscuit and the Baby*, Biscuit must learn how to handle his impatience to meet the new baby. He learns how hard it is to be quiet and wait, even though he must. Having a new baby in the house can be very exciting, but quite hard.

- How does Biscuit learn to wait to meet the new baby?
- When have you had to be patient?

Clifford the Big Red Dog series by Norman Bridwell (Scholastic) E

Boys love imagining what they would do with the giant dog in the Clifford series. Emily Elizabeth wishes her small puppy would grow big and be strong, and he does! He grows so big and so fast that before she knows it, he barely fits in her room, then her house! Normal Bridwell's now-classic series will keep your boys asking for more stories of Clifford and Emily Elizabeth's adventures. Underneath the lighthearted fun, there is also the very serious concern all children have about growing and their own sense of comfort with their ever changing size.

Curious George series by Margaret and H. A. Rey (Houghton Mifflin Company) E

Curious George and the man with the yellow hat eat delicious ice cream, visit the aquarium, go camping, and enjoy many other wonderful outings in this delightful series. Curious George's antics will keep you on your toes as you constantly wonder what could possibly happen next.

Talk About It:

In *Curious George and the Dump Truck*, Curious George only wants to learn more about the truck parked outside when he pulls the fateful lever.

- Have you ever accidentally caused a big mess or problem?
- How did you feel when it happened?
- How did you solve the problem? Did anyone help you?

Don't Let the Pigeon Drive the Bus by Mo Willems (Walker Books, 2004) E

What would happen if a pigeon drove the school bus? Will anyone let this determined pigeon try? He sure knows how to throw a pigeon-temper tantrum.
If you love this book, you'll also like:

- *Elephants Cannot Dance! (An Elephant and Piggie Book)* by Mo Willems (Hyperion, 2009)
- *Don't Let The Pigeon Stay Up Late!* by Mo Willems (Hyperion, 2006)
- *Leonardo, the Terrible Monster* by Mo Willems (Hyperion, 2005)
- *Naked Mole Rat Gets Dressed* by Mo Willems (Hyperion, 2009)
- *The Pigeon Finds a Hot Dog* by Mo Willems (Hyperion, 2004)
- *The Pigeon Has Feelings, Too!* by Mo Willems (Hyperion, 2005)
- *The Pigeon Loves Things That Go!* by Mo Willems (Hyperion, 2005)
- *The Pigeon Wants a Puppy* by Mo Willems (Hyperion, 2008)
- *There Is a Bird on Your Head! (An Elephant and Piggie Book)* by Mo Willems (Hyperion, 2007)

- *Today I Will Fly! (An Elephant and Piggie Book)* by Mo Willems (Hyperion, 2007)

Edwina: The Dinosaur Who Didn't Know She Was Extinct by Mo Willems (Hyperion Books for Children, 2006) E

Everyone in the neighborhood loves Edwina the Dinosaur. She bakes cookies, does favors, and helps old ladies cross the street. But Reginald Von Hoobie Doobie does not love Edwina; in fact, he knows that dinosaurs are extinct. Reginald tells all his classmates and his neighbors the truth about dinosaurs, but no one will believe him. Will Reginald ever find anyone to listen to him?

Fluffy series by Kate McMullan, illustrated by Mavis Smith (Cartwheel) E

Fluffy, the guinea pig who resides in Ms. Day's class, doesn't know what he's in for when he meets Ms. Day's students in *Fluffy Goes to School*. They are a precocious bunch of kids: not only do they bring him on their apple-picking expedition in *Fluffy Goes Apple Picking*, they also force him to find a girlfriend in *Fluffy's Valentine's Day*! Read these books and all of the others in the series to follow Fluffy's adventures in Ms. Day's class.

Talk About It:

Use the Fluffy series to talk about problem-solving skills or about the important lessons that friends can teach one another.

In *Fluffy Goes Apple Picking*, Fluffy worries that he is never going to get to eat an apple.

- How does he finally find a way to get an apple with a little help from his friends?
- Have you ever had to solve a problem like this? What did you do?

In *Fluffy and the Firefighters*, Fluffy needs the help of his friends to learn how to be a fire prevention hero without actually fighting fires.

- Have your friends ever helped you solve a problem?

Frog and Toad series by Arnold Lobel (HarperCollins) E

Frog and Toad are best friends who care deeply for each other. Frog helps Toad complete the items on his "to do" list, and Toad takes care of Frog when he is sick. Whether they are anticipating the arrival of the mail or preparing for the start of spring, Frog and Toad will remind all readers to celebrate their special friendships and help them navigate them when times get tricky.

If you love this book, you'll also like:

- *Alexander and the Wind-Up Mouse* by Leo Lionni (Dragonfly Books, 1969)
- *Bedtime for Frances* by Russell Hoban (HarperCollins, 1995)
- *Best Friends for Frances* by Russell Hoban (HarperCollins, 1976)
- *Caps for Sale* by Esphyr Slobodkina (HarperCollins, 1968)
- *Cat and Mouse* by Tomek Bogacki (Frances Foster Books, 1996)
- *Duck and Goose* by Tad Hills (Random House Children's Books, 2006)
- *Mouse Tales* by Arnold Lobel (HarperCollins, 1982)
- *Mouse Soup* by Arnold Lobel (HarperCollins, 1983)
- *Owl at Home* by Arnold Lobel (HarperCollins, 1982)
- *Uncle Elephant* by Arnold Lobel (HarperCollins, 1982)

George and Martha **by James Marshall (Sandpiper, 1974) E**

Two hippos show us the meaning of friendship. Sometimes it's hard, like when George has to pretend to like Martha's split pea soup or when Martha has to support George in his attempt to be the first hippo in flight! No matter the adventure, these two friends stick together and make readers laugh at every turn.

Henry and Mudge series by Cynthia Rylant, illustrated by Suçie Stevenson (Antheneum Books) E

Henry is a lonely only child with no friends on his street and not even a pet to console him. Luckily, a series of fortunate events bring Mudge, a 180-pound mastiff, to Henry's rescue. Life will never be the same! From the beloved author of *Gooseberry Park*, this series for new readers follows Henry and Mudge as they take advantage of everything the outdoors and their combined imaginations have to offer.

Talk About It:

- How do Mudge and Henry support one another?

How Do Dinosaurs Say Goodnight? **by Jane Yolen, illustrated by Mark Teague (Scholastic, 2000) E**

What would bedtime be like if you were a dinosaur? In the first of the How Do Dinosaurs . . . series, Jane Yolen asks this simple question. A dinosaur might want a bedtime story or a glass of water, or it might need help brushing its teeth or putting on its pajamas. Find out how funny saying goodnight can be when it's time for a dinosaur to go to bed.

If you like this book, you'll also like the rest of the How Do Dinosaurs . . . series, including:

- *How Do Dinosaurs Clean Their Rooms?* by Jane Yolen, illustrated by Mark Teague (Scholastic, 2004)
- *How Do Dinosaurs Eat Their Food?* by Jane Yolen, illustrated by Mark Teague (Scholastic, 2005)
- *How Do Dinosaurs Get Well Soon?* by Jane Yolen, illustrated by Mark Teague (Scholastic, 2003)
- *How Do Dinosaurs Go to School?* by Jane Yolen, illustrated by Mark Teague (Scholastic, 2007)
- *How Do Dinosaurs Laugh Out Loud?* by Jane Yolen, illustrated by Mark Teague (Scholastic, 2010)
- *How Do Dinosaurs Learn Their Colors?* by Jane Yolen, illustrated by Mark Teague (Scholastic, 2006)
- *How Do Dinosaurs Learn to Read?* by Jane Yolen, illustrated by Mark Teague (Scholastic, 2003)
- *How Do Dinosaurs Love Their Cats?* by Jane Yolen, illustrated by Mark Teague (Scholastic, 2010)
- *How Do Dinosaurs Love Their Dogs?* by Jane Yolen, illustrated by Mark Teague (Scholastic, 2010)
- *How Do Dinosaurs Play With Their Friends?* by Jane Yolen, illustrated by Mark Teague (Scholastic, 2006)
- *How Do Dinosaurs Say I Love You?* by Jane Yolen, illustrated by Mark Teague (Scholastic, 2009)

How Rocket Learned to Read **by Tad Hills (Schwartz & Wade, 2010) E**

Rocket loves to chase leaves and play like the good-natured pup he is! One day while napping, Rocket is awoken by a little yellow bird who picks him as her very first student. At first Rocket isn't interested in learning to read, but soon he becomes curious and excited to hear more of the little yellow bird's stories. Young readers will feel a keen sympathy and growing pride as they, like Rocket, become confident readers!

Hugging Hour by Aileen Leijten (Philomel, 2009) E

When Drool's parents go out and leave her with her grandmother for a babysitter, Drool tells her grandmother's pet chicken Kip that she feels like an orphan. What will distract her from her loneliness? Will it be fried ice cream? Maybe cupcake decorating? Hide and go seek? This book is a great choice if your child has trouble being left with a babysitter.

Knuffle Bunny trilogy by Mo Willems (Hyperion Books for Children) E

Trixie and her favorite stuffed toy Knuffle Bunny journey together to the Laundromat, to school, and all the way to Holland. Mo Willems uses humorously sparse text and an inventive illustration style to bring to life these three great adventures where a little girl and her inanimate friend learn important lessons about separation, sharing, and growing up.

Let's Do Nothing! by Tony Fucile (Candlewick, 2009) E

Pretending to be a statue in the park is a lot harder than Frankie expected. When his friend Sal suggests that they try to sit quietly and do nothing, Frankie just can't seem to stop moving. Watch as Frankie fights off pigeons and narrowly misses being hit by a dog relieving himself and Sal grows increasingly exasperated at Frankie's inability to just do nothing!

Little Bear series by Elsa Holmelund Minarik, illustrated by Maurice Sendak (HarperCollins) E

Little Bear visits his grandparents and hears great stories about Mother Bear in *Little Bear's Visit*, goes fishing in *Father Bear Comes Home*, and forges a new friendship in *Little Bear's Friend*. Whether he is playing all summer with his friend Emily, receiving loving kisses from Mother Bear, or finding just the right outfit for a snowy day, these delightful short stories depict the wonderful moments in Little Bear's childhood.

Talk About It:

Use these books to talk about the friends and family members who make you feel cherished.

In *Birthday Soup*, Little Bear fears that his mother has forgotten his birthday. What can he do? He plans his own party and makes his own soup, only to learn that his mother did, in fact, remember the occasion.

- How did Little Bear deal with his fear that his mother had forgotten his birthday?

In *Little Bear's Friend*, Little Bear becomes good friends with a young girl named Emily and her doll. They play together all summer, and Little Bear is despondent when Emily has to leave.

- How does Little Bear use a pen to feel less lonesome after his friend leaves?
- Have you ever missed someone very much?
- What did you do to help yourself miss this person just a little bit less?

Nanook and Pryce by Ned Crowley, illustrated by Larry Day (HarperCollins, 2009) E

Enter the epic adventure of Nanook and Pryce, who travel around the world on their iceberg without noticing the angry sharks and ravenous pelicans that tag along. For these two friends, it's all about the fish. With charming and clever illustrations, this book about two young fishermen will entrance you.

Talk About It:

- If you could go anywhere in the world right now, where would you go? Who would you bring with you?

Noodles series by Hans Wilhelm (Scholastic) E

Noodles the little white puppy has lots of adventures as he learns important lessons about friendship, sharing, the different seasons, and so much more. Your youngest boys will love how Noodles always manages to come out in the end a little wiser and with a plenty of fun memories, too!

Oliver by Syd Hoff (HarperCollins, 2000) E

Oliver travels with many other elephants all the way across the ocean to dance in the circus. When he learns that the circus already has too many elephants, Oliver feels discouraged. Will he ever find a way to live out his dream?

Owen and Mzee by Craig Hatkoff, Isabella Hatkoff, and Dr. Paula Kahumbu; photographs by Peter Greste (Scholastic Press, 2006) E

Can someone who is 130 years old be friends with a baby? Can a tortoise adopt a hippo? Not usually, but in this true story, Owen and Mzee defy the odds on both counts. When Owen the baby hippo was separated from his hippo pod after a tragic tsunami in December 2004, Mzee the great tortoise adopted him and began caring for him. A love story of unexpected proportions, the friendship of two very different animals is a reminder of the resilience of all living things even in the wake of great tragedy.

Papá and Me **by Arthur Dorros, illustrated by Rudy Gutierrez (Rayo, 2009) E**

This book takes a typical day and makes it magical. A young boy narrates his adventures with his father. While they speak both English and Spanish together, the universal language of unconditional love rings clear and true.

Talk About It:

- Share a relationship that is meaningful to you.
- Have you ever felt like your communication with a friend or family member has gone beyond language?

Pinky and Rex series by James Howe, illustrated by Melissa Sweet (Antheneum, Macmillan Publishing Company) E

Best friends Pinky and Rex have many adventures together. They overcome their fears and go to camp together, encounter a mean old witch, and even one day get married! Join Pinky and Rex as they navigate the joys and difficulties of growing up with courage and pluck.

A Sick Day for Amos McGhee **by Philip Christian Stead, illustrated by Erin Stead (Roaring Brook Press, 2010) E**

Amos McGhee is a grandfatherly zookeeper who always makes time to visit his dearest friends: the elephant, the tortoise, the penguin, the rhinoceros, and the owl. When Amos wakes up one morning with the sniffles, his friends decide that today they will visit him. Each one tries to bring Amos a little bit of comfort and cheer as he recovers from his cold. Erin Stead's poignant, gentle drawings bring this loving story to life as Amos and his animal friends spend an unusual day together.

The Wreck of the Zephyr **by Chris Van Allsburg (Houghton Mifflin Books, 1982) E**

How could a sailboat wind up wrecked at the top of a cliff? A wise old man tells the story of a boy who wanted to sail better than anyone else. When this boy goes out in a storm against the advice of a seasoned fisherman, he is knocked unconscious by the boom and wakes up on a mysterious island where the people know how to sail their boats through the air.

Talk About It:

- What do you think the boy learned at the end of his adventure?
- Do you have a guess as to who the old man really is? What clues does the author give you about the man's true identity?

For Emerging to Developing Readers

I Spy series by Jean Marzollo, photographs by Walter Wick (Scholastic) E →D

This browsing series is great for any resistant reader. Initially boys can engage in the text simply by looking for the hidden objects in the elaborate photographs. As their understanding and reading skills grow, your boys can begin deciphering the riddles and learning the nuances of each page. Each title in the series has a theme that the photographs and objects follow.

For Developing to Maturing Readers

The Invention of Hugo Cabret by Brian Selznick (Scholastic Press, 2007) D →M

This suspenseful book is set at the turn of the twentieth century in a train station in Paris. Hugo, an orphan, lives in the train station and wants to remain anonymous. To survive, he fixes clocks and walks off with what he needs. But Hugo is holding on to a wonderful secret passed down from his father. When he meets a girl and an old man, the safety of his secret and his world are jeopardized, and his life is forever changed.

Math and Numbers

For Emerging Readers

If Dogs Were Dinosaurs by David M. Schwartz, illustrated by James Warhola (Scholastic Press, 2005) E

Have you ever wondered how small a meatball would seem to you if you were so big that your hair was as thick as spaghetti? If mountains were really made out of molehills, how big would the moles be? Discover the answer to these questions and many more in this wonderfully funny book.

Talk About It:

This is a humorous and delightful book for the young math lover. Use it to guide a conversation about how math can be mind-boggling and exciting.

- Which new fact did you find the most interesting? Why?
- Are there any other questions about . . . that you have been eager to find out?

The Librarian Who Measured the Earth by Kathryn Lasky, illustrated by Kevin Hawkes (Little, Brown Books for Young Readers, 1994) E

Why do the stars stay up in the sky instead of falling? How far away is the Sun from the Earth? Eratosthenes was born full of wonder about the world that he found himself in. His parents thought that he would never stop asking questions. When he didn't get the answers that he wanted, Eratosthenes made it his mission to try to figure out matters for himself. His educational journey takes him from Cyrene (modern Libya) to Athens, and to Alexandria and beyond.

Sir Cumference series by Cindy Neuschwander, illustrated by Wayne Geehan (Charlesbridge Publishing) E

Follow the delightful, math-filled adventures of Sir Cumference, his wife Lady Di of Ameter, and their son, Radius. Solve the riddles, laugh at the puns, learn the formulas, or just enjoy the great stories.

Ten Black Dots by Donald Crews (HarperCollins, 1995) E

Can you count to ten? What could you possibly do with ten black dots? As you read through this book, find your own ways of using black dots. Enjoy this hugely entertaining book for a child who is learning how to count.

If you like this book, you'll also like:

- *1, 2, 3 to the Zoo: A Counting Book* by Eric Carle (The Trumpet Club, 1991)
- *Anno's Counting Book* by Mitsumasa Anno (HarperFestival, 1992)
- *Anno's Mysterious Multiplying Jar* by Mitsumasa Anno (Penguin, 1999)
- *Chicka Chicka 1–2–3 . . . And More Stories About Counting* by Bill Martin Jr. (Simon & Schuster, 2010)
- *Counting Coconuts* by Wendi Silvano (Raven Tree Press, 2004)
- *How Much Is a Million?* by David M. Schwartz (HarperCollins, 2004)
- *If You Made a Million* by David Schwartz (HarperCollins, 1989)
- *Just a Minute: A Trickster Tale and Counting Book* by Yuyi Morales (Chronicle Books, 2003)
- *Moja Means One: Swahili Counting Book* by Muriel Feelings and Tom Feelings (Puffin, 1992)

For Developing Readers

Chasing Vermeer by Blue Balliett, illustrated by Brett Helquist (Scholastic, 2004) D

Sixth graders Petra and Calder share love of art, blue candy, and their favorite teacher. When a valuable Vermeer painting is stolen from a museum, the two new friends use their mathematical talents to solve the puzzle of the missing painting. Follow the friends in their continuing adventures in *Wright 3* and *The Calder Game*.

Math Curse by John Scieszka and Lane Smith (Viking Juvenile, 1995) D

One day, Mrs. Fibonacci tells her class that you could think of almost anything as a math problem. So begins the curse: our narrator is doomed to see everything as a math problem, from getting dressed in the morning to choosing meal portions to dividing up objects. Some problems are easily solvable: "At 7:15, if it takes me 10 minutes to get dressed, 15 minutes to eat my breakfast, and 1 minute to brush my teeth, will I be on time for school at 8:00?" Still others don't seem to have mathematical applications at all: after counting her shirts, our narrator wonders when her Uncle Zeno will quit sending her ugly shirts. Whether you are a math lover or just the opposite, this book has something for you.

Talk About It:

- How do you use math in your everyday life? See how many math problems you can find (and solve, if you're feeling up to it)!

Marvelous Math: A Book of Poems selected by Lee Bennett Hopkins, illustrated by Karen Barbour (Simon & Schuster Children's Books, 2001) D

Each poem in this collection celebrates the many ways that numbers and mathematics add to our lives. From how we build houses to the famous Pythagoras to the wonder of passing time, Hopkins has put together a thoughtful grouping of numerical curiosity. Well-known poets like Janet S. Wong and Mr. Hopkins himself are mixed with new voices to create a fun, lyrical look at how numbers and words can go together.

Sideways Arithmetic From the Wayside School by Louis Sachar (Scholastic, 2004) D

Solve math brainteasers with the kids from Wayside School in this wonderful collection of short stories. Why would you need a spelling book to solve a math problem? Can you figure out what *Elf* + *Elf* equals? See how many of these problems and teasers you can crack!

What's Your Angle, Pythagoras? A Math Adventure by Julie Ellis, illustrated by Phyllis Hornung (Charlesbridge Publishing, 2004) D

What happens when you add "a-squared" to "b-squared"? When young Pythagoras meets a builder named Neferheferhersekeper, he discovers his vocation . . . he was born to study triangles! For readers who enjoyed Kathryn Lasky's *The Librarian Who Measured the Earth*, here's a similar tale of the power of undaunted curiosity and intellectual intrepidity.

If you like this book, you'll also like:

- *Alice in Pastaland: A Math Adventure* by Alexandra Wright (Charlesbridge, 1997)
- *Blockhead: The Life of Fibonacci* by Joseph D'Agnese (Henry Holt & Co., 2010)
- *Full House: An Invitation to Fractions* by Dayle Ann Dodds (Candlewick, 2009)
- *Mathematicians Are People, Too: Stories From the Lives of Great Mathematicians* by Luetta Reimer (Dale Seymour, 1990)
- *Multiplying Menace: The Revenge of Rumpelstiltskin* by Pam Calvert (Charlesbridge, 2006)
- *Mummy Math: An Adventure in Geometry* by Cindy Neuschwander (Square Fish, 2009)
- *A Very Improbable Story: A Math Adventure* by Edward Einhorn (Charlesbridge, 2008)

For Maturing Readers

Fractals, Googols, and Other Mathematical Tales by Theoni Pappas (Wide World Publishing, 1993) M

Using line drawings and humor, this book brings a variety of math concepts to life and even gives them personality. Whether your boy is whizzing through math class or still unsure of himself in that arena, this book is a fun way to take a new approach to learning and thinking about math. Pappas also gives a little bit of the history of math concepts, with comic illustrations included, reframing mathematics with rich context. This book is both a great tool for learning and a fun way to get inspired by the vast array of numbers and math that make up the world.

The Man Who Counted: A Collection of Mathematical Adventures by Malba Tahan, illustrated by Patricia Read Baquero (W. W. Norton & Company, 1993) M

This series of connected short stories is told in the motif of Arabian adventures and chronicles the travels of a man with remarkable mathematical skill, which he uses to solve conflicts and give wise advice to those he meets along his way. In each vignette a mathematical problem must be solved, and the hero uses insight from famous mathematicians throughout history to unlock the riddles. Readers who have numerical minds will enjoy trying to solve the problems with Tahan as they follow the stories.

The Number Devil: A Mathematical Adventure by Hans Magnus Enzensberger, illustrated by Rotraut Susanne Berner (Holt Paperbacks, 2000) M

Robert's dreams are suddenly very bizarre. Each night he finds himself in a land of numbers, and he must solve problems with the equally strange Number Devil. With each dream, concepts of mathematics are introduces and explained as Robert solves the problem at hand. Our hero must watch his step though, the Number Devil certainly lives up to his name if his demands are not fulfilled. Boys who excel at math as well as boys who struggle with it will enjoy the humor in Robert's strange predicament.

Mechanics and Technology

For Emerging Readers

Dinotrux by Chris Gall (Little, Brown Books for Young Readers, 2009) E

Half truck, half dinosaur, these mythical creatures wreak havoc as they trample across the earth. Hop on the safari that travels through the history of the Dinotrux and witness the trail of fiery destruction and disorder they leave behind. A perfect read for those who can't get enough of dinosaurs and trucks.

Hot Rod Hamster by Cynthia Lord, illustrated by Derek Anderson (Scholastic, 2010) E

Young readers will love this tale of a determined little hamster who loves cars and driving so much he decides to join a hot rod race meant, quite literally, for the big dogs. Cynthia Lord's sing-song text is cleverly tied together with the repetition of the interactive refrain, "Which would you choose?" Boys will answer eagerly as Derek Anderson's playful and bright illustrations of the small hero and his friends urge them on. Which would you choose?

I Stink! by Kate and Jim McMullan (HarperCollins, 2006) E

Garbage trucks sure stink, but they sure are fun! Watch this garbage truck eat all kinds of trash, keeping track of each thing he gobbles up from A to Z.

For Developing Readers

Honda: The Boy Who Dreamed of Cars by Mark Weston, illustrated by Katie Yamasaki (Lee & Low Books, 2008) D

From the time he was young, Soichiro Honda loved learning about how things worked. He watched the boats in the harbor, marveled at his father's creations as a blacksmith and, one day, observed a Ford Model T as it drove through town. After seeing his first Model T, Soichiro knew that he would someday learn how to make cars. He started in a garage as a mechanic and worked his way up the professional ladder to become a world-renowned manufacturer of motorcycles and cars.

Lego Star Wars: The Visual Dictionary by Simon Beecroft and Jeremy Beckett (DK Publishing, 2009) D

For diehard *Star Wars* fans, here is a comprehensive visual dictionary documenting every Lego tribute ever made to that story of a time long ago in a galaxy far, far away. Along with a picture of each Lego piece, detailed descriptions are provided relating the piece to the saga and specifying the film episode and relevant characters. A free Lego miniature of Luke Skywalker is included.

The Way Things Work by David Macaulay (Houghton Mifflin, 1988) D

This guidebook to pulleys, levers and all things that move will fascinate mechanically minded boys. This is a great browsing book, complete with cross-sections, diagrams and lots of labeled parts. If a boy has ever asked how something works, this is the perfect book for him. Macaulay might just inspire his readers to try to build some of the things he explains so well.

For Maturing Readers

Building Big by David Macaulay (Sandpiper, 2004) M

This volume of architecture spans the globe as it explains the mechanics of building some of the world's most famous structures. Macaulay has an incredible ability to break down the technical elements of the architectural tools and design. His descriptions and illustrations will allow any reader with a budding interest in building design to cultivate a better understanding of the artistry and thought processes behind the world's dams, domes, skyscrapers, tunnels, and bridges.

Future Tech: From Personal Robots to Motorized Monocycles by Charles Piddock (National Geographic Children's Books, 2009) M

Boys will love this colorful and insightful exploration into the technology that could be changing society in the near future. Piddock shares the current research and uses of robotics and nanotechnology, and also delves into the possibilities for these innovations in the future. The photographs and timelines throughout are perfect for the young man who loves facts and figures. Boys are sure to pore over this book and spend hours imagining what the future may hold.

Motor Novels series by Will Weaver (Farrar, Straus and Giroux) M

This series about car-obsessed teens living in Michigan is perfect for a young racecar fan. Though the storylines for each book in the series stand independently, readers will enjoy getting to know the characters as the series moves forward. From detailed descriptions of the car each driver races to the friendships and action on and off the track, the series has all of the elements mechanically minded boys love.

Mystery and Horror

For Emerging Readers

Alpha Oops: H Is for Halloween by Alethea Kontis, illustrated by Bob Kolar (Candlewick, 2010) E

In this out-of-order alphabet sequel to *Alpha Oops: The Day Z Went First*, each of the personified letters of the alphabet takes the stage "dressed up" in a different Halloween costume that starts with its respective letter. "H," for Halloween, starts the show, and "B" gets his moment of glory at the end when he says, "B is for . . . Boo!" The pictures, letters, and words are a perfect combination for boys who have a mastery of the alphabet and appreciate the scary parts of Halloween.

Bones series by David Adler, illustrated by Barbara Newman (Penguin Young Readers Group) E

Jeffrey Bones uses his powers of deductive reasoning to solve mysteries around his home and town. In *Bones and the Math Test Mystery*, Jeffrey finds his missing math test hiding in a very unusual place. Luckily, the young detective is able to retake the test and scores an "excellent" grade like his classmates. In *Bones and the Birthday Mystery*, Jeffrey asks questions and investigates clues to find his grandfather's birthday card and birthday present. Books in this series are fast-paced, easy-to-read, and great for boys who are just beginning to transition to chapter books.

Jitterbug Jam by Barbara Jean Hicks, illustrated by Alexis Deacon (Farrar, Straus, and Giroux, 2005) E

This book takes the idea of monsters hiding under the bed and turns it upside down. Bobo the monster is afraid to go to sleep because he thinks there is a boy "with pink skin and orange fur on his head where his horns should be" hiding under his bed. Bobo's grandpa, Boo-Dad, knows how scary boys can be. He tells Bobo how to frighten the boy away, but Bobo decides to take matters into his own hands. He's not so sure that the creature hiding under his bed is as scary as he seems. This funny inversion of the classic monster-under-the-bed story is sure to be a fast favorite for your boys.

Nate the Great series by Marjorie Weinman Sharmat, illustrated by Marc Simont (Yearling) E

Nate the Great encounters perplexing puzzles and has to find creative solutions to get out of tricky situations. With a bag full of tricks and the help of his friends, Nate the Great solves mysteries both big and small in this beloved series.

For Emerging to Developing Readers

Cam Jansen series by David Adler, illustrated by Susanna Natti (Penguin) E →D

With her photographic memory and eye for detail, Jennifer "Cam" Jansen is always finding and solving mysteries. In *Cam Jansen and the Valentine Baby Mystery*, Cam uses her photographic memory to figure out who has been stealing women's purses at the hospital. After she has solved the mystery, Cam meets her new twin siblings! Featuring a spunky heroine with an uncannily accurate photographic memory, short and easy-to-read sentences, and pictures that help clarify the plots, these books are well-written and fun transitional readers that help fill the gap between easy-to-read and middle-school-level books. The first ten books in the series have been recently reprinted with bright and eye-catching covers, perfect for young boys.

Invisible Inc. series by Elizabeth Levy, Illustrated by Denise Brunkus (Cartwheel, 1995) E →D

Chip is an invisible boy. He and his friends, Justin and Charlene, are dedicated to righting wrongs and to using their individual abilities—invisibility, reading lips, and good old-fashioned logic—to help people. In *The Snack-Attack Mystery*, the group figures out who is stealing snacks from their classmates' lunch boxes. In *The Mystery of the Missing Dog*, the trio uses its talents to find Max, Chip's invisible dog.

For Developing Readers

The 39 Clues series by Rick Riordan, Patrick Carman, Margaret Peterson Haddix, Gordon Korman, Peter Lerangis, Linda Sue Park, and Jude Watson (Scholastic) D

Instead of receiving a million dollars, orphans Dan and Amy Cahill decide to take on the challenge of locating the 39 clues to a large fortune that their late aunt left hidden all around the world. Together, Amy and Dan must use their wits and courage to locate and identify the mysterious clues before their very determined relatives. Between books in this series, readers can collect cards that contain clues to the mysteries and play online games at *www.the39clues.com* to keep them on their sleuthing toes!

A to Z Mysteries: The Missing Mummy by Ron Roy, illustrated by John Steven Gurvey (A Stepping Stone Book, Random House, 2001) D

Dink, Josh, and Ruth Rose visit the museum for Mummy Monday and quickly find themselves wrapped up in a mystery. During the trip, the mummy and valuable treasures are stolen from right under their noses. The three friends immediately set out to solve the case and recover the lost items.

If you like this, you'll like other books in the A to Z Mysteries series including:

- *A to Z Mysteries: The Absent Author* by Ron Roy, illustrated by John Steven Gurvey (A Stepping Stone Book, Random House, 1997)
- *A to Z Mysteries: The Bald Bandit* by Ron Roy, illustrated by John Steven Gurvey (A Stepping Stone Book, Random House, 1997)
- *A to Z Mysteries: Detective Camp* by Ron Roy, illustrated by John Steven Gurvey (A Stepping Stone Book, Random House, 2006)
- *A to Z Mysteries: The Talking T-Rex* by Ron Roy, illustrated by John Steven Gurvey (A Stepping Stone Book, Random House, 2003)

- *A to Z Mysteries: White House White-Out* by Ron Roy, illustrated by John Steven Gurvey (A Stepping Stone Book, Random House, 2008)
- *A to Z Mysteries: The White Wolf* by Ron Roy, illustrated by John Steven Gurvey (A Stepping Stone Book, Random House, 2004)

The Adventures of The Bailey School Kids series by Debbie Dadey and Marcia T. Jones (Scholastic Paperbacks)

The third graders at The Bailey School have had some interesting teachers. In each story, their new teacher has strange habits that seem almost supernatural. Mrs. Jeepers seems to have a lot in common with the undead in *Vampires Don't Wear Polka Dots*, and when they go to summer camp their counselor only seems to be partially human in *Werewolves Don't Go to Summer Camp*. The kids must unravel the mysterious true identities of the adults in their lives, and in each adventure in the series there is plenty of humor and action to keep boys turning pages as the action unfolds. Be it leprechauns or ghosts, dragons or zombies, you can count on The Bailey School kids to figure out who's who and what's what.

Geronimo Stilton: The Search for the Sunken Treasure by Geronimo Stilton (Scholastic, 2000) D

At the request of his aunt, Geronimo Stilton, publisher of the *Rodent's Gazette*, and his three friends Thea, Trap, and Benjamin set off to find a sunken treasure near the Ratlapagos Islands. Many years before, Geronimo's uncle disappeared while searching for the exact same treasure. Will Geronimo and his friends be able to find the treasure before the rotten rodents?

Goosebumps series by R. L. Stine (Scholastic) D

These short, creepy tales will have even resistant readers flipping the pages as fast as they can read them. Each magically horrifying mystery is a stand-alone story. In *Bad Hare Day*, Tim Swanson dreams of being a magician just like his hero, the magician Amaz-O. When Amaz-O performs nearby, Tim learns that Amaz-O is not a friendly magician. After stealing Amaz-O's bag of tricks, Tim must flee from the magician's wrath. In *Werewolf Skin*, Alex Hunter is a budding photographer. Alex ignores his aunt and uncle's warnings and goes out one night during a full moon to take some photographs. Little does he know, Wolf Creek has a big secret! Read all of R. L. Stine's twisted tales, and heed the series' tagline, "Reader beware—you're in for a scare!"

A Jigsaw Jones Mystery: The Case of the Food Fight by James Preller (Scholastic, 2005) D

A food fight breaks out among the second graders in the cafeteria. "Green Jell-O smashed. Spaghetti flew." Things get out of control, and the second graders blame Joey Pignattano for making them lose their recess. Jigsaw knows that Joey is innocent but the only way to prove it is to find the real culprit. Will Jigsaw be able to figure out who started the food fight in time to save recess? If you like this book, then read the others in the Jigsaw Jones Mystery series.

Talk About It:

Jigsaw knows that Joey just loves to eat; he does not start food fights. So when Jigsaw's classmates blame Joey for starting the food fight, Jigsaw is determined to help Joey.

- What would you have done if you were Jigsaw?
- How did Jigsaw ultimately solve the mystery?
- When did you know who the real culprit was?

Time Warp Trio: Summer Reading Is Killing Me by Jon Scieszka, illustrated by Lane Smith (Puffin Books, 1998) D

Despite their plans to have a calm summer without any trouble, Joe, Sam, and Fred find themselves caught up in a deadly game. The three friends definitely do not want to spend their summer doing their summer reading, so they hide the school book list inside a mysterious book. They don't realize that *The Book* hides a time warp. Not only do they fail to escape their summer reading, they are transported inside of it! Will the Time Warp Trio be able to escape the bizarre worlds of Frankenstein, Mary Poppins, and Peter Rabbit? The adventures continue in the Time Warp Trio series.

For Maturing Readers

Alex Rider series by Anthony Horowitz (Philomel) M

When Alex Rider's uncle and guardian is suddenly killed, Alex discovers that his uncle had been a spy for the British government. Alex is then given a task: to complete his uncle's last assignment by investigating the secrets of a man named Herod Sayle and his mysterious Stormbreaker computer. As the series progresses, Alex is called upon to solve more mysteries and unravel more secrets, armed only with ingenious tools and his own intelligence.

Brixton Brothers series by Mac Barnett, illustrated by Adam Rex (Simon & Schuster Children's Publishing) M

Steve Brixton loves mysteries and manages to find exciting adventures everywhere. In the first book in the series, *The Case of the Case of Mistaken Identity*, Steve stumbles across a mystery right in the library while doing research for a social studies paper. He must retrieve a historic quilt and prove that he is not working for an evil criminal mastermind before it is too late.

Cherub series by Robert Muchamore (Simon Pulse) M

In this series, teenagers double as CHERUB agents, spies who are trained to take on important cases and jobs. Because their tasks are so dangerous, the agents are unable to acknowledge the existence of the CHERUB program. The series begins with James, a struggling but smart young boy who has recently been recruited to join the program. Through James' adventures, we are introduced to a world of danger, suspense, and very daring teenagers.

The London Eye Mystery by Siobhan Dowd (Yearling, 2008) M

Salim is visiting his cousins Ted and Kat in England. When he wants to go on the London Eye, they decide to wait for him to return from the thirty-minute journey on the touristy ferris wheel but he never comes back! Where did Salim vanish to? Will Ted and Kat ever be able to find their cousin?

The Mysterious Benedict Society by Trenton Lee Stewart, illustrated by Carson Ellis (Little, Brown Books for Young Readers, 2008) M

Eleven-year-old orphan Reynie Muldoon decides to answer an ad recruiting gifted and talented children, and he and three other especially talented children are chosen by a man named Mr. Benedict to join a group called the Benedict Society. After undergoing rigorous training, the Benedict Society must infiltrate a very dangerous school called the Learning Institute for the Very Enlightened in order to save the world from a criminal mastermind who uses propaganda to deceive people everywhere.

If you like this book, you'll also like:

- *From the Mixed-Up Files of Mrs. Basil E. Frankweiler* by E. L. Konigsburg (Atheneum, 2007)
- *Mrs. Frisby and the Rats of NIMH* by Robert C. O'Brien (Aladdin, 1986)
- *The Mysterious Benedict Society and the Perilous Journey* by Trenton Lee Stewart (Little, Brown, 2009)

- *The Mysterious Benedict Society and the Prisoner's Dilemma* by Trenton Lee Steward (Little, Brown, 2010)
- Septimus Heap series by Angie Sage (Katherine Tegen Books)

Red Card: A Zeke Armstrong Mystery by Daniel J. Hale and Matthew LaBrot (Top Publications, 2003) M

Zeke Armstrong goes with his travel soccer team to an away game and finds himself in the middle of a murder mystery when his coach is suddenly killed. Zeke must solve the crime and lead his team to victory, but will he be able to do all of this before the killer comes after him? Find out in this action-packed mystery, and join Zeke as he solves many more cases in other Zeke Armstrong Mysteries.

Skeleton Creek by Patrick Carman (Scholastic, 2009) M

Where did Skeleton Creek, a small town in Oregon, get its sinister name? That is the question that Ryan McCray and Sarah Fincher set out to answer. Their quest to learn the truth takes them on a treacherous journey. Sarah films the trip, and readers can watch the films online as they read the book. Will the friends be able to uncover the history of their mysterious town? To uncover the exciting conclusion, read the sequel, *The Ghost in the Machine*.

Theodore Boone: Kid Lawyer by John Grisham (Dutton Children's Books, 2010) M

Theo Boone might only be thirteen, but he sure knows a lot about the law. He can't wait to grow up and become a real lawyer. Theo is about to find himself in court a lot sooner than he expected when he gets caught up in the middle of a major murder trial. He alone knows the truth and must discover a way to let others know, no matter what the cost!

Nature and the Animal World

For Emerging Readers

Actual Size by Steve Jenkins (Houghton Mifflin Books for Children, 2004) E

Is there really a moth as big as a bird or an animal with a two-foot-long tongue? What animal weights 600 pounds? What animal is only 1/3 of an inch long? Learn astounding facts and figures about some of the world's largest, smallest, and heaviest animals, and browse through pictures that bring these amazing creatures to life.

Bug Butts by Dawn Cusick, edited by Dr. Timothy Forrest, illustrated by Dr. Haude Levesque (EarlyLight Books, Inc., 2009) E

As it turns out, the rear ends of insects do some pretty amazing things! They can blow bubbles and even communicate with friends or enemies. This book is filled with a ton of fun and interesting facts about what bugs can do with their back sides. A truly funny and educational read for everyone!

Big Tracks, Little Tracks: Following Animal Prints by Millicent Selsam, illustrated by Marlene Hill Donnelly (HarperCollins, 1998) E

Become an animal detective and learn how to follow the tracks of cats, rabbits, and many other animals in nature. Learn how to identify the tracks of your favorite critters. What other information can you uncover about the animals featured in this book? Read it and track down the facts.

Bat Loves the Night: Read and Wonder by Nicola Davies, illustrated by Sarah Fox-Davies (Candlewick Press, 2001) E

Learn about bats and their nightly activities in an exciting narrative peppered with interesting facts. During the hours when humans and most other animals sleep, bats use their incredible sense of hearing to hunt for their food before the dawn arrives. The Read and Wonder series has so many great books that share the stories of different kinds of animals' lives.

Talk About It:

- This is a good book to read when you want to talk about nocturnal life.
- What new facts did you learn about bats? What else do you want to learn about them? How can you find out the answers to your new questions?

Look for more great Read and Wonder series titles, including:

- *Gentle Giant Octopus: Read and Wonder* by Karen Wallace, illustrated by Mike Bostock (Candlewick Press, 2002)
- *Grandma Elephant's in Charge: Read and Wonder* by Martin Jenkins, illustrated by Ivan Bates (Candlewick Press. 2007)
- *One Tiny Turtle: Read and Wonder* by Nicola Davies, illustrated by Jane Chapman (Candlewick Press, 2005)
- *Walk With a Wolf: Read and Wonder* by Janni Howker, illustrated by Sarah Fox-Davies (Candlewick Press, 2002)

Buffalo Song by Joseph Bruchac, illustrated by Bill Farnsworth (Lee & Low Books, 2008) E

At one time, huge herds of buffalo roamed freely through the West. By the 1870s, due to extreme overhunting, the large, powerful animals were almost extinct. Two members of the Nez Perce tribe, Red Elk and his father, Two Swans, came across one of the few surviving buffalo calves. Determined to save the calf's life, Red Elk brings him to Walking Coyote, who has dedicated his life to saving the disappearing creatures. Full of exquisite illustrations, this book is a perfect read for all who love nature, animals, and the stories of true heroes.

Farm by Elisha Cooper (Orchard Books, 2010) E

This is a look at farm life for a family of four from the months of March to November. Filled with details and facts all about farm animals, tractors, crops, and barns, readers will learn all about the happenings on a farm each day and through the seasons. This book is filled with beautiful illustrations and a lyrical writing style that will spark young readers' interest and curiosity about the world of farming.

First the Egg by Laura Vaccaro Seeger (Roaring Brook Press, 2007) E

What came first, the chicken or the egg? The story or the word? The paint or the picture? Finally, there are answers to these age-old questions, and they are in this delightful book. A perfect read for the curious young boy who is full questions about the world around him.

Gone Fishing: Ocean Life by the Numbers by David McLimans (Walker Books for Young Readers, 2008) E

Count from one to ten with the numerically-shaped marine creatures! While you're busy counting, be sure not to miss all of the details and fun facts you can learn about the tiger-tailed seahorse, the African penguin, and other cool marine creatures and their habitat.

Hottest, Coldest, Highest, Deepest by Steve Jenkins (Houghton Mifflin, 1998) E

If you love superlatives, you will love this book. What is the highest mountain? Where is the coldest spot on the planet? What is the most active volcano? Dramatic pictures help make the exploration of these marvels around the world even more exciting and kid-friendly.

Never Smile at a Monkey by Steve Jenkins (Houghton Mifflin Books for Children, 2009) E

Never smile at a monkey or pet a platypus: these are two of the many important lessons about what not to do when encountering potentially dangerous creatures in the wild. In this beautifully illustrated picture book, Jenkins shows young readers how many creatures that appear harmless may actually prove very dangerous to unsuspecting humans.

Spiders by Nic Bishop (Scholastic, 2007) E

Did you know that spiders have been around for over 350 million years? Gather fantastic facts about the more than 38,000 spiders that populate the earth. The bright and clear pictures bring even the most deadly spiders to life.

If you like this book, you'll also like:

- *Butterflies and Moths* by Nic Bishop (Scholastic, 2009)
- *Frogs* by Nic Bishop (Scholastic, 2008)
- *Lizards* by Nic Bishop (Scholastic, 2010)
- *Marsupials* by Nic Bishop (Scholastic, 2009)

What Do You Do When Something Wants to Eat You? by Steve Jenkins (Sandpiper, 2001) E

How does an octopus defend itself from a shark? How do other animals protect themselves from becoming another animal's dinner? Learn about the unique ways that animals from puffer fish to bombardier beetles arm themselves against their attackers.

Who Eats What? Food Chains and Food Webs by Patricia Lauber, illustrated by Holly Keller (HarperCollins Publishers, Inc., 1995) E

How does the food chain work? How are humans connected to tuna fish? Trace the intricate relationships between animals, plants, and human beings as they interact within the food chain. The clear and colorful pictures also provide lots of fun and useful information. Choose one or more of the activities that the author suggests doing after you have finished reading the book.

Whose Tracks Are These? A Clue Book for Familiar Forest Animals by James Nail (Roberts Rinehart Publishers, 1994) E

Discover the unique tracks left behind by many different animals. Become an amateur scientist and study all of the tracks that you can find in your backyard. Have you ever seen the footprint of a raccoon? What about the footprint of a fox?

Talk About It:

Are those tracks from a dog, a raccoon, or a cat? Learn fun and exciting ways to distinguish between the different prints left behind. Find a track somewhere outside, draw it, and analyze it.

- Study all of the tracks in the book and go on a nature walk. Identify some of the many tracks you encounter along the way.

For Developing Readers

Cave Detectives: Unraveling the Mystery of an Ice Age Cave by David L. Harrison, illustrated by Ashley Mims, photographs by Edward Biamonte (Chronicle Books, 2007) D

This narrative's mix of science and mystery takes young readers along on an archaeological investigation. Through a combination of photographs and illustrations, Harrison guides his audience from clue to clue. As the archaeologists piece together a story that happened thousands of years ago, before humans arrived in North America, Harrison describes the scientific tools and techniques necessary to uncover the ancient secrets of the Riverbluff Cave.

DK Eyewitness Books series (DK Children) D

How much water is in the ocean? What actually causes a hurricane? How many bones are there in the human body? Find the answer to these questions and many more in the wonderful Eyewitness book series.

Check out the following DK Eyewitness Books:

- *Chemistry* by Ann Newmark (DK Children, 2005)
- *Crystal and Gem* by R. F. Symes and R. R. Harding (DK Children, 2007)
- *Earth* by Susanna van Rose (DK Children, 2005)
- *Electricity* by Steve Parker (DK Children, 2005)
- *Human Body* by Richard Walker (DK Children, 2009)
- *Natural Disasters* by Claire Watts (DK Children, 2006)
- *Ocean* by Miranda MacQuitty (DK Children, 2008)
- *Universe* by Robin Kerrod (DK Children, 2009)
- *Volcanoes and Earthquakes* by Susanna van Rose (DK Children, 2008)
- *Weather* by Brian Cosgrove (DK Children, 2007)

Great Migrations: Whales, Wildebeests, Butterflies, Elephants, and Other Amazing Animals on the Move by Elizabeth Carney (National Geographic Children's Books, 2010) D

Many animals all over the world perform incredibly massive migrations every year. This book tells the stories of all these magnificent animals and their will to survive while traveling great distances. Filled with amazing photographs and important information, this book is a must read for those interested in animals on the go and what their annual journeys are like!

How to Scratch a Wombat by Jackie French, illustrated by Bruce Whatley (Clarion Books, 2009) D

What is a day like for a young wombat? Visit the secret world of wombats and learn everything you ever wanted to know about these mysterious creatures. Find out how singing helps bring wombats closer and how you can help protect these Australian natives. This is a perfect read for any wombat or nature lovers.

If you like this book, you'll also like:

- *Diary of a BABY Wombat* by Jackie French (Clarion, 2010)
- *Diary of a Wombat* by Jackie French (Sandpiper, 2009)
- *Edward the Emu* by Sheena Knowles (HarperCollins, 1998)
- *Hunwick's Egg* by Mem Fox (Harcourt, 2005)
- *Koala Lou* by Mem Fox (Sandpiper, 1994)
- *A Platypus, Probably* by Sneed B. Collard (Charlesbridge, 2005)
- *Possum Magic* by Mem Fox (Sandpiper, 1991)
- *We're Going on a Bear Hunt* by Michael Rosen (Little Simon, 1997)
- *Wombat Walkabout* by Carol Diggory Shields (Dutton Juvenile, 2009)

For Maturing Readers

Animal Fact File by Tony Hare (Checkmark Books, 1999) M

Like a car owner's manual for the mammal realm, this volume is practically bursting with diagrams and descriptions of the entire animal kingdom. Presented alphabetically, from aardvark to wombat, each animal is explained with illustrations of their external and internal appearance and a reference chart giving specific information about the species. While not every mammal is listed in this book, animal lovers will enjoy the facts and terminology Hare shares and the wealth of information for each creature included.

If you like this book, you'll also like:

- *Animal: The Definitive Visual Guide to the World's Wildlife* by David Burnie (DK Adult, 2005)
- *Animal Tracks and Signs* by Jinny Johnson (National Geographic Children's Books, 2008)
- *The Encyclopedia of Animals: A Complete Visual Guide* by George McKay (University of California Press, 2004)
- *National Geographic: Encyclopedia of Animals* by Karen McGhee and George McKay (National Geographic Children's Books, 2006)

Evolution: How We and All Living Things Came to Be by Daniel Loxton (Kids Can Press, 2010) M

This volume explains the theory of evolution with photographs, illustrations, and diagrams. The natural world and its history come to life on its pages. While the author is in firm support of the theory of evolution, he does not claim that science can answer all of life's questions and leaves room for spirituality's place in the world. Budding scientists and boys who are fascinated by fossils will love poring over this text and combing through the details. With all of the illustrative support, this book is great for browsing as well as for deeper fact finding.

Extraordinary Jobs With Animals by Alicia Devantier and Carol Turkington (Ferguson Publishing Company, 2006) M

This is the perfect book for any boy who wants to hold onto his passion for animals as an adult. Devantier and Turkington explore various jobs that involve caring for and working with wild animals. This thoughtful exploration includes detailed descriptions and luminous photographs. *Extraordinary Jobs With Animals* is sure to help any animal fanatic envision himself with a career he loves in a field that is anything but ordinary.

Going Blue: A Teen Guide to Saving Our Oceans, Lakes, Rivers, & Wetlands by Cathryn Berger Kaye and Philippe Cousteau (Free Spirit Publishing, 2010) M

This guide to conservationism is specifically crafted for growing readers who are interested in acting on behalf of the natural world. The book includes a basic introduction to the concepts behind global water conservation and clear ideas and examples of simple things young people can do to make a difference both in their communities and worldwide. The colorful photographs and diagrams bring the information to readers with a lot of visual appeal and useful facts. Readers can learn about important bodies of water across the globe, while planning their actions on a local scale. This book is sure to inspire boys to make a difference.

If you like this book, you'll like:

- *Dare to Dream! 25 Extraordinary Lives* by Sandra McLeod Humphrey (Prometheus Books, 2005)
- *It's Our World, Too! Young People Who Are Making a Difference: How They Do It—How You Can, Too!* by Phillip M. Hoose (Farrar, Straus and Giroux, 2002)
- *The Kid's Guide to Service Projects: Over 500 Service Ideas for Young People Who Want to Make a Difference* by Barbara A. Lewis (Free Spirit Publishing, 2009)
- *Kids With Courage: True Stories About Young People Making a Difference* by Barbara A. Lewis ((Free Spirit Publishing, 1992)
- *The Teen Guide to Global Action: How to Connect With Others (Near & Far) to Create Social Change* by Barbara A. Lewis (Free Spirit Publishing, 2007)

Poetry

For Emerging Readers

Black Is Brown Is Tan by Arnold Adoff, illustrated by Emily Arnold McCully (Amistad, 2004) E

Originally published in 1973, this was the first children's book to feature an interracial family. Arnold Adoff's poem celebrating the beauty of all races and all families rings as true today as it did when it first hit bookstores. Now reprinted with more modern illustrations, each page features the family going about their daily lives and enjoying one another's company as Adoff's rhythmic verse accents the themes of love and acceptance. Whether children come from interracial families or not, the poetry echoes the universal sentiments of familial love that are a comfort to all children.

Come to the Castle! A Visit to a Castle in Thirteenth-Century England by Linda Ashman, illustrated by S. D. Schindler (Flash Point, 2009) E

Told through the eyes of the Earl of Daftwood and his staff as they plan for a large party, these rhyming poems bring the Middle Ages to life.

FEG: Stupid (Ridiculous) Poems for Intelligent Children by Robin Hirsch, illustrated by Ha (Little, Brown Young Readers, 2002) E

Do you love alliterations, haikus, and odes? Read though this hilarious collection and find your favorite poems. Discover "How to Enter a Poem" or "F*E*G," the very funny alphabet poem.

Guyku: A Year of Haiku for Boys by Bob Raczka, illustrated by Peter H. Reynolds (Houghton Mifflin Books for Boys, 2010) E

This is a book of haikus with our littlest guys in mind. A haiku is a three-line poem where the first line is five syllables, the second is seven syllables and the third is five syllables again. The haikus flow through the seasons with a keen eye on the outdoors. Bob Raczka's accessible tome of short, sweet poetry is enhanced by Peter H. Reynolds' beautiful illustrations.

Looking Like Me by Walter Dean Myers, illustrated by Christopher Myers (EgmontUSA, 2009) E

Who is it that you see when you look into the mirror? In this wonderful poem, a father and his son team up to help you find the true beauty in each face that shines back in the mirror. This poetic picture book is a celebration of the bonds between father and son and the love that families share.

Odd Owls & Stout Pigs: A Book of Nonsense by Arnold and Adrienne Lobel (HarperCollins, 2009) E

Find out why a certain owl is always wet or why another likes to blow up and pop balloons. These short and slightly nonsensical rhymes and poems about owls and pigs will leave you laughing long after the last page has been turned.

If you like this book, you'll also like:

- *The Best of Ogden Nash* by Linell Nash Smith (Ivan R. Dee, 2007)
- *Cautionary Tales for Children* by Hilaire Belloc (Houghton Mifflin, 2002)
- *The Complete Verse and Other Nonsense* by Edward Lear (Penguin, 2002)

- *Falling Up* by Shel Silverstein (HarperCollins, 1996)
- *A Light in the Attic* by Shel Silverstein (HarperCollins, 1981)
- *Ogden Nash's Zoo* by Ogden Nash (Stewart, Tabori and Chang, 1986)
- *The Owl and the Pussycat* by Edward Lear, illustrated by Jan Brett (Putnam, 1996)
- *The Penguin Book of Nonsense Verse* edited by Quentin Blake (Viking Penguin, 2001)
- *The Tale of Custard the Dragon* by Ogden Nash (Little, Brown, 1998)
- *Where the Sidewalk Ends* by Shel Silverstein (HarperCollins, 1974)

Orangutan Tongs: Poems to Tangle Your Tongue by Jon Agee (Hyperion Book, 2009) E

Filled with terrifically tasty tongue twisters, this collection will keep you laughing. Find out exactly what noise annoys an oyster in "The Cranky Oyster" and learn just what a "dodo'll do" in "Dodos!" If you love words, this is the perfect book for you.

A Poke in the I: A Collection of Concrete Poems edited by Paul Janeczko, illustrated by Chris Raschka (Candlewick, 2005) E

These 30 concrete poems by many authors are wonderfully creative and funny. "Tennis Anyone" makes tennis come alive as the reader bounces from one side of the page to the other, while the poem "Sky Day Dream" grows smaller and smaller as it travels into the distance. Which will be your favorite?

The Underwear Salesman: And Other Jobs for Better or Verse by J. Patrick Lewis, illustrated by Serge Bloch (Ginee Seo Books, 2009) E

A wonderfully funny book of poetry full of puns and rhymes lets you meet great characters like Sloppy Joe the Butcher, the subway driver, and the marathoner. Find out all about these unique caricatures of everyday life!

For Developing Readers

Amazing Faces selected by Lee Bennett Hopkins, illustrated by Chris Soentpiet (Lee & Low Books, 2010) D

This compilation of poems celebrates the many faces that make the United States an amazing country. Each beautifully illustrated face's story is illuminated by the poetry matched to it. With each new page, the portrait of America grows in varying ages and races and genders. Hopkins has the collection culminate with Langston Hughes' poem, "My People," beside a crowd of faces waving the American flag. The message is clear; Hopkins and Soentpiet celebrate America in this work as a diverse and beautiful nation of people.

Dark Emperor and Other Poems of the Night **by Joyce Sidman, illustrated by Rick Allen (Houghton Mifflin Books for Children, 2010) D**

This collection of poetry explores the vibrant world that comes to life each night. Nocturnal animals take the spotlight, from bats and owls to crickets and spiders. Boys will love imagining this wild, nighttime community that thrives in the darkness that so many people and animals avoid.

Love That Dog **by Sharon Creech (HarperCollins, 2001) D**

Poetry is not for boys, right? With the help of his teacher, Ms. Stretchberry, and some writing role models like Walter Dean Myers, Jack learns that poetry actually might be perfect for boys. Written in free verse, this book is perfect for even the most reluctant poetry reader.

My People **by Langston Hughes, illustrated by Charles R. Smith Jr. (Simon & Schuster Children's Publishing/Atheneum, 2009) D**

In this book, Langston Hughes' poem "My People" is set to a collection of beautiful and inspiring photographs. Each pairing of words and images carries a powerful message and brings Hughes' message of hope and love to life.

If you like this book, you'll also like:

- *He's Got the Whole World in His Hands* by Kadir Nelson (Dial, 2005)
- *I Saw Your Face* by Tom Feelings and Kwame Dawes (Dial, 2004)
- *Let It Shine* by Ashley Bryan (Simon & Schuster, 2007)
- *Poetry for Young People* by Langston Hughes (Sterling, 2006)
- *Short Takes: Fast-Break Basketball Poetry* by Charles R. Smith (Penguin, 2001)
- *Soul Looks Back in Wonder* by Tom Feelings (Puffin, 1999)
- *The Sun Is So Quiet* by Nikki Giovanni (Henry Holt & Co., 1996)
- *Sweet Corn* by James Stevenson (Greenwillow, 1999)
- *Words With Wings: A Treasury of African-American Poetry and Art* by Belinda Rochelle (Amistad, 2000)

For Maturing Readers

The Rose That Grew From Concrete by Tupac Shakur (MTV, 2009) M

Tupac Shakur wrote the poems in this book when he was 19, before he became a world-famous hip-hop artist. Yet, they contain the same talent and energy that would electrify his music. The book is deeply personal, almost private: poems are copied directly from Shakur's notebook, preserving his handwriting, his edits, and, most of all, what it was like for him to be 19 years old.

If you like this book, you'll like:

- *Falling Hard: 100 Love Poems by Teens* by Betsy Franco (Candlewick, 2010)
- *Paint Me Like I Am: Teen Poems From WritersCorps* by Bill Aguado and Richard Newirth (HarperTeen, 2003)
- *Poetry Speaks Who I Am* by Elise Paschen and Dominique Raccah (Sourcebooks Jabberwocky, 2010)

You Hear Me? Poems and Writing by Teenage Boys edited by Betsy Franco, photographs by Nina Nickles (Candlewick, 2001) M

This collection of poems was written by boys, and so it has a bracing immediacy. The poems range across difficult situations: the perils of growing up, including sex and drugs. But the poems are mainly about what poetry has always been about: love and loneliness. Here is 12-year-old Quantedius Hall on what he wants: "Time Somebody Told Me / That I am lovely, good and real / That I am beautiful inside / If they only knew / How that would make me feel."

Realistic Fiction

For Emerging Readers

El Barrio by Debbi Chocolate, illustrated by David Diaz (Henry Holt and Company, 2009) E

Learn all about the rich and lively *barrio* that forms the backdrop for a young boy's life. Travel with him as he goes through his neighborhood on his way to his sister's quinceañera. At the end of the journey, he gets a special treat: "syrupy sweet *churros*."

Dear Primo: A Letter to My Cousin by Duncan Tonatiuh (Abrams Books for Young Readers, 2010) E

Two cousins, or *primos* in Spanish, write letters back and forth to learn more about one another. Charlie is American, while Carlitos is Mexican, and from the food they eat to the neighborhood they live in, there are so many interesting differences in their worlds to explore. Charlie loves to eat pizza, and Carlitos likes to help his mom make quesadillas. Carlitos swims in a small river, or *rio*, but Charlie uses a fire hydrant to cool off on a hot day. As they compare their lives, young readers will love the poetic and sometimes humorous descriptions each boy uses. In the end, Charlie and Carlitos may have more in common than they first thought.

Lionel at School **by Stephen Krensky, illustrated by Susanna Natti (Puffin Books, 2000) E**

Can Lionel survive his first day at school? Find out what Lionel decides to do to make the time spent in class pass as quickly as recess and follow our hero as he adjusts to the trials and successes of his school experience.

The Lost Lake **by Allen Say (Houghton Mifflin Company, 1989) E**

A young boy spends the summer with his father, who works all day in his study. Bored and stuck in the house, the boy longs for something to do. He is delighted when he and his father set off on a camping trip to rediscover a lake his father remembers from childhood. When they finally encounter the lake, it is nothing like his father remembers, so they venture off in search of a new lake. But will they be able to find one that lives up to his father's old memory?

If you like this book, you'll also like:

- *The Bicycle Man* by Allen Say (Sandpiper, 1989)
- *The Boy of the Three-Year Nap* by Dianne Snyder and Allen Say (Sandpiper, 1993)
- *El Chino* by Allen Say (Sandpiper, 1996)
- *Erika-San* by Allen Say (Houghton Mifflin, 2009)
- *Kamishibai Man* by Allen Say (Houghton Mifflin, 2005)
- *Night of the Moonjellies* by Mark Sasha (Purple House Press, 2007)
- *A River Dream* by Allen Say (Sandpiper, 1993)
- *Tree of Cranes* by Allen Say (Sandpiper, 2009)

My Weird School series by Dan Gutman (HarperCollins Publishers) E

Ella Mentry School is the setting for second-grader A. J.'s tales of crazy Miss Daisy and nutsy Mr. Klutz. Whether you run and hide or jump for joy when the school bus arrives every day, you'll love reading about this unusual school.

Talk About It:

- Who is your favorite teacher at school? Why? Do you know any weird facts about your teacher?
- What is your least favorite thing at school? What do you like best about school?

For Developing Readers

Alvin Ho: Allergic to Girls, School, and Other Scary Things by Lenore Look, illustrated by LeUyen Pham (Yearling, 2008) D

So what does Alvin hate? Elevators, substitute teachers, and kimchi make his list, but it's a pretty long list. One thing Alvin is definitively not afraid of is explosions. While at school, he is a silent student who avoids talking at all costs. But once he gets home, Alvin morphs into a brave and loud superhero: Firecracker Man! *Alvin Ho* is a great read for every budding superhero.

Bobby vs. Girls (Accidentally) by Lisa Yee, illustrated by Dan Santat (Arthur A. Levine Books, 2009) D

Have you ever found yourself in school with your sister's underwear static-stuck to your shirt? What would you do if you *accidentally* got stuck to a tree, and it just happened to be a very stinky tree? Follow the wonderful adventures of fourth-grader Bobby Ellis-Chan and see how he gets out of these sticky and stinky situations.

Calvin Coconut series by Graham Salisbury (Yearling) D

Follow the adventures of nine-year-old Hawaiian Calvin Coconut in this fun-loving series! Calvin has the difficult task of learning to navigate the complex, and often funny, world of fourth grade. Read along as Calvin manages to make every day an adventure!

Diary of a Wimpy Kid series by Jeff Kinney (Abrams Books for Young Readers) D

Middle schooler Greg Heffley shares the daily challenges he and his best friend Rowley face through cartoon drawings and diary-style entries. Greg explores timeless questions like "What does it take to become popular?" and "Why does his brother have to lie and tell his grandfather he loves watercress salad?" Greg and Rowley overcome every fresh catastrophe in a humorous way that every "wimpy kid" will love.

Hank Zipzer: The World's Greatest Underachiever series by Henry Winkler and Lin Oliver (Grosset & Dunlap: 2003) D

Hank Zipzer is a regular fourth-grader who means well but can't seem to do anything right. His misadventures are full of fun and humor, a lot of friends, and even a pet iguana! In the first book in the series, Hank is supposed to write a five-paragraph essay on his summer vacation. Not being a confident writer, Hank decides to build an interactive display of his trip to Niagara Falls. The project goes awry and winds up flooding the classroom! Don't worry, Hank and his friends always find a way to come out OK in the end!

In Memory of Gorfman T. Frog by Gail Donovan (Dutton Juvenile, 2009) D

Fifth grader Josh Hewitt just can't seem to stay out of trouble. After discovering a mutant frog in his pond, Josh is determined to find out if its fifth leg is the result of environmental contamination. In order to solve this mystery, Josh has to overcome a bunch of obstacles that stand in his way. One is his principal, who confiscates the frog. Another is his mom, who insists that he follow all of her rules. Will Josh be able to get the support that he needs from his classmates to solve this green mystery?

Leon series by Allen Kurzweil (Greenwillow Press) D

Leon has a mission: survive fourth grade. Most kids don't have much trouble doing that, but then again, they probably haven't met Miss Hagmeyer, a terrifying teacher who seems to have come straight from Leon's nightmares. Miss Hagmeyer and Lumpkin the Pumpkin, Leon's personal archenemy, conspire to make his life very difficult. Luckily, his best friends P. W. and Lily-Matisse are there to help him get by, even if his methods prove to be unconventional. If you enjoy *Leon and the Spitting Image*, be sure not to miss the sequel, *Leon and the Champion Chip*!

Mudshark by Gary Paulsen (Wendy Lamb Books, 2009) D

Mudshark, also known as Lyle Williams, is super cool and super observant. Whether he is keeping track of his triplet baby sisters, terrorizing the other players in a game of Death Ball, or hunting for the eraser thief at school, Mudshark's calm, cool power of observation and quirkiness make this an entertaining and delightful read.

Swindle by Gordon Korman (Scholastic, 2009) D

Griffin Bing is "The Man With the Plan." No matter the situation, Griffin's got things figured out. When he and his friend Ben find a Babe Ruth baseball card in an abandoned house, Griffin thinks he's about to be rich. The boys' hearts sink when an antique shop owner tells them it's a fake and only worth a little over $100. They accept their disappointment, until they watch the news that night and find out the shop owner lied and swindled them out of a card worth over $1,000,000. Right away, Griffin comes up with a way to get back what he believes is rightfully his. Plenty of mischief and mayhem will keep boys turning the pages as Griffin and his friends execute his latest plan! Griffin and his pals return in *Zoobreak* and *Framed*.

A Year Down Yonder by Richard Peck (Puffin, 2002) D

When she has to move from Chicago to her Grandma Dowdel's country home during the Great Depression, Mary Alice thinks her life is over. She doesn't think she'll be able to survive her grandmother's shenanigans without her brother to help her. Over the next year, Mary Alice comes to appreciate both country life and her Grandma Dowdel's clever antics. She finds a friend in her grandmother, who trips up the local bullies on Mary Alice's behalf, and ends up being very sad when she has to return to her home and parents in Chicago. Little does she know, Mary Alice will find herself back down yonder once more.

For Developing to Maturing Readers

Cosmic by Frank Cottrell Boyce (Walden Pond Press, 2010) D ->M

Life is tough for twelve-year-old Liam, who looks like he's closer to thirty years old. When Liam decides to enter the "World's Greatest Dad" contest, he and his friends find themselves in a whole new world as they wind up flying the rocket "Infinite Possibility" 200,000 miles above Earth's surface. Find out how they become a part of this exciting adventure in the pages of this humorous and touching story.

Fig Pudding by Ralph Fletcher (Yearling, 1996) D ->M

A large family brings unique joys and challenges. The oldest of six children, Cliff shares the highs and a lows of his family's past year with readers. Our 12-year-old narrator is smart, likable, and has a sense of humor about the antics of his younger siblings, even when they drive him nuts. The year has been full of memorable moments, some lighthearted and some tragic. When one of Cliff's brothers dies, readers will be moved as the family struggles to cope with the shock and sadness. The inclusion of life's hardest experiences only enhances the genuine reflection of life in a big family that Fletcher ably conveys.

Spider Boy by Ralph Fletcher (Sandpiper, 2009) D →M

Bobby and his family just moved from Illinois to upstate New York, and the spider-loving seventh grader is not sold on the change of scenery. Both Bobby and his pet tarantula haven't been eating much since the move, and Bobby is having a lot of trouble making friends at his new school. His classmates are not impressed with his encyclopedic knowledge of spider trivia. They dub Bobby "Spider Boy," and the class bully singles him out as his new favorite prey. Told through a combination of journal entries and third person narration, Bobby's story is one of perseverance and self-acceptance. As Bobby comes to terms with the move and his new life, he is able to confront his taunters and make new friends. Any boy who has ever had to make his way in a new place will understand Bobby's challenges and appreciate his strong sense of self.

For Maturing Readers

The Absolutely True Diary of a Part-Time Indian by Sherman Alexie, illustrated by Ellen Forney (Little, Brown Books for Young Readers, 2007) M

Arnold Spirit Junior suffers at the hands of bullies in his school on the reservation because he loves to draw and seems to be different from everyone there. When Arnold transfers to a predominantly white school off the reservation, he is shocked to discover how well he fits in. Armed with new friends, his family, and a sense of humor, Arnold faces encounters with his former classmates, the deaths of loved ones, and the struggle to find his place in the world.

Al Capone Does My Shirts by Gennifer Choldenko (Puffin, 2006) M

In 1935, twelve-year-old Moose moves with his family to Alcatraz, the infamous prison and home of well-known criminals like Al Capone. His father has a new job at the prison and Moose's family hopes that his autistic sister can attend a special school nearby. When his sister is not accepted to the school, Moose must care for her, but he's not alone. Luckily, Piper, the daughter of the prison warden, helps him handle his big responsibility and still have fun in their unusual home.

All the Broken Pieces by Ann Burg (Scholastic Press, 2009) M

Twelve-year-old Matt Pin, the son of a Vietnamese woman and an American soldier, doesn't really know where he belongs. During the Vietnam War, Matt was injured and airlifted to safety. Later, he was adopted by a caring family and went to live in the United States. Now that Matt is older, he tries to find a way to sort through all of the complicated pieces of his fractured life.

The Book Thief by Marcus Zusak (Knopf, 2007) M

Death, the narrator of this novel, tells the story of nine-year-old Liesel Meminger. Death meets Liesel after taking away her brother. Death becomes fascinated by Liesel after he watches her steal the Gravedigger's manual, even though she is unable to read. After Liesel is sent to live with a foster family, she finds solace in books and begins to steal more and more of them. Set in Nazi Germany, many of the characters in this book show the small but meaningful ways that so many resisted Nazi oppression during that time.

The Boy in the Striped Pajamas by John Boyne (Oxford University Press, 2007) M

Bruno is an eight-year-old boy who is upset when his family is moving far away from all his friends to a house in the country. Bruno thinks his family has moved near a farm but in reality it is a concentration camp, as his father is a high-ranking Nazi official. Bruno doesn't understand a lot of what goes on with his father and his work, but he decides that he wants to go visit the other children at the farm so he can have someone to play with. He soon meets the boy in the striped pajamas, and the two begin to develop a friendship. This is a beautifully told, heartwrenching story of family and friendship during World War II.

Burn My Heart by Beverly Naidoo (Amistad, 2008) M

Set in Kenya in the 1950s, this story depicts the complex friendship that grows between Matthew and Mugo. Matthew is the son of a wealthy, white farmer, and Mugo is the son of a Kikuyu servant in Matthew's house. Matthew and Mugo find their friendship tested during this tenuous time in Kenya. Will they be able to remain close in spite of their differences?

Drums, Girls and Dangerous Pie by Jordan Sonnenblick (Scholastic, 2006) M

Steven is gearing up for 8th grade when his younger brother Jeffrey is unexpectedly diagnosed with leukemia. The strain on his family and himself is only heightened by the myriad of middle school woes that plague every boy this age. As Steven watches his mother leave work to care for his brother and his father withdraw from the family, he is pained by his little brother's steady trials and becomes completely distracted from his schoolwork. Woven into this sad family drama is Steven's own trouble with girls, as he navigates between the girl he's had a crush on forever and the girl who is slowly catching his eye. Boys will love Steven's fresh, realistic narrative style and ride the emotional waves with him as his family and personal life all seem to collide. If you like this book, be sure to read the sequel *After Ever After*, a continuation of the story from Jeffrey's point of view, now in 8th grade himself.

The First Part Last **by Angela Johnson (Simon & Schuster, 2010) M**

Sixteen-year-old Bobby must learn how to raise his baby daughter Feather after the sudden loss of his girlfriend, Nia. With the support of his parents, he struggles to master the difficult childcare duties and to navigate the many changes in his life. Bobby's story allows older boys to explore the complexities that occur when life brings to bear consequences and challenges in unexpected ways.

Lawn Boy **by Gary Paulson (Yearling, an imprint of Random House Children's Books, 2009) M**

What would you do if you got an old lawn mower from your grandmother for your birthday? In Paulson's story, the twelve-year old narrator finds a use for his lawnmower and an exciting way to fill up the days of his summer vacation. The narrator explains how he went from having one client to becoming an entrepreneur overseeing fifteen employees, all in one summer. But will he be able to handle the pressures of a rapidly expanding operation, a stock portfolio, and a villain out to undermine his business?

My Side of the Mountain **by Jean Craighead George (Puffin Books, 2004) M**

City life just does not agree with Sam Gribley. Desperate to be in the wilderness, Sam runs away to the Catskill Mountains with little more than a penknife. Now he must learn how to live off the land. Sam survives even the most fearful storms with the help of Frightful, a wild falcon he tames and befriends. For anyone who is intrigued by the great outdoors, this book is a must-read.

If you like this book, you'll also like:

- *Call It Courage* by Armstrong Sperry (Simon Pulse, 2008)
- *Frightful's Mountain* by Jean Craighead George (Dutton, 1999)
- *Hatchet* by Gary Paulsen (Simon & Schuster, 2006)

- *The Incredible Journey* by Sheila Burnford (Yearling, 1997)
- *On the Far Side of the Mountain* by Jean Craighead George (Puffin, 2001)
- *The River* by Gary Paulsen (Yearling, 1993)
- *Tracker* by Gary Paulsen (Simon & Schuster, 2007)

Operation Redwood **by S. Terrell French (Amulet Books, 2009) M**

Can Julian Carter-Li stop his uncle from cutting down the beautiful, old Redwood trees that are home to his new friend Robin? After surreptitiously learning about the environmental cost of his uncle's actions, Julian and his friends try to save the Redwood Forest.

Talk About It:

- Have you ever wondered if your actions could help to save the world?
- How do Julian, Danny, and Robin work together to stop his uncle? What steps taken do you think were the most successful?
- Is there any environmental issue that you think you and your friends could work to address together? What steps might you take?

On the Wings of Heroes **by Richard Peck (Puffin, 2008) M**

Davy Bowman is a happy, average kid living in the Midwest in the 1940s, but his predictable world begins to change as World War II asks more and more of him and his family. Davy is eager to collect scrap metal to make shell casings and milkweed to stuff life preservers, but when his older brother is sent overseas to fight and his mother has to go to work, the world Davy knows suddenly becomes almost unrecognizable. The story is told with humorous encounters woven cleanly together with sobering tragedy, as Davy discovers what it takes to grow up in hard times. If you like this book, you'll love Richard Peck's other books including *A Season of Gifts, A Long Way From Chicago,* and *A Year Down Yonder.*

The Schwa Was Here **by Neal Shusterman (Puffin, 2006) M**

Anthony "Antsy" Bonano finds the perfect friend in Calvin Schwa, the boy who can almost disappear. Schwa has the ability to travel through life almost invisible to the world, and Antsy decides to become his agent. Over the course of Schwa's increasingly dangerous missions, they encounter Old Man Crawley and his blind niece Lexie. If you like this book, look for the continuation of Antsy's adventures in *Antsy Does Time*.

Slob by Ellen Potter (Philomel, 2009) M

Owen is the heaviest and smartest kid in his 7th grade class. He is often teased by his classmates and is always trying to avoid the school bully. Owen spends his free time trying to find the thief who steals his cookies, as well as inventing a TV that can show events that have happened in the past. Readers soon discover that Owen wasn't always overweight and that his life wasn't always this way. As Owen eventually finds closure on the troubling evens in his past, older readers have an opportunity to reflect on how they cope with challenges in their own lives.

Where the Red Fern Grows by Wilson Rawls (Bantam Doubleday Dell, 1961) M

When Billy Colman becomes the proud owner of two coonhounds, there's no coon left in the country that he can't "tree." Billy and his beloved Old Dan and Little Ann become famous in Oklahoma for their exploits and daring. But be warned: this is not only a story of love and mutual devotion. By turns tragic and touching, *Where the Red Fern Grows* is an unforgettable story of a unique friendship.

The Whole Sky Full of Stars by Rene Saldana, Jr. (Wendy Lamb Books, 2007) M

Alby and Barry have been friends since they were in the first grade, but as they grow older their differences begin to push them apart. Alby has a secret gambling problem and convinces Barry to box in some local competitions so that he can repay his debts. Barry has no idea that his friend is struggling and believes he will be able to use the money to help his mother. Older readers who are struggling with similar challenges as their friendships grow and change will genuinely understand how Barry and Alby so readily fall apart and come back together.

Science and Space

For Emerging Readers

Clouds: Let's-Read-and-Find-Out Science by Anne Rockwell, illustrated by Frané Lessac (Collins, 2008) E

Have you ever wondered about all the different kinds of clouds you see in the sky? Anne Rockwell shares the names of eleven different types of clouds, what they look like, where they are formed in the atmosphere, and what kind of weather they come with. Frané Lessac's friendly watercolor illustrations play up Rockwell's straightforward, yet engaging descriptions. The Let's-Read-and-Find-Out Science series is the perfect match for young readers who have a million questions about the world around them. The titles with the number one on the cover, like *Clouds*, generally deal with more concrete concepts, while the books with a two on the cover are slightly more complex. Both levels are appropriate for young, eager, inquisitive readers! If you like this book, look for other Let's-Read-and-Find-Out Science titles, including:

- *Ant Cities: Let's-Read-and-Find-Out Science* by Arthur Dorros (Collins, 1988)
- *Flash, Crash, Rumble, and Roll: Let's-Read-and-Find-Out Science* by Franklyn M. Branley, illustrated by True Kelly (Collins, 1999)
- *Gravity Is a Mystery: Let's-Read-and-Find-Out Science* by Franklyn M. Branley, illustrated by Edward Miller (Collins, 2007)
- *How Many Teeth? Let's-Read-and-Find-Out Science* by Paul Showers, illustrated by True Kelley (Collins: 1991)
- *The Moon Seems to Change: Let's-Read-and-Find-Out Science* by Franklyn M. Branley, illustrated by Barbara and Ed Emberley (Collins, 1987)
- *The Planets in Our Solar System: Let's-Read-and-Find-Out Science* by Franklyn M. Branley, illustrated by Kevin O'Malley (Collins, 1998)
- *What's Alive? Let's-Read-and-Find-Out Science* by Kathleen Weidner Zoehfeld, illustrated by Nadine Bernard Westcott (Collins, 1995)
- *What Is the World Made Of? Let's-Read-and-Find-Out Science* by Kathleen Weidner Zoehfeld, illustrated by Paul Meisel (Collins, 1998)

Dem Bones **by Bob Barner (Chronicle Books: 1996) E**

Why do humans have bones? How many can you name? Join the skeletons as they sing a traditional African American spiritual celebrating the bones in the human body. As you sing, read the information boxes that provide useful facts about our various bones.

Dinosaur Discoveries **by Gail Gibbons (Holiday House, Inc., 2005) E**

Are you fascinated with dinosaurs? Have you always wanted to know the difference between Theropods and Ornithopods? Do you ever wonder where dinosaurs laid their eggs or how big the Anchisaurus was? If you have always wanted to learn about dinosaurs—what they ate, how they lived, and what they might have looked like—then this is the perfect book for you. With bright and detailed illustrations, the book maps where dinosaurs lived, describes the three periods of dinosaur life, and compares many of the different dinosaur species.

Encyclopedia Prehistorica: Dinosaurs by Robert Sabuda and Matthew Reinhart (Candlewick, 2005) E

Do you love dinosaurs? Have you always wanted to watch them pop up right in front of you? This wonderful pop-up book contains pictures of the many species of dinosaurs with accompanying short tidbits about each creature.

Here in Space by David Milgrim (BridgeWater Books, 1997) E

What is it like to live in space? There are volcanoes, frozen oceans, and mighty pyramids. Sound familiar? That is because Planet Earth is located in outer space itself! With rhymes and great illustrations, the narrator explores the many wonders of Planet Earth in his journey to describe life in outer space.

Talk About It:

Become an explorer in your own backyard. Describe the amazing mysteries, sights, and monuments surrounding you. Put on your astronaut's gear and set off on a journey through the neighborhood.

- What amazing facts and magical wonders can you find just beyond your door?

Oscar and the Frog: A Book About Growing (Start With Science) by Geoff Waring (Candlewick, 2008) E

Oscar is a curious kitten who likes to make friends who help him learn new things about his world. When Oscar visits a pond, he has many questions about how things grow and develop. Luckily Oscar meets Frog, who can answer all of his questions, having recently gone through some amazing changes himself! From little insects to kittens like himself, Oscar learns that all living things grow and change over time. Oscar continues to learn new things in other Start With Science books by Geoff Waring, including:

- *Oscar and the Bat: A Book About Sound (Start With Science)* by Geoff Waring (Candlewick, 2009)
- *Oscar and the Bird: A Book About Electricity (Start With Science)* by Geoff Waring (Candlewick, 2009)
- *Oscar and the Cricket: A Book About Moving and Rolling (Start With Science)* by Geoff Waring (Candlewick, 2009)

- *Oscar and the Moth: A Book About Light and Dark (Start With Science)* by Geoff Waring (Candlewick, 2008)
- *Oscar and the Snail: A Book About Things That We Use (Start With Science)* by Geoff Waring (Candlewick, 2009)

Skeletons: Scholastic Science Readers by Lily Wood (Scholastic, 2001) E

The Scholastic Science Readers series was designed to engage young readers in the rich world of print as they learn all about a fascinating subject. In this book, Lily Wood shares a ton of fun facts about our skeleton and why it is so important. Each page features bright, eye-catching photographs, and at the end of each book in the series there is a handy glossary. This book is designated "Level 2," and you'll see others in the series designated "Level 1." Like the leveling system in this book, these are meant as a flexible guide to the complexity of the information in the book and should be used as a tool to help you match the perfect book to your young reader. More books in the Scholastic Science Readers series include:

- *Earthquakes: Scholastic Science Readers* by Deborah Heiligman (Scholastic, 2003)
- *Fall Leaves Change Colors: Scholastic Science Readers* by Kathleen Weidner Zoehfeld (Scholastic, 2002)
- *Rocks and Minerals: Scholastic Science Readers* by Edward Ricciuti (Scholastic, 2002)
- *Thunder and Lightening: Scholastic Science Readers* by Wendy Pfeffer (Scholastic, 2002)
- *Tornadoes: Scholastic Science Readers* by Brian Cassie (Scholastic, 2002)

There's No Place Like Space: All About Our Solar System by Tish Rabe (Random House, 1999) E

With the Cat in the Hat as a guide, you will travel through the infinite expanse of outer space. Explore the planets and the stars and do it in rhyme!

What Magnets Can Do: Rookie Read-About Science by Allan Fowler (Children's Press, 1995) E

Magnets are incredible tools with almost magical capabilities. You can make metal move without touching it just by placing a magnet nearby. There are so many surprising things you can do with a magnet, and this Rookie Read-About Science book by Allan Fowler shares both the fun ways to use magnets and the science behind them so young readers will feel ready to explore the world of magnets on their own or with you right away! If you like this book, check out the rest of the Rookie Read-About Science series, including:

- *All About Light: Rookie Read-About Science* by Lisa Trumbauer (Children's Press, 2004)
- *From Seed to Plant: Rookie Read-About Science* by Allan Fowler (Children's Press, 2001)
- *Look How It Changes! Rookie Read-About Science* by June Young (Children's Press, 2006)
- *Push and Pull: Rookie Read-About Science* by Patricia J. Murphy (Children's Press, 2002)
- *So That's How the Moon Changes: Rookie Read-About Science* by Allan Fowler (Children's Press, 1991)
- *Solids, Liquids, and Gases: Rookie Read-About Science* by Ginger Garrett (Children's Press, 2005)
- *What Is Electricity? Rookie Read-About Science* by Lisa Trumbauer (Children's Press, 2004)
- *What Is Friction? Rookie Read-About Science* by Lisa Trumbauer (Children's Press, 2004)
- *Will It Float or Sink? Rookie Read-About Science* by Melissa Stewart (Children's Press, 2006)
- *You Can Use a Magnifying Glass: Rookie Read-About Science* by Wiley Blevins, David Larwa, and Nanci R. Vargus (Children's Press, 2004)

You Are the First Kid on Mars **by Patrick O'Brien (Putnam Juvenile, an imprint of Penguin, 2009) E**

What is life like on Mars? What would happen if you took the four months to travel from Earth to Mars? What would you need? What would you see? Learn amazing and true facts about space travel to Mars in this wonderful book.

For Developing Readers

Beyond: A Solar System Voyage by Michael Benson (Abrams Books for Young Readers, 2009) D

Have you ever wondered about our solar system? Filled with useful information about the planets and stars that fill the night sky, the history of astronomy, and how everything works together, this book will leave growing readers with a ton of new facts to share and a good deal of excitement about outer space. The beautiful photographs and detailed charts are sure to entice even the most reluctant readers.

Cars on Mars: Roving the Red Planet by Alexandra Siy (Charlesbridge Publishing, 2009) D

Take a ride from Cape Canaveral, Florida, to the Gusev Crater and Meridiani Planum in Mars' Southern Hemisphere on the Mars Rovers. What will you see? Flip through real pictures of Mars and learn all you ever wanted to know about this exciting and mysterious planet.

How to Make a Universe With 92 Ingredients by Adrian Dingle (Scholastic, 2010) D

In this clever book, Adrian Dingle teaches his readers all about the elements and makes chemistry fun! Learn about how everything around us, from cell phones to humans, is made from just 92 elements. This book will bring the periodic table of elements to life in a way that is surprisingly fun and accessible.

Lucy Long Ago: Uncovering the Mystery of Where We Came From by Catherine Thimmesh (Houghton Mifflin Books for Children, 2009) D

Have you ever wanted to see what human ancestors looked like? Meet Lucy, the extraordinary fossilized hominid who roamed the earth 3.2 million years ago. With fantastic pictures and interesting facts, learn all about the discovery, reconstruction, and steps taken to understand what the fossil can teach us about life so very long ago.

Talk About It:

- How do you think 47 bones can teach us so much about our past and life on earth 3.2 million years ago?
- What did scientists learn from the fossils? What could they not learn? Which facts did you find most interesting? Why?

A Zombie's Guide to the Human Body by Tom Becker and Mercer Mayer (Scholastic Reference, 2010) D

This complete guide to the human body is detailed from the perspective of a zombie. Filled with photographs and interesting facts, growing readers will learn all about how their bodies work while also getting tips on how to avoid being a snack for Professor Zombie. This cleverly twisted text on anatomy is sure to leave a smile on your little guy's face!

For Maturing Readers

365 Simple Science Experiments With Everyday Materials by E. Richard Churchill, Louis V. Loeschnig, and Muriel Mandell (Black Dog & Leventhal Publishers, Inc., 1997) M

Have you always wanted to know why there are cracks between the stones on a sidewalk or how to milk a potato? If you love performing science experiments, then this is the perfect book for you. These 365 fun, easy, and creative science experiments are richly engaging.

Oh, Yuck! The Encyclopedia of Everything Nasty by Joy Masoff, illustrated by Terry Sirrell (Workman Publishing, Inc., 2000) M

Everything you ever wanted to know—and everything you never wanted to know—all in one volume! What is a zit? From cannibals to cockroaches and beyond, if you have a penchant for slightly off-color trivia, this book is a good investment. If it's any comfort, *The Encyclopedia of Everything Nasty* also offers solid advice at the end of every entry on how to deal with the nastier side of things, like what to do when you have a zit, and the science is completely accurate!

There's a Fungus Among Us! 24/7 Science Behind the Scenes by John DiConsiglio (Scholastic, 2007) M

Based on real medical files, the 24/7 Science Behind the Scenes series takes growing readers on a journey into the complex yet fascinating world of scientists who research the bizarre and gross. In *There's a Fungus Among Us!* readers can learn about the 100,000 species of fungi that exist in the world, the kinds of fungi that can be dangerous, and how some fungi have killed people! With a vast assortment of scientific factoids and data, fungus will never seem the same to your budding scientist. Other titles in the 24/7 Science Behind the Scenes series include:

- *Dusted and Busted! The Science of Fingerprinting: 24/7 Science Behind the Scenes* by D. B. Beres (Scholastic, 2007)
- *Help! What's Eating My Flesh? 24/7 Science Behind the Scenes* by Thomasine E. Lewis Tilden (Scholastic, 2007)
- *Killer Lipstick and Other Spy Gadgets: 24/7 Science Behind the Scenes* by Don Rauf (Scholastic, 2007)
- *Toe Tagged: 24/7 Science Behind the Scenes* by Jaime Joyce (Scholastic, 2007)
- *UFOs: 24/7 Science Behind the Scenes* by N. B. Grace (Scholastic, 2008)

The Way We Work by David Macaulay (Houghton Mifflin, 2008) M

Meet . . . yourself! This book takes you on a tour of the body. From cells to organs to the immune system, you never dreamed that you were this complex. A perfect read for the amateur biologist or anyone who is curious about the way life works.

Sports

For Emerging Readers

Bats at the Ballgame by Brian Lies (Houghton Mifflin, 2010) E

Baseball has gone batty! These bats love to play America's favorite pastime, and batty baseball wouldn't be complete without mothdogs and cricket jacks! The acrylic illustrations and rhythmic poetic style will absorb readers. Boys will get a huge kick out of Brian Lies' batty twist on familiar baseball terms and players.

Casey at the Bat: A Ballad of the Republic Sung in the Year 1888 by Ernest Lawrence Thayer, illustrated by Christopher Bing (Handprint, 2000) E

Although over a hundred years old, this story is just as enthralling and captivating as it was when it was first published. Wonderful illustrations and a delightful retelling of the classic ballad make this book a must-read for all who love baseball.

Talk About It:

- What do you think about Casey as a person?
- Would you want to be his friend? Why or why not?

- How do you think it would feel to be in the audience at that game? What would you say or do?
- How do you think Casey felt in the end? How would you feel if you had done what he did?
- If you were him, would you have done things differently? Why or why not?

The Fastest Game on Two Feet: And Other Poems About How Sports Began by Alice Low, illustrated by John O'Brien (Holiday House, 2009) E

In poetic form, Alice Low shares the origins of several popular sports games. Ranging from ancient athletics to sports you can watch on television today, little readers will be fascinated by how these sports began and why they remain popular.

P Is for Putt: A Golf Alphabet by Brad Herzog, illustrated by Bruce Langton (Sleeping Bear Press, 2005) E

Learn about the sport of golf, the rules of the game, and its most celebrated players in this informative and beautifully illustrated alphabet book. *P* might stand for putt, but what does putt mean? Who putts, and how do they do it? If you liked this book, read *K Is for Kick: A Soccer Alphabet, H Is for Home Run: A Baseball Alphabet*, or any of the others in this great series.

For Developing Readers

Baseball Card Adventure series by Dan Gutman (HarperCollins Publishers) D

With the help of old baseball cards, Joe Stoshack discovers he has the power to travel back in time and meet famous baseball players. In *Shoeless Joe and Me*, find out whether Joe can prevent "Shoeless" Joe Jackson from making the biggest mistake of his career. In *Honus and Me*, Joe finds Honus Wagner's rarest and most valuable baseball card and is faced with the difficult decision of selling the card to help his mother or telling the owner of the card about his discovery. Enjoy the spirit of adventure, the excitement, and the lessons that each of these wonderful books adeptly teaches as you make your way through the series.

Talk About It:

In *Mickey and Me*, Joe must come to terms with his father's injuries from a car accident. Learning how to cope with a family member or friend's illness or injury can be incredibly scary and difficult. Joe learns that by helping someone else, he can in fact help himself overcome a difficult time.

- How did Joe's time travel help him to cope with his father's accident?

In *Jim and Me*, Joe and his nemesis Bobby Fuller travel through time to meet Jim Thorpe, the Native American baseball and football champion who lost all of his medals in a scandal. Bobby and Joe try to help Jim before it is too late.

- What would you have done to help Jim ?

Catch That Pass **by Matt Christopher (Little, Brown Books for Young Readers, 1989) D**

Jim could be a wonderful linebacker for the Vulcans. He has big hands and he can move quickly. But he is also very afraid of being tackled. During a game against the Cadets, Jim drops the ball just before he is about to be tackled. His teammates and his brother, the Vulcan's coach, want to know why he dropped the ball. Can he tell his friends and brother his embarrassing secret? Will he ever learn to be unafraid on the field?

Talk About It:

Finding the courage to master a difficult play can be a daunting task, but sometimes help comes from a surprising source.

- Who do you talk to when you need to find the courage to overcome something difficult?
- How does Jim learn to overcome his fear?
- What does the boy in the wheelchair teach him?

The Super Sluggers: Slumpbuster **by Kevin Markey (HarperCollins Publishers, 2009) D**

Banjo H. Bishbash is the star third baseman and home-run leader for the Rambletown Rounders. When his hitting streak ends one day and he gets into a slump, he winds up on the bench. Will he get his groove back in time for the big game?

Soccer Cats series by Matt Christopher, illustrated by Daniel Vasconcellos (Little, Brown Young Readers) D

Tag along with the members of the Soccer Cats, a summer soccer league, on and off the field. In the first Soccer Cats adventure, *The Captain Contest*, the team must select a captain. Who should it be? Dewey or Bundy? In *Switch Play*, Ted must learn how to handle the overwhelming jealously that he feels when his twin sister receives heaps of praise for her soccer skills. Each of these delightful books will appeal to the young soccer lover.

Talk About It:

The members of the Soccer Cats learn about sportsmanship, friendship, and courage. Use the books to talk about any of these lessons.

In *Master of Disaster,* Jason is forced to become the starting goalie instead of his usual role as the team's prankster. He worries that he will fail miserably.

- How does Jason learn what he needs to know before the big game against the Panthers?
- What does Jason learn that will help him in the future?
- Have you ever been in a similar situation? What did you do?

In *Hat Trick*, Stookie really wants to score a "hat trick," three goals in one game, just like his older brother Greg. But during the Soccer Cat's next game, Stookie learns from his coach and his teammates what it really takes to be a team player.

- What do you think about what Stookie did after the game?
- What would you have done?

You Never Heard of Sandy Koufax?! by Jonah Winter, illustrated by Andre Carrilho (Schwartz & Wade: 2009) D

Unravel the mystery of Sandy Koufax, the all-star Jewish baseball player who overcame physical shortfalls and anti-Semitism on his rise to greatness. Little is known about this extraordinary player, but through wonderful illustrations and rich language, he comes to life.

For Maturing Readers

The Batboy by Mike Lupica (Philomel: 2010) M

Brian Dudley gets his dream job this summer. He is going to be the batboy for the Detroit Tigers! Unfortunately, Brian quickly learns that his hero Hank Bishop is not the player he thought he was. While Brian struggles to communicate with Hank Bishop and his dad, a former baseball player, he learns several important lessons about heroes and those you love.

The Brooklyn Nine by Alan Gratz (Dial Books for Young Readers, 2009) M

Nine chapters tell the story of nine generations of a family who live for the nine innings of a baseball game. These chapters weave together the story of a Brooklyn family's relationship to baseball.

The Greatest: Muhammad Ali by Walter Dean Myers (Scholastic, 2001) M

When twelve-year-old Cassius Clay's prized bicycle was stolen, he told Joe Martin, a police officer who he hoped could help him to recover it. Martin couldn't find the bike, but he offered Cassius boxing lessons at his local community center so that he could defend himself from future thefts. From the beginning, the boy who would grow up to become Muhammad Ali showed his promise. He wasn't the fastest or the strongest, but he worked harder than of any of the boys in his boxing class. Muhammad Ali's work didn't end when he left the boxing ring. Ali was ultimately famous not only as an athlete, but also for his courageous stand against the Vietnam War and the racist policies of the United States government in the 1960s.

Talk About It:

- Have you ever had to practice something for a long time before you got it right?
- Who is your hero?

Last Shot (A Final Four Mystery) by John Feinstein (Yearling, 2006) M

Steve loves basketball. He learned to read so he could follow the events on the sports pages, and he loves to write about the basketball games he has seen. So when he wins a writing contest and has the opportunity to go to New Orleans to report on the Final Four for his school newspaper, Steve is ecstatic. But when he and his fellow contest winner Susan Carol overhear MSU's coach tell their star player he must lose the game, the mystery of March Madness begins. Will Steve and Susan be able to solve the mystery before the final game?

Talk About It:

Last Shot provides the perfect venue for talking about gambling in sports. Use the book to talk about the pressure that Chip felt from his coach.

- How did he handle the situation?
- What could he have done differently?

Although they have to go through a lot to do so, Steve and Susan Carol manage to save the game and help their friend.

- What lesson did they learn about not giving up, even though the situation proved difficult?
- How would you have handled a similar situation?

Million-Dollar Throw **by Mike Lupica (Philomel, 2009) M**

Thirteen-year-old Nate Brodie appears to have it all—he is the star of his football team and has the perfect best friend, Abby McCall. However, Nate's family is about to lose their home, and Abby has a rare illness that is causing her to lose her eyesight. Nate learns about one way that he can help his family and his best friend—make a million dollar shot during a pro-football game. As a star quarterback, he should be able to accomplish this feat, but as the pressure mounts, his confidence begins to fade. Will Nate be able to find the strength to help his loved ones? If you like this, check out more sports fiction by Mike Lupica: *The Big Field, Safe at Home, Travel Team,* and *Heat.*

Sports Shorts **by Joseph Bruchac, David Lubar, Marilyn Singer, Terry Trueman, Dorian Cirrone, Tanya West, Alexandra Siy, and Jamie McEwan (Darby Creek Publishing, 2007) M**

These eight short stories by children's book authors provide wonderful insight into the blunders and joys that come from playing sports. With humor and honesty, each author recounts a single moment or game from his or her childhood that epitomizes the experience of a young athlete.

Talk About It:

This is the ideal book to read when you want to talk about those painfully embarrassing gaffes or great athletic achievements that take place on the playing field.

In "Bombardment," Joseph Bruchac recounts precisely how he felt when he was, as usual, the last one chosen for the dodgeball game.

- How did he eventually overcome this humiliating moment?
- What would you have done in the same situation?

Magazines

For Emerging Readers

Boys' Quest (Bluffton News Publishing and Printing Company) E

Boy's Quest magazine is a bimonthly publication that prides itself on going to print without advertisements: its pages are devoted in their entirety to the entertainment of young subscribers. Each issue is chock full of jokes, poems, riddles, and science trivia all related to themes that never repeat, ranging from electricity to optics. It's probably the most wholesome periodical out there.

Spider (Carus Publishing) E

Geared towards kids 6–9 years old who are just beginning to read on their own, *Spider* is a compilation of poems, stories, and articles meant to encourage the early reader. The magazine is a great value, with a good quantity of articles packed into its 40 pages and no advertising whatsoever. The first story in each magazine features the Danderville Twins as they try to solve a problem with the help of their friends. Stories are written with large type and colorful illustrations to attract a young reader. Spider and her cartoon friends live in the margins of the pages and are so popular with readers that they receive their own fan mail. Also recommended is the entire Carus Publishing family of magazines:

- *Click*—science and exploration for ages 3–6
- *Ladybug*—an introduction to reading for ages 3–6
- *Ask*—an interactive magazine featuring the key players in art, science, and innovation both past and present, for ages 6–9
- *Appleseed*—nonfiction reading and social studies for ages 7–9
- *Cricket*—encourages exploration through puzzles, recipes, experiments and articles for ages 9–14
- *Dig*—articles discuss archaeology around the world and its impact on our modern lives for ages 9 and up
- *Cobblestone*—American history for ages 9–14
- *Faces*—in each issue, world culture articles explore life, culture, and history in a different country for ages 9–14
- *Calliope*—world history for ages 9–14, including maps, pictures, illustrations, and interviews with historians and archaeologists
- *Odyssey*—theme-based issues exploring the cutting edge of modern science for ages 9–14
- *Cicada*—poetry, nonfiction, and fiction stories written by teenagers for teenagers

For Developing Readers

Boys' Life (Boy Scouts of America) D

A monthly magazine published by the Boy Scouts of America, *Boy's Life* recently celebrated the one hundredth anniversary of its first publication. It is published in two editions geared toward 6–10 year olds and 11–18 year olds respectively, although some content is common between the two versions. Each issue highlights an important aspect of maintaining physical health and features sections devoted to coverage of trips taken by scouts around the country and recent entertainment news, among other subjects.

Muse (Carus Publishing, Sponsored by Smithsonian) D

A truly multifaceted magazine for kids interested in history, science, and the arts, *Muse* is published nine times per year with articles covering a wide variety of topics, each incorporating thought-provoking questions for kids to ponder. The magazine's margins are the playground of the Muses, nine cartoon characters, each with a snappy sense of humor.

Ranger Rick (The National Wildlife Foundation) D

Ranger Rick offers features on interesting animal facts that are sure to make a nature lover out of every child. Combined with the *Ranger Rick* Web site's interactive games, quizzes, and contests, this magazine is engaging both for kids and their parents. The wide selection of activities make this magazine and Web site a great option.

Sports Illustrated for Kids (The Time Inc. Magazine Company) D

A kid-appropriate version of the regular *Sports Illustrated*, this magazine features the expected array of glossy photos, interviews, and articles traversing the spectrum of both amateur and professional athletes. Notably absent, however, are any of the sensationalist features on athlete behavior that may be considered inappropriate by parents. The articles focus on the people behind the magic and the joy of competition through quality journalism that will help kids develop strong reading skills. Combined with a flashy but straightforward interactive Web site perfect for the avid young sports fan, this magazine really delivers.

Sports Magazines for Individual Sports

For a list of magazines on individual sports visit http://www.ebscomags.com.

Walking Beyond the Towers:

The Impact of Boys as Readers on the World

When my husband and I had our first baby, it was highly unusual for any man to spend as much time parenting as he spent in the office. Over these past nineteen years, much has changed. And in our family, it changed hugely along with the changing times. When Katie was seven, Jim and I both decided that together we wanted to create a new paradigm for the raising of our children. We recreated our work arrangements so that we could share equal responsibility in raising our daughters. This was only possible because we began to truly co-parent. From Jim, I have learned a huge amount about what it means to nurture and to raise children. He is a deeply tender and loving father. He encourages his girls to take risks and be bold. Interestingly, I had always been curious about the way he reads, which is very different from the way I read. He browses, I delve. He likes statistics, I like character relationships. But the interesting thing is that in life, he and I are more alike. We both browse, we both delve. We both love facts, and we both love relationships. The gender differences that we sometimes put up as barriers to understanding fall very quickly when parenting a child equally. He cried over *Anne of Green Gables* along with the rest of us. I cried when the Boston Red Sox won the World Series for the first time in years along with the rest of us.

I am grateful to Jim's parents, Cindy and Lou Allyn, for parenting Jim in such a way that he was immensely comfortable with a masculinity that encompasses many aspects of himself. He has never been in any way cowed or threatened by living with three women who like to go for afternoon tea or watch romantic silly movies. He taught both girls how to kick a soccer ball and how to drive a car. I hope they will grow up to teach their daughters and sons to do the same, and I hope they will teach their sons and daughters that it is a blessing to find a man who will cry over *Anne of Green Gables*.

Jim taught our daughters how to do lots of brave things, but if one of the bravest things he teaches them is how to transcend gender stereotypes, then that will be a lasting legacy, not only for them but for everyone else who has been blessed by his great softball coaching and so many of his other gifts. By reading, we all become smarter. We take in more information. But also, we become more humane. We learn about the stories of others and how people live all around us. We become able to care more deeply, and reading builds our capacity for compassion by teaching us about the world. We raise our children to be the kind of parents who will break through further gender stereotypes for the next generation.

Boys who read widely and wisely, joyously and purposefully, are the same boys who will some day raise children wisely and well, make interesting work decisions, and step forward into the world with kindness, intention, and boldness.

I hope this book in some way contributes to the nurturing of boys who will be bold enough to embrace all of these things, and who will step forward onto the rope, between the towers, in their own moments of daring and exploration, fearless and free, guided by the love of and power of words.

Additional Resources

BookHive.org

This easy-to-navigate site is filled with useful children's literature resources. Browse the reviewed kids' books in their database by first choosing one of 30 different categories (ranging from "Earth Friendly" to "Historical") and then by selecting the audience (babies through sixth grade). BookHive also offers lists of their top picks for each grade level, audio files of stories told by professional storytellers, and discussion questions for approximately 15 intermediate-level chapter books.

Boy Writers: Reclaiming Their Voices by Ralph Fletcher (Stenhouse, 2006)

Reading and writing are inextricably interconnected. As we cultivate the reader in boys, we can also cultivate the young writer inside each one of them. *Boy Writers* provides plenty of answers for teachers looking to help boys become enthusiastic about writing. Educator and children's author Fletcher recommends honoring their own style of writing and allowing boys to write about their interests. The author comments on real examples of boys' writing throughout the book and provides plenty of ideas that teachers can readily implement in the classroom.

Bright Beginnings for Boys: Engaging Young Boys in Active Literacy
by Debby Zambo and William G. Brozo (International Reading Association, 2008)

Educators Zambo and Brozo present this essential literacy guide for teachers of K–3 boys. The authors discuss how the development of boys differs from that of girls and give advice on how to improve instructional methods and reading curricula in order to best meet the needs of their male students. Inserted throughout the book are anecdotes of real boys' experiences with reading at school, and the appendix provides a list of books with positive male role models.

GettingBoysToRead.com

This community-based blog is a great resource for teachers, parents, and librarians who are looking for more ways to help boys become interested in reading. Videos and articles like "Boys Need to MOVE IT: How to Use Movement to Help Boys Become Better Readers" are filled with interesting tips for developing boys' literacy skills.

GuysRead.com

Popular author John Scieszka is the mastermind behind this Web site, a page devoted to helping guys find books that they'll love to read. Boys can browse lists of favorite books that other boys have recommended, and they can even start their own official chapter of GuysRead with friends and make their own contributions to the Web site! Categories for perusal include "Books with at least one explosion," "Outer space, but with aliens," and "Realistic kids in realistic situations." There is also a blog full of GuysRead news and fun, book-related downloads.

How to Get Your Child to Love Reading: For Ravenous and Reluctant Readers Alike by Esmé Raji Codell (Algonquin, 2003)

This guide is perfect for parents looking for innovative ways to nurture a love of reading in their younger children. School librarian Codell reviews over 3,000 books from a wide range of topics and even delves into nonfiction subjects such as science and food. Sprinkled throughout the book are countless imaginative, reading-based activities. Though this guide is aimed primarily at parents, educators will find this book useful for its reading lists and creative ideas like "author/illustrator studies" and "poetry breaks."

KidsReads.com

This fantastic site has it all—reviews of hundreds of popular titles for developing and maturing readers, author biographies, trivia games and word scrambles for various book series, advice for starting children's book clubs, and more. Click on "Cool and New" for a list of books released in the previous month. Also, search "great books for boys" for more suggestions of chapter books for older readers, especially action and adventure stories and fantasy books.

PBS Teachers (PBS.org/Teachers) and **PBS Parents** (PBS.org/Parents)

Chock-full of lesson plans and other resources for teachers of all grades, PBS Teachers is noteworthy for its videos and interactive web activities that will stimulate students' interest in what they are reading. In addition, both parents and teachers of younger kids can benefit from the book-search tool on the parents' page. From the PBS Parents home page, navigate to "Education" and then to "Reading and Language" to search for books based on the desired level (babies to third grade) and theme.

Read.gov

A Library of Congress site, Read.gov includes kids' book lists on American history topics that many boys will find interesting, such as sports, inventors, and the Civil War. The site also provides access to digital copies of rare, classic picture books, including *Humpty Dumpty* and *The Three Little Pigs*.

Reading Don't Fix No Chevys: Literacy in the Lives of Young Men
by Michael W. Smith and Jeffrey D. Wilhelm (Heinemann, 2002)

Two educational researchers and former high school teachers search for solutions to the literacy gap between boys and girls by discussing and analyzing the experiences of 49 male students from all sorts of backgrounds. In the case of boys, they find, school often just doesn't maintain their interest. This book is a compelling choice for teachers because it offers practical ideas for educators based not on numbers but on a personal investigation of how boys feel about and participate in school.

ReadKiddoRead.com

Bestselling novelist James Patterson dedicates this site to his own children's books picks. He organizes his suggestions for kids of all ages into four main categories—non-fiction, realistic fiction, adventure/mystery, fantasy—and provides reviews for each listed title. The site also features interviews with prominent children's authors and links to book-specific lesson plans. Check out the "Boys Spotlight" page, a discussion forum with tips and ideas for how to get boys reading.

Scholastic.com

Scholastic's website offers a wide variety of resources for educators, parents, and kids. On the "Teachers" page, one can find plenty of reading lesson plans for K–12 students, in addition to a broad, searchable database of book lists submitted by educators. The "Books and Reading" section of the "Parents" page features book lists organized by theme, as well as articles on how to turn children from Pre-K through 8th grade into thoughtful, interested readers. Finally, "The Stacks," Scholastic's page for kids, allows young readers to explore their favorite Scholastic books and series through interactive activities.

Starfall.com

Starfall is perfect for parents and teachers of emerging readers. Students who are learning to read can independently discover all sorts of bright, colorful picture books, poems, riddles, and more right on this site. Selecting any word in one of the digital books gives its sound, and some of the pictures even come to life with a simple click!

Teaching Reading to Adolescent Black Males: Closing the Achievement Gap
by Alfred W. Tatum (Stenhouse, 2005)

Tatum combines his own experience as a black student with reflections on his career as an urban educator to provide thoughtful recommendations for tailoring English curricula to the needs of African American boys. One of his main pieces of advice is to assign books that deal with the poverty and violence that many of these students endure. Throughout the book, Tatum suggests stories that will appeal to black male students and also mentions ways to tailor instructional methods to the needs of these learners.

To Be a Boy, To Be a Reader: Engaging Teen and Preteen Boys in Active Literacy
by William Brozo (International Reading Association, 2010)

This book, an updated edition of the original 2002 publication, is in many ways a counterpart to *Bright Beginnings for Boys*, but for middle and high school students. Here, Brozo discusses ten different positive male archetypes and reviews books with characters that fit these models. Other chapters present ideas on how to incorporate visually-driven texts into reading lessons and how to make boys' literacy a community endeavor.